LOVE ON THE *line*

A BEAUMONT LEGACY NOVEL

VAI DENTON

Love on the Line

Copyright © 2024 by Vai Denton

All rights reserved. No part of this book may be used or reproduced in any manner whatsoever without written permission from the author, except as permitted by U.S. copyright law. Without limiting the author's and publisher's exclusive rights, any unauthorized use of this publication to train generative artificial intelligence (AI) technologies is expressly prohibited. This book is a work of fiction. Names, characters, businesses, organizations, places, events and incidents are either the product of the author's imagination or are used fictitiously. Any resemblance to actual persons, living or dead, events, or locales is entirely coincidental.

Editing: Rachel Bunner (@rachels.top.edits)

Proofreading: Chelsey Brand (@theimperfictionist) and Laura Hartley

Cover design: Cindy Ras (@cindyras_draws)

ISBN: 979-8-9904429-1-7 (paperback)

ASIN: B0D4KZHGNB (ebook)

First Edition: November 2024

10 9 8 7 6 5 4 3 2 1

Author's Note

Love on the Line is the second book in the *Beaumont Legacy* series. It is recommended that you read this book after enjoying *Gridlocked on the Gridiron*, the first book in the series. Otherwise, there may be some spoilers. That said, this book can be read as a standalone and will have no cliffhangers.

Your mental health is incredibly important to me, so please take the following content warnings into consideration before continuing: death of a parent (off page, prior to the start of the book), alcohol use, grief, anxiety (including on page panic attacks), explicit sexual content.

For anyone who has been made to feel like they take up too much space — Take. Up. Space.

Chapter One

Maya

Maya's face was plastered to the cold living room floor when she awoke, head pounding, stomach turning, and for the life of her, she couldn't remember what debauchery had taken place the night before to leave her in such a state. She rolled over onto the rug, reaching in the direction of the couch until her fingers found the edge of a blanket, and she yanked it over her body.

The movement caused her wrist to twinge painfully, despite the brace it was in. And that was when Maya remembered.

There had been no debauchery, no fun with her friends. She hadn't seen her friends in weeks. Not since she'd learned that her wrist injury was the end of her tennis career. Even physical therapy wouldn't help it heal completely.

No. This feeling was grief and wallowing and anger and exhaustion. Her head pounded from dehydration, and her stomach was turning because she'd been subsisting off peanut butter and jellies and gummy bears for days. It was all she could afford now that she was off the pro tour.

Professional tennis wasn't all people believed it was. Just because she'd played on the tour didn't mean she was flush with cash. Only the top hundred players were so lucky. With the cost of coaches, training facilities, physiotherapists, travel, and meals, Maya had hardly been getting by. Which is why, when she'd learned that she was done, she'd used a majority of her money to get to her dad's empty house in Los Angeles.

As far away from her friends and family as she could be.

After her computer had died for the fifth time in as many days, she'd decided the living room was a better place to rot. The TV wouldn't die on her, and she was much closer to the food when her stomach grumbled.

Maya couldn't complain too much. The cold was a welcome reprieve from the emptiness she'd been feeling for days as she'd cycled through seasons of her favorite sitcom like she was competing for an Olympic medal.

She curled into a ball, leaving a hole in her blanket just big enough to breathe through as she dozed off again, the sounds of two characters fighting lulling her back into the darkness she was getting all too familiar with. Maya couldn't have been asleep for longer than a few minutes before she felt the blanket ripped from her body.

"Jesus Christ, Mai. We thought you were *dead*." Her oldest brother Colton's voice jolted her from a REMless sleep.

Maya opened her eyes and groaned, seeing the curtains thrown agape and sunlight spearing through the room like it was looking to burn her to ash.

"Why are you on the floor?" At the sound of Landon's voice—her other brother—she sat up quickly. Her brothers had never been more than cordial to each other, and though Colton had made attempts to mend their relationship, the fact that they were willingly in the same place when, surely, they both wanted to be elsewhere was alarming enough to make her contemplate how long she'd been dodging their calls.

Maya cleared her throat, trying to disperse the cobwebs in her mind she was sure had been created by her lack of mental stimulation and abysmal macronutrient consumption. "Uh..."

Her brothers exchanged a look. Again, alarming.

"I wanted to feel the cold," was what she managed as an explanation.

"So you decided to lie on the rug and wrap yourself in a blanket?" Landon placed the back of his hand against Maya's forehead, a gesture she didn't think he'd ever done for anyone. "She's warm," he said to Colton, like she'd disappeared.

Colton frowned. "Mai, are you sick? Why haven't you been answering our calls and texts? I know you're going through a rough time right now, but you can lean on us. You know that, right?"

This was the exact reason she didn't want to be on the East Coast where Colton, his girlfriend, and Maya's entire group of friends lived. Maya had never been one to talk about her issues, especially not with the people closest to her. She had always been the invisible Beaumont child, and she liked it that way. She'd gone through life like that, her problems invisible to others, and she was content knowing she was never burdening the people around her. They had far better things to worry about than her.

The last thing Maya wanted to talk about was that she was a failure. That the one talent she had was now moot because she wouldn't be able to use it for anything. That dropping out of school to pursue her dream had *not* panned out for her. She had already been telling herself that enough.

The fact that they were both here, changing their daily lives for her, brought back that familiar feeling she'd been outrunning for years.

Maya was usually the one holding their little family together, going out of her way to call as often as she could manage while playing tennis. She'd spent years, since she'd been twelve, forcing herself to be the independent one. The one who took care of others.

Now that they were here, she was once again the burdensome little sister they had to worry about, not the full-grown woman she'd become.

Maya cobbled together her best, most convincing smile. "I'm not going through a rough patch. Nothing's going on. You came here for no reason. Please locate your nearest exit and go *away*."

Landon snorted. "You always get extra witty and weird when you're upset. We're not going anywhere until you tell us how you've been doing."

As if to prove his point, he sat on the couch beside her head, clicking out of her comfort show in search of something else. *Rude.* Colton continued to stand, his worried look fixed on her.

"Maya, please. I know tennis is really important to you. We just want to help," he pleaded.

This was another problem: they could never really understand what this injury meant for her because they would never be able to put themselves in her shoes. No matter what happened to them, they would still have money and fame.

"If your career ended tomorrow, you would have something to fall back on. Both of you. I don't have that same luxury," she snapped at him.

Colton reared back a little like he was surprised by her words. To be fair, she never talked to them like this. And that only made her feel worse because this situation wasn't their fault, and it wasn't fair to take it out on them.

Maya knew no matter how stubborn she might be, she wasn't more stubborn than Colton. She would have to tell them eventually. Better now than to have him stay for hours trying to pry it from her.

He was a championship-winning quarterback. He had better things to do.

She sighed, leaning back against the couch and pulling the blanket they'd abandoned at her feet over herself protectively, as if it would prevent her next words from burrowing deep beneath her skin.

"I don't know what to do with myself. Tennis is all I have. It's all I am. What now? I don't know where to go from here," she blurted honestly.

Landon had stopped scrolling, sitting on the coffee table so he could look at her. Colton dropped down beside her, clearly waiting for her to say more. But what more was there?

Tennis had always been her safe space, and now it was gone. She would never play at the same level as the rest of her friends again. She would never again enjoy the adoration of the fans, the competition in her veins, the feel of the ball hitting her strings so perfectly that they sang.

Maya pushed a knuckle into her leg, hard, trying to shove away the burn of unshed tears behind her eyes. "I didn't know the last time I played in front of a crowd like that would be the last time, you know? I didn't know that would be my last time playing doubles with Delilah," she said, referring to her closest friend on the tour. "You spend your whole life training for something, put everything else on the back burner, decide you don't need a college degree because those years are prime tour years. And then it's all gone in an instant."

Sandpaper bit the back of her throat, and she choked down a sob. "I have no degree, no other prospects. I don't know what to do with myself now. I'll be lucky if I can even play *rec league.*" Her voice broke on the last two words, and she was embarrassed at the emotion she was displaying. She hadn't cried like this in front of either of them since Ryan had ended things with her over a year ago.

Maya felt strong arms wrap around her, pulling her slouched body into a chest and holding her tight. Then she was rocking slowly. She didn't have to open her eyes to know which brother held her. Colton's consolatory words and movements hadn't changed since he'd held her together after their mom had died.

Only when the well inside her had dried up did she pull her face from her hands, her cheeks tight with tears, eyelashes clumped together and heavy with the weight of the salt. Landon looked at her solemnly, holding out a hand for her to clasp.

"I'm so sorry, Maya. I just...I really am so deeply sorry. There's nothing I can say beyond that." Landon had never been good at expressing his feelings, and she appreciated him trying to articulate them for her benefit. She squeezed his hand weakly.

The three of them sat like that for a moment before Colton spoke softly. "I know I could never understand what you're going through, but we need to know you're taking care of yourself. Peanut butter and jelly and candy are not going to help you get better, and even if you can't go back to the tour, you should heal for the future. Have you been drinking water? Going to physical therapy?"

Maya grimaced, the feeling of three missed calls from her physical therapist like a tangible weight pinning her to the floor. For a flash, she felt bitter anger sweep through her before it burned out. She glared at him even though she knew he was right. He smiled sadly, like that had been answer enough.

"Just try? Please? To take care of yourself. I hate you being here all alone, but at least Landon is an hour flight away. And you know you're always welcome at my and Lucia's house."

"I'll try," she mumbled, breaking eye contact and resting her head on his shoulder, not wanting the conversation to continue. She didn't need a reminder she was worrying him. It only made her feel worse.

Maya hadn't been making any effort to rectify the issue so she could play at a lower level. She'd found zero motivation when she'd thought about the fact that no matter what she did, her surgeon had told her it would only get worse if she went back to play on tour.

What was the point?

The sound of Landon's stomach growling garnered a chuckle from them all. Her brothers were up in an instant, Landon searching through the empty pantry, Colton moving to peer out the curtains that hung over the two windows beside the front door.

"Yeah, they're gonna be here for a while. We should order in," he said.

Maya stood, grabbed the almost empty peanut butter and jelly jars, and pushed them in front of Landon, whose face scrunched like she'd offered to stab him through the heart with a steak knife.

"Who's gonna be here for a while?"

"Fucking paparazzi," Landon grumbled, smacking at her hand when she tried to start making another PB&J.

"Hey! I've been eating these for days and I'm fine. Stop treating me like a child."

"Treating you like a child? You're the one eating PB&Js and gummy bears daily. What do you want for lunch? You choose." He was already pulling his phone from his pocket and handing it to her.

Maya chose, then passed the phone to Colton, who had joined them in the kitchen. Maya began walking back into the living room, but Landon stopped her by stepping in front of her and putting his hands on her shoulders.

"Maya, I have to tell you something."

"You followed Colton's example and found a woman you want to settle down with?" she mused wryly.

"Yeah, right."

"A man you want to settle down with?"

"Not quite."

"You've taught yourself to knit, and now you're making sweaters for penguins."

He removed his hands from her shoulders but pointed at her. "You're doing that thing again where you try to repress your feelings with your sense of humor."

"You're just mad I do it better than you."

"True, but still not what I was going to tell you." He leaned closer like he was going to tell her a secret and then whispered, "You smell horrible."

Something like a laugh flew past her lips. Or maybe it was a gasp. She couldn't be sure. She batted at him. "Rude."

"That might be true too, but you need a shower because"—he waved his hand in front of his face while pinching his nose with the other, like he was trying to rid himself of her stench—"I didn't want to say it when you were crying, but it's putrid."

"Dick."

"Stinkerbell."

Even Colton laughed at that, though he looked apologetic when she glared his way.

"Assholes."

She barely heard Colton's "I didn't even say anything!" as she ran up the stairs to her bedroom, her Crestview Tennis T-shirt covered in new stains and smelly in a way that was definitely not socially acceptable.

When she stood in the scalding water, staring up at the shower head, she marveled at the way her brothers had managed to help her forget—even for a few minutes—that despair that'd settled over her like a steadfast storm cloud.

Problem was, they had their own lives and couldn't be with her all the time. She didn't *want* them to have to be with her all the time. Their company was great for keeping the emptiness at bay temporarily, but Maya still felt it tucked inside her, waiting until they left to be let loose. She knew the moment they were out the door, it would come crawling back and sink its teeth into her until she was nothing but a void, rotting on the couch once more. Even now, as she lathered her hair and cleaned the saltiness from her face, she felt it creeping in again.

She wondered if it would ever go away.

Chapter Two

Cooper

The Barrett household, headed by Sabertooths O-line-man Rudy and his wife Jenna, always seemed to be the championship-watch-party house. Normally, if they hadn't just lost in the conference final, they'd be expected to watch at the facility, but it seemed the coaches pitied them after the loss.

Cooper couldn't say he cared. He was content with two championship rings, and this would hopefully mean the media would take a step back and stop plastering him all over the place with crazier and crazier headlines. Put the focus on other players in the league who'd committed far worse atrocities than consensually enjoying women.

Wishful thinking if the paparazzi outside the gated house were any indication.

He walked into the large downstairs living room and waved to Colton, who sat on the floor in front of the couch, between

Lucia's knees. After Colton lifted his hand, he looked back at Lucia like a lovesick idiot as she talked animatedly with Jenna. Cooper grinned.

Colton and Lucia had hated each other for years because her ex-fiancé had been Colton's rival in college. Then, a little less than a year and a half ago, Lucia had joined the Sabertooths analyst team after her ex had cheated on her, taking on the responsibility of working with Colton when he'd struggled on the field. What had begun as a fake dating deal to fix her reputation and get back at her ex had led to very real feelings, and Lucia had recently moved into Colton's house.

Colton was a changed man, and he'd joined the ranks of their teammates in meaningful, committed relationships.

It was bittersweet seeing so many of Cooper's friends in love, knowing his only relationship had existed because Gabi, his college girlfriend, had liked the idea of dating a football player. He had thought he was okay with the temporary love he received for his body or football, but ever since watching his closest friend fall in love, he wondered if maybe he was ready for something a bit more permanent.

Time kept passing and he kept telling himself he'd find someone, but how could he know if the women he went out with were interested in *him* rather than his job or his money?

Cooper snagged a barstool behind the living area, leaning his back against the cool marble bar top. He swirled his beer around in the bottle before settling it on his lips, recognizing the growling of his stomach despite having eaten two plates of the gigantic spread Jenna had laid out for them. Even during the offseason, he consumed far more than the average man, his self-imposed—and often Colton-imposed—lifts keeping him in shape.

His hand twitched near his pocket, and he made a concerted effort not to break the record for number of times checking the news on oneself in a day. Cooper knew it was a self-destructive habit. Every time he saw a headline linking him with someone new, he shoved down that thing in his chest that wanted something *more* for himself. Didn't they ever get tired of reporting who he was spotted with and speculating who his "flavor of the month" was?

He'd tried to ignore the barrage of comments about his sexual exploits and millions of women objectifying him on his social media profiles as if he were nothing but a beautiful figurehead, but more and more, Cooper wished to toss his phone and get off the grid so all the attention would stop following him everywhere he went.

Colton stood, grabbing a beer from the fridge in the bar area alongside their running back, TJ, before they both joined Cooper.

"Five-to-one odds someone throws a punch today," TJ continued their conversation, sliding onto a barstool. "Fuck it, ten to one if it's someone we know."

Colton shook his head. "I'm not betting with you ever again, TJ."

"What? Why? What'd I do?"

Colton looked to Cooper as if to say *Is this guy for real?* and then responded, "I've won at least three bets against you, and you've never paid me."

"We didn't shake on it! That's the rule."

Colton grunted, sliding onto the stool on the other side of Cooper.

TJ turned his attention to Cooper. "Whatcha sulking back here for? Couldn't find someone in Charleston you haven't hooked up with to bring to the party? Honestly, same."

The comment was meant to be a joke, clear from TJ's chuckle and Colton's exhale. Cooper mustered a smile, even as his hand tightened a bit around the glass.

It was Cooper's own damn fault people made jokes like this at his expense. This was the narrative he'd created. He may as well have been the inventor of the casual relationship, a string of broken hearts left in his wake. Not that he ever made them any promises. No, they always knew what they were getting with Cooper Hayes. A good time, and nothing more.

Even so, that didn't stop the sting he'd been feeling from the moment he'd been declared his hometown's pretty boy, as if he could provide nothing more than what he offered physically. He was tired of the label, tired of feeling like there was no brain in his head.

"Something like that," Cooper remarked, eyes back on the television as the halftime show came to an end.

Raucous laughter broke out in the kitchen. TJ perked up. "Maybe *they'll* bet with me," he muttered, heading in that direction.

After a moment, Colton asked quietly, "You okay?"

Cooper only nodded, swallowing a sip of beer over the lump in his throat. He'd never confided in Colton that he wasn't a fan of the lifestyle he'd resigned himself to. Cooper had always felt it was stupid to complain about having women throw themselves at him when Colton had very serious issues that were due far more attention.

Now that Cooper was ready for a change, he wasn't sure Colton would understand. Colton had never dated much and had focused almost solely on football before Lucia, so he'd only hooked up with a few women here and there. Plus, it was such a small issue, there was no reason to bring it up.

"Yeah, I'm good," Cooper added with more conviction.

"You ready for the shoot?"

Colton and Cooper were set to film a commercial in Los Angeles in a couple of days. It'd slipped his mind entirely until now.

"Ah, hell. I told my parents I'd see 'em for my sister's birthday, but I'll have George change my flights so I leave from LA that evening," Cooper replied, referring to his agent. He shot a quick text to the man, ignoring the previous text George had sent him. It was a headline that linked Cooper with Tara Carr, an established pop singer, and below it was a thumbs up.

George loved all the media drama that Cooper hated.

"I'm excited to see Maya. I know it's only been a few days since I was out there, but I think she really needs people with her right now. She's usually so social, you know?"

Cooper nodded, his stomach twisting at the thought of Colton's little sister. He was glad he'd be going straight to Tennessee from the shoot because the last thing Cooper needed was to have her in his head once more.

Every time he'd seen her since her birthday a couple of summers ago, what they'd almost done had haunted him. It took him weeks to get it out of his head each time.

How her hands had felt in his hair on the dance floor of the bar on her twenty-third birthday when they'd gotten away from her friends and brothers. How her hips had felt against his as she danced. How she had looked over her shoulder at him, pouting until he got closer. And how he'd almost indulged, almost kissed her, his lips just a small exhale away before he'd run a hand through his hair and pulled away.

Damn it, he was doing it again.

"How's she doing with the injury? I meant to ask."

Colton took a swig of his beer, then frowned. "Not great. It's been less than two weeks since she found out she won't be able to play anymore, when before, she thought it was something physical therapy would fix. She's rightfully devastated, and now, she isn't really taking care of herself. Hasn't even gone back to PT."

Cooper's heart ached for Maya. She'd been battling this wrist injury since July. Maya had hurt it during a tournament, had surgery, and then had focused on physical therapy. Then when she'd played again in early January, she'd injured it even worse.

He didn't know what he'd do with himself if he got hurt and couldn't play in the league, but Maya's love for tennis was something else entirely. Far more intense than his feelings for football.

Maya loved tennis more than Colton loved football, and that was saying something. The last time Cooper had seen her, only a few weeks ago when she'd come to their last game, she'd just gotten imaging done but was hopeful about her recovery.

Absolutely heartbreaking.

Coverage for the second half was beginning, and Lucia turned to wave at Colton, who immediately stood. "My lady awaits. There's space on the floor if you want to join me." He inclined his head to where he'd been sitting.

Cooper followed him, all the while trying with everything in him not to think of Maya, hurt and alone in Los Angeles.

Cooper's luck, however much he might have had, ran out when the shoot went late and he missed his flight to Oakridge Springs, Tennessee. He felt bad, especially since he usually only stayed with his family for a few short hours. As much as he loved them, he couldn't spend very long in his hometown without getting that familiar itch.

The one that made him feel like nothing more than the mayor's pretty-boy, football-playing son. The one that had made him go to the University of Alabama so he could *get out.*

Even worse than that? Colton had invited Cooper to stay with him at his dad's house in LA. The same house in which Maya was currently residing. Colton had spoken to Maya alone for half an hour while Cooper ate leftovers from the dinner they'd picked up. Then, Colton had gone upstairs to call Lucia and fall asleep, leaving Cooper and Maya together.

Alone.

For the first time since they'd almost kissed.

For the past year and a half, Cooper had always found ways to leave before it got to that point. Or he'd made sure to stick with Colton rather than stay back to talk with her like he might've before his near-disastrous infraction.

He had never known how to act around Maya, not since he'd met her three and a half years ago. Cooper had been entranced by her, drawn to her energy and sarcastic sense of humor. Her passion when she talked about tennis. Her kindness to everyone around her. How she had tucked her long, black hair behind her ears and leaned in close so she could hear what Cooper was saying. She'd been bright and open like a sunflower, so happy just to exist.

And Cooper knew now he needed to leave. Follow Colton upstairs and head to bed.

Only, something about the way she was slumped on the couch, glazed eyes watching the television, kept him anchored across from her.

He hated seeing her like this.

Cooper dug his nails into his palm. This was Maya, Colton's little sister. Cooper had spent many an evening talking to her about her travels while she'd been on tour to countries he'd never even thought to visit. While they may not have communicated except when she visited her brother, and almost never alone, they were almost friends, certainly more than acquaintances. They were close enough that he could check in on her.

"How are you?" he asked.

She didn't even turn to look at him. "I'm good."

Cooper knew he was probably pushing it, especially after the recognition only moments earlier that they were nothing more than sort-of friends, even if that friendship was nearing four years. Still, he pressed. "How are you, really?"

Maya finally looked at him. "Colt told you?"

Cooper nodded.

She blew out a breath, looking away. "I'm figuring it out. Or trying. I don't know. I don't really have any other answer than that right now."

Cooper flicked his eyes to the screen too, hoping his next words weren't as transparent as they seemed to him. "I know my brother regrets that he didn't follow his doctor's orders right after his injury. He waited months, and that time cost him years in the long run. I think if he'd known what he knows now, he would've made sure he was doing everything he could to get better."

Maya was silent, and when he turned to look, she was frowning. "So Colton told you about more than just the injury."

"Don't be mad at him. He's worried about you."

"What happened to him? Your brother. If you don't mind talking about it..."

"Bull ridin'." Cooper was only a couple of years younger than his brother, so he'd already been in college when it'd happened. "He didn't compete at a super high level, but there was something about it Dylan couldn't part with. And one day, he was thrown too hard, and that was it. He fractured half the bones in his body, and even after the surgeries, he was in bad shape."

She'd leaned closer as he'd spoken, as if something he'd said had resonated with her. "What did he do after the surgeries?"

"I wasn't around much, but Ma and my sisters said he was very...angry. Dyl had always been broody, but I guess after his injury, he wouldn't talk to anybody. Wouldn't do anything but lie in bed and curse himself day and night. He'd wanted badly to continue for a couple more years, but it was the end of the road for him. It took him months to get into physical therapy. They said if he'd started sooner, he would've gotten his mobility and strength back quicker. But because he waited, it took him years to get close to where he was before. Still might be workin' on it, honestly."

He hadn't talked much to his older brother after he'd left Tennessee, most of his news about the ranch coming from his mom and gossiping sisters. He'd always felt bad for not doing more after his brother's injury, but just like with Maya, he didn't know how to help besides being there as support. And according to his family, that wouldn't have been much help. Especially not when they'd never had a relationship like that, even before he'd left.

Dylan had always hated that Cooper had been on a trajectory out of their little country town. And honestly, Cooper had always felt guilty that he'd been the one to get out, especially because he knew it meant his parents kept a tighter hold on the rest of them.

"That feels eerily similar to me. Are you sure you're not just making up a story to convince me to go to physical therapy?"

He almost laughed, especially when he saw the slight upturn of her lips at the question, but he just shook his head. "Promise. True story. He's okay now, running the ranch with my dad. They've made it clear they'd like for me to come back and help out too, but that's not really..." He shook his head, not wanting to get into why he never returned home for longer than a few days.

"Anyway. All I'm saying is I get why you're upset. And I get why you don't want to go to PT." Cooper shrugged. "It's easier to pretend everything's fine and it was all just a misunderstanding than to have to confront reality."

Maya sucked in a breath, and Cooper realized he may have gone too far.

"Sorry, I didn't mean to—"

"No, you're right though. That's what I'm doing." She smiled at him sadly. "Did you major in psychology or something?"

Cooper chuckled. "Colt asks me the same thing sometimes, but no. Just a product of being in the middle of a lot of sibling conflict, I think."

"Key difference though."

"What's that?"

"Your brother had something to look forward to. Something to give him hope. To rally behind. I don't. I don't have a fallback. I didn't get my degree. I dropped out of school. Tennis has always been my one and only strength." She clenched her jaw. "And now that's gone."

"I can't imagine it's the only thing you're good at. You're resilient. You can do anything you set your mind to. You could always go back to school." Upon seeing her disgusted face, he continued, "But there are plenty of things you can do without a degree. If tennis is your biggest passion, why not coach?"

She shrugged after thinking about it for a moment. "Maybe. But I want to do something real and important. Something that's meaningful, you know?"

"I'm sure anyone you'd teach would find it meaningful."

Maya hummed in response, focusing back on the television. Cooper waited to see if she would say anything else, but she seemed to want the conversation to end. Respecting her unspoken wishes, he said good night and went up to get ready for bed.

He'd pushed enough for one day.

Chapter Three

Maya

Maya blinked at her best friend in utter disbelief. Unless she was dreaming, Delilah, all curly golden hair and bright blue eyes, was standing on the porch, right in front of her. Close enough to touch. Close enough to hug.

She must've been dreaming.

It'd been five days since Colton and Cooper had flown back to the East Coast, and though Maya had had short phone calls with both of her brothers since, she'd been going a little stir-crazy alone in this house.

Delilah hadn't said anything about being able to visit her, especially not now when she was supposed to be at the tournament in Dubai. Maya made a noise in the back of her throat.

Delilah, seeming to sense Maya's disbelief, charged toward her and wrapped her in a big hug. The moment Delilah's happy cloud enveloped her, Maya reciprocated, tears welling in her eyes.

It had only been a month since Maya had seen her, and yet it had felt like an eternity. Her doubles partner, her best friend, the person who she'd spent more of her adult life with than her own family, was *here*.

"H—how? How did you get away?"

Delilah pulled back, her signature smile on her face. She always had a way of making anybody feel like they were the most important person to her.

"You needed me," she answered simply, her hands slipping into Maya's.

"No, seriously."

Tennis wasn't a sport one could just leave during the season. The tour was intense, and players were at a tournament almost every week. There was no getting away when you were making a run at the top one hundred, as Delilah was currently doing and as Maya had been starting to do before her injury. Players went to every tournament, looked for every opportunity to get more points so they had a shot at even one of the four grand slams. Potentially dropping in the rankings by not playing wasn't an option.

Delilah squeezed her hands. "Okay, fine. I'm in the main draw for Indian Wells, so we agreed I'd take a couple of weeks off to train and focus on physio," she responded, talking about the tournament in California in March.

"Main draw is amazing, Del. And nobody questioned you coming to see me?"

"Well, of course I had to fight a little to train in California instead of at the academy, but I'm the one paying them, so what can they do about it?" She laughed.

The Morozov Academy was where Maya had befriended Delilah and the other girls in their group. It was where they and many other men and women on the tour trained when they weren't on the road, and during the offseason.

Suddenly remembering they were still standing with the door open, Maya joked, "Do you want to come rot with me on the couch?"

"Actually, I promised I would do something active if I came here for the next couple of hours. Want to go for a run?"

Maya snorted. "How about a walk?" she compromised, because she had no interest in being active at all. But Delilah always knew how to get Maya to do things that were good for her, even if she didn't feel like it. "Let me change real quick. One second."

She shut the door behind Delilah before she hustled up the stairs to find a clean pair of shorts and a new shirt, hoping her friend hadn't noticed the clothes she'd opened the door in weren't in the best shape.

Maya had been trying to keep her promise to her brothers. She'd been showering more—which still wasn't very often, but she also barely moved from the couch—and she'd even purchased some cheese so her sandwiches weren't all PB&Js. She'd given thought to Cooper's words and had plans to go to physical therapy in the near future. She wasn't ready yet, but she knew the wallowing had to end soon.

Especially now that her panic attacks were making a reappearance every time she tried to figure out what to do with her life. She'd been on the verge of one when Delilah had shown up, feeling like she had been twelve again, waking up in the middle of the night struggling to breathe, pleading with someone, anyone, to make it go away. Colton would come rushing in and hold her to his chest, coaching her on how to breathe through them until she could relax and fall asleep once more.

Except she wasn't twelve anymore, and she couldn't rely on others to get her through this.

She frowned at where her thoughts had led her, like the moment her friend's radiant presence had faded, she'd fallen back under the dark cloud of despair that'd been following her around for weeks. Maya changed quickly and stepped into her running shoes before meeting Delilah at the bottom of the stairs.

Delilah's eyes landed on the wrist brace Maya grabbed off the entry table along with her keys, and Maya nearly sighed in relief when her friend's expression didn't change to one of pity.

The brace had been a nice change from the cast Maya had worn through the end of January. Maya had gotten another surgery, but even with it, her doctor had told her it hadn't healed properly.

Hence why she couldn't play on the tour anymore.

His only advice had been to keep it braced and to go to physical therapy so she could regain some functionality in the future, and she'd clearly only been doing the former.

"Ready?" Delilah asked, tossing her ponytail over her shoulder and marching toward the door before Maya could respond. Her friend had already descended the concrete stepping stones in the front lawn and begun walking down the street by the time Maya had gotten the door locked.

A cool February breeze snaked through Maya's hair, and she breathed in the slightly smoggy Los Angeles morning air. The sun shone brightly through barely there clouds, bathing the streets in a warm glow. Two- to three-story houses sat atop well-manicured lawns, and the sidewalk and streets were some of the most pristine in Southern California.

It paid to have a father who came from money, she mused.

"How are the girls?" Maya inquired.

"They're doing pretty well! Nicola's still pushing to get into the top ten, but she dropped to forty-two, and she's been struggling a bit with that."

Maya felt for Nicola. She'd worked so hard since she'd won big in the juniors, but she never seemed to be able to get back up to the top. It was why she'd moved to the Morozov Academy this past November. She and her coaches had wanted a change for her, and even though Maya had only known her for a couple of months, Nicola had become an integral part of their group in her eyes.

"Harper and Sahar are good too. Harper and I have been grinding to move up into the top one hundred. Sahar's still top fifty, I think. They're all in Dubai right now. Not much has changed since we saw you last, honestly. You know how busy the tour is. We've only been able to train together a few times."

"And Anya?" Maya questioned before she could filter herself. Delilah would know exactly what she was asking, and it had nothing to do with Anya's tennis.

A little over a year ago, Maya had been hooking up with Ryan, a guy on the men's tour who had trained with them at the academy. After developing feelings for each other, he'd told Maya he wasn't ready for a relationship. As if that hadn't made her feel unwanted enough, only a few months later, he'd started dating Anya, the daughter of the owners of the academy and the woman her friends mutually agreed was their frenemy, on and off the court.

Well, except Delilah. Delilah was friends with everyone, which meant Anya was often included in the few outings and birthday celebrations the tour allowed them.

"She and Ryan are...okay," she said slowly, like she was trying to choose her words carefully. "I think they've been fighting. They both lost pretty badly at the Australian Open and have been struggling a bit on the tour. You know how it is dating another player. It's good when you're doing well at tournaments and bad when you're not."

Maya tried not to be so happy about that.

"But enough about that. How are *you*?" Delilah turned her head to look at Maya as she asked. Just like before, there was no pity, only genuine concern, and Maya loved her friend all the more for it.

Like with her brothers, Maya didn't want Delilah to worry about her, but she also knew that, like her brothers, Delilah would be able to sniff out a lie if she pretended she was fine.

Honesty, then.

"I'm—" She searched for the right word. "I'm trying to be okay. The stress of not knowing what to do next is getting to me a bit." Maya shrugged. "I never imagined my life without tennis. I still can't. I knew I'd retire one day, but I figured I would have made a bit more of a dent in the tennis world than this. I couldn't even break 150," she mumbled the last sentence.

Delilah stopped abruptly, and Maya looked back at her questioningly.

"Maya! I can't believe you're thinking about yourself like that. Do you know how impressive it is to be one of the best two hundred women in the world? There are over twenty-five hundred women on the tour. You were in the top eight percent and well into the top teeny tiny percent in the *world*. You've played in two grand slams now. Billions of people on this planet can't say the same."

Delilah hadn't mentioned Maya had barely made it through the first round of one and lost in the first round of the other, but Maya got the point. Her cheeks burned in embarrassment because her friend was absolutely right.

She ducked her head, and Delilah placed an arm around her shoulder, continuing their walk around Maya's neighborhood.

"And you know what I think?" her friend continued. "I've seen you coach, and I wouldn't be surprised if, one day, you're on tour with a player you're coaching."

Maya turned that over in her mind. She liked coaching, she really did. She just wanted to do *more*, find something that helped people *more* than that. Maya wanted to give back to the community she loved so much in another, bigger way. She just couldn't quite figure out what that bigger way was.

"Coaching." Maya nodded. "I can see it. Maybe I can start there and find something that excites me like the tour did along the way."

Her friend squeezed her shoulder lovingly. "Exactly."

Delilah began filling her in more about the tour and gossip about people at the academy. With so many competitors in one place training to be the best, it was no surprise there was often drama. But, when Delilah casually brushed over her father asking her for money, it was Maya's turn to stop her.

"Del, what? He asked for money *again*?"

Her father was the definition of a deadbeat drunk, and her mother had been out of the picture since her youngest twin siblings were born. Delilah had grown up the oldest of four children, and from a very young age, she'd had to take care of her siblings. She'd worked hard to make ends meet for her family, and when a young couple had discovered how talented she was on the court and had sponsored her move to a training facility, then the academy, it'd been the big break she'd needed to keep her siblings safe and healthy. All her money had been going to her coaches and her family, which is why she'd shared a tiny apartment just outside the academy with Maya.

The fact that her father was asking for more than the money she'd already sent him pissed Maya off, but she knew Delilah was too sweet to say no.

"It's...complicated. I just want to make sure they have enough to eat and go to the best schools and get the best of everything. They're all in college or going to start soon, and I just want to be sure they have everything they need, you know?"

Maya slipped her uninjured hand into Delilah's to comfort her the way she always comforted Maya. "I know you do. You're the greatest big sister in the world."

They walked hand in hand, talking about more drama and plans for the tour, and Maya was thankful her heart didn't shoot up to her throat the way it usually did when she thought about how the tour was no longer her future. Not that she was coming to terms with it, exactly, but with Delilah by her side, it didn't hurt quite as badly.

They walked the full two hours Delilah had been allotted, and as Maya watched her drive the rental car out of her neighborhood, the sight of a reporter and cameraman—no doubt wondering if her brothers were inside—made her frown. A good reminder to talk to her father about getting a security system in the house, she supposed.

Chapter Four

Cooper

Opulence was Cooper's agent's favorite aesthetic, and it was evident even from the foyer of his office space. Floor-to-ceiling windows peered out over downtown Charleston, and chandeliers that looked entirely misplaced in an office setting hung from the pristine, glass ceiling.

Normally, Cooper didn't come to see George. Most of their conversations happened over the phone, text, or email, especially with Cooper's busy schedule. But now it was the offseason, and that thing that had been nagging at Cooper had grown so large, he hadn't been able to sleep the last couple of nights.

He was exhausted, figuratively and literally.

Cooper had gotten so used to the media and everyone in his life seeing him as the playboy jock, he'd just accepted all it had come with.

He'd left Oakridge Springs to get away from it—away from people wanting something from him because his father was the mayor or because he was the star tight end or because he looked a certain way. When Cooper started at Alabama, he'd thought things would be different. He'd thought he found someone who cared for him the way he cared for her, but then that had crashed and burned, and by the time he got to Charleston, he'd accepted this was the life for him. He'd enjoyed the nights with women who had wanted him for his body, money, or his fame because at least it had felt like he'd been getting love.

Sure, it had been temporary, but it'd been better than none at all.

But then he'd watched Colton, who had never cared much for relationships, fall in love with someone so right for him, and Cooper had realized the love he thought he'd been getting was nothing at all in comparison.

The want for something more than quickies and late nights had been a simmering current creeping through him to that point. Only now, as he realized what life could be like if things were different, was the need for change becoming unbearable.

Cooper didn't want to keep finding someone new to sleep with in exchange for fleeting moments of feeling cared for.

And maybe talking to Maya a few days ago had pushed him to do better too. Though he couldn't explain why, since they hadn't spoken about him much at all.

George's office door swung open, and he stepped out in a suit, his brown hair all over the place like he'd been running his hands through it in frustration. The look he sent Cooper, something like exasperated confusion, only confirmed that George was stressed.

But Cooper knew he was George's biggest client, and he hoped that would be enough to convince him.

"Hey, Cooper. What can I do for you today?"

Cooper stood, shaking George's hand and walking into his office.

"I was hoping to talk about some of the media work I've been doing. Or rather, maybe taking it in another direction."

George sank into his chair, steepling his hands and setting them on his desk, his face souring.

"'Taking it in another direction.'"

Cooper nodded. "Yeah."

"What does that mean exactly?"

"Well...I'm tired of the constant headlines, man. I'm tired of every Charleston news site, and even a ton around the country, acting like the only important thing about me is that I'm a serial dater."

George's eyes narrowed. "As opposed to...?"

"I don't know. I'm more than that. I'm more than football, even. Maybe I could do extra outreach or something to show I'm not just that one thing."

"But what's the point, exactly? Why does it matter what they print about you if it's making us this much money?"

Cooper frowned. This is what he'd been worried about. He'd known George had always cared most about the money.

Until now, Cooper hadn't really minded that. George was good at his job. Great, even. He took care of many aspects of Cooper's life, like handling travel for shoots and the like, finding people to deal with his finances, and negotiating the best deals in all of Cooper's contracts.

Plus, George had been with him since he'd joined the league. Sure, he was a bit of an ass, but they'd never really had issues working together, and he'd truly eased Cooper's life significantly. They'd been on the same page until now, and with only a few more seasons in the league, Cooper wasn't sure he wanted to deal with the hassle of finding someone new.

"I'm just tired of it. I want to do something that shows them that's not all I am," Cooper repeated.

"Look, I hate to say it, but even if you were to get into a relationship, which I don't recommend, things probably wouldn't change. You'd probably be battling this for years, with constant speculation that you're cheating. I say you just keep enjoying what it gives us."

Cooper glared down at the thick, oak desk in front of him. That was not what he'd wanted to hear.

"So, what then? Just deal with it until I retire and hope it ends there?"

"Cooper, be rational. Unless you have a real reason to change how things are now, why try to fix something that isn't broken? Your reputation is part of the reason you're asked to do so many commercials and other shoots. You should be happy with it. You get all the money and women you could ever want with none of the expectations that you'll become something more for them. Do you know how many men *wish* they could be in your shoes?"

Cooper sighed. This was a lost cause with George, and maybe even to the world. He'd dealt with this most of his life. People had been calling him a heartbreaker since he'd been six, while everybody else was praised for their academic achievements. This was not so different.

Whenever there was an opportunity for outreach, whether going to the children's hospital or coaching young kids or helping local businesses, Cooper was there. He'd never done it for the press, had never shown up to an event with the hopes a camera would find him and show the world he was caring, because that would have taken away from what he'd been doing anyway.

Because he did care.

But it clearly didn't matter that he could be so many other things, because this was all the world saw him as. And it shoved any hopes of change right back down his throat.

Cooper stood. "You're right. I don't know why I thought things could be different." He shook hands with George, who looked far more pleased than he had a few seconds earlier.

"I'm glad to hear it. And don't forget about the shoot tomorrow. I'm having Felicity send you information about it tonight."

Cooper nodded, already headed out of the office, giving George's secretary, Felicity, a brief nod before he walked into the elevator.

It had been dumb of him to even come.

Chapter Five

Maya

Maya stared up at her ceiling, tucked tightly under her duvet, counting the glow-in-the-dark stars her mother had helped her stick there when she'd been seven. Counting them took her mind off the panic, just like Colton had taught her one of those late nights a handful of weeks after her mother had died.

Before her father had told her Colton's sleep had been more important than her night terrors.

She counted them over and over, breathing in deeply, holding, breathing out deeply, holding. Just like her brother had taught her. The paralyzing panic subsided slowly until her tunnel vision cleared and she could feel her body again.

Get up, she thought to herself. *Get up, get up, get up.*

What would Colton have thought of her? Landon? Lucia? Cooper? Her friends? Worse, what would her mother have thought if she saw Maya as she was? None of it, not even the biting feeling of knowing they would all have been disappointed in her, pushed her out of her bed.

Being with Delilah yesterday had made her want to try harder, just like her brothers and Cooper had made her feel. But now that she was alone in the house, she'd fallen back into the same thoughts and worries as before.

What now? Her money was dwindling, and she could barely bring herself to think about physical therapy. After talking to Delilah, she'd very nearly called her physical therapist. But today? She knew she needed to, but all she could think about was that her dream was dead. What was the point of physical therapy if she couldn't play at the level she wanted to?

Of course, if she was going to coach for a little until she found what she really wanted, she had to start soon. Cooper's words about his brother's injury rang in her head.

"They said if he'd started sooner, he would've gotten his mobility and strength back quicker."

God, what was wrong with her? She was up and down constantly. Her good days felt good, and her bad days were *ugly*. She knew she needed to just bite the bullet and go, so what was stopping her? Frustration at herself turned to anger before it subsided into nothingness.

Her phone buzzed on her nightstand, and Maya's eyebrows pinched when she saw it was Landon calling. She'd always been the one to reach out, but like he'd known she needed someone, here he was.

"Hi?" she said, her voice tilting up at the end as if she were questioning the call.

"What, I can't call my favorite sister?"

Maya smiled just a bit at that. "Sorry, hi." This time, there was no question.

"Better. How are you?"

"I'm okay," she lied. He didn't need to know the thoughts that'd been flying through her mind the last few minutes. He'd only worry.

"Are you being *honest*?"

"Maybe. What about you? How are you?"

"I'm good. Offseason is offseason. We only really have a few free weeks before training and camp, so I'm trying to enjoy them while I can. Speaking of which, I was planning on coming down to hang out in the next few weeks." He paused, almost like he was trying to convince himself to continue. "Would that be okay with you?"

Maya smiled softly. Landon, who to everyone else was so rough around the edges, could be very sweet on the inside. She didn't have the closest relationship with him, especially since she and Colton had always been closer and his and Colton's relationship was lukewarm at best, but she and Landon were certainly trying.

Maya hated the idea that he might be coming to check on her. But the part of her that wished she could go back and keep her brothers together, keep them friendly and keep their unit close, wanted to see him. Wanted to rectify what she hadn't been able to while she was playing tennis.

"Of course! Colton and Lucia are forcing me to come to Charleston in a couple of days, which, honestly, I think will be good for me. I need to get out of the house," she rambled, then realized this might be making him feel excluded. Maya knew he probably hadn't been invited, and she'd never really gotten a read on how that sort of thing made him feel, since he always *seemed* okay. "Anyway, you can come next week or the week after if you'd like."

"Great, I'll text you when I decide on a day." He was silent for a moment and then said their mother's goodbye quietly, "Love you to the moon."

"Love you to the moon," she echoed before they hung up. Typically, she heard her mother's part of the phrase, "and back," in her head. But since her wrist had started hurting in July, long before the final injury in January, her mother's voice had disappeared entirely, even in their favorite goodbye.

The call had seemed to give her the motivation she'd needed to get out of bed. Maya headed downstairs and grimaced at the empty bags of gummy bears and bread littering the counters of the kitchen. She threw them into the trash bin and then stared at the couch, where her mother had oiled her hair while they'd watched TV together. Maya gritted her teeth to prevent the tears from falling.

It seemed she only had three emotional states nowadays: anger and sadness traded places often, emptiness peeking in infrequently. What happened to the five stages of grief? Why was she not moving from one to the other seamlessly? It was more like someone had written out the stages and scribbled on the page, sending her all over the place.

The evening sun shone through the trees in the backyard, casting a pretty glow on the lawn. She missed lying out on the grass and reading a book, or hanging out in the backyard and watching the clouds go by.

There'd been a lot of that after her mother had passed. Her father hadn't so much as looked in her direction other than to agree to pay her tuition and get her a credit card connected to his account—things that had taken months for him to actually complete.

Their father had kept Colton and Landon too busy. Where he had been ever-present for them, their father had been entirely absent for her, which meant after her mother had died, she'd been left to amuse herself.

Her mother. Her best friend. Her first hitting partner. The woman who had spent every waking second devoted to her children, Maya especially. The ache of her loss was forever present in Maya's daily life. Win or lose, Maya was on that court for her mother and because of her mother. Win or lose, her mother was who first came to her mind.

The months after losing her had been the hardest, but Maya had thought she'd gotten through that pain. Now that she spent day in and day out doing nothing but sleeping, staring into space, crying, and wondering about her future, the loss had begun to feel fresh again. All she wanted was for her mother to sit behind her, massaging coconut oil into her hair while they watched cartoons or *The Princess Bride.*

Why had Maya stopped hearing her voice encouraging her? What would she have said if she had been there with her? It'd been so long since she'd read her mother's journals from during her time in chemotherapy that she'd forgotten the shape of her mother's sentences, their ins and their outs.

Maya was up the stairs in a matter of seconds.

The door to the master bedroom had been closed since her father had moved away her senior year, when he'd followed Colton to Charleston. She'd only ever gone in to read her mother's journals, put off by the strange, cold feeling of being in the room.

Maybe the journals would reignite her mother's voice in her head.

Maya opened the door slowly, feeling a gust of cool air hit her as she did. After stepping inside, she headed straight for the box under her mom's side of the bed.

She'd never thought to take the journals from the room, certain it was their rightful place all throughout high school. But now, as Maya sat on her heels on the floor of this chilly, unpleasant room, she decided it was time they came with her. It wasn't like her father would care anyway.

Maya tucked the three leather-bound journals tight against her chest as she walked out of the bedroom, closing the door behind her with her foot. Although the journals were all practically the same from the outside, Maya knew their order by heart.

She opened the first, smiling at the loopy script she'd missed seeing, even as her vision blurred with tears.

Hello, my little ones,

I've finally decided to write in these journals I've had lying around for years. I can't even remember where I got them, but I figure I better use them while I can.

Being away from you is one of the hardest things I've ever had to do, but I hope the chemo does what it's supposed to and then I can come home to cheer on Colton, cook with Landon, and oil Maya's hair in front of the TV. I hope you're all happy at home and that your father is stepping up and taking good care of you without me there. Just because I'm not there to remind you doesn't mean you shouldn't be doing your homework (looking at you, Landon).

Also, Nani and Nana may come by more now from Michigan, so make sure to make them feel welcome. They'll be so excited to see you.

Maya's eyebrows pinched, and she wondered what Nani and Nana, her grandparents, were doing now. They'd visited during her mother's chemo, but never after. Where were they living? What had happened to make them stop contacting her and her brothers entirely after her mother had passed? Had she done something? Or had they just been too heartbroken and hadn't wanted to be reminded of the loss?

She swiped away a tear.

Anyway, it's my first full day of treatment and I'm quite fatigued, so I don't have much to say today other than I love you. I'm going to try out daily journaling and see if it works for me.

Sending you all big hugs and kisses, and remember, if life gives you melons, you might be dyslexic!

Love you to the moon and back,

Mom

Maya wiped another tear from her cheek quickly, worried about the already crinkled pages that were full of tears from when she'd been younger and first read her mother's words. That was her mother's way—vibrant despite the pain and sickness. She had always tried to make Maya and her brothers laugh, even when she was hurting.

PS don't forget to do something today that gives back to others.

And there was one of her mother's favorite phrases. She had uttered it often, especially when she would take Maya to volunteer at a soup kitchen, or when they'd go on long drives around the city, dropping off meals to people in need.

Maya flipped through the pages, reading entry after entry, consuming the words swiftly. She wanted to read every last letter, and then maybe she'd be able to figure out what her mom would have told her to do now.

After she'd finished all the journals and still couldn't hear her mother's voice or feel the gentle brush of her fingers pushing her hair back, Maya started again. And again and again.

She read long into the evening, clinging to the love between the pages, preferring the sadness that settled around her over the anger and emptiness her mother's voice chased away.

Chapter Six

Cooper

The dragon-themed mini golf park was already crowded by the time Cooper showed up, children of Sabertooths players running around with their little clubs and multicolored golf balls. He smiled at a couple of his teammates and their families before heading to the line to pick up a club.

Normally, charity events were a bit fancier, with far fewer children, but if there was one thing Devin, their starting wide receiver, knew how to do, it was put together a fun time. Cooper wasn't sure he would've even come if the event weren't for charity, his legs aching from a particularly difficult lift and his spirits low from the phone call with his mother he'd had to end early as he'd pulled into the parking lot of the bought-out park.

The first thing she'd said to him when he'd hopped on the phone was ask, lovingly of course, if he was using protection in his escapades, because while she wanted a grandchild, she didn't really want one out of wedlock.

That was a great start to the conversation. Not at all part of the reason he didn't go home or anything.

The next thing she'd said to him was that his father was asking, for the millionth time, if Cooper thought he'd retire soon so he could make a bid to take over as mayor of Oakridge Springs.

Hard pass.

Still, he'd spent the entire conversation promising that yes, he had been staying safe—though he hadn't so much as kissed a woman in a few months. Yes, he would give retiring and running for mayor some more thought, along with all that came with moving back home.

Though Cooper felt he did good work as a football player, his family had only entertained it because of how it'd helped Cooper's father in his political career. Now that his father's final term as mayor was coming to a close, they refused to acknowledge it as anything but a waste of his potential.

Cooper knew saying otherwise would only invite conflict with his parents, and he already felt guilty for leaving his siblings and their tight-knit community to pursue a life away from the ranch.

Cooper grabbed the putter and golf ball from the desk worker, and when he turned, found Colton and Lucia beelining toward him.

And then there was Maya, her injured wrist in a brace, a tiny frown on her face like she wasn't quite comfortable with her surroundings.

Okay, maybe there were other reasons for him to be here.

It'd only been a week and a half since he'd seen her in LA and yet that feeling flowing through him felt an awful lot like excitement.

Cooper hugged all three of them before Colton and Lucia walked to the desk to grab their items.

"I didn't even realize you were in town," Cooper said, smiling warmly at Maya as she took in the people all around them. They were lucky there was such a big course in Charleston, because this group of the team and their families would have been a bit large for a standard mini golf course. Probably too big for a *regular* golf course.

"Yeah, Colton and Lucia wanted me to visit again, and I figured it would be good to get out of the house." Her shoulder lifted before she turned to look at him.

"You mean one of them bought you a ticket without really asking because they missed you?"

Maya let out an almost laugh, a quick huff of air. "It's like they can't get enough of me."

"Making up for lost time, I think. I know Colton wishes he could've seen you more these last few years." He'd said as much on many occasions, especially recently. "Plus, offseason starts to get busy quick, so the more time he has with you now, the better."

"That's true. And I'm glad to see them. I was a stewing mess in the house, so it's nice to have some semblance of a purpose."

"You feeling any better?" Cooper had promised himself the next time he talked to her, he wouldn't press so hard. He'd overstepped a week and a half ago when they'd spoken at her house, and he didn't want to do that again.

Still, he needed to know she was okay.

Maya glanced at him warily. Her gaze remained steady before she responded, "A little. I'm going to look into tennis centers that need coaching staff. And I set up a physical therapy appointment for when I get back, if that's what you're asking."

Cooper shrugged, hoping there was even an ounce of nonchalance in the gesture. "I'm glad, but your recovery is yours alone, and I shouldn't have overstepped the way I did."

"I appreciated it, actually. I've been kind of in and out of it recently, struggling to see my future as anything but what it could have been. Your tough love was helpful. I think it was one of the things that motivated me to get my act together."

Cooper tried not to grin at that. "Just glad to be of help."

Colton and Lucia walked back over, the former handing Maya her club and ball before he led them to one of the three starting points. There was, unsurprisingly, a bit of a line, so Cooper turned back to his conversation with Maya.

"Are you a big mini golfer?"

So dumb. He'd never had trouble talking to women, but for some reason, when Maya was around, his tongue got twisted up and he said anything he could to keep the conversation going.

Maya narrowed her eyes at the course. "I'm the reigning queen of mini golf in my friend group, but I'm not sure about this. I don't understand the charity aspect of it at all."

Cooper chuckled, because he'd had Devin explain it to him twice, and even now, he still didn't fully get it.

"From my understanding, we all play, and then the five football players with the worst scores on each course will make a donation to the charity. Along the way, people can place bets on holes or the course in general, all of which goes to the charity. And then I think anybody who didn't have to donate during the game but wants to, can do so at the end."

He could practically see the gears working inside her head as she tapped her pencil against her chin.

"And family members? How do they factor in?"

Colton turned at her question. "Fun night for the kids, no risk. Only the players' cards matter."

Lucia elbowed him. "How dare you."

Colton held his hands up in surrender, a smile stretching across his face. "You're right. You could never be a risk and your card is the only one that matters."

Maya snorted, exchanging a glance with Lucia.

"So when I beat you guys, there's no glory?" Maya asked.

Colton and Lucia chuckled, and Cooper raised an eyebrow at the question. For someone who had been so low the last few weeks, this was a side of Maya he hadn't expected today.

"What do you want *if* you win?" Cooper asked.

Maya's eyes met his for a couple of seconds and in that time, he wondered if their almost-kiss was flashing in her head too. If the pull to each other they'd both been suppressing for years was back in full force for her like it was for him.

At the small uptick in the corner of her mouth, he was sure it was.

"You first."

Cooper thought for a moment as they took a step forward, the line before them dwindling. Colton and Lucia stepped up, bickering over who would putt first. "Well, now that I know you're planning on coaching, if I win, and when your wrist is better, I'd like a tennis lesson," he drawled.

She shook her head, but a wider smile was playing on her lips. "You could've asked for so many better things."

"There is nothing I want more than a tennis lesson. From you."

That might not have been entirely true, but he had meant it. Even if it *had been* just a tactic to see her more often.

He liked being friends with her. Or whatever this was.

Maya's smile widened as they stepped up again, now right behind Lucia, whose face was contorted into one of intense concentration while she readied her club. She was doing a great job of ignoring Colton trash talking her from where he'd picked up his ball.

"Your turn," Cooper said, keeping an eye on how far Lucia swung back in case she tried to take one of them out.

"When I win..." She tapped her pencil against her chin once more. "*When* I win, you double what you planned to donate to the charity today."

Something like exhilaration skittered in his chest at her words.

"You could've asked for so many better things," he repeated her words back to her, and the glimmer in her eye made that feeling in his chest grow.

Colton and Lucia collected their golf balls and moved to the line for the next hole as Maya stepped up, setting her pencil and papers on the small table beside her. She tapped the ball, grinning when it landed in the hole on her first try.

Spinning around to look at him triumphantly, she said, "Nothing's better than donating to charity and helping others."

As if those words had kickstarted something in her head, her eyebrows pulled together and she began twirling a strand of her hair around a finger of her free hand. Cooper wondered what she was thinking but didn't question her change in demeanor. He walked over, grabbed and pocketed her ball, then stepped up and smacked his into the hole in one drive as well. He marked a one on his scorecard, and when he turned to look back at Maya, she still looked pensive.

"Tiger? Tiger Woods? Is that you?" He waved her golf ball in front of her face.

Maya snorted, grabbing it and shoving past him.

When they reached the next hole, where another line awaited them, Cooper asked, "What's on your mind?"

"I was just thinking...well, I don't know. It might be dumb. It seems complicated, and I might not be able to do it."

Colton turned to look at his sister questioningly. "Do what?"

Lucia turned around as well and smiled encouragingly. Maya shrugged, almost like she was embarrassed to have their attention now. "I've just been thinking about what's next for me a lot. I thought coaching made sense for a while, but I've really wanted to do something more meaningful, you know? And then I got to talking with Delilah—you guys know Delilah." The three of them nodded, all having met her best friend at some point over the years.

"Well, she didn't have the greatest home life growing up, and she got super lucky with tennis. It was like her and her family's ticket out of that life. But not everybody has that chance, and I'd love to do something like that for under-privileged kids in Los Angeles. Raise money, find coaches, let them try something new and have the opportunity to show their stuff. Maybe be that ticket out for some of them while helping the whole community."

Cooper was stunned silent.

"Maybe that doesn't make sense, I don't know. I haven't figured it out yet. It was just a thought."

Colton was the first to speak. "No. It's a *great* idea. That sounds like the perfect way for you to do what you love while helping others, Mai."

Lucia nodded and agreed, squeezing Maya's free hand briefly. "It's great, Maya. I love that idea. If you think you'd need any kind of help, just let us know. I'd love to be a part of something so beautiful."

Pink colored Maya's cheeks. "Oh, well, I don't know…"

"She's serious. Anything you need help with, you let us know. Money, time, connections, just tell us," Colton chimed in.

Maya pointed ahead, where it was Colton and Lucia's turn to putt, and then she turned to Cooper. "What do you think?" she asked hesitantly.

Many of his friends had charities they'd helped create, were the face of, or donated to, but none had talked so reverently about helping others.

She was incredible.

He almost said as much but instead went for, "It's an amazing idea. It'll absolutely make a difference, and to even think of something like that is…" *Incredible.* "It's really great."

Maya was almost beaming. "Thank you! I'm going to start researching tomorrow. I know there's probably so much that will go into it." She paused. "I guess it's a good thing I have nothing but free time."

Cooper was still mulling over her selflessness when she stepped up to take her turn. They traded turns at each hole, and each time, he matched her strike for strike until the eleventh, where she took two more strokes than him. Maya snatched his card and scribbled something onto it, pouting.

When they finally finished the course, Cooper pocketed both their scorecards, smiling at the frowning face she'd drawn on his.

Cooper beat her by two strokes, and he would absolutely be asking for his tennis lesson the moment her wrist was ready. He'd even gotten her number, just for that purpose.

And he doubled his donation to Devin's charity anyway.

Chapter Seven

Maya

Searing pain slammed through Maya's wrist as Grayson, her friend and new physical therapist, tried to figure out her wrist's limits.

"Ouch," she croaked.

Maya's motivation had been peeking through and then dissipating since her brothers had first visited her a month ago. Delilah's visit and Cooper's story about his brother had helped with her motivation too, but what had finally pushed her was the idea she'd come up with a few days ago to start a charity. The moment she'd gotten back to Los Angeles, Maya had outlined her next steps, and going to physical therapy was at the top of the list.

She could be strong for her brothers. For her mother, who she knew—even without being able to hear her—was watching her.

For herself.

And for all those children she might be able to help one day.

It wasn't like the emotional turmoil she'd been feeling had just suddenly gotten better. Maya still didn't feel like much more than a shell of herself. But basic tasks *had* gotten marginally easier, and she pushed through them the best that she could.

"Sorry," Grayson murmured. His eyes cut to hers below his light-brown, shaggy bangs, and she couldn't help but look away, knowing she would break under the disappointment she saw there. Maya had met Grayson when he'd worked on the tour, and they'd become good friends. He'd established a practice in Los Angeles and had been generous enough to offer to see her for free every other Tuesday until she was back on her feet.

"Maya, it's been seven weeks since the surgery. You should've been in four weeks ago when the cast came off."

She grimaced. Grayson was absolutely right, and Maya had no excuse. Her first appointment should've been right before her brothers came to visit, but instead, she'd been wallowing in the world's biggest pity party on the floor of her childhood home.

"I know," Maya mumbled.

"Okay, well, your range of motion is clearly inhibited. Let's check your grip strength and then get started on the basic exercises you *should have* been doing at home," he declared pointedly.

With a sheepish smile, Maya tucked her hair behind her ear and picked up the little machine she was meant to squeeze in order to get a reading on her strength. At Grayson's frown, she knew it was not nearly what it should've been.

"Maya, have you been doing *anything* you were supposed to? Even the band work?"

Her finger found the tips of her hair, wrapping them around it as she once again did everything she could not to make eye contact with him.

"Not really."

"And why's that?"

"Haven't really had much motivation since Dr. Jeffords...since I found out I can't play tennis anymore."

"Well, not on the tour. You'll still be able to play at a less competitive level. But I understand. A lot of athletes feel that way," Grayson murmured. "Does you coming in today mean you've found a reason to try?"

Maya's mind flashed to herself on a tennis court with a bunch of kids laughing and smiling around her. Then, for some unknown reason, it flashed with Cooper's face, his dirty-blond hair mussed from running his hands through it, blue eyes sparkling, face cloaked in a hint of stubble.

"Something like that."

Grayson held out a hand to help her off the tall exam table, walking over to the other side of the room to grab a set of bands, two-pound dumbbells, and a squeeze ball. He set them down beside her.

"You know what to do."

For the first time in two months, since before she'd reinjured her wrist, Maya winced through her exercises, hoping that, with every rep, she was building herself up enough to one day play the sport she loved so much, even at a lower level.

Maya let out a hiss of pain as she sat at her dining table, wrist still sore from her physical therapy appointment earlier that morning. She knew if she'd decided to go sooner, it wouldn't have hurt so badly, but she tried to be proud of herself for going at all.

She laid out her ideas and to-do lists for the charity so she could take them all in. Maya had researched how to start one the last few days, and it'd only made her less sure she was capable of doing this.

Maya called her sponsors to ask if they would be willing to donate once she got a new bank account up and ready for the cause, but they told her that now that she wasn't playing, they had no reason to commit to that. Disheartening, but not all that surprising. They *did* offer to provide a few rackets and baskets of balls, which she was thankful for.

Next, she turned to her network, though she hated begging for favors from everyone she knew. It was embarrassing and went against everything she had made of herself, but she didn't have much of a choice.

Inevitably, she got questions about her injury and recovery, and she pretended she was doing better than she was because she didn't have time or energy to get into how difficult it had been so far.

Few knew of foundations that donated to charities such as this one. Even fewer thought they'd ever be able to coach. After all, most were from the academy in Florida and were on tour. They all offered their well wishes and told her they'd reach out if they were ever in the area, but Maya didn't want to hold her breath.

At the very least, she hoped these calls were generating buzz in the community, enough to convince even one person her cause was a worthy one.

Next, she texted her friends about the idea. Maya told them she knew they were too busy to help day to day, but she'd love it if they'd come by if they were ever free. She also let them know there would always be a place on the board for them.

Maya would have to keep the charity small, nothing fancy, no big organization. Maybe one day she could expand, once it grew legs and showed people what it could do. But at the very least, she would need a vice president and some coordinators to help her out.

She was frustrated. Everything required money, and money's what she *didn't* have. Even the items Maya had worked through weren't figured out. She didn't have set coaches, she didn't know if she had enough equipment, she didn't have funding. And she still had to figure out transportation, advertising, and a facility that would let her use their courts a few hours a week. Not to mention garnering enough interest to draw in the families of kids in the community.

Maya set her head on the table and took two deep breaths in and out. She wouldn't give up. She'd worked her whole life so she could make her own way in the world. She'd spent more blood, sweat, and tears than most people out on that tennis court so she could get a scholarship to Crestview, then she'd worked harder than anyone on her team to make it to the pros. She'd learned to do things on her own.

Her brothers' legacies were football, but hers was going to be this damn charity, because if there was one single thing she'd taken away from her mother's life, it was the need to give back.

Maya opened her computer and started making note of all the courts in the area, specifically ones closer to the less affluent neighborhoods in Los Angeles. Just as she typed in the number for the first one, Delilah's contact flashed across her screen.

Before Maya even had a second to greet her, Delilah asked, "Is it true? Are you really starting a charity for underprivileged kids?"

Maya's eyes welled up a bit, and she cleared her throat. "Yeah, Del. After we talked and I remembered how much it impacted your life, I thought it might be a great way to help kids like you here, even if it just helps families with after school care, you know? And if I can actually get it up and running, which is proving more difficult by the second, then I can still be in this world, still coach but do something that truly helps people," Maya rambled.

There was a sob and then, "You are one of my most favorite people, Mai."

A tear slipped down Maya's face before she could stop it. "And you're mine."

Delilah murmured fervently, "Anything you need when I'm free, just tell me. Any time I can get away from tournaments and training. You just tell me what I can do and I'll be there. I'll talk to some people to find coaches around you."

Maya wiped at her face once more, resting her elbow on the table, her face in her palm. "Just knowing I have your support is all I could ever ask for. I hope I can do you justice with this."

A hiccup from the other side of the phone. "Don't you say things like that to me right now! I'm already very emotional," Delilah all but wailed.

Maya smiled, and she knew no matter how hard this path was going to be, she would put in the work to make a difference. For her mother and for Delilah, and for all the kids like her best friend who just needed a chance.

"I mean it, Del. You're so inspiring."

"I love you, Mai. So much. I was mid practice match when I saw your text, and now I'm getting glared at, so I have to go and attempt to get it together enough to finish, but I can't wait to be a part of this. Keep me in the loop for everything."

"I love you more. Kick whoever's ass you're playing."

Delilah snickered. "Roger. See you soon."

"See you soon," Maya echoed before clicking out of the call. Nicola, Harper, and Sahar had all sent sweet messages during the conversation, offering their help whenever they were available.

Despair slipped away as Maya made separate notes beside transportation and advertising that read *need funding and courts first*, and then she called the first facility she'd found, feeling almost rejuvenated.

It would all be worth it. She knew it would be.

Chapter Eight

Maya

Twelve calls later, and Maya's happy spirits were beginning to wane again. Not a single facility was able to offer a discount for the courts, and many of them didn't have the availability she would need to coach kids after school. A couple of facilities said they didn't know the answer and would get back to her, but they seemed to be trying to get her off the phone, so she didn't put too much stock in that.

Maya blew out a breath as she tapped the second to last phone number into her phone, her left fist wrapped around the wooden edge of the dining table as if it would keep her upright when another facility needed to be crossed off.

She refused to let her new dream die so soon.

The line rang a few times before a woman answered, "Serve It Up, here to serve. How can I help you?"

Maya released a breath, ready to start the spiel again. "Hi, my name is Maya, and I'm calling to see if you do discounted rates for local charities. I'm in the early stages of starting one, something small, with the goal of coaching underprivileged children in the area after school. I'm looking to nail down a few details, like courts where I'll be able to host the lessons, coaches who may be interested in volunteering a few hours of their time, and other things like that."

There was a pause. Then the woman responded, "Sorry, I'm just writing this all down and taking a look at our calendar. Could you give me an idea of when you'd need the courts?"

"No worries! Ideally, we'd like to use the courts one to two evenings a week after school. I know that's typically your busiest time, so we're happy to take any hour or two you may have available here and there. Depending on how much it costs to rent the courts—"

"Nonsense. We take Tuesdays and every other Thursday off after noon. Typically, nobody's around to run things here, but I'd be happy to come in and help out those days for a cause like this. I'll talk to the owners about pricing, but four to six hours a week on days we don't typically have lessons anyway shouldn't cost much."

Excitement zipped through Maya. This was the first time she wasn't immediately shut down, and she almost couldn't believe it.

"Oh...well, that would be amazing, actually. I'd love to come by and talk more with you sometime soon if that would be okay? And just so I know who I'm talking to, could I get your name?"

"Silly me! I'm Viola Pearson, manager here at Serve It Up. You can come by any time in the next few weeks to chat and look at courts. Hopefully by then, I'll have a schedule and rate for you. How does that sound?"

"That would be perfect. Thank you so much, Viola."

Finally, a big win. Sure, it wasn't confirmed, but Maya had needed this.

"Of course! I just need your first and last name, a phone number, and best email."

Maya gave her the information.

"You wouldn't happen to be Maya Beaumont, professional tennis player, would you?"

Maya was surprised. After she'd used her last name for the seventh facility in a row and received no indication that anyone knew who she was, she'd stopped mentioning it. For one, it felt icky to use her time on the tour to secure courts, but more than that, she felt a twinge of sadness that no one seemed to know who she was. Like nothing she'd accomplished meant anything to anyone but her.

She should've been used to it by now. Her brothers were professional football players, so it wasn't unusual for her to be out of the limelight in comparison. Plus, no one, not even people in the tennis world, paid attention to players' names unless they were playing in grand slams, which she hadn't been doing much of. Still, it stung.

"I—Yes, I am." Maya chuckled, almost in disbelief.

"Oh my." Maya heard shuffling and then scratching, like Viola was writing something else down. "Well now I'm *definitely* going to get you those courts. You just come whenever you want next week and we'll get everything figured out. I will ask for one thing though."

Maya's heart sank, and she hoped it wouldn't cost too much. "Of course."

"I would *die* if I could get a signed tennis ball from you, and I'd *love* to pick your brain about the tour a bit."

Maya blew out a relieved breath. She tried to tamp down on the giddiness that filled her at knowing she had at least one fan. "Absolutely! I can do that for you."

"Perfect. Well, Maya Beaumont, I hope to see you very soon."

"You too," Maya responded before the call disconnected.

She looked out the window, noting it was now dark, and rather than seeing out into the backyard, Maya only noticed the smile that stretched across her face.

Finally.

Maya knew she would need to get a job coaching on the side, no matter what happened with charity funding opportunities down the line. She made a note to ask Viola when she talked to her in person.

She had forgotten what it was like to be busy. To have a purpose, something to look forward to.

The day had been a roller coaster, and even though she was happy to have gotten a win, the feeling that she couldn't accomplish a single thing without funding was dampening her spirits significantly.

Maya heaved a sigh. She'd done enough research for the day, and what she'd learned was that this would be challenging. Incredibly so. But she also knew it would be very rewarding.

From the age of twelve, Maya had had trouble asking for help, plain and simple. The moment she'd realized how her panic attacks were negatively impacting Colton, she'd slept with her bedroom door closed and sat in the bathtub when it came time to calm herself so she didn't bother him.

Maya never again wanted to feel the way she'd felt that night, like the silly little sister who was ruining her brother's chances on the field by screwing up his sleep schedule. Finding ways to do life on her own, invisible and amenable, was her motto.

Asking her brothers to help with the charity was out of the question. They'd done far too much for her in her lifetime and had their own lives to deal with. Plus, Maya didn't want to mix family with business. It would make things weird and had the real possibility of creating tense situations.

Her eyes landed on the unopened text from Cooper, checking in on her charity-starting process, her heartbeat picking up at the knowledge that he was thinking about her. They'd been texting more since mini golf, just three or four texts a day, mostly checking in or, less often, Cooper joking that he was ready for his tennis lesson.

She wanted to talk to someone about the charity, and if she told Colton about how difficult it was going to be, he'd sweep in stubbornly and force his help, financial or otherwise, because that was just his way.

But Cooper wouldn't be like that. He was a friend more than a brother.

Kind of.

It was a weird word for her and Cooper's relationship. They'd spent enough time together in the past few years that they were no longer really acquaintances. And yet "friend" didn't fully embody the flicker of feeling she'd gotten when he was at the house, talking her through his brother's story. It didn't properly explain how, even though she still felt the emptiness and anger lurking when she was with her brothers, something about being around Cooper seemed to chase it away entirely. Even getting a text from him during a lull in her day seemed to make her feel better.

Then there was their very real almost-kiss. It had been the most on fire and out of control she'd ever felt, and he'd barely touched her, never even let his lips brush hers. She didn't think that was normal for a platonic relationship.

But that's why he'd pulled away, she guessed. To keep that line between them clear.

So, she texted her *friend*.

Chapter Nine

Cooper

The moment Cooper saw Maya's *It could be better* text, he was video calling her, his chicken and vegetable dinner abandoned on the kitchen island. He'd spent longer than normal in the weight room, trying to work off the shitty feeling that'd been eating at him the last few weeks. It hadn't worked; all it'd done was force him to eat dinner sometime near eleven.

She picked up on the second ring, hesitantly answering, "Hello?"

"Hey, Mai. Sorry if you're busy. I'm more of a caller than a texter, and you seemed like you needed someone to talk to."

She propped the phone up on the table in front of her, and he took in the tired droop of her shoulders, her long hair up in a ponytail.

"Hate that you figured that out from one text," she said, grimacing.

"Call it intuition."

Maya sighed, looking away. "I've just been calling practically everybody I know to find funding and coaching and everything else I might need for this. I found a facility, and while the manager seemed enthusiastic, I have no idea what their rate will be for the courts." Her mouth twisted to the side. "Why's it so hard to do something good for others?" She'd asked it so quietly, he'd barely heard her.

"Mai, it's only been a few days since you started researching. The fact that you've already gotten a potential facility is impressive as hell."

She shrugged. "Maybe. I also got my sponsors to donate a few rackets and baskets of balls, which was nice."

"See? That's great."

"I didn't mean to bother you when I texted you that. I've just been on a roller coaster of emotions today, and I don't feel like talking to my brothers about it right now."

Cooper tried not to let his chest swell too much that she'd chosen to talk to him over Colton and Landon. "You're never bothering me. I asked because I know how difficult it can be, and that's from people who have whole teams helping them get it set up."

Not for the first time, Cooper recognized how remarkable Maya was. The fact that she was working so tirelessly at a cause that was so selfless made Cooper want to do something too.

He had more money than he knew what to do with at this point, and if it could help her—and by extension local kids—by donating some, why would he not?

"Let me pay the upfront costs."

Maya reared back, almost falling out of her chair. "What?" She shook her head like she hadn't heard him correctly before asking again. "What?"

"I can pay for the facility, transportation, and a fundraising event to get you up and running."

"Stop saying that like you're reading me the weather! That's thousands of dollars."

Cooper shrugged, grinning. "What, like that's a lot?" At her glare, he said, "Maya, I'd rather it go to something like this than something stupid like me buying another car. The last thing I need is another car. So, really, you'd be doing *me* a favor."

His whole life, people had wanted to take and take and take, and so he'd given and given and given. Friendship with the mayor's kid? Alright. Money? Sure. His body? Okay. For once, he was offering something he wanted to give to someone he wanted to give it to.

Her face was still twisted into downright shock. It was adorable. Her refusal to accept and surprise that he would even offer was proof that she wouldn't use him like others who always expected him to give, always expected to take. It only made him want to help more.

"Why would you support a tennis charity on the other side of the country?"

"Because I want to help you. And because I want to do something I'm proud of."

Maya scoffed. "Two championship wins isn't enough?"

"Something meaningful. Impactful. I want to be like you." And maybe he was being a little selfish too, but it might even get his parents off his back. Prove to them that he *did* do things that were worthwhile as a football player.

Cooper was ready to do more, be more than a guy who played ball and slept with pretty girls. He knew everyone had a reputation, good or bad, and it was time to show there was a different side to him than others knew.

But more than that, he hadn't been kidding when he said he wanted to be like Maya. Cooper wanted an ounce of her selflessness and compassion.

And yes, he cared about her, and if this helped her *and* others, that would make it all the more worth it.

"I don't know..."

"Think it over for me. I'll talk to the Sabers' philanthropy department tomorrow to see if they have any tips, even if it's just tax stuff."

Maya pulled her hands into the sleeves of her sweater, nodding slowly. "Okay. Thank you so much, Cooper. I appreciate your offer, but—"

"Think it over," he repeated softly, more firmly.

She nodded again. "Okay. I know it's late there, so I'll let you go, but thank you for talking to me. It made me feel a lot better."

"I'm glad."

"Oh, and...sorry to ask this of you, but do you think you could hold off on mentioning this to Colt? I think it would hurt his feelings if he knew I'd talked to you about all this before him."

"Yes, of course." He didn't love keeping secrets from Colton, but he understood her concern.

She waved before ending the call, and Cooper thanked his intuition, or whatever it was that'd told him he needed to call her.

The next day, Cooper woke up in a great mood, and even enjoyed a light lift. It all came crashing down quickly, though, when his mother called once again to act as the mouthpiece for his father's agenda. Unfortunately, his parents were aware his contract was up this season, and though he was pretty certain it would get extended, his mom and dad seemed set on the idea that this was God's way of telling Cooper it was time to come home.

Cooper was inclined to disagree, blasphemous as it might have been. Despite him explaining that he was on the way to the philanthropy offices to help get a charity set up as they spoke, she still emphasized he would be doing more important work by coming home. Though she didn't specify what that important work would be.

As if leaving his closest friends and a sport he loved to play would be so easy.

Cooper walked into the philanthropy offices, and he tried to let go of the negative feeling that'd built in him while on the phone, forcing a smile for the man behind the front desk. "Hi, I'm—"

"Cooper Hayes, I know," the guy said, setting a stack of stapled papers to the side. "How can we help you today?"

That recognition would never get old. "I was hoping to talk to someone about how to get a charity set up."

"Oh! Did you want someone to set something up for you or..."

"It's for a friend. She's starting a small tennis charity, and I wanted to see if I could get tips on where to begin."

The guy blinked at him a few times before looking at his computer screen. Then he pointed down the hall. "Krista is available now to answer questions about that. Second door on your left."

Cooper looked down at the man's name plate. "Thanks, Josh. Appreciate it."

Cooper followed the directions and walked into the office of a fifty-something woman with gray hair slicked back into a bun and what seemed to be a permanent frown on her face. Even though he thought she was smiling at him, she still looked upset.

"Hi, Mr. Hayes. How can I help you?"

Cooper explained himself once more, and Krista nodded toward the chairs in front of her desk.

"I'm going to print some tax documents your friend should complete, as well as the manual we typically have our newer employees follow when they're getting something like this set up. Will your friend's charity be based in Charleston?"

Cooper shook his head. "Los Angeles, actually."

Krista tapped a pen against her nose twice as she hummed. "Okay. Let me ask around to see if I can find any nonprofits or foundations that might be open to supporting a charity like this. I will say, it's going to be difficult for your friend to start on her own. There's a reason we have an entire department dedicated to working with players to get theirs set up."

Cooper tried not to let that dishearten him. He would keep that from Maya when he talked to her next.

"I assume the answer is no since she's not a part of the organization, but there's no chance we could help her get started, is there?"

Krista almost seemed apologetic as she shook her head. "I'm sorry, I don't think so. If she were starting it here, it would be more likely, as we do help with many non-Sabertooths local charities. But unfortunately, if it's going to be based out of Los Angeles, we won't be able to."

"I figured as much."

Krista pulled a stack of papers from the printer, handing them across the desk to Cooper. "Some ways you can help are to make sure she sets up a strong mission statement, encourage her to research the cause, and make sure she looks into other organizations with similar goals."

Cooper pulled out his phone and began typing. "Sorry, I'm just taking notes."

"No need to apologize. This is all in that manual as well. I've printed the documents she'll need to submit to the state of California to get tax-exemption status. That'll help when she's receiving donations. It sounds like she won't be putting together a board of directors, but she should definitely find local coordinators who can help with things like marketing and outreach."

Cooper nodded, flipping through the packet she'd handed him. "Okay."

"She should also come up with a fundraising strategy, and I highly recommend an opening event, like a gala. You can invite Sabertooths players and staff and people she may know in that area to raise money to help fund it for a while until she's getting steady donations. Of course, I don't know her personal financial status, but that's costly on its own..."

Krista looked at him expectantly, and he set the papers onto the desk. "Yes, I'm hoping to help fund the event and anything else she may need to start, like paying for tennis courts and transportation."

"Good, good. She'll need to make sure she's compliant with local legal regulations, which means she'll be filing and reporting on the charity annually. I recommend finding a good tax attorney to help.

"And like I mentioned, she's going to want to find people who can help get the word out and volunteers to be there during the lessons, including coaches and probably some other staff. I don't know much about tennis, but I imagine that'll be helpful."

When it seemed Krista was done speaking, Cooper stood, extending his hand for her to shake. She seemed surprised but did so. "Thank you so much, Krista. This is immensely helpful."

"Happy to help! If you need any more advice, feel free to come back, or I can put your friend in touch with someone who runs similar charities in our department."

"That would be amazing. Thank you again."

Cooper stepped out of the office feeling significantly lighter and like he might actually be able to help Maya in more ways than one.

Chapter Ten

Maya

Landon looked at the contents of the fridge incredulously before turning to Maya with his hands on his hips. "How am I meant to work in these conditions? There's nothing here I can make for us."

"Who said you were making food? And I've barely had time to shower, let alone go get groceries."

Landon sniffed at the air before screwing up his face playfully. "And once again, you smell ripe."

Maya threw the rest of the bagged loaf of bread at him, and he caught it easily. "I just showered, asshat. And strike two for that one. If I hear one more thing about me showering…" She tried looking at him menacingly but knew that had never been her forte.

Despite his teasing, happy wasn't a strong enough word for what she felt now that he was here. She'd missed out on a lot with her brothers, but even more so with Landon, and being in LA with him again made her feel nostalgic for the rare times they'd hung out after Colton left for Crestview. Sure, she'd made efforts to keep in touch with them while on tour, but those had mostly been superficial. This felt like it had the potential to remedy whatever had separated them all those years ago.

He placed the bread back onto the counter, closing the fridge door. "Hey, you're the one who brought it up."

"Let's just go get food," she grumbled, moving to the foyer to grab her keys.

"Whatcha wanna get? I'm down to go anywhere but downtown." His whole body shuddered as he followed her, like he was remembering something horrifying. "Downtown LA is lawless."

"Why don't we just go to Dino's?" The two of them had often snuck out to Dino's Diner since their father hadn't allowed Landon to eat out much. *If we're going to do something nostalgic, we may as well do it properly, right?*

"Hey! I almost forgot about that place. Is it even still around?"

Maya locked the front door and they jumped into her car, still outside the garage from when she'd picked Landon up from the airport.

When she typed it into her phone and the navigation popped up, she answered, "Allegedly."

"Alrighty then." Landon grinned. "Let's get some food poisoning."

It didn't take long to get there, and the drive was familiar, though she had always been the passenger. The diner was run down, the tall sign out front hanging askew, lights flickering, and when Maya looked too hard at the window in front of where they'd parked, she noticed what looked like packaging tape across the cracks in the glass.

Nice.

Even the staff seemed surprised to have customers, and the only other people in the tiny restaurant were a few very old couples.

Landon led them to a booth, where water and menus were dropped onto their table. Maya made an effort to flip through it, but she knew she wanted the banana chocolate chip pancakes with eggs, bacon, and hashbrowns, just like old times.

"Not to sound like a snob, but especially now that I try to make my own food, this all looks disgusting." He pulled his baseball cap low over his face, though there really was no chance anyone here besides *maybe* the staff would know who he was.

Maya rolled her eyes. "You do sound like a snob. One meal won't kill you."

Landon's menu dropped to the table, and he stabbed at a picture with his pointer finger. "This just might."

She tried to suppress the laugh that bubbled out of her when she realized he was right. It was a plate of steak, but it almost looked green. Why would Dino's even serve steak?

"It's like something out of a Dr. Seuss book," he muttered, still looking at it.

"Mm, green steak and ham. Your favorite."

"Right…Think I'm gonna have to pass on my favorite today. Not sure I could stomach that. I have practice tomorrow, and I'd rather not throw up during."

Maya shrugged. "Clearly, you're no longer built for Dino's."

"A real tragedy."

"Hi, are we ready to order?" a pretty waitress with curly hair asked, chipper, her eyes on Landon, whose smile was already widening at her.

He leaned toward her and whispered conspiratorially, "What do you recommend?"

"Depends on what you're wanting."

"Something that won't make me sick?" Maya kicked him under the table, but the woman smiled knowingly.

"I'd stick to pancake meals, and probably steer clear of most of the meats."

"Something told me I'd be meeting an angel today. Let's do a fruit stack, just the pancakes, eggs, and hashbrowns."

She nodded, writing in the little notepad before smiling at Maya, who gave her order quickly.

When the waitress hurried away, Landon set his chin in his palm. "You feeling any better?" he asked quietly.

Maya looked down at the table, fiddling with the ends of her hair. "I am," she answered, surprised it was somewhat true. She wasn't wholly better, and she still had days she wanted to smash every tennis racket she owned, but she also had good days. Productive days, where she felt like she actually had a future.

It'd been less than a week since she'd talked to Cooper over the phone, and she'd been poring over the materials he'd sent her from the Sabertooths' philanthropy department since. Maya had planned to visit the courts yesterday, after the Serve It Up rate sheet had come in much cheaper than she'd expected, but Viola was coming off an illness, so they'd rescheduled to later in the week.

Things were slowly coming together.

Landon smiled, and Maya could see how genuine it was, like knowing she was happy could change his own mood. "I'm so glad. You said you've been busy? What's been going on?"

"I...um..." She didn't know why she was nervous to talk about it. Pushing through it, she continued, "I'm starting a charity. Nothing big. Something local. I want to coach kids in the area who don't have access to the sport."

"Oh, wow! That's amazing. I figured you'd coach, but I didn't even think of something to that scale. Pretty damn cool, Mai."

His words nearly choked her up, and she looked out the window, which, luckily, was not being held together by tape. "Yeah, I'm excited about it. It's been a lot of work, but I can't wait until it's set up and I can be back in the tennis world again."

"I don't think being injured means you're out of that world."

Maya shrugged again. "Feels that way sometimes." All the time, really. Only when she was talking to people in the community, like her friends or those at the tennis facility, did she not feel that way.

"Are you still keeping up with the girls? Do you think going to see them play would make you feel less like that?"

Maya had thought about it, especially since Indian Wells was currently taking place in California, but she worried about going back right now. It'd been a little over a month since she'd moved to Los Angeles, and though she had been able to watch her friends play on television, she knew being there, watching in the stands, being near her coaches and Anya and Ryan and all the people she knew on tour would be too painful. She wasn't ready yet, not for the pitying looks or the hurt that would inevitably follow when she felt the competition swirling through her veins with nowhere to go.

"I don't think I'm ready for that just yet."

Landon nodded. "Fair enough. What work have you done for the charity so far?"

She told him all the calls she'd made. How she'd found a facility she was excited about and gotten equipment she needed. How she'd found a way to have kids bussed straight from certain schools. Maya didn't mention how expensive she suspected it would be or how she still had no idea what she would do about the cost. She didn't want his money, her brain still trying to find a way to make it work without taking Cooper up on his offer.

Like he could read her mind, he said, "Sounds expensive."

"Oh, you know. Some money here and there."

"Do you have the money to front those costs?"

"I—I'm figuring it out."

He didn't respond, but by the way his eyebrows drew together, she knew she hadn't been convincing. "Cooper and Colton offered to help, separately, but I'm not sure I want to take money from anybody."

"Then I won't offer, even though I could if you needed."

Maya sighed, grateful. "Thank you. I just want to be able to do something on my own, you know? You guys have made your mark on the world. It's my turn, and if I take help from either of you, it won't feel like I'm making my own way."

"I get it. So don't take money from me or Colton. Let's pretend mixing money with family could go wrong, even though you know Colton and I wouldn't care. Why not Cooper?"

Maya thought about her relationship with Cooper. How he'd always made an effort to ask her about her life when she'd come visit Colton. How right it'd felt when he'd been pressed against her in the bar. How close it had come to something more.

Their waitress set their food onto the table, and Maya shoved those thoughts down.

"I'm worried it could get messy," she responded cryptically.

Plus, Maya knew if she took money from him, she'd spend the rest of her life working herself to the point of exhaustion to pay him back.

Landon's smile told her he knew exactly what she meant. "Well, messy relationships are no secret to me, so I get it. But I think if you're going to get this done, and you don't want to take money from me or Colton, and you've done as much research as you have into foundations with no luck for finding donors, this might be your only option. I'm sure you can find ways to keep costs down." He looked at her meaningfully. "Just don't feel like you shouldn't pursue your dream because things could get 'messy.'"

Maya cocked her head at that statement, tucking it away for later when she was alone and could think a bit harder about it.

"Maybe. Anyway, tell me about you. I'm tired of talking about myself."

"Not much to tell, really. Football's been good. Dad's been on my ass more now that Colton isn't paying as much attention to him, but that's nothing new. I'm getting very good at ignoring his calls."

Maya knew this was the other side of being a Beaumont. Any time she felt sad that she'd only had one parent, she remembered that her brothers, who'd gotten all of their father's attention, only mattered to him when it came to football. She knew if they'd had the opportunity to choose, they would've wished to be in her shoes instead. To have the freedom to do what they wanted, to not have to spend every minute of their free time on an inherited dream.

She didn't miss talking to her father. When she'd been on tour, trying to keep the family together, calling once or twice a month, Maya had made an effort to include him. On the rare occasions he'd answered, he'd hardly said a word anyway.

"I'm sorry. I'm glad you're not answering every single one like Colt used to. I'm glad you're both finding ways to deal with him."

Landon nodded as he began eating, and Maya followed his lead. They made small talk, mostly about his teammates, the parties he'd been to, and how much he was enjoying San Jose. Maya listened closely, pocketing every new piece of him he was sharing.

She'd missed being close to *both* her brothers. Which is why, when there was a lull in the conversation as they finished their meals, she said quietly, "I'm really sorry we grew apart after Mom died. That Colton and I stuck together through it and you sort of got pushed out because of your relationship with him. It's one of my biggest regrets about that time."

Her brother shrugged like it didn't matter, but she knew it had to have affected him in some way. His fingers drumming on the table made it clear he was uncomfortable, but still, he said, "We were coping the best we could. Losing Mom was hard on you, and you and Colton had always been close. It made sense you guys leaned on each other."

Maya wouldn't tell him the reason she and Colton had gotten so close during that time was because he'd watched her fall apart almost every night and held her together when she couldn't do it alone anymore.

Even after Colton had left, she hadn't wanted to lean on Landon. At that point, Landon had started cooking for her when he wasn't too tired after practice. Maya hadn't wanted to ask for more. She hadn't wanted to ruin his life too.

Maya pulled at a few strands of her hair. "But you were hurting too. So, I'm sorry for not being there for you. I know you and Colton have your beef, and I'm not going to pretend I understand it. Or that I have any right to judge either of you, since your childhoods were vastly different from mine. So while I can't change what happened after Mom, I do want to fix things now."

"Maya, you were the youngest. You needed *us*. I failed you by not being there for you like Colton was. You have no reason to apologize."

Maya's hand stilled, her fork dropping the couple of inches onto her plate. "You knew about that?"

Landon's eyes were sad, his smile pained. "Of course I did. I didn't know what to do. Colton always seemed to know how to help, so I stepped back. I figured you didn't need us both." He pushed his plate away from him. "And after he left, when I didn't hear you at night anymore and you seemed to go on with life, I figured you didn't need me."

Maya didn't realize she was crying until she felt a drop land on her hand. She wiped at her face, looking up at the ceiling, which was just a bunch of colored pipes. "I didn't want to ask for help after Dad got mad at Colt. But I did—I *do* need you both. You're my big brother, Landon. Me being close with Colton doesn't make that any less true."

Her brother's eyes flicked away from her, and she saw more emotion in them than she could ever remember from him.

When he finally made eye contact again, he grinned like nothing had happened. "Guess it's a damn good thing we're less than an hour flight away then, right?"

Chapter Eleven

Cooper

Stepping out into the March evening sun, Cooper swiped away from the texts with his mother, hoping he'd remember to respond when he was less annoyed with his parents. He noticed the woman leaving the facility at the same time as him, and he made an effort to step away from her, trying to put some distance between them in case there were any paparazzi outside the building. It was something he'd noticed he'd been doing more and more.

No need to be linked to someone he'd never even spoken to.

His phone vibrated, and when he realized it was Maya calling, he answered immediately.

"Maya? What's wrong?" They'd still been texting a few times a day, but the last time they'd spoken on the phone was a week ago, when Cooper had called and offered to pay the upfront costs of the charity.

"Oh, uh, sorry. Nothing's wrong. I probably should've texted you, but I've been doing a lot of thinking. Well, actually, I was looking at every single foundation and nonprofit that might help fund the charity and kind of came up empty, so I'm agreeing to your offer. With some conditions."

Cooper felt his heart rate pick up a hair as he made it across the expansive Sabertooths stadium parking lot toward the restaurant where he was meeting the guys, a grin on his face. "Shoot."

"The first is that I will be paying you back. I've charted how much this will all cost over the coming months. The price of courts and transportation is uncharacteristically low because the facility is being kind, so operating this charity shouldn't be too expensive. If I'm taking money from you, it'll only be enough to pay for a small fundraising gala, as well as the startup costs. Once we get donations, I'll be set for a while and then can hope for rolling contributions as we show how important our work is." There was a noise like she was shifting the phone. "I hope. And I'm going to coach on the side, so it may take a while, but I'll pay back every last penny."

"Maya, I—"

"Non-negotiable, Coop. I can't accept your help unless I find a way to pay you back eventually."

Cooper decided not to fight her on it now, though he knew he'd never accept the money. He was doing this because he wanted to, not because he felt obligated to. For once, he was doing something for someone because *he* wished to.

"Fine. What's your next condition?" He jogged across the street before turning down a wide alley with little shops.

"If we do this, I want you to be a cofounder. All the stuff you've sent me from the philanthropy department has helped me immensely, and especially since you're funding the first bit, I'd love for you to be my copilot."

"Maya, that's okay. All I'm really good for is the money anyway," he joked. "I'd be of no help to you."

Maya was silent for a moment. "What the hell are you talking about? Why do you put yourself down like that?"

Cooper almost ran into a telephone pole at the change in her voice. She sounded legitimately upset.

Before he could respond, Maya continued, "You're intelligent as hell, and you'd be a great cofounder." His cheeks heated at the praise. "If we're doing this, you're my partner. You don't even have to do any of the work if you don't want to or don't have time."

He knew he'd have some time to help her, even if it wasn't always in person, especially since offseason camps didn't start for over a month. But if she said she trusted him, once again, he wasn't going to fight her.

"I'd like to help, then."

"Great! Later this week, I'm going to go talk to Viola at the tennis center I was telling you about to get the ball rolling on a schedule and advertising."

"When do you think you'll be doing that?" Cooper asked, pulling his phone away from his ear to look for flights to Los Angeles.

"Probably Friday? Viola said she'd be available then."

"Perfect, I'll be there."

"What? Cooper, you don't have to fly here for this. I can talk to her on my own."

He chose a flight and booked it. "Cofounder, remember?"

"Yeah, but when I said that, it was because of what you've already done and like...your ideas on things. Not so that you'd come here when you're busy with football."

"Maya?"

"Yes?"

"I'll see you Thursday night."

Maya laughed and then sighed. "Okay, Coop. See you Thursday."

Thursday night had rolled around, and with practice earlier in the day, the long flight, and the dullness of having to go through George's "to-do" emails, Cooper must have fallen asleep on the couch. The lamps in the living room were dimmed, and the back porch light was on. He couldn't see much past the pool, but he thought there was movement in the hot tub, the lights inside the stone area on.

"Maya?" he called into the darkness. "Are you upstairs?"

Silence said she wasn't, so he stepped out onto the porch, enjoying the cool breeze that kissed his cheeks and arms. Cooper approached the hot tub slowly, and when he was a few feet away, he saw Maya almost entirely submerged, her head resting against the stone of the hot tub, eyes closed.

She looked relaxed, far more so than the last couple of times he'd seen her. He liked it. After everything she'd been dealing with recently, she deserved it.

Maya cracked an eye when he got close. "The old man rises from his slumber."

His lips parted. She stood, and he forced himself to look away from the swell of her breasts in the flimsy bathing suit she wore, but it was too late. When he closed his eyes, he saw the drops of water as they fell down her body steadily, already ingrained in his mind. He heard movement in the water, and when he opened his eyes, she sat on the bench behind her, as if giving him room to join her. He closed his lips when he could hardly find words to respond.

Maya smirked. "It's okay if you can't hang," she challenged him. "If I were old, I'd be tired at eight too."

He cleared his throat. "I'd hardly call someone four years older than you *old*."

She looked at a spot across from her, goading Cooper to prove himself by getting in. After a moment of thought, he ripped his shirt and jeans off, leaving him in boxers, and slipped in, keeping a healthy distance from the leg she swirled. He prayed she hadn't seen the way his dick strained at the cloth, still trying to push the image of her out of his head.

He *had* to stop thinking about her.

Maya was so far off-limits that it was unreal. She was Colton's little sister, and more than that, he wasn't sure he was a good fit for her. While he was done with the "girl in every port" lifestyle, he hadn't been in a serious relationship since college. And even that had only ended in hurt for him. He didn't have much to give her, and Maya Beaumont deserved everything with someone who was absolutely crazy for her, ready to yell it from rooftops.

It had been a bad idea when they'd almost kissed a year and a half ago, and it was a bad idea now.

"How are you feeling?"

Maya brought her foot back toward her body. "A little better. Definitely not perfect, but the work I've been doing has been a great distraction. And going to physical therapy helped. I think being cooped up inside was making things worse."

"I can imagine."

"How's Colton doing? I haven't talked to him much since mini golf."

"He's doing really well, honestly. I'm glad he and Lucia finally moved in together because he was becoming such a whiny bastard the nights she slept apart from him."

Maya watched her hand rise through the water, then flipped it palm down. "They seem really happy. She's good for him.

He set boundaries with Dad for the first time ever, and I know it was because of her."

"Yeah, your dad's a real...character."

"No need to filter yourself. He sucks. I know he was hard on them long before, but things got so much worse when Mom died. Colton's entire life was micromanaged, and Landon barely fared better."

"And yours?"

"Hmm?"

"What was *your* life like with him?" Cooper had heard a lot about Troy Beaumont from Colton's perspective, but whenever he and Maya had talked, it had mostly been about her life on tour and the countries she'd enjoyed visiting.

She shrugged. "Oh, you know. He wasn't around much. Always at their practices or games. I barely had to see him, luckily."

Maya must have seen the angry look on Cooper's face, the hard set of his jaw, so she continued, "Colton tried his best to be there, but I was taking too much attention away from his football. And by the time Dad moved to Charleston to be with Colton my senior year, I could take care of myself."

Cooper's brows furrowed. "Colton told you that you were taking too much attention away from his football?" That didn't sound like him at all.

She shook her head. "Oh, no. He would never. My dad heard him helping me get to sleep after a particularly bad panic attack one night after Mom died. I was struggling pretty badly, even four months later, and he always helped me get them under control. But when Dad found out, he told me I was screwing with Colton's sleep schedule and I needed to deal with my problems on my own like everybody else." She shrugged again. "So I did."

The willpower it took for Cooper not to get Troy Beaumont's phone number and rip him a new one was honestly worthy of applause. He clenched his jaw more, if that was even possible, gripping the concrete bench he sat on to stop him from reaching toward her and comforting her.

Cooper couldn't imagine treating his daughter like trash because she wouldn't be a great football player like his sons, and then when she needed him most, telling her to deal with her pain on her own because she was impacting her brother's football.

How fucking disgusting. A disgrace of a human being.

And after all of that, forcing her to grow up on her own, believing her feelings and experiences weren't as important as other people's, and leaving her in this house alone at seventeen years old.

The baby of the family who had to grow up quickly because her father hadn't stepped up the way he should've.

Cooper inhaled a calming breath, knowing his anger would do nothing to help. Her dad was a piece of shit. Cooper had learned that in his few interactions with him and after hearing all the shit he used to say to Colton before Colton had finally put his foot down and all but kicked him out of his life. But now, hearing how he'd treated Maya as well, her father would be lucky if he didn't get socked the next time he showed up at a Sabertooths game.

"Where were your grandparents?"

"Dad's parents died when I was younger. Mom's parents were in Michigan last I heard. They were always away when I was growing up, which was fortuitous for Dad, since he didn't like us seeing them."

"I'm surprised they weren't here more after your mom..." Cooper tried to find a word that wasn't as harsh as *died*.

"You can say she died. It's what happened. And yeah, I don't know." Maya looked up at the sky, her head resting on the outside of the hot tub. "It was almost like they disappeared from our lives after Mom. Never could figure out why. Though maybe it was because we weren't as Indian as the rest of our cousins. Or maybe it was just too hard to see us when Mom was gone. Who knows."

Cooper hoped neither of those were the case. They would be doing themselves a disservice in not getting to know their grandchildren, especially Maya. He knew they would have been proud of her if they had the opportunity to be.

"Have you thought about reaching out?"

Maya picked her head back up and began playing with the water again, studying her hand as the water forced resistance in her movement. Cooper would have given anything and everything to know what she was thinking.

"Sure, some. Especially after Mom died. But now I figure if they'd wanted to talk to us, they'd have reached out, right? Is it my responsibility?"

"I'm honestly not sure."

Her leg brushed his, and he nearly jumped. He did *not* appreciate the way his body seemed on edge around Maya. He didn't remember it always being like this, but it would certainly be a hindrance moving forward.

This situation needed a sticky note slapped onto it that read *this can only end poorly*.

"Were you able to see your family?" Maya asked. "I know you were annoyed when you missed your flight to see them last month."

Cooper grimaced, looking toward the shed behind the hot tub. He still hadn't planned a trip home, not ready to explain to his parents, once again, that what he was doing was important to him, whether or not it was important to them.

"No, not yet."

Maya cocked her head. He marveled at how near predatory she looked. "Scared of seeing an old flame?"

"An old flame? Now who sounds like an old geezer?"

She splashed at him.

"Nice deflecting, cowboy."

"Things are strained with my parents right now. Or at least they will be once I go home. And Oakridge Springs has always been the town I left behind for a reason. It's a *very* small town, and I've just built up a bit of a reputation."

"A reputation."

"Yeah. You know, you do something enough, it stops becoming surprising and it starts becoming…expected. And sometimes, I just want to go home, see my family, and be done with it. I don't want all the rest of it that comes with living in Oakridge Springs."

"Clearly, nobody in the town knows you well enough to recognize you're not your reputation. Which means they don't deserve any better than a cold shoulder from you."

Cooper marveled at her willingness to support him, despite not knowing how he'd gotten the reputation in the first place. Something knocked in his chest at the resolute set of her beautiful features, like nothing would change her mind about him.

"Unless I deserve the reputation I have because it's based entirely in fact."

Her lips thinned, and he thought she leaned closer, just a hair.

"If I ever go to Oakridge Springs, Tennessee, they better watch out, because I'm going out swinging if I hear anybody say anything about your *reputation*."

Cooper's mouth twitched up into a smile. Did she want to come with him to Tennessee?

"I have the same reputation in Charleston—there are just more people there so it's less in my face. It's not a big deal."

He regretted bringing it up at all. He wasn't interested in talking to Maya about his time with other women, even if he and Maya could never be more than friends.

"I know you mentioned something going on with your family too, but this feeling *is* a big deal if it makes you not want to go home." Her voice dropped. "It's a big deal if it makes you feel like you're lesser because of it. Don't let anyone make you feel inferior because of the choices you make about your own body."

Maya was staring at him with the fierceness of the sun. Cooper couldn't hold eye contact, his body made nervous by her sincerity, so he looked up at the sky, trying to count the few stars that survived the LA light pollution. "It's one of the reasons I want to help with the charity. I'd like to think maybe I could be known for something good. Something better than *this*." He gestured at himself, though he didn't really know what he meant by the word.

"I know the charity will be yours, but I'm hoping that with me helping...I don't know." He blew out a breath before convincing himself to look back at her. "I want people to see me as more than that. I don't want to be that guy anymore." Even if it would piss George off to lose the money that reputation made "them."

"It's just as much yours as it is mine, Cooper."

He smiled at her softly. "Yeah, okay."

She looked pensive but didn't say anything else.

"Should we discuss what we're going to say to Viola tomorrow? Or plan the fundraising gala?" Cooper wondered.

"Tomorrow morning. It's much too late for shop talk now."

Maya pushed herself up so she sat on the brick wall of the hot tub, most of her body out of the water. This time, it was clear she was doing it on purpose. He felt her watching him, watching as his eyes traveled the length of her body, taking in her peaked nipples and the goose bumps cropping up on her arms, slipping down to the toes that still circled in the water below her. Alarm bells rang in his mind as his eyes met hers once more, and there was that predatory look in her gaze again.

"Good night, Coop," she whispered.

"Good night, Mai." It came out gruffer than he'd intended, and he stuck his nails into his leg to jolt him from the thoughts he absolutely should *not* be having.

He closed his eyes as she got out of the hot tub, trying so hard to push away the image that now seemed to be burned in his brain, not ready to see what she looked like as she walked away.

How much trouble was he about to get himself into with this charity?

Chapter Twelve

Maya

Was Maya embarrassed about her display in the hot tub yesterday? Sure. Had she known when she'd gotten in that she would do something like that? She would have liked to believe the answer was no. But she just couldn't shake the feeling that being in the hot tub with him had chased away the feelings of powerlessness and intense sadness that'd still found her, even if to a lesser extent, since she'd seen him last.

The sadness had still been there, yes, in a miniscule form that she wasn't sure would ever go away. Just like the sliver of grief she'd befriended after her mother passed, always present but not necessarily in a bad way. It'd stuck around, but Maya had learned how to function with it.

But something about being in Cooper's presence and conversing with him sent that feeling of powerlessness scurrying away. He made her feel capable and intelligent and worthy. It wasn't at all what she'd been expecting, especially when the only feelings she'd had for him before then had been lust-induced.

And if she was being honest, putting on that show for Cooper had taken away that weird, little sister feeling that'd been brought on by his helping her with the charity. It'd made her feel like a woman who was his equal, and she rather liked that feeling. It'd also started a small storm in her stomach that didn't want to go away, brewing larger and larger.

Which was terrifying. Especially now that they were working together, she wasn't sure feelings of any kind for him were a good idea.

Maya smiled at the man in question, who held the door to Serve It Up open for her, and she tried to shove down those rapidly surfacing thoughts. Cool air hit her as she noticed the children milling about, some chasing each other across the center. When she approached the front desk, the middle-aged woman with dark, frizzy hair behind it smiled wide. She looked like she'd just come inside, sweat beading along her dark skin, and when Maya looked at her nametag, it read *Viola*.

"Good afternoon. I'm—"

"Maya Beaumont. It's really you." Wonder painted Viola's face, and she extended her hand. Maya shook it as firmly as she could with her wrist in a brace.

"Hi, Viola. It's so nice to meet you in person."

"And I am over the moon to meet you! I can't believe we have a real celebrity here today."

Maya tried not to laugh, knowing Cooper, who stood right beside her, was far more of a celebrity than her. "Well, I don't know about that, but I'm excited to be here. This is my cofounder, Cooper Hayes."

Cooper extended his hand, a charming smile on his face. "Hi, great to meet you. Thanks for all your work for the charity already. We really appreciate it."

There was no recognition as she shook his hand, though her smile stayed wide. "Great to meet you too. We're so excited to host these lessons, and I've already started working on advertising. The moment your charity has a name, you let me know, because I'm going to be plastering signs everywhere it's legal."

Maya loved Viola's energy, thankful to have found someone so eager to help so early on. Especially someone so entrenched in the local tennis community.

"Also, I know you okayed the rate I sent over. Do you want to take a look at the courts before we draw up the paperwork and finalize days and hours?"

"That would be *perfect*, thank you." Maya followed Viola out into an area with benches and vending machines, noting there were sixteen courts as the website had indicated, all well-kept.

As they walked, Maya wondered aloud, "Viola, I meant to ask—do you currently have any coaching spots available? Now that I'm not on the tour, I'd love to do some extra coaching work."

Cooper's knuckles brushed against hers as they walked side by side, and Maya didn't know whether it was accidental or not.

A part of her hoped not.

"I can let you know if I hear of anything. Honestly, if I send out your qualifications in our newsletter, you're going to have people clamoring to take private lessons with you." Viola shot Maya a wide grin. "Speaking of your qualifications, what was it like beating Anya Morozov in the Wimbledon first round last year?"

Maya contained her grimace, not at the mention of Anya, her kind-of friend who was now seeing her almost-ex, but at the reminder of the match that had started all of this. When she'd first strained the ligament in her wrist. Despite the painful reminder, nothing ugly or dark reared its head inside her or tried to pull her back down into that old pit of despair.

"Anya's actually a friend of mine so it was a little bitter-sweet." Lie. She'd loved wiping that conniving smirk off Anya's face. "But it was a fun match for sure. I didn't play my best in the second round, though." Because of the pain in her wrist, but also because she'd been playing the world number one.

"I stand by the fact that your second serve in the third set at two-all was in. I know they have machines for line judging nowadays, but it looked like it was a mile in," Viola declared, arms crossing over her chest.

Maya was impressed Viola remembered something seemingly so insignificant to anyone but her. She thought only she and her coaches would remember that painful double fault. That'd been the change in momentum her opponent had needed to move on to the next round.

"Well, I don't know about that. It was definitely a tough loss, but I'm proud of the way I played considering…my injury."

No look of pity, just understanding. "You played incredibly. Just like in the first round of the Prague Open against Taylor Whitmore."

And on and on they went, talking about Maya's tournament wins and losses, even after they reached the end of the sixteen-court facility. Viola knew Delilah's and Nicola's stats from the past couple of years as well, and while she said she didn't watch men's tennis much, she'd seen Ryan here and there. She also had a friend of a friend who knew Maya's old coach.

It was nice having someone in the tennis world to chat with, who understood when she made mention of her heroes and the people who'd inspired her. The girls had been busy the last couple of weeks, so she hadn't been able to talk to them as much, though their group chat was as lively as ever.

When Maya turned to check on Cooper, he was leaning against the gate of the last court, a mischievous smile on his face. He looked at Viola as he asked, "Should we have Maya show us her stuff? I know I'd love to see her coach."

Viola looked between the two. "Sure! You can use this court and the balls in that basket there." She pointed at a basket full of balls beside the net with three rackets leaning up against it.

Cooper cut his eyes to Maya, then said, "What do you say, Mai? I seem to remember a certain bet where a tennis lesson was promised."

Maya frowned at him, looking him up and down. Granted, in those tight jeans and even tighter fitted T-shirt, he looked better than any man she'd ever met on a tennis court, but it definitely wasn't appropriate attire for a lesson.

"You're not exactly dressed for tennis, Coop."

"Oh, come on. Just a couple of balls. Call it testing out the courts, and then I'll take *half* a lesson later."

She knew the moment his smirk widened that she was going to say yes. Still, she made an effort to grumble about it as she shut the gate to the court behind her, Viola opting to stand behind to watch.

Maya picked up a ball and bounced it with one of the rackets, happy when there was no prick of pain inside the brace. Even happier to enjoy the singing of strings against the ball.

She'd missed it far too much.

The court felt exactly right under her tennis shoes, and blood rushed through her like she was returning home. Like every cell in her body recognized she was back in her safe space.

Maya passed the racket to Cooper, holding back a laugh at his mismatched outfit. "Come stand on the baseline."

She tossed a ball toward him to see how he'd fare. He managed to land the racket on the ball, but not even his athleticism could make up for his poor form, and the ball went flying onto another—thankfully empty—court. Maya saw Viola behind the fence suppressing a laugh, and Maya was attempting to do the same.

"Okay! Good start." Maya approached Cooper, who was glaring down at the racket like it was its fault he didn't know how to hit a tennis ball. She grasped the head of the racket and began moving his fingers so his grip was a little better.

"Now set your feet like this." She widened her stance, bending her knees. He followed her.

"Good. Now as the ball comes toward you, you'll want to set your racket back." She motioned so her imaginary racket faced the fence behind her. He copied her again.

"Yes! Watch the ball as it comes toward you. When it bounces and gets to its highest point, hit it and follow through, like this."

She did the motion, and once again he copied her. She stepped away and grabbed a ball from the basket, tossing it toward him. He did the steps, just as she'd shown him, making good contact with the ball, but it still soared into the far fence.

"That's better! And that's just a forehand. Almost everything changes for your backhand."

"Let me perfect this first. Fix my grip again."

She approached him, looking at his hand on the racket. It hadn't changed much, but she shifted his pointer finger so it was a bit higher above the rest of his fingers. When she grinned up at him, he was already looking at her, a serious expression on his face. His lips curved into a smile as she scanned his face, her hands still on his, holding the racket with him.

"You're doing really well." Her grin widened. "For a football player."

His eyes looked down toward her lips, just a flick in their direction before they were back on the rest of her face, but she felt her whole body ignite, that brewing storm growing antsy in her belly.

Cooper grinned cockily, and warmth bloomed in her chest, slow and steady as it spread. "If we were playing against each other, I'd let you score all the points so I'd always be in love."

Maya smacked a hand over her mouth to stop herself from cackling at his ridiculous words. She took a step back, needing to put some distance between herself and the man who warmed her whole body from the inside out. "How long have you had that one percolating?"

He shrugged, bringing the racket back so it was centered in front of him. "I'm too embarrassed to tell you. Next ball, please."

She fed him a ball, and another and another. Then she showed him how to hit a backhand, all under the watchful eye of Viola, who still looked a little awe-struck that Maya was there with her.

Maybe it was the person she was coaching, or maybe it was coaching in general, but Maya was finally beginning to feel another little piece of herself falling back into place. She laughed at his very tall, athletic form looking so unathletic as he attempted her sport, and for the first time in a while, she was so excited about something that the near-constant emotional turmoil was almost fading away.

She might not ever feel the jubilation she had while on the tour, but maybe she could be happy in another way. She could be back in her community again, even if not in the same capacity. And maybe that could be enough.

Chapter Thirteen

Maya

Having Cooper stay at the house for the next few days while they hammered out some more logistics and paperwork was a blessing and a curse. Maya loved not being alone in the big house, loved the feeling that she was safe here with him.

But it also meant seeing a half-naked Cooper walk past her from the bathroom to the guest room while she stood by and tried not to stare, the muscles of his abdomen straining, his thick shoulders and arms shining with droplets of water. It meant lying on the lawn, pretending to read a well-worn novel she hadn't touched since high school as he worked out in the home gym her father had put up in their backyard.

Now, as they sat together at the dining table, she tried to focus on her computer screen and not the way his biceps looked in his Sabers T-shirt.

Focus. Focus, she told herself. *Viola is working on transportation and advertising. What's next?*

Her eyes strayed across the table of their own volition, and she stifled a groan, annoyed with herself. Maya stood, pacing the length of the dining room to put some space between them. She needed to think clearly, and that was becoming increasingly difficult the more time she spent in his company.

Maya couldn't remember the last time she'd felt this bothered by a man, if ever, but she knew what she and her going-to-need-new-batteries-soon vibrator would be doing tonight—a reminder to buy a rechargeable one as soon as possible.

Cooper cleared his throat, finally looking up from his laptop. "Are...you okay?"

"No. I mean yes. Yes. I'm great. Better than great."

"Oh-*kay*," he responded, drawing out the last syllable. "One of the companies I contacted to help with the event got back to me, and of all of the ones we've looked into, this seems like our best option."

Maya stopped pacing. "Okay, perfect. Are you still sure the end of April is okay?" They'd talked about when they should have the fundraising event over the last couple of days, and while she wanted to have the gala as early as possible, she knew he would be busy with the draft.

"Yeah, the woman I talked to thinks we should plan to have it right at the start of May and that an evening event will be best. She sent some stuff for us to consider in the meantime, if you want to work on that tonight."

"Good. Yes, let's do that."

After they'd gotten back from Serve It Up two days ago, they'd dove right into their work, going down Maya's to-do list that seemed to grow by the day. It was exhausting and exciting at the same time, and even better, only hours after they'd left the tennis center, Viola had called and let Maya know she already had three people interested in taking lessons with her with more calling in by the minute.

Viola must have really talked up her qualifications, but Maya wasn't going to complain because this was what would ensure she could pay Cooper back for all he'd been willing to give.

She and Cooper had been working all day, but with him going back to Charleston the next morning, they'd agreed to work late into the night to make sure they finished everything they could.

Maya sat back down, and Cooper turned his computer so they could both look at it. They went through the handbook the woman had sent, identifying themes and decor they liked. Or rather, that Maya liked, because Cooper kept waiting for her to choose and then would agree with her adamantly.

"Coop! Pick something on your own."

"Nah, this isn't really my forte. Ma told me I'm not allowed to plan parties in general, and I think, for everyone's sake, that's probably for the best."

Maya cocked her head inquisitively. "What did you do?"

"Let's just say that me, petting zoos, and magicians do *not* mix."

Maya laughed, a hand on her chest at the ache that had begun lessening there. The new feeling was warm and had begun settling around her comfortingly. "Please say more."

Cooper sighed. "So keep in mind that I was, like, fifteen. I was planning a party for my youngest sister, Daisy, and I guess I didn't do my due diligence in the slightest because the magician I found not only did *not* inspire awe with his illusions, but he managed to make the cake disappear. Permanently, and not in a magical way. Turns out, he was a pretty clumsy performer and dropped it right there in front of her...after he'd already set a few decorations on fire. Poor Daisy spent an hour crying."

"What does that have to do with a petting zoo?"

"Mm, another one of my mishaps, I'm afraid. I guess I didn't do a good enough job of making sure the goat enclosure was properly secured before the party. The decor-on-fire situation did not go over well with the goats. They sort of escaped. And chased all the guests. Which only made more of a mess."

This time, Maya's head fell back as she laughed, uninhibited, feeling the good kind of tears forming in her eyes. Cooper joined her, the deep noise reverberating through the dining area, setting her insides alight and turning them gooey.

"Poor Daisy."

"Oh, she was so upset. She wouldn't talk to me for days after." That made them both laugh harder. When they'd calmed down, their eyes met and held. A moment, and then another. And then another.

"No party planning for Cooper, then," Maya murmured softly.

"'Fraid not. But I'll be cheering you on in all the decisions you make."

"A tragedy to lose out on your creativity. A magician *and* a petting zoo? What ever will our donors think of our gala without the might of your creative genius behind it?"

"We'll just have to tell them my genius was lost in a magician's fire and that you were born without any. It'll be tough for them to hear, but hopefully they'll be so sympathetic to our plight, they won't even care what we're raising money for."

After a moment, when Maya couldn't find anything else to say, she chuckled. "So, you're a little chaotic but memorable."

She hadn't meant it in any certain way, but if the look on Cooper's face, stricken and a little mischievous, was any indication of how he'd taken it, Maya was sure she'd just crossed their imaginary line.

The one Cooper had drawn in the sand almost two years ago.

His eyes were fixed on her, dropping down as she licked her lips nervously, the hand he still had on the table balling into a fist, the muscles of his corded arm straining.

"Sweetheart, any time spent with me is unforgettable."

Words became a foreign concept to Maya, as did breathing. She made a concerted effort to inhale, eyes never leaving his. A little smirk was forming on his face, like he knew exactly what he'd done to her.

Danger, a little voice said in the back of her mind. *Bad idea*, it continued.

She cleared her throat. "Right. Well, let's finish this so that poor woman can get started on a gala that includes neither magicians nor animals one would find at a petting zoo."

Chapter Fourteen

Cooper

Frankie's was unsurprisingly empty, since Colton's birthday fell on a Thursday. Cooper had originally planned to meet Colton at his house for the dinner that Lucia and Maya were preparing, but it seemed Colton had been kicked out of the kitchen, so Cooper had agreed to meet him at the only club in Charleston that catered exclusively to athletes. No non-athletes allowed meant no chance of paparazzi or of being posted all over social media.

To Cooper? It was a godsend.

Cooper sat on a barstool in the corner of the quiet club, untouched beer in front of him as he scrolled through the news. He knew it was dumb, but his self-control disappeared for a moment as he searched for his own name. Nothing new came up since the last time he'd checked, and he didn't know if that was good or bad. A part of him had hoped things would already be changing for the better, but that was a ridiculous hope, since he hadn't actually *done* anything of value yet.

He swiped away a text from George asking him why he hadn't been out with anyone recently. Cooper sighed. Another person whose texts he was dodging. Unfortunately, that wouldn't last for long, since he spoke with his agent almost every day.

A hand patted him on the shoulder and then Colton was beside him, slipping onto a barstool.

"Sorry I'm late."

Cooper shook his head. "I just got here too. You're good."

Colton asked for a beer and then looked around. "Wow, it's nice and quiet, huh?"

"Well, it *is* almost dinnertime on a Thursday evening. Not exactly prime time."

Colton grunted, taking a sip of the beer the bartender set in front of him.

Cooper held out his bottle for his friend to tap with his own. "Happy birthday, man. Hope it's been a good one. I'm having your present sent to your house tomorrow after practice."

His friend nodded, staring down at the bar top. "Appreciate it. But know that if it's another car, Lucia might have words with you."

Cooper snickered before noticing Colton wasn't joining him. "What's wrong? You're gloomier than usual."

"Just thinking about how close we're getting to retiring age."

Cooper raised an eyebrow. "You're thinking about retirement? I never thought I'd see the day." He chuckled.

Six years ago, Cooper had been drafted to the Sabertooths right out of college. Colton, who was only a year older, had been the grumpiest twenty-four-year-old Cooper had ever met. With all the time they'd spent together on the field, in the weight room, and in team bonding, Cooper had realized that grumpiness had come from a drive like he'd never seen; Colton was fiercely competitive, and football was his outlet.

It had taken a few months of trying to break through Colton's shell—the man had had very few friends and rarely went out with the team if he could help it. But Cooper had kept trying, and finally, Colton had opened up, and their relationship on and off the field had been the better for it.

Colton shrugged. "Thirty does that, I guess. I used to be so concerned about what I'd accomplished and what I had left to do. But now a part of me just wants to enjoy another season or two before I start traveling with Luc. I don't know, is that crazy?"

"I don't think it's crazy. I think it's surprising to hear from you, but I'm glad you're taking it a little less seriously now."

A couple of years ago, nothing would have been good enough for him to be ready to retire.

"Setting boundaries with my dad helped, I think. I don't feel as stressed when he calls, especially because I don't answer as often. Can't bring myself to cut him off entirely, but still. All around less pressure."

Cooper nodded, taking a sip of the cool beer. He wondered if it was a sign he needed to work on boundaries with his *own* family.

Colton continued, "I'm sorry I haven't been as present since Lucia moved in. It's so easy to want to go straight home after practice and lift now that I get to see her every day, but I feel like we haven't hung out much recently."

"Nah, I get it." And Cooper really did. He had nothing but good things to say about Lucia, and he could only hope that one day, he could find someone who made him feel that way too.

He tried not to let the momentary flash of Maya's face in his mind affect him.

"I know you do, but I'm going to do better. Should be easier too now that she's settled in. But you've been busy too, huh? You didn't tell me how things went in LA."

"You haven't talked to Maya about it?" Maya had already been in Charleston for a little over a day, staying with her brother.

It'd been more than a week of only seeing Maya over video calls in the evenings while they worked through charity stuff, and Cooper had been looking forward to being with her in person for days.

"She told me you guys accomplished a lot, and she seems really excited. But I feel like she's holding back a little. She said you're a cofounder now?"

Cooper suspected this would be a sensitive subject, but he'd never lied to Colton.

Well, almost never. Cooper pretended omitting the time he and Maya had almost kissed in this very club didn't count as a lie.

"Yeah. We did a lot of paperwork, some event planning for a fundraiser, and found where she'll be having the actual lessons."

"She said she got a local donor to help her out with initial costs?"

Cooper didn't know if the almost accusatory tone was all in his head.

"Uh, I offered, actually."

It was silent for a moment, and when Cooper turned to look at his closest friend, he saw the flash of hurt. He almost wished he *had* lied.

"I'm confused. When I offered to help pay, she said she would find another way."

"I think she was just worried about mixing business with family." At least, that was a part of it. Cooper got the feeling Maya struggled to accept help in general, like she wanted to do everything herself so she didn't have to take up space in anyone else's life.

He hated that she did that. Especially when she had so many people who loved her and *wanted* her to lean on them.

When Colton didn't respond, Cooper said, "I really don't think she meant anything by it, man."

"I know she didn't." Colton frowned. "I wish she felt comfortable talking to me about it, though."

"I think I was just there when she had the idea at Devin's event. And she had a couple of questions about setting up that I was able to get the information for. I think she knows you're busy, or at least worries you might be, and doesn't want to add to it."

His friend frowned even more, if possible. "And you're okay with helping? You don't mind?"

Cooper wanted to tell Colton he was doing this for himself as much as he was for Maya, because he wanted to show the world he could be good. He could *do* good.

But, despite how close he and Colton were, Cooper had never expressed how much he hated all the labels put on him. Especially because he hadn't really realized how badly he'd wanted the change until recently. Cooper would tell his friend about it, but his birthday wasn't the right time.

"I'm happy to help. We both know I have more money than I'll ever need, and it's for a great cause. Plus, I'm honored to help Maya."

Finally, the frown disappeared, and Colton nodded. "Okay, thank you. I appreciate it, and I'd rather it be you, me, or Landon than someone random. At least this way, I know she's working with someone I trust. Someone who sees her like a sister and will treat her with that same respect."

Shame slammed through Cooper, because in *no* way did he think about Maya the way he thought about his sisters. He was a shit friend for the things he'd continued to let pass between him and Maya.

He swallowed over the guilt of knowing that he was not as good a friend to Colton as Colton was to him. "Of course."

It only took a few more minutes to finish their beers, and then they were taking a car back to Colton's for dinner.

As they were finishing up their meal, Maya was talking about the charity, and Cooper was struggling to concentrate on her words. With each sentence about all she'd achieved, she brightened more and more, and like the beautiful sunflower she was, she bloomed as she spoke, her face lighting up. The smile on her face was genuine and radiant, and Cooper felt as if he'd been punched in the solar plexus.

Every day, trying to hide how much he wanted to be near her became harder and harder, from himself and probably the world.

He couldn't take his eyes off her as she talked animatedly about the work she'd already accomplished for the charity and how excited she was to get it up and running. The ache to reach out and touch her was stronger than usual, so he slipped his hands under his legs and looked straight ahead.

To where Lucia watched him knowingly, a slight smile on her face.

Shit.

Trying to appear nonchalant, Cooper began collecting all the dishes on the table.

"Oh, Coop, there's no need. I can do that." Lucia tried to stop him, but he sidestepped her grab for the plates.

"Like hell you will. You cooked us a great meal, and now I'll be cleaning."

Maya stood, grabbing the cups and other dishes she could manage. "I'll help."

He almost said something to remind her that *she* was one of the people who had cooked, but the resolve on her face told him not to.

Cooper heard Lucia's grumble, but she didn't rise from her chair to assist them in the kitchen. He placed the dishes beside the sink, grabbing the sponge and beginning his work soaping and scrubbing. Maya took the cleaned plates and wiped them down with a towel before placing them back into the cabinet.

On the third plate, Maya accidentally grabbed Cooper's hand as she tried to get the plate from him. She giggled, the pink of her alcohol-addled cheeks deepening. "Sorry." But she didn't let go, and when Cooper glanced at her, she was staring at his hand in hers. She used her thumb to gently trace his veins. The light pressure was enough to shock Cooper into dropping the fork in his other hand.

At the sound of it clattering, her eyes found his, and the tension between them stretched until the air around them was so thin, Cooper could hardly find any to breathe. He was utterly fixated on her. He couldn't have taken his eyes off her even if he'd wanted to, which he didn't.

Neither of them moved.

The way she was looking at him reminded Cooper of her twenty-third birthday party, and his thoughts flitted to that moment, that almost-kiss. He couldn't help but wonder how different things would be if he hadn't pulled away that night. If he'd let himself indulge in what they'd both clearly wanted.

Without thinking, he asked in a whisper, "Do you ever think about it?"

From the hazy look in her eyes, she knew what he was talking about, but she still asked, "About what?"

"That night. At Frankie's."

Maya looked like she was debating something, and for a very long time, she said nothing. When she finally seemed to decide, she pulled away slightly, removing her hand from his and carefully pulling the plate from his hand, making sure not to touch him again.

"Coop, I don't think…"

A mistake. A huge mistake. His dumbass big mouth. "No, you're right. Sorry." He turned back to the sink, scrubbing at the next plate hard, punishing it for his own idiocy.

Before she took the next plate, she whispered, "Of course I think about it." She said it plainly, as if those weren't the most dangerous words to be spoken between them. "It's always floating around when it shouldn't be. Especially when Colton's here, and I have to remind myself he would lose his mind if he found out." Her voice dropped even more. "And most especially when you're around."

His breath caught in his throat. This was dangerous territory, and he knew that, but ever since she'd come to Charleston earlier that year, wrist in a cast and a light in her eyes that was only just starting to come back, it'd played in his head far more than it should have.

But that was all it could ever be: thoughts. He'd just promised himself he'd do better for Colton's sake. Plus, Cooper couldn't help but feel Maya deserved more than someone whose entire life appeared to be football, women, and sex. What would people start saying about her if they were ever linked in the news? Would she be able to handle that kind of media?

They finished the remaining dishes in silence, and when they returned to the living room, Colton had a look on his face like he wanted to be locked in his bedroom with Lucia. He tore his eyes away from her and looked back at them.

"We're heading to bed, but feel free to watch whatever you want. Coop, don't even think about driving home because you've had too much to drink and we have a late start tomorrow anyway. Take the room you always do." He gave Maya a quick hug, patted Cooper on the back, and practically dragged a wine-happy Lucia behind him, her laugh echoing around the dining room as she waved goodbye over her shoulder.

"So gross, but I love them together. I really do. He's never been so happy." Maya flicked off all the lights but the one in the foyer, providing just enough light to find the guest rooms.

They reached her room first, and she leaned back against the closed door, making no move to open it. Maya looked up at him, and without even a thought, he was in front of her. It went against everything he'd just told himself, but it was like there was a current thrumming between them, pulling them together. Like opposite ends of a magnet.

Still, he kept his hands at his side, waiting for her to make the next move.

She ran a thumb over his bottom lip lightly, the corners of her mouth quirking up into a small smile. His hands twitched.

"Why did you pull away that night? Why not kiss me?" She'd whispered it so softly, he'd had to lean forward half an inch to hear her, his forehead nearly touching hers.

He closed his eyes, running a hand through his own hair. "Because of Colton. And because I can't let you be associated with me and my—"

"If you say reputation, I'll pinch you. Hard. We talked about this."

Cooper looked down the hall, where he was sure his best friend was *not* having a deep conversation with the woman he cared for. "I've spent so much of my life being used for one thing after another. If it wasn't trying to befriend me to get something out of my dad, the mayor, then it was what I could provide with my face, my body, or my status as a football player. You spend your whole life being told that you're the 'pretty boy,' that you're gonna break hearts, it starts to become who you are."

He knew it was dumb to complain about being perceived as attractive, but over time, his self-worth had become interwoven with his looks, and his life had become a series of objectification after objectification. As if his personality were secondary to what he looked like.

It felt good to tell someone. Cooper had kept it bottled up for so long, only coming even remotely close to telling someone when he'd asked George to help him make a change.

But this was Maya, and something about her always made Cooper feel like he could be honest. She was so good at putting everyone at ease, at making sure they knew she'd never judge them.

Maya didn't respond after a few seconds, and worried she would point out what a first world problem that was, Cooper continued, still not looking at her. "I know how ridiculous it sounds. I know it's coming from a place of privilege for that to have been my biggest issue growing up. But sometimes it's hard to believe you're anything but a *thing* when people put the word 'actually' in front of any compliments they give you. 'You're *actually* funny. You're *actually* smart.' Things I believed about myself that were slowly eroded away when it became clear that they weren't what people wanted or expected from me."

Cooper had tried to get away from it all after high school. Had run away to Alabama to start again. He'd thought he'd met the love of his life in college, someone who'd genuinely cared for him as a person, but when he really thought about it, Gabi had barely even thought of him as her boyfriend.

He paused before he said the last words, his face scrunched in embarrassment. "I didn't think there was any-thing about me that could ever deserve a kiss from you. So, I pulled away."

After Gabi, Cooper had come to the conclusion he wasn't meant to be in a relationship. Or rather, there was no one made for him the way he'd thought there would be. No one for him like Lucia was for Colton and vice versa. His life had become a revolving door of casual relationships because the universe had made it abundantly clear he was not meant to have anything serious or real.

But now, seeing what he might one day have, he didn't know anymore. There were too many thoughts going back and forth in his head.

When he glanced at her again, she looked angrier than he'd ever seen her, her eyebrows pinched together tightly, lips beginning to form a scowl.

"You *are* funny. You *are* smart. You're sweet and caring and willing to do anything for the people close to you. *None* of that is secondary to how you look and what you can provide to others. You are far more than that. There is nothing in you that makes you undeserving of love."

He looked down, and she placed a reassuring hand on his chest. "If you want others to stop seeing you that way—as the man with a reputation for keeping things casual—you have to stop seeing yourself that way too. *You* have to see yourself as funny and smart and all of those other things. And others will see it too. Fuck your reputation. And fuck anybody who could ever see you so two-dimensionally."

Cooper's heart ricocheted around his chest at her words. They may have known each other for years, may have been attracted to each other from the start, but this was something different. Something more intense.

For the first time since college, Cooper could see himself with someone who cared about *him*, who saw *him*. With Maya, he had a personality beyond what everyone else, even his own family, saw him as.

How much longer could he keep using the excuse that she was Colton's sister to stay away from her?

Not much longer, it seemed.

He cupped her jaw, tilting her head up slightly. Her eyes flashed, and he waited to see if she would pull away. When she didn't, her eyes fluttering shut, he brushed his lips against hers softly. It felt more like a caress than a kiss, but every point of contact between them began to tingle.

This was exactly what Cooper was afraid of. This pull to her confused him, made his head hazy. He knew he shouldn't be kissing her, felt the knife of betrayal leaving him and finding his closest friend's back, but just the brush of his lips, just a taste, and now he wanted it all. Want consumed him, shredding through his resolve because, for once, he felt important to someone in a way he hadn't often, if ever, felt.

A door, likely to Colton's bathroom, closed and echoed across the house. Cooper's eyes closed, and he heaved a deep sigh through his nose.

He couldn't do this to Colton, *especially* not on his birthday. Cooper had to keep fighting it.

Or at the very least, figure out how he could convince Colton that he was worthy of her.

"Good night, Maya," he whispered against her lips. Seconds later, he was in his guest room, waiting to hear the sound of her door closing behind her.

He couldn't explain the feeling in his chest as anything other than anguish.

Chapter Fifteen

Cooper

By the end of March, the Sabers were starting some light practices on the field, which Cooper was excited about, even if he was looking a little rustier than usual. While he liked lifting, he'd missed being on the field, turf under his cleats and grass ahead of him as he dodged defensive backs.

Cooper headed straight home after he showered. He'd been up far later than he'd planned thanks to a call with the event planner and Maya the night before. He hadn't realized he'd fallen asleep on the call until he'd looked through the five messages from Maya telling him to open his eyes and making fun of him for being an old man.

He missed her. The last time he'd seen her was two weeks ago at Colton's birthday dinner. She'd had to leave for LA for a couple of tennis lessons and to work with Viola on charity logistics. Preparations were really beginning to ramp up, and

Cooper cursed the distance, because he truly wanted to be there to help.

It was an odd feeling, missing her, because he was sure he'd never missed a woman in his life besides his mom and sisters. Yet, over the evenings of event planning and the excited phone calls in the middle of the night when she'd figured something out that would make the charity run smoother, they'd slowly unearthed the little things about each other most people wouldn't ever get to know.

She liked gummy bears, but only the red, yellow, and white ones. The green and orange ones ended up in a plastic baggie somewhere in her room, deemed unfit to be eaten unless she were in a pinch and couldn't get her fix. In elementary school, she put gum in Kayla Johnson's hair after Kayla bullied another girl reading in the cafeteria—something she was not proud of, even if she had been smiling as she said it. She had wanted to be a swimmer like her mom, only when she'd tried, she'd nearly drowned, and no amount of coaching seemed to help.

Losing tennis was like losing her mom all over again because she'd spent so many years playing *for* her mom, and it'd become her safe space when her mother had passed away. She hated telling her brothers how she felt, even though she went out of her way to ask them about themselves, because she hated the idea of worrying them at all.

Though that last one was something he'd gathered from her actions, not really her words.

He'd told her about his older brother and three younger sisters. About how he'd climbed a tree chasing his brother and had broken his arm in four places. That his favorite way to spend an evening was on the beach, watching the tide come in and out peacefully. She'd been surprised by that but had said it only made her like him more.

Cooper had stuttered over his words after she'd said that, like a high schooler who couldn't get his bearings after his crush spoke to him.

He'd never expected to hate the distance so much, but while Colton might've been his best friend, Maya had slowly been worming herself into that spot too. In a completely different way, Maya was becoming one of his closest friends. Someone who he felt comfortable telling anything, even the things he might not talk so much to Colton about, like his family life, and why Oakridge Springs was such a sore spot for him.

He hadn't realized how badly he'd needed someone like that, and now that he had her, he didn't know how he'd gone so long without her.

Despite the fact they spent nearly every night on the phone and that he'd grown to crave her voice being the last he heard before he slept, they hadn't talked about the kiss at Colton's house. It was clear they were both avoiding it, though he didn't know her reasoning.

Cooper hadn't brought it up because he shouldn't have done it. He'd decided that if Maya was who he wanted, which he was growing surer of by the day, he needed to prove to the world—and especially to Colton, Maya, and himself—that he was worthy of her. And right now, that wasn't the case.

He went through the rest of the evening like a zombie, responding to George's many emails with signed contracts. Cooper ignored the other email from George that included a list of women Cooper could take out since he hadn't been photographed with anyone recently.

His agent was apparently quite worried about the "rampant speculation" around Cooper's love life.

After falling asleep at his dining table, he got up and readied himself for the evening, chugging two protein shakes before brushing his teeth and falling into the king-sized bed he'd spent an entirely unnecessary amount of money on when he'd first purchased the house.

Just as he set his phone down for the evening, a call came through. At first, he was sure it was his mother, calling for the second time today to ask him if he'd given more thought to retiring since there still hadn't been any movement on an extension on his contract, despite George's promise that things were in the works. But when he grabbed his phone, he saw it was a video call from Maya.

His heartbeat rocketed like it always did when she called so late, forever worried about what harm might befall her while she lived alone so many miles away. Cooper couldn't stand the thought, swiping his finger across the screen, only breathing a sigh of relief when he saw her unharmed.

"Mai? Are you okay?"

"Hi, I'm so sorry to bother you. I keep hearing creaking in the house, and I know it's just settling, but I'm about to die of thirst and I need to get water, but I didn't want to do it alone. I call you at this time sometimes so I thought it might be okay..." She looked more and more embarrassed the longer she rambled.

"You could never be a bother. Go grab some water, I'll stay on."

Once again, the urge to ask her to spend more time in Charleston shoved its way down his throat, but he closed his lips over the words that attempted to escape. Even if he hadn't been asking for selfish reasons, either to spend more time with her or to know she was safe in Colton's house rather than alone across the country, it wasn't his place to ask that of her, especially when she was just beginning to establish herself in Los Angeles with the charity, Viola, and the tennis community.

It was dark, but she kept the phone close to her face, her brow furrowed.

"Turn on the lights. And can you do me a favor?"

"So bossy." Light flooded the room around her, and she looked down at him, then pulled the phone away from her. "That was a horrible angle. But yes, what can I do for you?"

"Can you check all the windows and doors and make sure they're locked properly?"

She let out a light laugh. "I'm the only person living here and would know if any of the windows or doors weren't locked, Coop. Such a worrywart."

"Sweetheart, please," he pleaded, not even realizing his mistake until the words had been out of his mouth for seconds. That was now the second time he'd slipped up and called her that, though this time was far more meaningful than when he'd teased her about how memorable of a time he could be.

She blinked down at him once, twice, then let out a chuckle that sounded a little more forced than the last. "Oh, uh, okay. Yes, sure." She began the process, slowly making her way through every room in the house, flicking on the light before checking the windows and even balcony doors, just to assuage his fears.

"Oh! I came up with a name for the charity. Let me know your thoughts." She paused. "On the Line." Maya was beaming at him as she waited for his reaction.

"I like it. Give me the backstory."

Maya continued checking windows and doors as she spoke. "It's perfect for a tennis charity because it's a very common tennis term, whether you're lined up on the line or hit a great shot on the line. Or you have everything on the line."

"Oh, see, I thought maybe it was because we're always on the phone," he teased.

She paused, looking down at him in confusion. "What does On the Line have to do with a phone?"

Cooper was really about to date himself with this one. "You know. The landline phones where you have to stay close because it's attached to the line. And people would always say 'get off the line.'"

Maya shook her head.

"Oh, so you're a *baby*. How can you not know about land-line phones?"

A smirk grew on her pretty face, and Cooper knew what was coming. "No, you're just an old man."

"Again, only four years older than you."

"Did you ever have to hang the phone up on the wall?" she asked, like she already knew the answer.

Cooper had, of course, but only when he'd been younger. To be fair, he'd lived in a little town, nothing big like Los Angeles.

"Yes," he answered resignedly.

"Old."

He rolled his eyes as she checked the last room of the house, still giggling. "*Anyway*, I like On the Line. I think it's perfect," he said, hoping to move past the teasing.

"Thank you! It just hit me and I thought so too." Maya paused, squinting at him, though a smile still played on her lips.

"Also, don't think checking all the windows and doors is an every-night thing. I'm a little too lonely and sad to add much more than washing my face and brushing my teeth to my nightly routine." She smiled like it was a joke, but he knew the words were true, and his chest ached at the thought of that. That in a world full of people Maya could easily make friends with, in a world where she already *had* so many friends, she'd been so alone.

She'd mentioned something about it a couple of nights ago but hadn't explained further than that, much to his dismay. He'd very nearly booked a flight then and there so she wouldn't feel so alone, but at least he would be there in a few days for their press conference.

"If you're thinking of telling me to move to Charleston or spend more time at Colton and Lucia's house, don't even say it. The charity is in LA, and the last thing I want is to be putting Colt and Luc out."

Now, that was *uncanny*. Either she could read his face like a book, or she'd just gotten to know him so well that she could read his mind. He liked the idea of both of those a bit too much, so to cover that up, he grinned. "Who said anything about Colton and Lucia's? I have four perfectly good guest bedrooms." After flicking on the light switch beside him and sitting up, he held his phone out to show off how little of his own bed he took up. "And a very large bed."

She stopped moving, her mouth in an 'O' of shock. When she collected herself a few seconds later to the sounds of his laughter, she said, "Cooper Hayes!" Maya finally cracked, a hint of a smile trying to come out, and then she rolled her eyes. She flipped the camera and panned around the open floorplan of the house. "Everything's locked, cowboy. Now am I allowed to get water?"

When she flipped the camera back, he saw the little tank top and even tinier shorts she was wearing before she pulled the phone closer to her. Filthy thoughts flooded his mind, but he once again tried to push them down, even as he felt blood rushing down below the waistband of his shorts.

"Am I giving the orders?" he drawled.

"You told me to lock the windows and doors and I listened, so apparently."

"I can tell you to do anything?" His dick was fully at attention now, his voice lower than a few moments ago.

The look in Maya's eyes seemed to mirror his. "Depends on what it is." She tucked a strand of hair behind her ear that'd loosed itself from her ponytail, and if Cooper hadn't known better, he would've thought she was angling her camera just a *little* bit lower, her chest just *slightly* more visible. He'd never been so attracted to someone's collarbone before, but he was quickly learning there was nothing about Maya that wasn't attractive—and he'd certainly tried his hardest to find something when his thoughts were too much.

Her teeth sunk into her bottom lip, and the feeling that ripped through him at the sight also wiggled loose the thought he'd had since this whole ill-advised flirtation had started: he needed to find a way to prove he was good enough for her.

He cleared his throat, adjusting his shorts to accommodate himself a little better. "Why don't you get that water now?"

Disappointment clear as day flashed across her beautiful face. In a moment, he'd made her, his sunflower, wilt, something he'd promised himself he'd never do. Frustrated with the situation and even more so with himself, he rolled his shoulders, keeping his eyes on Maya as she filled up her bottle, turned off all the lights, and walked up the stairs to her bedroom.

Yeah, he was five-finger-punch-from-Colton fucked, and he was starting to care less and less.

Chapter Sixteen

Maya

The uneven stone of the Beaumont house's front stairs nearly laid Maya out flat as she chased after Cooper into the early April afternoon. She was lucky she hadn't twisted an ankle already.

"Coop, slow down! I still have to fix my hair."

"Hurry up, sunflower. We're gonna be late to our own press event." He opened the passenger door of her car and motioned for her to get in. "And you look stunning as you are."

Her heart fluttered like a butterfly at the praise and at the name, just as it had when he'd accidentally called her *sweetheart* on their phone call earlier in the week, the slight Southern twang just poking through in his exasperation with her. She swallowed at the memory, tucking it away for later. When she didn't need to be ready to talk to the media.

Once Cooper had her car out of the driveway, she pulled open the mirror and stared at herself, making sure the light makeup she'd applied to her eyes hadn't smudged in her rush out of the house. She didn't normally care *that* much about how she looked when she left the house, but for the first time in her life, she was nervous to speak to the press.

Though that was likely due to the fact that Cooper's name on the charity meant there were far more paparazzi and tabloids than there ever were at tournaments.

"I meant what I said, Mai. Leave your hair down like that. I like it." Damn him and the way his words made her body feel.

"It's not very sporty. Doesn't really match my outfit. I look like a poser." She'd donned one of her billion tennis dresses and shoes, and she knew walking up in it with her hair down would make her look like someone who did *not* belong on the court.

Cooper set a warm, calloused hand on her knee, and Maya's breathing stilled. "Your track record speaks for it-self. You've won more tour matches than any of these peo-ple, so screw what they think."

She sighed, but she knew he was right. She looked better with her hair down than she did with it in a braid anyway.

"Should've at least brought a hat, then," she grumbled.

He didn't respond, but the right side of his mouth ticked up slightly.

When they finally arrived at Serve It Up, having ex-changed very few words due to Maya's feelings of impend-ing doom, she nearly locked herself in the car.

"You okay?" Cooper asked, eyebrows drawn. He looked at her like he'd weather any storm to make sure she was okay—even when he knew she could survive by herself—just so she'd have someone with her on the other side.

"That's a lot of reporters." She nodded her head to where a large group of people with microphones and cameras and clipboards stood. Most of them appeared local, and none of them seemed to be sports reporters specifically, so they would probably have no idea who she was unless they'd done their research.

Whether that was a good or bad thing, she didn't know.

"Ah, that's not too many, honestly. Average at best."

His words didn't make her feel any better, and her knee began to bounce as she thought through their mission statement over and over again, not wanting to misspeak on live television. Annoyed by the stiff brace on her wrist, she ripped the Velcro and dropped it to the floor of her car, frustrated.

It's not like she was playing tennis. Plus, Grayson, her physical therapist, had told her only days earlier that she could begin seeing how her wrist felt without it.

Cooper's hand squeezed her knee, the pressure reassuring. "You can speak as much or as little as you want. I can answer any questions they have for the both of us, okay?"

She mulled that over for only a second before her leg stilled and she nodded. "Okay. Let's get this over with."

They were out of the car and across the parking lot mind-bendingly quickly—or Maya's brain was just processing at the speed of molasses—and before she knew it, she stood beside Cooper in front of the crowd of people, an excited Viola waving from her periphery enthusiastically.

At least the lessons Maya had started giving at the center made this place feel a bit more like she was on her turf.

True to his word, Cooper fielded the first couple of questions, though standing there without something to say made her feel like an idiot. A lot of the questions seemed to be more about Cooper's life and football than the charity.

The weight of a panic attack building only made her spiral further, the buzzing beneath her skin and ringing in her ears practically unbearable.

Breathe, she heard Colton's voice reminding her. *In, hold, out, hold.*

Maya tried, hardly listening to the reporters and their questions. This much fixed attention on her was shutting her system down. She'd done small press conferences before, but no one really paid attention to those.

But this? People would be paying attention to this.

Plus, it sometimes felt like reporters preyed on people's downfalls, and she really didn't want to say or do anything that could lead to negative press for On the Line.

Maya snapped out of it somewhat as the group of them laughed at something Cooper had said, seemingly completely at ease with the crowd. He was probably so used to this kind of attention that it was nothing. As he smiled and laughed with them, his eyes turned to hers, twinkling even as they asked a clear question: *okay?*

There he was, worrying about her, anchoring her in place so she didn't drift in the sea of anxiety that tried to pull her down.

She nodded subtly.

"Why don't we get some questions about the charity?" Cooper asked. Maya dug her nails into her palm so she could focus better on the world outside of her, rather than inside her mind.

"Sure! What are your roles in the charity?"

Maya cleared her throat, nodding subtly again, and Cooper understood, letting her answer. "I'm cofounder and director but will also be coaching once we get up and running. Cooper is also a cofounder and has been an immense help in the process."

Cooper inched slightly closer to her, almost imperceptibly.

"Can you tell us a little more about the charity?"

Maya took another breath in, then out. She twirled her hair around her finger mindlessly, but she knew she could answer this one in her sleep. "On the Line is a local organization that will look to pair underprivileged children in the area with tennis coaches. The hope is that by providing lessons and after school care to these children, they'll have an opportunity to learn a new skill and potentially find a sport they can play for years while also easing the financial burden for their parents. Tennis isn't the most accessible sport, but it is a beautiful one that every child should have the opportunity to learn, if they want. So that's what we hope to do."

Despite the nerves, her response was perfect. All she'd had to do was think of little Delilah and she was reminded of that passion that'd been building in her for On the Line since the idea was conceived.

"And you said you're going to be coaching? What are your qualifications for that? Do you coach locally?"

Maya's head snapped to the person who'd asked the question, a mousy man with long, brown hair and wire rimmed glasses. She'd been right. These people had no idea who she was. She was used to not being recognized generally, but for someone to not know going into this press conference when she was spearheading so much of it was a slap in the face.

"N-No. I'm—"

"Are you and Cooper in a relationship? Is that why you've been given this role?"

The buzzing under her skin became worse, like winged insects trying to loose themselves from her body. The ringing in her ears intensified, and no amount of breathing or counting imaginary glow-in-the-dark stars was helping.

There was a cold, hard edge to Cooper's words as he said, "Maya is a top-ranked professional tennis player. She is highly qualified to lead this charity, as well as to coach. The idea for the program was hers and hers alone, and she is very passionate about the mission statement, as are all of us with On the Line."

When Maya glanced at him, his jaw was clenched, a flash of anger on his face before he was able to hide it.

The reporter had the decency to look surprised, but continued nonetheless, "But that doesn't really answer my question. Are you two in a relationship?"

Why was this happening? Why weren't they asking questions about the reach and who would be benefiting from their work? About expansion and bringing a beautiful sport to a wider group of people who might not otherwise be able to learn it?

It made her angry. She'd put so much love into everything to this point. Why couldn't they see that?

"I fail to see the relevance of these questions. As Cooper said, we're very excited to be able to bring tennis to more people in the community. We're passionate about—"

"Cooper Hayes doesn't really date though, does he? So, is this more casual? We know he doesn't do girlfriends, so—"

"Excuse me." Maya wasn't one to interrupt, but after the number of times she'd been cut off in the last minute, combined with what the reporter in the back was saying, she was fuming, almost feeling the smoke coming out of her ears. Gone were those anxiety symptoms, replaced with red hot anger.

She took a step in front of Cooper, a feeling of protectiveness joining that anger. "I'm sorry, I don't know what's going on exactly, but we were told this was a press event to spread the word about what we're trying to do. Not that it's *any* of your business, but Cooper and I have a professional relationship and have been friends for years. What we do in our free time has no bearing on our mission, and these questions are futile. If you'd like to ask something about the charity, please do so now. Otherwise, I think we're done."

There were far worse things swimming in her head that she wanted to say, things like *fuck you for talking about Cooper like that*, but she knew a blow up on television was the last thing they needed. She took a couple of breaths in and out as the reporters mumbled amongst themselves.

Cooper stepped beside her, his hand brushing hers lightly before drawing back, as if it were accidental. She knew it hadn't been, and just the second of it had sent the anger rushing out of her, cloaking her in comfort.

He looked expectantly at the crowd, though she saw the slight slump of defeat in his shoulders, and all she wanted was to reach out and hug him. How dare they talk about him like that? It was disgusting, and it was even worse that it was the one thing he was trying to turn around. Yet there it was, being flung in his face again, basically advertising that he was only good for a good time and nothing else.

Some of the other reporters asked questions that actually related to the charity, and Cooper fielded most of them. When Maya chanced a look at Viola, her anger and disappointment were palpable.

The whole thing didn't last more than fifteen minutes, but by the end of it, Maya was drained and still a little peeved. As the reporters dispersed, she walked toward Viola, embracing her for a little longer than she usually would.

Viola's arms squeezed her once before she whispered, "Don't you worry about them, hon. They're maggots, and they're just lucky I didn't get up there myself and yell at them. Only held myself back because of the charity."

Maya pulled away, a small smile on her face as she glanced back toward Cooper, who was looking off into the parking lot, clearly lost in thought.

"I just hope even one person sees it. The important part of it at least."

Viola stuck her chin in Cooper's direction. "Is he going to be okay?"

"I hope so."

Viola looked between the two of them before nodding once. "You should head home for today. Nothing productive is going to get done after that. I'll keep getting the message out to as many people as I can, and we can put up more flyers around the area in the next few days. Don't you worry about a thing. The fundraiser is going to go well, and it'll all work out."

Maya nodded, giving Viola one last side hug. "Thank you, Vi. See you soon," she murmured, her thoughts already back on Cooper.

If they'd ever left him.

The ride home was as quiet as the one there, though this time, they were both taking space to process what had happened. Maya tried not to worry about the insinuation that she was sleeping with Cooper for her job, but it kept bubbling up, and more than making her sad, it *pissed her off*.

How had it all gone so wrong so fast?

As they reached the house, Maya resisted the urge to flip off the people with cameras who stood barely down the street from them, clearly hoping to get a picture of Cooper. They walked into the house, and she closed the front door and gave him a warm smile before brushing past him toward the stairs. He seemed like he still needed space, and she would be glad to give it to him.

"Maya, wait."

She stopped on a dime, scared to see the look on his face when she turned around. All she found when she did was concern and reverence.

"You okay, sweetheart?"

Maya inhaled a short breath at the name and at the tone of his voice. It sounded like he was holding himself back from reaching for her. Just like he had been the past few weeks. She was tired of holding back though. Sure, he was Cooper, Colton's best friend, but he was also Cooper, the kind man who'd listened to her talk ad-nauseum about tennis with a smile on his face. The man who talked to her every night like his free time was built for her and her alone. The man who could make her smile no matter how sad she was.

Cooper could hold himself back, but she wouldn't do the same. Maya moved a step toward him, wanting to place a hand on his weary face. He looked as drained as she felt, even if he tried to hide it.

"I'm okay. Are you?"

He nodded once, but she could tell it was a lie. Her right hand landed on his stubbled cheek, a thumb brushing over his cheekbone, up toward his hairline, and then back down a few times.

There was a rumble in his throat, almost like a groan.

"Maya." He'd whispered it so quietly, like it was a secret he wanted, needed, to keep to himself. Indecision flickered across his face like a candle in the wind.

Maya hated seeing such a confident man shaken up like this, but she was glad it was her who got to be with him through it.

His head sunk down toward her shoulder, and she wrapped her arms around his neck, warmth spreading through her body when she felt his arms encircle her waist. Back was the storm in her belly, though calmer, mellower.

He was leaning down, half of his body weight leaning against her, and she wished she could take it all so he could rest.

"I'm so sorry, Coop." Her hand ran through his hair rhythmically, soothingly.

"It doesn't matter what I do, this is all they'll see me as. Cooper Hayes: Sabertooths playboy who's around for a good time or not at all. Cooper Hayes as a whole person with dreams outside of his next hookup? Unfathomable."

He turned his head slightly so his nose was buried in her hair, and then he inhaled a slow breath.

"Fuck them."

"I told you, everyone loves to talk about that reputation."

"*Fuck.* Them," she hissed, her hand stopping its run through his hair to cup the back of his head. "They don't deserve a single ounce of your attention. They don't know you like I do, Coop. They don't get the privilege of knowing how special and caring and hilarious you are. It's their damn loss."

He exhaled, pulling her tighter to him. "You're an angel. *My* angel."

Maya didn't know if it was his breath on her neck or his claim, but she shivered involuntarily, hand tugging at his hair a little. "Coop," she moaned.

Cooper pulled back, a pained expression on his face. He swallowed once, then shook his head like he was trying to rid himself of the same thoughts racing through her mind. One of his arms released her, though the other one anchored her to him. He placed a soft kiss on her right temple.

"Come on," he whispered against her hair. "Let's eat while we watch some TV."

Even during dinner, his body never left hers, a leg pressed to hers if his arm couldn't be. Maya didn't know what any of it meant, too terrified that, if she so much as opened her mouth to question it, their closeness would disappear in a cloud of smoke. Poof.

Instead, she enjoyed the warmth of his body beside hers and the sounds of his breath evening out on the couch.

Weathering the storm alongside her.

Chapter Seventeen

Maya

"Cooper, please be serious," Maya begged exasperatedly the next day, walking over to where her phone camera was recording them for the fourth time. They'd had a quiet evening, but this morning, he'd seemed to be in brighter spirits, which had brightened her day too.

Cooper tended to have that effect on her.

"I'm sorry, Mai. I just don't think we should be recording this very important video on your phone. No matter how new the phone may be."

"Jane said it would be endearing as long as we *get it right*," she responded as she looked at the video, referring to their event planner. "And I'm open to suggestions as long as they're *real* ones."

They had finalized the agenda for the opening night gala, and since there weren't any children who could speak to how the lessons impacted them yet, they'd decided to film a video themselves. After a helpful call with Delilah, extensive out-lining by Maya, and very minimal help from Cooper, they'd decided to talk about the mission, the challenges faced by underprivileged kids in accessing sports programs, and the impact of tennis lessons on an individual child and the community as a whole.

Only, it had been four takes, and they hadn't even gotten through the first sentence.

She set it back up on the windowsill in the dining room, thankful for the great lighting. "Okay, ready? Recording."

Maya pressed record and then ran over to where Cooper stood.

"Good evening, everyone. I'm Maya Beaumont, and this is Cooper Hayes. We want to start by giving you a heartfelt thank you for coming to our event tonight. This charity means the world to us, and we can't wait to show you all the good we can do with it."

Her eyes cut to his in the mirror of the phone video, waiting for his lines, but the confused look on his face had her bending over with a palm slapped over her mouth, trying not to laugh out loud.

"Cooper, *please*." She laughed as he turned slowly to face her, that confused expression still on his face. When he started walking toward her like a deranged zombie from a 2000s movie, she gave up and collapsed on the ground laughing. "You're an idiot."

Cooper chuckled. "Okay, this time I promise. Don't even turn it off, we'll just roll now." He looked at her expectantly, tapping his foot. "Tick tock, come on Maya. We're on a timeline here with the sun," he mimicked her from earlier.

She shot him a middle finger but got up, dusting off her jeans and white T-shirt. Maya tried not to love how much their outfits were matching. They looked like dorks in the best way.

"Alright. Take six." She started her paragraph and thankfully got through it once more without an issue. She looked to Cooper again to start his lines.

"Hi, I'm Cooper, and I—"

"Cooper! This is starting to feel like weaponized incompetence. How you get all those commercials done is beyond me. This is atrocious."

He raised his hands in surrender, though there was a small tilt to the corners of his lips. "Hey, what'd I do wrong that time?"

"I already introduced you! Don't start your lines with 'Hi, I'm Cooper,'" she said, dropping her voice down a few octaves and mocking his Southern drawl.

"I don't even sound like that."

"You most definitely do, cowboy."

Cooper put his hands on his hips. "Hey, we ranchers are a hardworking people. Just because the rest of the country likes to use our culture and clothing for fashion doesn't mean us *real* cowboys aren't out working the land and taking care of the animals."

Maya puffed out her chest, trying to stifle her laugh once more. "'It don't mean us *real* cowboys ain't out working the land,'" she again mocked him. "You are the most white-collar man I've ever spent this much time with besides my brothers. You have three overpriced cars, a massive mansion, and use an app to order your food most of the time, if it's not already made for you at the facility."

He narrowed his eyes, moving toward her slowly with his arms outstretched like he was about to grab her. She ducked and ran across the room, giggling.

"I said '*doesn't*' and '*aren't*.' Just because I like nice things *doesn't* mean I'm not still a rancher." He stopped giving chase, gesturing at his outfit. "Look at my clothes. This is all I wear."

And she thanked every religion's god for it, twice, because those jeans fit snug as hell, and his cowboy hat really did give him that rugged handsomeness she loved so much.

"Just because you have one cowboy hat and a few pairs of Levi's *don't* mean you're cultured in the ways of the ranchers. If I called your family right now, they'd tell me you're the least cultured of them all."

Again, he moved toward her with his arms outstretched, though this time, he went for deranged zombie once more.

"I'll do you one better. I'll take you to Tennessee and show you my ranch and my family, and then we'll see who's talking."

Was Cooper offering to...take her home? Maya's insides twisted at that.

Right as he reached her, she ducked before grabbing a dining chair, holding it up to protect herself. "You'd be so busy staring at my ass in those skintight jeans and cowboy boots, you wouldn't be able to do a single second of work."

His smirk was downright evil. "Don't tempt me with a good time, *sweetheart*," he drawled, purposely allowing his accent through a bit more.

Maya didn't respond, setting the chair down and positioning her hands in the sign for time out. "I'll let you dress me up however you like if you finish this video before the sun sets. Jane's going to kill us if we don't send it to her today."

Cooper rushed at her, grabbing her around the waist and setting her back on her mark, seemingly incentivized by her promise.

"*Any* way I want?"

It was her turn to smirk evilly. "Let's film this damn thing."

Her phone was still rolling, so she did their introductions again, smiling wider because she was so proud of herself for not missing a single word despite how Cooper was now looking at her—though she did wonder if it was borderline inappropriate for him to stare at her like that for the video.

She also wondered if those were his bedroom eyes, and then she closed her eyes for a second to rein in that line of thought.

Cooper started on his lines, and it seemed like he was going to finish the second paragraph of the script, but as if she'd now been conditioned to laugh every time he took his turn, she stifled one, ended up snorting, and then was once again bent over laughing.

"Now I get why actors struggle so much in their bloopers—it's so hard not to laugh," she panted as her body kept shaking with mirth until her laughter became silent, and then Cooper was laughing at her.

Finally, when she wasn't looking, he swooped her up and threw her over his shoulder.

"Coop! Put me down! What are you doing?"

"You're trying to mess me up so that we don't finish this video in time and then I don't get to choose what you wear."

"That's ridiculous!"

He began walking around the living room, purposely jostling her, even as his hand rested on the back of her thighs. Heat speared her lower belly at the contact. "Stop laughing so we can finish."

"You're the one making me laugh," she cried, hands smacking at his back so he would put her down.

"I didn't even do anything that time. I was literally perfect."

"Yeah, but it was residual from the last few times. Put me *down*," Maya demanded as he nearly rammed her into a doorway.

"Promise you'll be serious."

"*You* promise!"

"Maya Beaumont, so help me God, I will keep you up there all evening."

She relaxed her whole body, sighing dejectedly. "I promise to be serious."

"Good." He tossed her onto the couch in a way that reminded her how much she liked to be thrown around, and even more so when a tall, muscular, and rugged man in jeans and a cowboy hat stood over her, looking her over eagerly.

They were *not* serious for the rest of the evening, and Cooper did *not* get to dress her, the video long abandoned for another day.

Jane could wait one more day...Maya hoped.

By the time the sun set and they'd ordered their food, her stomach ached from laughing and she'd cried the happiest of tears since beating Anya in the Wimbledon first round.

Chapter Eighteen

Cooper

A couple of weeks later, Cooper flew into Los Angeles for the day so he and Maya could meet with their event planner. The gala was only two short weeks away, and the pressure was on.

After the meeting, where they'd gone through every minute detail so Jane could ensure everything went according to plan, it was like a stopwatch had begun ticking, letting them know their free time together was coming to a rapid end.

Thanks to the Friday evening traffic, it was over forty-five minutes to the place Maya described as "the best ice cream of her life." Though they'd spoken on the phone nearly every day, the ride gave them an opportunity to catch each other up on the little details.

As usual, Cooper was starting to get that antsy feeling he always did when he had to leave soon. Draft day was fast approaching, and getting away from Charleston and the Sabers had been getting more difficult. He hoped it would be better during the couple of months after the draft, but he knew once summer hit, he'd rarely be able to leave.

The thought of not seeing Maya as much made his whole body ache.

When they finally parked, she was practically skipping with excitement. Cooper was glad to get glimpses of this Maya. It'd been a few months, and there were still times when she seemed to be grieving, but the charity appeared to be distracting her. Despite only having one quick coaching session, he knew she'd make an amazing coach.

Maya would make an amazing anything, though.

When they got to the front of the line, she didn't even sample any of the flavors, choosing a scoop of lavender vanilla ice cream with gummy bears on top. Cooper tested a few before landing on the salted caramel.

It was just okay. He imagined the reason she loved this place was because it offered the mutant ice cream she seemed to be enjoying so much. Still, he finished the small scoop quickly and tossed out his trash.

Maya stuck a spoon of the monstrosity into her mouth as they exited the shop. "The beach is right down the street if you want to stop there." She pointed ahead of them. "I know you like the beach. But only if you want to."

"Only if you promise you'll throw all those gummy bears into the ocean."

She gasped. "How dare you even think of something like that? Gummy bears belong on lavender vanilla ice cream."

"Lavender does not belong in vanilla ice cream, and gummy bears belong on an island far away from ice cream."

"You're just jealous you have such bland taste. It's too bad you weren't blessed with taste buds like mine, or you could be enjoying the goodness that is *this*." Maya put a spoonful in her mouth, sucking on the spoon, closing her eyes and moaning. It took great effort for Cooper to cut his eyes away before his brain started working through its many fantasies that only seemed to be getting worse the more time he spent with Maya.

Only now, half of those fantasies weren't even remotely sexual in nature, and often, they involved them getting food together, cuddling while watching TV, or enjoying a night at a bar knowing they could go home with each other.

It just wasn't the right time. Maybe once the fundraiser was done and On the Line was up and running, things would be different. Maybe the *Tribune* would stop reporting about the parts of his life that mattered least.

Like the post from today that looked a lot like a conspiracy theorist's work, trying to figure out if he and Tara Carr were together.

Bizarre and kind of sad that reporting on his relationship status was someone's life's work.

Cooper followed her down the sparsely lit road to what appeared to be a private beach. "My taste buds are perfect, thank you. I just don't like toxic waste. And have you been here before, or are you trying to get us in trouble?"

She grinned over her shoulder at him. "Who said those were mutually exclusive?"

Maya walked through a hole in the fence with a sign that read *No Trespassing. Private Property*, stopping as Cooper took it in. She smirked, and despite the shadows, he knew she was calling him a chicken.

"Come on, old man. There's a hole in the fence. It's practically begging us to come through and enjoy the view."

"Yeah, that's my fear. Next thing you know, there's gonna be a guy with a shotgun coming after us," he murmured as he once again followed her, ducking through the hole.

"Such a worrier. This is California, not Tennessee. The people living in this house probably don't even own guns." Maya ended the thought with another moan as she put one of the last few bites of her scoop into her mouth.

A breeze blew through her long hair, and the moon illuminated the small stretch of sand that led to calm waves. She took a seat a few yards from where the waves were breaking, motioning him to join her.

"It's so calming," she hummed as she set her cup down beside her.

"Does my presence bother you so much that you have to come to a private beach to get calm?" Cooper asked as he sat.

"Yes, I can't *stand* to be near you for longer than a few minutes before I'm rushing elsewhere for peace and quiet. Haven't you noticed?"

"I've been so busy doing the same, I guess I haven't been paying attention."

Maya pouted. "You wound me."

"You're too pretty to let the thoughts of any man wound you."

She turned to face him, eyebrow raised. "Are you flirting with me?"

"Sweetheart, I've been flirting with you against my better judgment for months. Maybe even years."

She paused for a moment, and in the light of the moon, he could see the reddening of her cheeks. "Do friends often flirt with each other?"

His heart fell to his stomach at the question. Maybe she hadn't pulled away the times they'd almost kissed, and maybe she'd stayed tucked beside him on the couch after the disaster of a press conference, but clearly, she didn't feel the same heat for him that he did for her. But when he looked at her before he responded, the smirk on her face told another story.

"Are we really *just* friends?"

He didn't know why he asked it, because he'd continuously promised himself that *yes*, until he could prove to everyone that he was worthy, they would be *just* friends.

Maya looked at him thoughtfully before pulling him close by his Sabertooths sweatshirt, her eyes falling to his lips for a moment before they were back up, looking into his eyes. Cooper sat rigidly, wondering if he needed to pull away from her for what felt like the tenth time in the two and a half months they'd been growing close.

"I guess that depends on one's definition of friends." Her words were hushed, and before Cooper could process what was happening, she was pulling off her shirt.

It was as she pulled the zipper of her jeans down that he asked in a raspy voice, "What are you doing?"

"Getting in."

"What?"

"Come on. Let's swim."

A few moments later, after he'd taken in the fact that he'd just seen his closest friend's little sister strip down to her tiny underwear and walk with a purpose toward the water, he heard a splash, and she disappeared under the waves.

Something felt off. Maya was certainly fun, even wild at times, but this felt different, like she was overcompensating for something. Pushing limits she might not usually push.

Cooper stood, pulling his sweatshirt and shirt off quickly, then stepped out of his jeans, leaving them in a pile with her clothes. He walked slowly toward the water, sighing thankfully when her head emerged a few feet in.

When he finally made it to her, walking with slow, determined steps, he asked, "What's going on, Mai?"

She didn't meet his eyes. "What do you mean?"

He grabbed her chin lightly, pulling her eyes to meet his. "Maya."

She sighed. "I like being with you, okay? I get lonely when you're gone, even with Viola and the tennis center and the lessons. Even when I'm busy or when I'm with others, I miss you. I know you have to leave tomorrow, and I guess I just didn't want our time together to end so soon."

She pushed away from him, and he let go of her chin. "You just got in today, you know? I'm used to getting you for a couple of days at least," she finished quietly.

A sharp stab of pain slammed into his gut, and guilt washed over him like the waves that moved them, wishing he hadn't pushed her to talk and yet thanking the stars above she'd finally said what he'd been thinking.

"Sweetheart, I would've stayed up all night with you if you'd asked."

Bright, hesitant eyes looked at him, as if trying to confirm his words were real. She opened her mouth and then closed it, searching his face before she turned to the dark horizon.

"I don't know if you remember a couple of Thanksgivings ago when I showed up at the Barrett house in distress."

"I remember." Cooper had been outside playing with some of his teammates' children, and when it was time to come in and eat, she'd been standing there, looking distraught and like she'd been crying for days. It'd been the first time he'd seen her since her birthday, when they'd nearly kissed, and his heart had stopped at the sight of her.

Maya had been hauntingly beautiful, and no matter how many times he'd quietly asked her how she was during dinner and trivia, she'd just shaken her head.

"I'd been, um, I'd been seeing this guy. Kind of. He was on the men's tour and so we'd been friends for a while before we started...hooking up."

Cooper's hands clenched of their own volition at her words. Did he want to hear about this? She looked so vulnerable that he just nodded encouragingly, even though he was sure he didn't.

"So, we were hooking up for a while, and we agreed it was just a friends-with-benefits situation, so it was my own damn fault. Unsurprisingly, I got attached. After we...you know...he would always make up an excuse to leave. As soon as it was over, he was gone. And I got it, because that's what we'd agreed on, but there was still a part of me that wished he'd lingered. Wondered if it was something I was doing.

"Later, he told me we couldn't hook up anymore because he'd developed feelings but still didn't want anything serious. That's why I showed up that day."

Cooper's nails bit into his palm as he tried not to lose his cool, unfurling one hand to push a wet strand of hair behind Maya's ear while she looked out over the ocean.

"Of course it wasn't something you were doing, sunflower. Never you." He wondered if he'd ever made a woman feel that way. Knew he probably had. The thought flitted in and out of his head like a hummingbird before he focused his attention back on her. "And if you ever want me to stay with you, doesn't matter for what reason, you just tell me, and I'll do my best to stay, okay?"

Cooper didn't want Maya equating him with this guy ever again, because he'd meant what he'd said. If she asked him for the moon right now, he'd try and find a way to get it for her.

"Thank you."

Maya pushed her hands up toward the surface of the water, then pushed them back down, up and then down, displacing the water enough to sway them.

"My mom was truly the only person who ever made me feel like I was a priority without a thought when I was growing up. Sure, Colton and Landon did their best, and I appreciate everything they've done for me, but they were older, busier, and dealing with their own stuff. Dad hasn't cared about me from the moment I was born. If I couldn't play football and continue his legacy, what good was I? So, yeah, Mom was the one who was always there, championing me, making sure I knew how much she loved me." She continued looking away from him toward the ocean.

Cooper couldn't stop himself from holding her any longer. He wrapped an arm around her waist, tucking her body into his and setting his head on top of hers. It didn't feel right voicing the words that were on the tip of his tongue, that *he* wanted to make her a priority, not when he wasn't sure what he was ready or able to give her. He hoped holding her would show her, at least, that no matter what, he was there for her.

"And then Mom died, and I was alone. My mom's side of the family never reached out, whether because they couldn't stomach seeing us after having to bury her or something else, I don't know. But either way, I didn't hear anything from them. And so, once again, I felt lost and alone. Even in college, my team's love for me and interest in me always felt conditional upon my abilities. But at least when I was playing, I felt wanted. Needed, even.

"And then I met the girls, and I had a place. I had my people. I felt loved, even if we were often too busy to talk, even if it was just a wave from another tennis court down the way. And then all that stuff happened with Ryan dating Anya, one of the girls at the academy. That was hard for a while, but I still had my girls. But then I got injured, and it felt like I'd lost the people who loved me again."

She was quiet for a moment, and Cooper placed a kiss to the top of her head, sensing that she had more to say.

"I know I still have my friends, but they're so busy, we can hardly talk now that I don't travel with them. It's almost like the universe was trying to tell me, each and every time, that I didn't deserve that love. That if I ask for too much, I could lose everything."

He kissed the top of her head again, moving his pointer finger in figure eights on the bare skin of her waist. She'd barely taken a breath as she spoke, like she was airing it all to him, everything that lived in her head.

"I had no idea. I wish I could've been there for you during all this, sweetheart. I wish I'd known so I could've held you like this when you needed it." He wrapped his other arm around her waist, needing her as close as he could get her.

"But now that I am, I want you to know that you are an incredible human being. One of my favorites. You've been through so much and have come out the other side so much stronger. Screw Ryan and Anya. And I don't mean to speak ill of elders, but if your grandparents don't care to learn who you are now, screw them too. You're too vibrant and amazing to be pulled down by the opinions and whims of idiots. You're Maya fucking Beaumont, and if anybody ever makes you feel like you're not special again, they're gonna have more than your brothers to contend with."

This was one of many reasons he'd called the paper of that reporter—the one who'd accused Maya of sleeping with him for her job—to speak with his superior. That anyone could ever make her feel so small was unacceptable.

Like she was weary from spilling her guts, or maybe Cooper had just finally said the right thing, Maya rested her head against his chest, and they breathed in the salty air together as they looked out over the ocean. His sunflower, always so beautiful and vibrant despite the many layers of grief that lived underneath. The ones she rarely let anyone in to see.

As if prodded by her honesty, and despite never having expressed it to anyone, not even Colton, he said quietly, "In college, I dated this girl, Gabi. Well, at least I thought we were dating. To her, I guess we were just sleeping together. I was the person she posted to social media and went to sorority parties with but not the person she wanted to be with. I thought she was the love of my life, but to her, I was some trophy. The Bama tight end she could enjoy evenings with, but who wasn't exactly long-term relationship material."

Maya pulled back, anger clear on her face. "She *said* that?"

Cooper nodded. "She said she'd gotten the following she'd been looking for on her socials and didn't need to be seen with me anymore. It wasn't until then that I realized she'd never once said she loved me back."

"And that's why you feel like casual relationships are all you're good for," she breathed out. It wasn't even a question. She'd shrewdly figured him out so easily, so quickly.

Cooper didn't respond, worried Maya would tell him she agreed. He knew she wasn't like that, knew she'd only ever made him feel worthy of love and kindness, but he still waited with bated breath to hear those fateful words he was so used to hearing. It was what the media, no, the whole country, believed. He wouldn't have faulted her for it.

"You deserve the world, Coop." She cupped his cheek, rubbing a thumb over his stubble. "You deserve the fucking world. Someday soon, I really hope you see that."

They stood like that for minutes, until someone from the shore shouted at them to get off their property, and then they were racing to get their clothes on and get back to Maya's car, twin smiles etched onto their faces.

Chapter Nineteen

Maya

The event hall was packed with people laughing loudly as they mingled with other invitees of the evening at round tables. Between her brothers, Cooper, her friends, and herself, they'd managed to convince over seventy athletes, staff, and tech investors—courtesy of Landon in the Bay Area—to listen to their pleas and potentially donate to the cause.

Maya turned to Viola, who had stayed steadfastly by her side through the welcome reception, opening remarks, video presentation, keynote speaker—*the* Nicholas Aetos, the top male tennis player in the world, an appearance gifted by her friends—the two auctions, and now, as their guests enjoyed dinner.

"It's going well. It's going well, right? I feel like it's going well."

Viola's hand found hers and squeezed. "Breathe, hon. It's going very well. Everyone here seems happy, and the auction put you very close to your goal."

Maya took a breath in, smiling at this woman who had quickly become a friend. "Put *us* very close to *our* goal," she reminded Viola. After all she had done, Maya had asked her to be outreach coordinator for the charity, a position she was currently crushing.

Viola squeezed her hand once more. "Exactly. All is well. We can always talk about lowering the cost of the courts if that becomes an issue too. But I don't think it'll come to that."

Maya nodded. "Okay. You're right."

"Why don't you find Cooper? He's been looking at you all night."

Maya stuttered on her next words before she closed her mouth. She'd been doing her best *not* to look at him all night, because every time she did, she noticed how handsome he looked in a suit and could barely breathe. They'd hardly had a moment to speak about anything other than the gala since he'd flown in, and even though they'd talked almost every night of the two weeks they'd spent apart, Maya felt almost shy around him.

"Probably has a question. Or just checking to make sure I'm okay."

"Mm-hmm," Viola hummed.

"You'll be okay if I go?"

"Oh, please. I'm perfectly content people watching, you know that. It's like watching reality TV in here with all these minor celebrities."

Maya snorted but began looking for Cooper. Her eyes fell on Landon, who was speaking to a group of people who appeared to be hanging onto his every word. Colton and Lucia had had to say goodbye after the live auction to make their flight to Rome—a gift to her for all her draft work, Colton had said.

She found Cooper, and just like she knew she would, Maya struggled to breathe as she watched him talk animatedly, a charming smile on his face. Approaching him, she noted the woman he was speaking to, with her long auburn waves falling to mid-back and the prettiest fox-like features. An unpleasant feeling reared its ugly head somewhere deep in her chest, and it took everything inside her to quash it and plaster a big smile on her face as she took in the woman's hand on his arm.

She *really* did not like that.

When Maya finally reached his side, he turned to her, his eyes lighting up, though a hint of worry flitted across his expression. She took that to mean she was baring her teeth a bit too much rather than smiling, so she turned to the woman, pulling it back a couple of notches.

"Hi! I'm Maya," she said through the smile as she held out her hand.

"Abigail." The woman shook Maya's hand. "I was just telling Cooper how much I enjoyed the guest speaker, and he said you might be able to put me in touch? I'm a sports journalist and would love to talk to him."

"Of course I can. Do you have a business card?"

Abigail finally removed her hand from Cooper's arm as she searched through a small black clutch that Maya wouldn't have minded swiping from her, knowing how well it would go with her long, red evening gown. Maya saw Cooper watching her in her periphery but kept her focus on Abigail until she had the card in her hand.

"Here. I appreciate it so much." Abigail leaned toward Cooper. "And my personal number is on the back." The sultry expression on her face was fixing for a smack, but Maya had never been violent, so she kept the fake smile plastered on her face.

When the woman finally walked away, Maya ripped the card in half and shoved it into the tight bodice of her gown. "Mm, that's a shame. It was almost believable." She turned so she was facing Cooper.

"Is my sunflower jealous?" The lines beside his eyes as he grinned at her only served to make his clean-shaven face more handsome, and her heart thrashed against her ribcage. If he looked mouthwatering in jeans and a tight T-shirt or his football uniform, she didn't even know what word to use to describe him in a suit.

Maya scoffed. "I don't know what you're talking about, my motor functioning is just impaired from all the alcohol I've consumed. It was an accident."

His knowing smile widened. "You haven't touched any of the alcohol, Mai."

She narrowed her eyes. "Have you been watching me all night?"

"Always."

The storm in her stomach raged, and she had to break their eye contact. Jane ambled toward them, saving Maya from responding. Their event planner extended a small index card with a crudely written number. Maya struggled to decipher it, but when she finally did, she stared at Cooper with open-mouthed shock.

The number was far higher than they'd been hoping for.

Cooper's expression matched hers, and she had to will herself not to squeal loudly right there in a room full of some of the richest people in the country.

Jane cleared her throat. "There's a celebration room for you through that door." She inclined her head to their right, where two venue staff members stood. "You've got a few minutes to celebrate before acknowledgements and thank yous, if you'd like."

It only took them a few seconds to get through the door, waving at people who called out to them or raised a glass in their direction. On the other side, there was a small closet before them and a long hallway to the right.

"Do you think she was talking about the close—oh," she cut herself off as Cooper dragged her by the hand into the closet, closing the door behind her and backing away from her until his back hit the wall of the little room, running a hand through his hair.

She stepped forward, batting his hand away. "Careful! Your hair is so perfect right now. Don't mess it up."

His lips pulled into a smile, and she beamed back, completely uninhibited. The joy she felt after seeing that number and knowing how many children's lives she could hopefully enrich beat almost every other achievement she'd had in her life.

"We did it, Coop."

Cooper brushed the few strands of hair she'd pulled out of her half-up half-down hairstyle behind her ear, like he wanted to get a good look at her, his smile shifting into something more tender.

"Yeah. We did," he whispered.

Cooper had been there with her, a driving force alongside her, helping her get something Maya never could've imagined for herself only a couple of months ago. And here he stood, more handsome than any man she'd ever seen, and all his focus was on her too.

Maya didn't know what kissing him would entail, other than the complications that came with him being Colton's closest friend and them working on the charity together, but she knew she wanted to. She was tired of pushing away the need that thrummed between them.

Her thumb reached out to brush against his bottom lip, and warmth wound tight behind her belly button at his sharp inhale and the subtle change in his eyes. Desire hung heavy around them, pulling his forehead to rest on Maya's like she was his gravity. He closed his eyes, inhaling another sharp breath.

Quietly, Cooper murmured, "I'm sorry. I can't stop myself anymore. If you don't want this, I need you to tell me right now so I can walk away, because I can't stop thinking about you and what you might taste like." His hand slid to cradle the back of her neck.

Want, bright and hot, pulsed through her at his words. She felt her nipples harden and push at the cups of her gown, and the lace of her panties rubbed perfectly against her center, drawing a sigh from her lips. "Finally," she breathed.

The word was hardly out of her mouth before his hand was digging into her hair and his mouth was upon hers, his other hand wrapping around her waist and pulling her body flush against his.

Just as she'd imagined, kissing Cooper was like playing with fire. Her skin heated deliciously, her whole body alight in his hands as his lips pressed to hers firmly, warmly.

Maybe it was a bad idea, maybe she would one day regret the passion behind this kiss, the raw need. But every cell in her body lit up with his flame and burned the doubts away, leaving her with only desire. The desire that'd been building in her for months. Every time his hand had brushed hers. Every time they'd hugged goodbye. Every near kiss. It all culminated to this point.

Screw the consequences.

Maya flicked her tongue over his bottom lip gently, needing him to know how badly she wanted him. She grabbed a fistful of his pristinely pressed button-down, loving the feel of his beating heart beneath her hand. His groan into her mouth was music to her ears, and the hand around her waist slid to her ass, pushing her into the bulge in his pants.

It was her turn to moan, feeling the slickness between her legs at the knowledge that she did that to him. His tongue matched hers in every stroke until she was pressed up against the door and ready to rip off his clothes right there in that closet, and hers with them.

He pulled back, leaving her panting.

"Wha—"

A knock sounded from the door against her back, and she remembered where she was.

She took in his disheveled state, reaching up to fix his shirt and the tie that was just slightly askew. Noting the lipstick that painted his lips a shade of pink, she swiped at them with her thumb, chuckling.

"How's my hair?" she asked.

His voice was strained as he attempted to get the word out. "Perfect."

She knew he was lying, so she tried to pat it down.

"Guys? It's time for thank yous."

They took one last look at each other, and when he stepped away and nodded, she turned and pulled the door open.

Jane's eyes ran over them like she knew exactly what she'd interrupted. She reached over Maya, and only when Maya felt a sharp tug did she realize Jane was fixing her hair. Maya threw an annoyed look over her shoulder and was met with a sheepish smile from Cooper.

"For future reference, the celebratory room, also known as the back room or set up room, is down the hall. But the closet's good too," Jane teased.

Cooper snorted behind her.

"Right. We're ready," Maya said, not even sure they were.

Luckily, as they reemerged into the main event room, no one seemed to notice them besides Viola and Landon. Viola also looked like she knew their shame, but Landon either wasn't very perceptive or he didn't really care because he walked up to Maya with his signature cocky smirk on his face.

"I've got to head out for the evening so I can make my flight back to San Jose, but I wanted to tell you how proud I am of you. You've come so far in the past three months." He opened his arms for a hug, and she stepped into them, tears welling in her eyes at his words. "Mom would be proud of you, munchkin."

Maya had tried to stop the tears from falling and ruining her makeup, but that was the final push, identical tear drops making their way down her cheeks. She smiled up at her brother, wishing, not for the first time, that his not-so-great relationship with Colton hadn't put a wedge in their own. If only she could've had this all these years.

Well, she was thankful to have him back now.

Maya sniffled. "Thank you. Love you to the moon," she whispered.

"Love you to the moon." He squeezed her hand and then walked out of the room.

Maya had all of a few seconds to get herself presentable, taking Cooper's warm and reassuring hand as he helped her up the stairs to say their thank yous.

She almost felt like she was taking a step into a new future.

Chapter Twenty

Maya

Maya couldn't tell if the tense silence on the way back to the house was anticipatory tense or *we shouldn't have done that* tense. Cooper appeared to be very in his head as he drove them.

"That went well," she offered, to try to break the silence.

He mumbled something vaguely like *mm-hmm* but said nothing else.

Maybe this silence *was* bad. Maybe he'd only kissed her because she'd been leaning in and he hadn't wanted her to feel badly but now he regretted it. Sure, he'd said some things that had made her think otherwise, but something inside her was telling her that maybe it'd been a heat-of-the-moment kiss.

As they pulled onto her street, Maya asked quietly, "Do you regret it?"

Cooper's eyes snapped to her, his hand flying over the console to rest on her knee. "Never, sweetheart. Of course not. I'm just thinking."

Maya nodded once but looked out the window as they pulled into her driveway, still not sure how the rest of the night would go. Maybe he didn't regret it, but that didn't mean he was ready to do anything more.

Maya put a hand over her face when a flash went off to her right, and Cooper stepped around so he blocked her, guiding her with a hand on her back up to the front door. "Gonna buy you a security system. I hate this."

Maya shook her head. "I'll get the garage door fixed in no time, and then I'll go through there instead of up to the front door. It's no biggie."

She didn't need him worrying about her. Maya locked the door behind them and began moving up the stairs, hoping she didn't look as crestfallen as she felt.

"Sweetheart."

When she turned back around, his hair was wild, like he'd managed to run his hands through it fifteen times in the seconds it had taken her to get halfway up the stairs.

"Hi," she said dumbly. Her brain felt scrambled taking him in. *It should be illegal to look that fucking good.*

"Hi."

She blinked, not sure where to go from there.

"I'm sorry," he whispered, so softly she almost missed it.

Her heart dropped. "Hey, no, I get it. I was leaning in, and you wanted to protect my feelings. I get—"

He held a hand up to quiet her.

"You have no *idea* how badly I wanted that kiss. There is nobody in this world who wants something as badly as I want you," he all but growled.

Relief filled her at the affirmation, though she was still confused why he'd apologized.

"So then *take* me."

His gaze slowly slid down her body and then back up, taking his sweet time enjoying the view. "No."

Maya crossed her arms over her chest. "Why not?"

"There isn't enough time in the day to go through all the reasons this is a bad idea."

She scoffed. Cooper kept seeing her as Colton's sister, and if that was one of his big reasons for holding back, she was over it.

"I'm not going to beg you. You said you want me, then prove it. Just because I'm Colton's little sister doesn't make me a kid. I can make my own damn decisions. And I'm choosing you. I want you. If you can't say the same and mean it, then yes, we should stop whatever this is."

Cooper's jaw clenched, and in only a few strides, he was one step below her, a gentle hand applying next to no pressure to her throat. Just the brush of his fingers was enough to send a zing of excitement through her body, her blood boiling in anticipation of what he would do next.

His hand tightened slightly, though still gentle, and his lips found hers in the most passionate kiss she'd ever had. Maya's head emptied as her sole focus became keeping herself upright. A few moments later, when he pulled away, kissing and dragging his teeth down her jaw and neck until she was nothing but a puddle, her knees finally gave out.

Cooper's other arm wrapped around her waist to keep her standing, her center grazing over his leg. He buried a hand in Maya's hair, pulling her head back so he could have better access to her neck. A needy moan escaped her open mouth as she let her head fall back, enjoying the bite of his teeth and the soothing strokes of his warm breath and tongue as he kissed it better.

"Look at what you do to me," he breathed into her neck, lifting her head so she looked at him.

Maya peered down at his dress pants through lowered lashes, seeing the way he strained against them.

"That's twice now tonight. You felt that and really thought I don't want you? I'm in a perpetual state of wanting you. The devil on my shoulder wants me to do depraved things with you, but the angel keeps telling me that you're better than me. That Colton won't talk to me again if I let this go any further. That I don't deserve to kiss you until I rectify how the public sees me."

Her tongue swiped across her lips quickly, his eyes following the motion. "Let the devil win. Imagine how much more fun

it'll be." Her reedy voice was foreign to her ears. She sounded like a fucking seductress, and she loved it.

Anything to make him see she wasn't just Colton's little
sister.

He seemed to like it too, his hand gripping her hair
tighter, tilting her head back slightly to lick up her neck and
suck her earlobe into his mouth, warm breath in her ear.

"Maybe so." He seemed to recover slightly, placing both
of his hands on her waist to steady her on the stair above
him. His hands stayed there, fingers caressing her.

Maya remembered what he'd said about *deserving* her,
her brain finally catching up. She grabbed hold of his dress
shirt with both fists and frowned at him. "Please hear me
when I say that I don't give a fuck how the public sees you,
and I wish you would stop caring too. I don't care what they
call you or what they'll say about me or us. I care about you,
how you feel, and how you make *me* feel. There is nobody
more deserving of me than you, Coop. I thought I'd made
that clear."

His eyes flicked back and forth between hers. "How do I
make you feel?"

"Like I'm on fire. Like I can't breathe. Every time you
pull away, it only gets worse, like my body *knows* how good
it would be to kiss you and never stop." Quieter, she continued, "Like I'm safe and worthy."

Cooper's hands left her, flitting through his hair once more.
Maya placed her hands in his and squeezed, looking into his

eyes meaningfully, hoping he could read how true her words were.

"Mai, you can't say things like that to me..." Cooper groaned, looking away.

"I mean it. Every word."

Finally, he sighed, his hands finding her waist again. "If I'm going to be with you, I'm going to be *with* you. I don't want casual with you, sunflower. I want to take my time enjoying everything. Your smiles, your laughs, your moans." His voice dropped. "Your screams of pleasure. I want to show you how wanted you are. Will you let me do that, sweetheart?"

Maya nodded, struck dumb by his confession. Words failed her entirely as she watched his kiss-stained lips curl into the sexiest of smirks, like he knew how badly he tied up her insides.

"Yes," she managed.

"You got a crush on me or somethin'?"

She'd missed his teasing while he'd been gone for the draft. She never wanted him to leave again so she could have it forever.

She was so far past crushing on Cooper Hayes. Nothing could've prepared Maya for the feelings she was having for him, that had been tossing and turning inside her for weeks, maybe months.

This was no crush. This was far more, and she couldn't believe it could be hers.

"Or something," she whispered, and his smile widened.

"Good. Now let's get into comfy clothes and fall asleep on top of each other."

Cooper helped her unzip her dress, stepping back and looking away as it fell. Maya faced him, letting the dress drop down slowly and pool around her feet on the floor, nothing but panties covering her body. The bodice of the gown had been so tight, she hadn't needed a bra. When they'd been quiet for a few moments, Cooper's eyes flicked back, and his expression turned pained.

"*Maya*," he groaned, though his eyes stayed on her, drinking her in. He took a step forward, hand reaching out, then he backed up again, shaking his head. "I'll shower in the guest bathroom."

Her heart broke for him as she wondered if he was holding back, keeping the physical part out of it, to protect himself. To not have the same thing that had happened in college happen to him again.

A little over half an hour later, they'd both taken separate showers—much to Maya's dismay—and changed into sweatpants, settling into her bed shoulder to shoulder, staring up at the glow-in-the-dark stars on her ceiling, and intertwining and disentangling their fingers over and over, like a promise.

Maya whispered into the dark, "How do we handle this? Publicly, I mean. And with Colt." She couldn't imagine her brother would react well to this.

Cooper blew out a sigh. "I don't think I'm ready for people to know until something changes with the media. I was trying to stay away from you until then too, but it's been torture." He squeezed her hand. "I know you hate when I talk about my reputation, but I can't let you be associated with where I'm at right now. Just give me a little time to keep working through it so I can prove to the world that I'm good enough for you. Colton may never see it, but I have to keep trying."

Maya turned her head to look at him, taking in the structure of his profile. Strong, defined cheekbones and jawline, almost-straight nose, his clean-shaven face starting to regrow its usual stubble. A pang of hurt hit her square in the chest, like her body believed he didn't want people to know about her. But she knew that wasn't true and even understood where he was coming from, though she didn't agree.

Plus, she already felt more cared for than she had with Ryan. Cooper wanted her so badly and yet was holding off so he could improve himself to be better for her.

Even if she didn't think he needed any improvements at all. "Okay."

He almost looked shocked. "Okay?"

Maya nodded once. "But not because I don't want to be associated with your reputation. I've made it clear I don't care about that, but I understand what you're saying. And I really don't want the start of the charity impacted by this either. I don't want speculation. I just want these kids to get the lessons they deserve. Plus, Colt might go ballistic, and we don't need that right now."

The last thing she wanted was for On the Line to seem less legitimate because of their relationship. It'd already been insinuated at the press conference, and she didn't need it "confirmed."

Cooper nodded, his thumb rubbing circles over the top of her hand. "Agreed."

Maya wanted them to have a fighting chance. There were infinite variables that could change the course of whatever this could be. Her brother. The press. The charity. Her fear of accepting things from Cooper, especially the money she'd been trying to make up through tennis lessons. His fear that he was undeserving of her love. The fact that it was already early May, and soon he would be too busy to come see her. All of it and more had the power to knock them down before they'd found their footing.

"So, we keep it private, then. We fly back and forth as we're able under the guise of working on the charity and see what happens." Maya stated the words, though they were more like a question. She wanted to make sure they were on the same page.

Cooper frowned. "I don't like 'see what happens.' I want you, no matter how many damn flights I have to take to get to you."

Maya's lips ghosted over his sculpted shoulder. "I think I can be okay with that," she teased.

She could handle having him quietly. Reporters and people in his comments could say what they liked; Maya didn't care. At the end of the day, at least for now, she knew she was his and he was hers.

Chapter Twenty-One

Cooper

The amount of speculation surrounding Cooper and Maya's relationship was reaching epic proportions, which is exactly what Maya hadn't wanted. Rather than reporting on the opening gala as an evening of hope and a chance to do good, all the media had seemed to care about the past week was determining whether they were together, and if they weren't, why Cooper hadn't been seen with anyone else in months.

Originally, he'd agreed to three or four post-gala press inquiries to get people talking about On the Line, but this only seemed to have emboldened media outlets and paparazzi to approach him with questions everywhere he went. Questions that never seemed to center on the charity or its important message.

As if he wasn't getting enough of this from his parents, who seemed to put on blinders when it came to anything good he did in his daily life.

Cooper ran a frustrated hand through his hair as he sat beside Colton at team dinner, feeling the dreaded tie he'd put on for the stakeholders constricting him in the worst way. Cooper's phone was open to another photo of him entering the Los Angeles Beaumont house, one of many that had been posted over the last week and plastered everywhere, and he hated it for himself, but even more for Maya. It worried him that now anyone could find out where Maya lived with just a little bit of digging.

"Why are they saying all of those things about you and Maya?" Colton asked, nodding his head toward Cooper's phone.

A flash of guilt had Cooper turning his phone off and flipping it over, going for an air of nonchalance as he shrugged and said, "You know how they are. They love to sniff out things that aren't there."

Colton nodded his head thoughtfully. "True."

Cooper sighed, hating how easily the lie had slipped out. Being dishonest with Colton, especially about this, felt wrong, but he needed to fix this media shitstorm first. And Maya and he had agreed to keep things private for now.

Dinner ended a little later than Cooper had planned, and all he wanted to do was make it back to his house so he could call

Maya. He said a quick goodbye to his teammates and beelined toward the car he'd called, not interested in making small talk.

A small group of paparazzi followed after him, and he attempted a smile he hoped wasn't too fake. He thought he caught another "flavor of the week" question but kept walking.

Sure, it was frustrating that no one seemed interested in seeing another side to him, but even more frustrating was that a charity whose mission he was quickly growing to believe in couldn't get even a percentage of the attention it deserved.

Maya had been right when she'd said going public would be bad for On the Line. Clearly, the only thing that mattered to people was his relationship status, and he imagined if they got wind of them together, it would derail their mission entirely.

"Or maybe you've been too busy with your charity's co-founder to seek anybody else out?"

Cooper's hand stilled on the knot of his tie, the hand at his side itching to clench into a fist. He'd just made it out of the narrow downtown side streets of Charleston and could see his car only a few feet away. But despite his media training, despite knowing better than to engage with them, something, maybe honor, forced him to turn around slowly and glare at the spindly man whose expression was far too smug.

"What are you talking about?" Cooper ground out.

The man had the audacity to smile wider, like he'd caught Cooper, and the expression pushed at a memory.

This man was familiar for some reason.

"Don't you think it's odd that you've only been seen with *her* since all of this started?"

The longer Cooper looked at the guy, the more familiar he became, until Cooper finally realized…"Aren't you based out of LA?"

This was the man who'd spent the entire press conference outside of Serve It Up talking to Maya like she'd slept her way up to her position rather than earned it. The very same man whose superior Cooper had spoken with to make sure it didn't happen again.

Something in the reporter's face changed, hardened. "I'm on leave from my paper in Los Angeles. They thought it best I take some *time off*."

Cooper hadn't meant to get him fired, if that was what he was implying, but he couldn't say he was sorry if he had. Every word out of this guy's mouth was ridiculous.

Cooper turned back around and kept walking until he was at the car, sliding in and texting Maya that he would call her when he was home.

The whole interaction with the press had him falling back into his old ways of thinking. The day after the gala, they'd stayed in the house together, talking, cuddling, and kissing the day away. He'd told her about his fears, and she'd told him about hers, and they'd worked through them.

But now they were back, eating at him. She claimed his reputation didn't matter, but clearly he was still just the ladies' man of Charleston. How would she do with that hanging over them when they finally went public? He was worried she'd hear about it enough times that it would finally sink in and then she'd be hightailing it right out of their relationship.

Even if she honestly wouldn't care about that, Gabi's words kept replaying in his head. He'd been able to keep their sharp points from piercing through for years, but now that he was ready to try for Maya, they played on repeat in his head. What if he *wasn't* relationship material?

What if he tried and tried and tried to be what Maya needed and it wasn't enough for her? Would he be able to handle losing her after putting in the work and pushing aside these feelings?

He groaned, running a hand down his face. It was all moot because he was already in a state of falling, and no matter the outcome, he knew having her in any capacity, for however long she gave him, had to be enough for him.

Then there was the part of him that wondered, especially since he *still* hadn't heard about his contract, whether he should look into one of the Los Angeles teams. Cooper hadn't asked George about the contract in the last few weeks since there had been so much going on with the draft and the charity, and because George had been getting ever more aggressive about Cooper's personal life.

Could he leave all his friends behind? Start new with a different team when retirement was somewhat on the horizon?

Cooper slumped in his seat. The driver, Alonso, smiled at him kindly in the rearview mirror, and Cooper did his best to reciprocate.

Cooper didn't know how long he cycled through the same thoughts, each time trying to shove them down further and further and slam the door in the face of them, but it didn't seem to hold, no matter how he tried to quiet his mind. It was pointless.

When he finally arrived at his house, Cooper took off his shoes and ripped at the suffocating tie around his neck, tossing it to the ground. He pulled his phone out of his pocket as he threw himself onto his couch and video called the one person he knew would make his day better.

She picked up on the fifth ring, just when he thought she was busy. It took a second, but when Maya's face appeared on his screen, he could tell she'd been crying. Concern speared through him immediately, taking in her surroundings to assess what could be wrong.

"What happened?"

Maya opened her mouth to talk, but a sob came out instead, and she bit down on a knuckle as she set her phone down on the desk in her bedroom. She appeared okay physically at least, and while that was a relief, his insides were churning with worry.

"Sweetheart, please tell me what's wrong."

Through another sob, Maya managed to say, "I thought I was better."

He frowned. "Better? What does that mean?"

"That I was done feeling all of these"—she waved her hand around herself—"things. Feeling sad about missing tennis. Feeling lost. I thought all my work on the charity had fixed it all. Made those feelings go away." Her body shook, and she turned away, like she didn't want him to see her like this.

Maya continued, voice shaky, "I've felt so good the past few weeks, almost like everything was better. But today, I don't know what it is, I just can't seem to stop thinking about it. About the thrill of competing, sliding back and forth on the court and feeling a ball hit my strings so perfectly. I can't get it out of my head, and I'd give anything to have it back."

"May—"

"I know that's not how it works. It certainly wasn't what happened after my mom. I was up and down and all around the five stages of grief. I don't know why they act like it happens in that order, it's a fucking rollercoaster." She'd stopped crying, her last sentence angry before her shoulders slumped in defeat. "I just thought this would be different. I thought I was better," she repeated.

"There's nothing wrong with grieving, sweetheart. Like you said, grief isn't linear. You're going to have good days and bad days, and some of those bad days are going to come when you finally think the sun is shining and everything is bright and new again." He didn't know where the words had come from, because he certainly hadn't experienced loss or grief like hers, but he spoke like he was put on the earth to comfort her.

"You're gonna wake up after a night of feeling on top of the world, and it's gonna feel like the world is closing in on you, like you can't get a breath out. And that's okay. It's okay to feel that way. Nobody's gonna tell you it isn't. I know it's hard, but you're so strong. The strongest person I've ever met. And if anybody can get through this, it's you."

She blinked at him a couple of times before she let out a watery chuckle. "Damn, Hayes, you're good."

Cooper breathed out a sigh, thankful to get her close enough to a smile after her tears. Not being with her as she cried was one of the worst feelings imaginable. It was like a betrayal to watch her hurt and not be able to pull her into his arms and whisper into her hair. Everything about being in a long-distance relationship pissed him off.

Like she could read his mind, she whispered, "I wish you were here. I miss you."

Cooper clenched his jaw, feeling tears prick the back of his eyes at the vulnerability in her voice. "I miss you so much, sunflower. I haven't been able to get you out of my head since I left you."

She sniffled. "Long distance sucks."

"It does."

"Fall asleep on the phone with me?"

"Wouldn't want it any other way."

But first, he bought a ticket to Los Angeles with a round trip of under twenty-four hours. Offseason practice was getting more intense and his duties in Charleston were starting to pile up again, but it was his turn to brighten her day the way she always did for him.

Chapter Twenty-Two

Maya

The day after her meltdown, Maya tried to get back into her routine, giving three tennis lessons and working through some final charity logistics with Viola. Then, when she checked On the Line's email, she found one from her grandmother, her nani, who Maya hadn't spoken to in over a decade.

Her grandparents had apparently seen one of the press conferences about the charity, and upon realizing she was in Los Angeles, decided to reach out since they now lived nearby.

A part of her, the part that had felt abandoned by them, was angry. The other, bigger part of her recognized that she was as much at fault for not reaching out to them as an adult. Sure, she hadn't known they'd left Michigan, but nowadays, finding their contact information wouldn't have been such a challenge, and she hadn't even tried.

Mainly because she was terrified of knowing whether they'd truly lost touch or had *made* the decision to stay away.

She'd come home to think through their offer for her to go over for lunch, and she was still mulling it over hours later as she lay in the hot tub.

Maya was just starting to relax when she heard the side gate closing. Her eyes flew open.

"Son of a bitch!" she cried as she took in the man striding toward her, her heart racing both because she was startled and because she'd missed his rugged sexiness deeply.

She stared at the face of the man who'd held her together over the phone yesterday, a bouquet of sunflowers in one hand, a big bag of gummy bears in the other, cowboy hat over his dirty-blond hair, and a sheepish grin on his face.

Her cowboy.

"Hi, sweetheart," Cooper drawled in that intoxicating accent of his. "I found the spare key."

"Y-you," she stuttered, still in shock.

"I had to see you. You said you missed me, and that was all the tempting I needed."

Her chest seized, and she jolted up, jumping out of the water and into his outstretched arms before she could think about how she was ruining his clothes. Her legs wrapped around his waist tightly, her arms around his neck and her face buried in it, breathing him in.

She felt him kiss the side of her head before he whispered, "Was today any better?"

Maya peeled herself off him, grimacing at the wet stain left behind. "Oh god, I'm so sorry." When he waved it off, she smiled at him. "Today was a little better. A lot better now. Though I did get some interesting news."

"Oh, yeah? What's that?" The smile that pulled at his lips was heart stopping. She was lucky to still be alive.

"My mom's parents reached out. They said they moved here recently and would love to see me if I'm interested."

Shock was clear on Cooper's face as he reached out to hook their pinkies together. Maya loved that now that he *could* touch her, it was almost like he always *had to* be touching her. She led him into the house.

"Wow. That's...Wow. How are you feeling about that?"

As Maya had thought through the last couple of days and how sad she'd been just yesterday evening, she had wondered if it was some kind of sign. She'd never given much thought to a higher power, but she couldn't shake the feeling that somehow, some way, her mother had known how badly Maya needed her as she'd sobbed through the grief last night.

And maybe this was her mother's way of guiding her to the people who had known her best.

"I've been going back and forth. I don't know what their reasoning is for reaching out, but I figure I should at least talk to them. Hear them out and decide from there, right?"

Cooper placed the bag of gummy bears on the kitchen counter. "I think whatever you feel comfortable doing is what you should do. Have you talked to Colton and Landon?"

Maya nodded. "I texted them. Landon said it's completely up to me whether I go or not. Colton hasn't responded." She paused. "I've just been thinking about it a lot the past few hours and...I think I'm going to do it. Meet them. Probably tomorrow, since they invited me for lunch. I just think the timing of them reaching out feels so right, and with how much this injury has made me miss my mom, I can't not."

Cooper bent down, catching her lips in a gentle kiss. After a second, he pulled back a hair, whispering against them, "I'm so proud of you for figuring that out. And I hope they have a damn good reason for waiting so long." He kissed her nose and stepped back. "Do you want me to come with you? I can change my flight in an instant." He handed the sunflowers to her.

Maya took them, holding them to her chest lovingly. She didn't know why he called her sunflower, but she liked the nickname. "No, no. It's going to be emotional, I'm sure. And something I have to do by myself."

Cooper nodded understandingly, though Maya could still see concern in his eyes.

"I can't believe you flew all the way here just because I said I missed you," Maya whispered in awe. She pulled out a painted vase from one of the cabinets, filling it with water, adding the flowers, and then setting it onto the counter above the sink.

How anyone could have ever told him he wasn't relationship material was beyond her. This was the sweetest thing he could've done for her. The sweetest thing *anyone* had ever done for her.

"I told you I'll do anything I can to make sure I'm here if you need me. I meant that."

Maya took in the crinkle around his eyes, the way his hat was a little lopsided after she'd jumped into his arms, the lips she'd imagined on her body countless times. He'd shaved for her, and like he knew what these tight shirts did to her, he'd worn a white one, every part of it hugging his sculpted upper body.

She jumped onto the counter beside the sink, pulling him closer by his shirt. When he was inches from her, she whispered, "Well, thank you for making my day."

Maya marveled at how pretty he was as he closed his eyes. She followed suit, her hands tossing off his cowboy hat and slipping into his hair as she kissed him. They'd only been apart for a week, but it had been a week of having to stay inside to steer clear of the media and trying not to worry that people cared more about whether they were dating than how impactful On the Line could be.

She needed him.

The kiss, at first slow, turned hard and fast, and Maya slid herself across the counter until her legs were wrapped around his waist. She grinded herself against him, desperately seeking friction until she was hardly able to keep up with his deft kisses and bites of her lip. Her nails dug into his scalp, and he groaned like she was driving him crazy, his hands tightening around her waist.

Maya wanted him to let go for *once*. She didn't care about anything but him and her. She wanted to finally have what she'd been imagining every night while her vibrator had brought her to an orgasm she knew would be lackluster in comparison to the real thing.

His hand came up to cup her face, and as one of hers slipped down his chest to his muscled stomach, he pulled away, panting.

She frowned, reading the hesitation in his eyes. "You know you don't have to prove anything to anyone, right? I know you're right for me. Isn't that enough?"

Cooper grimaced, pulling her off the counter and setting her on her feet. "Sweetheart, let's see what happens once On the Line is up and running. I just want to prove to everyone, especially Colton, that he shouldn't be worried when it comes to me and you."

He cupped her cheeks, placing a soft kiss to her lips before stepping back a few feet, rubbing against where his jeans were tented, like he was in pain. "I want you to know that not touching you, tasting you, not having you in that way is killing me. Just because I'm not laying you out and fucking you until you scream doesn't mean that's not true. But this is my first time trying this in years, and I want to make sure I do it right."

Maya sighed but she knew, once again, that this was about his past. He'd spent so much of his life feeling used, and she didn't want to be like the rest of the people he'd been with. She nodded.

A car alarm went off outside, startling them. Maya huffed a laugh, then asked, "How did you get in holding all this without being seen?" She gestured at the bag of candy and flowers, knowing there were at least a few people with cameras waiting outside the house.

"I got dropped off a block away and snuck up to the side gate. I think they were waiting for a car to come right up to the house. They're parked outside your neighbor's house, on the other side from where I was dropped off."

"Smart."

Cooper shrugged, like he didn't believe the word should be applied to him. "What were your plans for the night? What do you want to do?"

She took a couple of breaths, still letting her body catch up to what was happening. Or rather what was *not* happening. "I was planning on trimming my hair and then doing a face mask, but we don't have to do that."

"You know, I used to cut my sisters' hair when they were younger. I learned from a video and got really good, if I do say so myself."

Maya snorted, shooting him an incredulous look. She wasn't sure she'd trust him near her hair.

"What? You don't think I can do it?"

"I'm honestly not sure."

"Let me prove myself to you. I gotta make myself indispensable. Let me be your hairstylist."

Maya looked at the confidence on his face, and even though she was sure she would regret it, she led him up to her bathroom and handed him the scissors. She brushed through it until it was completely untangled, and then she nodded for him to start.

It was just hair after all. How badly could he mess it up?

Only, the faces he kept making, a cross between concern and confusion, did *not* make her feel better. And, as it turned out, he *could* mess it up quite badly. When she turned to look at the back of her hair in the mirror, she saw him grimace. Maya slapped a hand over her mouth in horror, her eyes widening.

Her normally long, straight hair looked like a child had taken scissors to it, some pieces much shorter than others.

"Oh my god, Cooper. Oh my god, it's horrible. It's so bad." She burst out laughing, slapping the sink with her other hand.

"I thought I was following the video so well! Look." He pulled up a part of the video, showing her what he'd tried to do. "Look, I did this exactly! I don't know why it didn't work."

"Cooper, you understand I can't go out in public like this, right?"

He sighed dejectedly. "Yeah."

"Okay, I'm gonna try it myself and see if this is fixable."

Cooper scratched the back of his neck. "So, that's a no on me being indispensable in the hair arena?"

Maya patted his cheek, still trying to hold in a fit of horror-induced giggles as she took in her new look.

"My sweet summer child, you are never going near my hair with anything sharp ever again."

He set his hands on her waist, pulling her flush to him. "All I've ever wanted to be is Edward Scissorhands. You're crushing all my dreams."

Maya pecked his lips once, twice, thrice. "What are some of your other dreams? Maybe I can make those come true."

Cooper's thumb ran over her jaw, and his forehead met hers. "I have no doubt about that. You're all I dream about anymore."

The storm in Maya's stomach erupted at his confession.

Again, she couldn't believe he didn't see that he was more than enough for her. She would find a way to show him.

But first, she needed to fix her hair.

Chapter Twenty-Three

Maya

*B*uzzzzz. *Buzzzzz.*

Maya groaned, an eye opening as she realized her phone was vibrating on her nightstand. Cooper, who was already awake and scrolling through what looked like news sites, chuckled and smiled at her as he passed her the phone.

"Ah, shit," she mumbled. "It's Colt."

Cooper was already shifting. "Want me to go downstairs?"

Maya shook her head. "No, no. Maybe just don't talk?"

Cooper huffed a laugh, and Maya answered. "Hey, Colt."

"Hey, Mai. I know you're a busy bee with the charity, but we haven't talked since the fundraiser, so I'm just checking in."

"Hi. Did you see my text about Nani and Nana?"

"Yeah, was also checking in about that. You sure you're okay to go by yourself?"

"Oh, yeah. I'll be fine. I'm excited to talk to them, especially about Mom. I think it'll be good for me." She paused. "For us."

Colton was quiet, and Maya couldn't be sure what he was thinking. "Yeah."

"How was Italy?" she asked, changing the subject. Cooper stretched, and a long, muscular arm settled over her stomach.

"Beautiful. Lucia had a great time, which is all I cared about."

"Aw. Did you guys take lots of pictures? I'd love to see them all." She'd only seen the couple that Lucia had posted to her socials.

"I'll send you some, but Lucia can show you the rest when you're here next. Speaking of which, are you coming to Charleston to celebrate the Buck Isaac Award? I think I texted about it a couple of weeks ago."

Maya remembered having to look up the award being presented to her brother for his leadership, then had immediately used points to buy her tickets. "I'll be there. The charity will be up and running by then, so I won't be able to stay as long as usual." When she looked over at Cooper, he was frowning, but Maya couldn't tell if it was at her words or his phone. She squeezed his arm.

"I get it. I'm glad it's coming together for you so quickly, and we're just glad to see you."

"Thank you! I'm excited too."

After a pause, "Alright, well, call before then if you can. And stop stealing my best friend."

Maya laughed uncomfortably, and Cooper shifted like he'd heard. She knew Colton was joking, but it was a little too close to the truth.

Colton continued. "I miss you. Love you to the moon."

"Love you to the moon," she echoed softly, and it was Cooper's turn to squeeze her.

When Maya set her phone down, he pulled her into his body, her head resting against his chest. "Okay?" he whispered into her hair.

"Okay."

"Want to go back to sleep until I have to go to the airport?" She was dropping him off at eleven, right before she met up with her grandparents.

"A man after my own heart. Yes, please."

✦

Maya stared at her grandparents' two-story stucco house from her car, mind clouded with all the questions she had for them. She wanted to know anything and everything that could teach her about her mom—her culture, her home life, the people she'd loved outside of Maya's siblings.

But she was nervous. What did she say if they asked why she hadn't reached out? Maybe this was a bad idea. Her stomach turned over and over, and not in the way it did when she was with Cooper.

No. She'd thought this through, and this was what she wanted. She'd started making a network of friends in Los Angeles—okay, mostly just Viola—and she wanted to have more people she could talk with. Her breakdown over the phone with Cooper a couple of days ago had come from being alone in the house too much, she was sure of that. She needed a bigger network if she was going to be putting down roots here. And the charity was one very large root.

Deep breath in. Deep breath out.

When her head was clear, she stepped out of the car and made her way to the door. A few seconds after knocking, the door opened wide, revealing a smiling woman dressed in an Indian-style shirt.

Maya smiled back. She hadn't seen her nani in a very long time, but it was astounding how her grandmother looked practically the same.

"Hi," Maya breathed out.

She was gathered in a hug quickly, squeezed so tightly, it was almost uncomfortable. When her nani pulled away, she placed a gentle hand on Maya's face.

"You always looked a bit like your mom, but now I see even more of her in you."

Maya's eyes watered at that. She'd always thought she was a mix of her parents, not looking much like either of them. And as she got older, she cursed the bits of her father that she saw in herself. But to know that she still carried her mother's features put the most bittersweet of feelings into her chest.

Behind her nani was her grandfather, Nana, who also looked nearly identical to her memory of him.

"Come, come. Come inside." Nani ushered her through the foyer of the house, past the living room, and into the dining room. Small casserole dishes sat on top of towels, their glass lids made opaque from the steam of the food. The house smelled like spices and incense, and just like when Maya was little, there were statues and banners of Hindu gods everywhere she looked.

When Maya sat down, her grandmother set a plate in front of her and began spooning rice and vegetables from two of the dishes, as well as a yellow liquid which she put over the rice.

Maya wasn't very hungry, her nerves suppressing her appetite, but she had a vivid memory of getting in trouble for refusing her nani's food when she'd been younger, so she thanked them both and began taking bites of everything.

It was *incredible*. She'd had some Indian food growing up and had even had it at restaurants and when she'd played in the Mumbai Open the year before, but she was used to the creamy curries over rice. This was completely different but just as delicious.

It felt like being home, even though her mother never made Indian food for them.

"Thank you so much. It's all amazing."

They made small talk for a few minutes as she tried to eat as much as she could without exacerbating that lingering nervous-pukey feeling.

Her grandparents asked about her brothers, and she told them, including about Colton and Lucia. Maya asked how they had been and why they'd decided to move to LA, learning they'd wanted to live in a warmer climate, and that her cousins were nearby.

A thought that excited her greatly.

When she'd finished what she could of the food, they moved to the living room, her on the couch, them in the leather rocking chairs in front of her, smiles on their faces. She couldn't help but feel a little awkward in their home, years of distance between them.

What did one say to long-lost grandparents besides small talk?

Luckily, they seemed to know what was warring inside her.

"Nana has recorded all your matches. We watched as much as we could when we learned you started playing outside of college. And the boys—Nana always makes sure to have their games on when they're playing." Nani's smile hadn't dropped since Maya had entered the home, and Maya began feeling more at ease.

"Thank you. I'm so glad you guys got to watch me play before I—" She faltered. Shaking her head, she backtracked. "Well, I'm thankful you watched me." And she was thankful they hadn't asked about her injury.

"Of course we did! We're so proud of you three." Nani's voice broke on the word *proud*, and Nana reached his hand out to place it on hers.

"How many people can say their grandson has two championship wins, eh?" Nana asked, clasping his wife's hand.

Maya chuckled. "Right."

She looked around the room while she waited for them to speak, noticing the beautiful and intricate tapestries hung on the walls.

When they didn't reply, Maya turned back and said, "I really am sorry I didn't reach out sooner. We didn't have your number, but I'm sure I could have found it if I tried a little harder. With college and then the tour, I just never..." She trailed off, embarrassed.

It was quiet, and she was convinced she'd said something wrong when they exchanged a glance.

Finally, Nani murmured, "Troy told us you three didn't want to see or speak to us after Kavya passed. He told us we reminded you too much of your mother. We weren't sure if we believed him, but we wanted to respect your wishes just in case it was true."

Maya sat up straighter at the words. Her father had been causing problems for the three of them for a long time, but she'd had no idea that he had gone to such lengths to keep the boys focused on football.

That had to be his reasoning for this.

And what was his excuse for keeping *her* away from them? He'd never cared about what she did before. Any rage she'd felt toward them was sapped, funneled right back into her growing hatred for her father.

Once, not so long ago, she'd really tried hard to get him to see her. Until Colton had finally set boundaries with the man, she'd tried to get dinner with him any time she was in town. She'd called him at least once a week, even after he'd refused to pick up or stay on the phone with her for more than five minutes at a time. She'd stayed with him and tried to be the perfect houseguest, hosting her brothers for family meals.

But now, all she would see when she thought of him was her grandparents believing their grandchildren didn't want to talk to them. And she *hated* him.

Her mouth opened and closed. Then it opened again. "I—He lied. I never said that, and Colton and Landon never would have said that either."

Nani smiled sadly, as if she'd already figured that out. "We tried to contact Colton, but we never heard back, so we thought your father had spoken honestly. We're glad to have you now, though."

Colton hadn't responded? She'd have to ask him about that. "But *why* would Dad have said that? It seems like something he would do to make sure Colton and Landon focused on football. But why me? I...I needed someone then."

Her grandparents exchanged another glance.

Nana spoke quietly. "Your father is...well, he always tried to keep you away from us. We wondered if he didn't want his children, the boys especially, to be too interested in the culture. Like he was hoping to keep you...Like he wanted American children and he worried what might happen if you looked to your roots."

Nani nodded. "He told Kavya she couldn't give you Indian names. She wanted to give each of you an Indian middle name then, but he said no to that too." Her smile had disappeared during the conversation, but it was back as she whispered conspiratorially, "Your father doesn't know Maya is also an Indian name."

Maya's head reared back. "It is? What does it mean? Mom...she never told me that."

"In Sanskrit, it means illusion or magic. Kavya liked it because it's another name for one of our goddesses—Lakshmi."

Lakshmi. Maya often regretted not knowing more about her mom's culture. She'd gone to temple with her mother once when she had been much younger, but that was the extent of her experience.

She smiled at her grandmother, who was pulling a thick book from a cabinet below the television. "I'd love to learn more about the gods. And the food. Everything. I wish I'd learned earlier, but..."

"Kavya wanted to teach all of you. But you were always the one she was sure would want to learn."

Maya closed her eyes for a moment, vowing to herself to do better for her mother. Learn more about her roots.

Nani sat beside her, setting the thick book onto Maya's lap. When Maya opened it tentatively, she realized it was a photo album with pictures of her mother, grandparents, and others. She flipped through the photos wordlessly, tears in her eyes.

She saw a picture of her mom, dressed in a Crestview swimming T-shirt with a swim cap on her head, a huge grin on her face as she lay across the ground in front of her family. Maya let out a watery laugh and looked between her grandparents. "You guys seem so close here."

Nani leaned over and looked before nodding. "We were still living in Michigan then. That was the last time we were all together like that," she said, and Maya could read between the lines to figure out what she *wasn't* saying. Her mother probably met her father soon after, and then they'd barely gotten to see her or their grandchildren.

Trying not to think about all her mother had sacrificed, she responded, "She must have been a great swimmer. I had friends on the swim team at Crestview, and they were nationally ranked."

Nana nodded, still in his chair across from her. "She was like a fish from the moment she was born, that one. Learned how to swim faster than her brother and sister. They didn't want to race with her anymore after a while. Tall, too. Just like you."

Maya remembered her mother giving up on Maya learning how to swim. She had been the opposite of a fish, struggling in every facet, every stroke, to the point that her mother had decided to find a new sport for her. "Mom knew I wouldn't be any good at swimming pretty early. We took Mommy and Me tennis lessons, and when she saw how quickly I progressed, she kept taking lessons so I would always have a hitting partner."

Maya's eyes hadn't stopped watering since the photo album had come out, and now she felt a tear slide down her cheek.

"I miss her." She knew they would understand. Her brothers had had their mother for longer, and of course they missed her, but her mother had been Maya's *best friend*. She was sure no one *except* her grandparents could understand that pain.

Nani laid an arm on her shoulder, pulling her body closer and rubbing her arm soothingly. "Us too, bacha. Us too."

Maya continued flipping through the pages of the album, wiping her tears with her shirt so she didn't damage any of the photos. By the end, her mother was no longer in the pictures on family vacations, even as her siblings had little children in their arms.

She started to ask about them, her cousins, right when the doorbell went off. Nani removed her arm from Maya's shoulders, walking the few feet to the front door.

Maya looked up as Nani and a beautiful Indian woman about Maya's age walked in. She wore a blazer buttoned in the front, long black pants, and heels. The woman looked vaguely familiar, but Maya couldn't place her.

"Maya, this is your cousin, Devika. She's your mom's sister's daughter. You met...Prana, when would they have met?"

Without waiting for Nana to answer, Nani said, "You met when you were much younger."

"Maya! Nani and Nana told me you'd be here, so I thought I'd stop by during lunch." Devika walked toward the couch with her arms outstretched, and Maya set the album down, standing and walking into her cousin's embrace. She didn't remember anything about the last time she'd seen her, but it felt like hugging a friend.

"It's nice to see you again, Devika," Maya declared as they pulled apart.

"Call me Devi." She turned to their grandparents. "Did you already eat?"

Nani spoke in another language, and Devi ran into the dining room. Maya and her grandparents sat down and continued talking as Nana put family home videos on, and Devi joined them with a plate of food shortly after.

"Maya wants to learn about Hinduism. You should take her to temple and to that restaurant down the street," Nani said to Devi.

"Yes!" Devi exclaimed. "There are tons of events in LA all the time. And there are some restaurants I've been wanting to try in the area."

"I'd like that." Maya smiled. This would be good for her. She'd been wanting to learn more about her mother, more about herself, and this was the perfect way to do it.

Maya spent another couple of hours with her grandparents and cousin, watching home videos of her cousins and talking about her mother. After she finally said her goodbyes, a box of food in her hand, she checked her phone.

She had a message from Devi, who she added to her contacts. Cooper had also texted her that he was back home and ready to call for the evening whenever she was. They'd taken to going about their evening routines together on the phone, her reading a book and him playing video games, or sometimes syncing up a movie they wanted to watch together.

Maya missed him already, especially after meeting her family. She wished he could hold her while she told him everything she'd learned, but she was also thankful to have a life apart from him. It felt healthy and safe, and she was glad to be relying on herself again and finding people to spend her time with so she didn't spend her whole life wishing she were with him.

She hopped into her car, knowing that feeling would only last so long, and that someday, if they wanted to stay together, they'd have to find a way to shed the distance.

A problem for later, she supposed.

Chapter Twenty-Four

Cooper

Devin's house was packed by the time Cooper arrived at the party later that week, and he saw Lucia, Jenna, and some of the other partners of players dancing in the living room, where Devin had pushed all his furniture against the wall. Cooper knew he should look for Colton, but since he and Maya had agreed they wanted to be together in some capacity, Cooper hadn't been hanging out as much.

He'd turned down going on a double date with one of Lucia's physio friends. Less than a week ago, he'd taken a flight to see Maya when most of his teammates had gone to dinner together. He'd been too tired the evening he'd come back to meet his friends at Frankie's. He hadn't been joining Colton for their usual optional lifts—though those were getting less and less optional as June camp grew closer.

It hadn't necessarily been purposeful most of the time, but Cooper *hated* keeping secrets from his closest friend, and the longer they continued, the worse it would be when Colton inevitably found out.

A part of Cooper wanted to let everyone know how much Maya meant to him, but he stood by his reasoning for waiting. If nothing changed for Cooper after the first couple of weeks following On the Line's launch day, he'd talk to Maya about biting the bullet and telling her brother.

Cooper was sure Colton was suspicious, and it was only a matter of time before his friend found out and confronted him. So Cooper grabbed a beer from the massive chest in the kitchen and tried to get his story straight while he looked for him.

He clinked his bottle with TJ and a few of the other offensive Sabertooths players who had grouped together right outside of the kitchen, talking and laughing over the loud music, before walking past them.

A year ago, Cooper would have been with them or dancing with a bunch of girls or using one of Devin's many guest rooms, which Devin had so elegantly dubbed his "teammate sex rooms." The thought made Cooper feel sick, and all he wanted was to be in Los Angeles with Maya in his arms. Or even better, to be with her in front of his friends here in Charleston without worry that Colton would be hurt or that the media would have a field day.

When Cooper finally found Colton, his friend was already approaching him. Cooper took a breath and gave Colton what he hoped was an easy smile.

"Hey, Colt."

"Coop." Colton nodded, pulling him into a quick hug. "Everything okay?"

Cooper nodded into his beer. "Of course. Why wouldn't it be?"

Colton shrugged. "You've been gone a lot recently, it feels like. I know you've been in LA helping Maya some, but it seems like more than that."

Trying to think quickly, he responded, "Ah, it's just family stuff." At least that wasn't a complete lie.

His parents, in an effort to prove themselves right about how he was throwing away his life, had resorted to communicating with him via articles about his exploits. None of them were accurate, but his parents didn't seem to care.

One of these days, Cooper was going to pick up the phone and tell his parents exactly how he felt. He just wasn't sure he had the courage to deal with the guilting that would inevitably occur after.

Cooper owed a lot to his parents. His father had grown up poor but had worked his way up the ranks of a construction company until he'd owned it. At that point, he'd built half of the city of Oakridge Springs, and once their family was financially stable enough, he'd bought Hayes Ranch. While his father had always dreamed of having a ranch, he was also motivated by making sure his children didn't live the same life of poverty he had. And through it all, his mother had been a beacon of positivity, even in the early days when Dylan and Cooper had been young.

Cooper wanted a relationship with them, and his siblings too. He just wasn't sure how to keep them without moving back home and giving in to their wants and wishes.

"Oh." Colton nodded. "You want to talk about it?"

Cooper didn't talk much with anyone about his family. Even Maya only knew some of the story, though he planned to tell her eventually, when it came up a little more organically. But talking to Colton about it, especially before now, when it hadn't been quite so bad, had never seemed necessary.

He wondered why.

"My dad wants me to come back to run for mayor. He thinks I've wasted my time playing football and that I'm only ruining my political chances by continually 'making my exploits available to the media,'" he said, the last portion with finger quotations.

"Damn. That's harsh." Colton took a sip of his drink, looking toward Lucia. "What about your contract? Will they back off if it gets extended? I will personally have words with whoever I need to to make sure you stay here."

Cooper sighed. "George just keeps saying they're working on it. He's been annoying the shit out of me recently so I haven't talked to him much, but I need to call him." He'd been holding off now that he and Maya were together. Cooper hadn't yet decided whether to look into a move to LA. A part of him wanted to, but knowing Maya, he wasn't sure it was something *she* would want.

But even if his contract did get extended, his parents might back off until they sniffed out his interest in retiring, and then he'd be back here again, with the expectation that he'd come home.

Which is why he needed to sit down and talk to them. Eventually.

Colton hummed. "And when you say exploits, you mean…"

"With women, yeah. I think they see the headlines and believe I'm just fucking around. They don't care about the charity or outreach or any of it because what's in the news? What's bad for politics? My *exploits*."

"But you've been dialing it down recently, right? I mean, at least when I've seen you, it hasn't been as obvious what you're getting up to as it used to."

Cooper looked at his friend, confused. Colton continued, "I just mean, at these parties, you used to have girls draped all over you. All the time. We'd talk for a little while and then I wouldn't see you again. It's been different recently."

Cooper nodded, glad that at least his friend had noticed the change. That made him feel a lot more confident in telling Colton about him and Maya. Eventually. "Yeah, I'm trying to make a change. Don't want to be like that into my thirties. Figured it was time to do something different."

"Well, you know I support you either way, but I'm happy for you. You thinking about dating someone?"

He watched Colton's reaction carefully as he responded, "Maybe."

He wasn't surprised to see the flicker of shock, but it still hurt. Cooper wished he'd talked to Colton about this sooner. Even his own best friend didn't see him as a one-woman man.

"Wow. Someone specific?"

"No," Cooper lied, shaking his head.

"Alright then." Colton held out his drink for Cooper to cheers. "To a new Cooper. Maybe you could start by coming out with me, Lucia, and Lucia's friends."

Cooper chuckled. "Fair enough."

Colton looked around the party before turning to Cooper.

"And Maya? You've been seeing her more than I have—does she seem okay?"

Cooper thought about Maya preparing for tomorrow's big launch, her face split with a smile, beaming with pride for the legacy she was about to begin. If he hadn't had practice, he'd have stayed the whole week to help her.

"Oh, uh, she seems okay. Better than three months ago, for sure," Cooper said, looking toward where a group of people were hooting and hollering around Devin. "I only see her here and there though."

A complete lie. Cooper video called Maya every single day without fail, even if just to say good night.

He was the worst friend ever.

Trying to take the heat and attention off himself, he asked, "You think we got a chance at another championship this year?"

Colton shrugged like it hardly mattered, and that change from before, when all he cared about was winning, shocked Cooper just like it always did. "I don't know. I figure you and I try a couple more times before we go out in style. I'll accept three or four rings."

"We better stop Devin from hazing the rookies tonight then."

Lucia walked over, and Colton held an arm out for her to walk into. Cooper's chest ached as he watched them come together so naturally, so publicly.

Colton smiled at the group. "Nah, a little Devin hazing never hurt anybody."

Chapter Twenty-Five

Maya

There was a buzz rumbling through Maya as she looked at the school bus outside of the tennis center, and she wasn't sure if it was from nerves or excitement. Probably both. Launch day had finally come, which meant she was about to meet the first group of twenty children *her* charity was helping.

And while Maya was sad Cooper wouldn't be able to make it, she was ecstatic Delilah and Nicola had been able to come around their tour schedules. Their teams had agreed to let them fly in for the day before they had to go back to Florida to train for Wimbledon.

Maya jogged from the parking lot to right outside the office, where two of her closest friends stood, and without a thought, she threw her arms around them both.

"You're really here," she breathed, closing her eyes and imagining she was back on the tour, just one last time, enveloped in a hug in her tennis gear.

Delilah laughed, trying to wrap her arms around Maya as Nicola cracked a soft smile and patted Maya on the arm.

"Of course we are. We're so proud of you, we *had* to be here. You know Harper and Sahar would be here too if Berlin weren't so very far," Delilah said, squeezing Maya tight.

Maya pulled away and asked, "Ready to meet the kiddos?"

They both nodded.

"Oh, also, my friend who manages this center is absolutely going to ask you to sign a tennis ball for her, sorry. She's done a lot for me though, so hopefully that's okay."

"Are you kidding? I never get to talk to fans. I can't wait!" Delilah responded, already pulling open the door to the center, Maya and Nicola following behind her.

The kids, all elementary school-aged, were running around, their backpacks on the tables that took up the back area of the center. Viola was behind the counter, as she usually was, stacks of tennis rackets in front of her. When she saw them walk in, she smiled wide and waved.

"Oh, come in, come in! We've got the courts set up with baskets for the three of you, and here are rackets for the kids." Viola nodded toward the rackets.

Turning to address the children, she said, "One, two, three, eyes on me," and a hush fell over the center, kids stopping mid-stride. "Great job! You're my best group yet. If I put you in group one when you came in, please follow Ms. Maya to court one!"

Maya waved so they knew to follow her, grabbing the rackets Viola handed her with a matching smile and walking backward to make sure she could memorize the faces of her group. Viola asked group two to follow Nicola to court two, then group three to follow Delilah to court three.

Out on the court, Maya had each of them give her their name a couple of times until she'd memorized those as well.

"Have any of you had tennis lessons before?" They all shook their heads, so she smiled and passed out the rackets, showing each of them how to hold it.

"Okay, let's get a line started right here." She walked over to the center of the court and had them line up ahead of her.

"I'm going to throw a ball to you, and I want you to try to hit it like this." She showed them the motion, her wrist only barely twinging thanks to physical therapy, and then she had them practice, spacing them out a bit more when Jimmy almost smacked Andrea in the head. "Okay, one at a time, show me how you would hit a ball."

They did so, and when she'd helped them fix their grips sufficiently, Maya grabbed the basket and began tossing the balls to them. Most struggled to get their racket on the ball the first few times, but after a couple more rounds of trying, Maya coaching them, picking up the balls, and trying again, they were beginning to get the hang of it.

Jimmy walked up, and his toothy, six-year-old smile made her heart warm. When the frame of his racket thwacked the ball, he giggled, and Maya joined in.

"I hit it that time. Coach Maya, did you see? I hit it that time!" Jimmy's excitement was infectious, and she held her hand out for a low five, his little hand slapping at it.

"Great job, Jimmy! You keep at it and you're going to be a pro in no time." She smiled as she watched him hop to the back of the line.

She continued feeding the balls to the children, and when the basket was empty and the kids were trying out the new move she'd taught them to pick up a ball without bending over, Maya looked to the court beside hers, still a little shocked to see Delilah there giving lessons too. Across the walkway was Nicola, who was smiling more with the children than she did with most adults.

Unexpectedly, Maya felt tears prick her eyes, and she smiled, because for the first time in a while, they weren't tears of grief or frustration. How lucky was she that she got to feel this happy accomplishing a dream she hadn't even known she'd had until a few months ago?

Cooper had been right about good days and bad days. Some days, she woke up and felt like she had to crawl back out of the well of emotion. Other days, she felt on top of the world. A lot of the good days were because of this charity, the work it was already doing, but also what it had the potential to do. Maya had carved out a new path for herself, one she'd never seen in her future, but it was quickly beginning to feel so right for her.

Sure, twenty kids wasn't a lot, but Viola and Maya had already been contacted by five or six coaches from all over the city

who were interested in helping, and Maya knew that someday soon, On the Line was going to help many more.

It was like the sun had come back out and the feelings of
anger and grief had skittered away again. Never gone, but
held at bay for longer and longer, just like the ones that had
been with her since her mom had died.

Once the basket was full again, she continued tossing
balls to the seven kids on her court, correcting their form
the best she could for it being their first day. Viola walked
by, monitoring the lessons with a big smile.

Maya let the kids take a quick water break, laughing at
their squeals of delight as they ran back into the air-conditioned center. Los Angeles in May was no picnic on the
tennis courts, but Maya loved the feel of the sun beating
down on her.

With a tennis racket in her hands, a hard court beneath
her shoes, her hair in a braid, and her best friends on the
court beside and across from her, Maya was finally back.

After arriving at Maya's house and showering, Delilah,
Nicola, and Maya had decided to stay in for the evening.
There was a reporter who looked vaguely familiar standing
outside the house, even though neither her brothers nor
Cooper were with them.

Delilah and Maya lay with their backs on the floor, legs up against the couch, watching the TV upside down, partially finished frozen margaritas beside them. Nicola lay on the couch, a bowl of chips balanced on her chest and a hand on Delilah's leg, placed there after Delilah had drunkenly complained that she needed physical touch immediately.

Maya had missed this dearly, and even though Harper and Sahar weren't here, it felt like old times when they would have a few days here and there to spend together at the Morozov Academy, the girls piling into the tiny apartment Delilah and Maya had shared.

"I missed you so much," Delilah said sleepily, threading her fingers through Maya's. "What's been going on outside of the charity and seeing your family again?"

Maya had debated all night whether to tell them about Cooper.

She wasn't sure what would happen to her and Cooper once they were public. Maya knew he wasn't Ryan, that things were different between them, but she couldn't help but wait for the other shoe to drop and for him to realize he didn't want to be with her.

Maya looked between her friends, knowing without a doubt they would keep it a secret. She hadn't shared it with anyone else in her life, and the urge to talk about it was strong, especially with her closest friends. So she told them about it and why they weren't allowed to tell anyone.

Nicola scoffed playfully. "Worst kept secret of the century, Mai. The one time I hung out with you both, you looked like you wanted to rip each other's clothes off." That would've been at New Years, right before Maya reinjured her wrist.

Delilah giggled.

"It's not *just* that though. Sure, that part is fun, even if we haven't gone all the way, but I've genuinely never felt like this about someone outside of you guys. He feels like one of my best friends. Like if the six of us went out together, he'd fit right in."

Delilah sighed dreamily. "Oh, to love a brother's best friend."

"Yeah, but when are you going to tell your brother? I have to imagine it'll only be worse the longer you wait, no?" Nicola asked, ever the pragmatist.

Maya knew the time was coming to tell Colton, but she was terrified. She was a grown woman, but Colton was still very protective of her, and even if he weren't, she imagined it would be uncomfortable for him. Hell, if one of her friends started dating Landon, she'd feel a little weird about it, even if she'd be happy for them.

"Not sure yet," she murmured. "Soon, I think. We *just* admitted we have feelings for each other. I'm scared of rocking the boat on something so new."

"Makes sense," Nicola responded over the crunch of a chip.

"And you guys? What's been going on on the tour?"

"Dating wise?" Nicola asked.

Maya shrugged. "Anything. I've missed our apartment talks."

Delilah sat up on her elbows before pointing accusingly at Nicola. "You have to tell her!"

"Oh, I love the sound of this. What happened?"

Nicola rolled her eyes as Delilah exclaimed, "Tell her, tell her! Or I will."

"Alright, fine. I may or may not find a certain Morozov a little bit sexy."

Maya gasped, knowing how much Nicola hated Anya. "You think Anya is hot?"

"As if."

"She has a crush on Anya's *brother*," Delilah practically yelled, like she couldn't stop herself.

"I'm not eight. It's not a crush. I can just admit when I think someone's attractive, and annoyingly, now that he's everywhere I turn, I am admitting I'm attracted to him." Nicola sighed, gazing up at the ceiling. "It's not like anything's going to happen."

Delilah pouted but lay back down. "At least you have prospects. Most of the guys on tour are full of themselves."

Just as Maya opened her mouth to ask a question, her phone flashed with a call from Cooper. She frowned. She'd told him she wouldn't be able to talk tonight, and he'd told her he was glad she was having fun, so if he was calling her, it meant something had happened.

She excused herself for a second, feeling the slight dizziness of the second margarita finally hitting her. "Coop?"

"Hi, sweetheart." His voice sounded strained, and Maya's frown only deepened. "I'm so sorry to bother you. I'll only be a minute."

Trepidation filled her veins. "Coop, what's going on?"

"It's...it's my dad. He had a heart attack."

Maya blinked, instantly sober. "Oh, Coop. How can I help? I can be on a plane to Charleston in the morning." It'd only been a few days since he'd come to surprise her, and they hadn't planned to see each other for a couple more weeks—until the end of May, when Colton accepted the Buck Isaac award in Charleston.

"Do—" He cleared his throat. "Could you come to Tennessee? I just bought my ticket to get in tomorrow and can meet you at the airport. If you want to come."

"Of course I want to come. I'll get a ticket now." Her heart broke for Cooper, who sounded distraught, and she wanted to hold him. He'd been supporting her so much recently, and she ached to do the same for him.

"I just bought it for you. I'm sending you the info." He cleared his throat again.

She was already accepting too much help from him. Maya didn't want him to have to pay for her ticket too. "Wait, Coop, you didn't have to—"

"You're doing me a favor. Of course I did. Now go hang out with the girls. Thank you for answering."

Maya took a few more steps away from the living room. "I can stay on with you if you want to talk."

"Thank you, sweetheart. I'm going to try to sleep. I miss you, and I can't wait to see you."

"I miss you too."

When Maya returned, her friends were out cold. She texted Viola about her change of plans and packed a bag, so worried about Cooper's father, she didn't have time to contemplate that she was about to meet his entire family.

Chapter Twenty-Six

Cooper

George was droning on and on about Cooper's media presence over the phone as Cooper searched the tiny Oakridge Springs airport for Maya, whose flight had landed only half an hour after his.

He still hadn't fully processed the news that his father was in the hospital, and he hadn't cared about anything George had said until Maya was mentioned.

"What did you just say?"

"I was just saying that since you've already been seen with her and there's so much speculation, we should work on a way to spin it. You don't seem interested in any of the other women Tessa and I have been trying to get you to go out with anyway." Cooper couldn't be sure, but he thought Tessa was a publicist with the Sabertooths.

Odd that his agent hadn't even thought to ask what Cooper's relationship with Maya actually was.

"George, I don't care about the media right now. My dad's in the hospital, and my latest hookup isn't really somethin' on my radar. I asked you to get me an update on my contract extension, and if that's too difficult for you, I'm happy to look for another agent."

Cooper watched Maya step out of the tunnel, eyes searching for him across the small building. Even though she wore a T-shirt and jeans, she stood out like the only person in the room.

George stammered, "I'm still working on it. I'm just negotiating some things, but I'm sure we'll have a final version by the end of June."

"Great." Maya smiled when she saw Cooper and began walking toward him quickly. Cooper spoke quietly. "And keep this on the down-low, but see what either of the Los Angeles teams would be willing to offer. If I need another option, those would be my choice."

There was silence on the line. When George finally answered, Cooper was already gathering Maya in his arms, her hands running over his back soothingly. "I didn't realize it was so serious."

"It is. But I'm not lookin' to advertise that right now. Just get me the offers." Cooper hung up and tucked the phone into his back pocket, breathing Maya in, enjoying the smell of coconuts and citrus.

"Hi, sunflower."

"Your accent is thicker here."

He huffed a laugh. Colton had told him that once.

She pulled back and smiled reassuringly. "Ready? Or do you want to hang out for a second?"

"I'm ready." He hoped. Cooper wrapped an arm around her shoulder and led her to the doors. Right outside, a driver holding a card with Cooper's last name stood, and they were quickly helped into the car.

Maya watched the rolling pastures pass, her hand firmly tucked in Cooper's, grounding him.

His relationship with his father wasn't great now, but that didn't change that he was his father and that at some point, they *had* been close. Before Cooper had left for college and everyone had taken offense to his leaving.

Cooper's father had done a lot for him and his family, and he wanted to make amends as best he could.

Only when they rolled up to Hayes Ranch did Cooper realize something was off.

The driver only smiled when asked what was going on. Maya's expression of confusion mirrored his own.

The moment Cooper's mother walked out onto the porch, curly auburn hair pulled up in a clip, apron over her clothes and a smile on her face, Cooper knew he'd been lied to.

"Ma?"

She smiled and ambled over to him, throwing her arms around him. "Hi, pumpkin." Her eyes lit up as they landed on Maya. "And who's this?"

He hadn't had a chance to let them know he was bringing her after she'd agreed the night before.

"This is Maya." There was an edge to his words, but if his mother noticed, she didn't react.

Maya smiled, and his mother wiped her hands on her apron before holding them out for Maya to shake. "We're so glad to have you both. We were just gettin' ready to serve dinner. Come on in."

"Ma, what's goin' on?" Cooper asked as they entered the home. "You said Dad had a heart attack."

Pictures lined the walls, most from when he and his siblings had been younger. When they walked into the dining room, Cooper's sisters were already seated and his father walked in from outside, like he'd been working the ranch with Dylan, who was right behind him.

"We thought your father had a heart attack, but luckily it was just some chest pains."

Cooper's eyes narrowed. "And at what point did you realize it wasn't a heart attack? Before or after you called me?"

The look his mother sent his father was answer enough. They'd lied to get Cooper to come home. Anger slid through Cooper's veins, even as he hugged each of his sisters.

"None of that matters now. We're just glad you're finally home. Come sit—Lily Ann's already graced the food."

Cooper made quick introductions for Maya, glaring at his father the whole time. He then pulled a chair out for her, and everyone began piling food onto their plates.

This wasn't uncommon. Cooper had had many tense family dinners, since nobody in his family ever stood up to his father. While a part of him wanted to address the blatant lie, he also didn't want Maya to be uncomfortable.

"So, son, how's Charleston treating you?" his father asked.

Warily, Cooper answered, "Good. Camp will be picking up soon, so I'll be gettin' pretty busy again." He glanced at Maya, but she was listening to something his youngest sister, Daisy, was whispering to her, a smile on her face.

"That's only if your contract's extended, correct? Which, as of now, isn't the case."

Cooper stared at the man he'd once looked up to. "My agent is sure it'll be extended. And if not, there are other teams."

His father hummed. "And Maya? What do you do? How'd you two meet?"

Maya glanced up from her conversation with Daisy. "My brother is on the team with Cooper. I was playing tennis professionally up until recently, and now I'm running the charity Cooper and I started together, teaching tennis to children."

"Ah, so you're in Charleston too?"

"Uh, no, sir. I'm in Los Angeles, actually."

He watched his parents glance at each other questioningly, always communicating silently.

"Ma, that's the charity I've been tellin' you about. Maya and I cofounded it. It's already doin' great work for kids in Los Angeles."

His mom smiled at him and nodded, but she didn't respond. Always waiting for his father, always the shadow that agreed with his every word.

"So it sounds like you don't have to be there in person for it then. That right?" Cooper's father asked, and Cooper knew exactly where this was going. Before he could even respond, his father continued, "This is why I asked you to come home. As I'm sure your mother has told you, I plan to step down as mayor, and I want you to move home and run in my stead."

"You didn't ask me to come home. You faked a medical emergency. And why can't Dylan do it?"

"Well, *maybe* if you answered your phone and bothered to come home, I wouldn't have to go to such lengths to get you here. Dylan has been doin' most of the ranch work since you left. And you were always the charismatic, well-liked one anyway."

Dylan's knife scraped against his plate, and when Cooper cut his eyes to him, his brother was glaring at *him*, as if it were his fault others thought that way.

Cooper set his fork down. "Dad, I've talked to Ma about this. I'm not plannin' on retiring from the league yet. I wanna keep playing."

His father shook his head. "To what end? We've entertained this for years. We let you go into the world, fulfill this dream of yours, whore yourself out to every questionably eligible woman in Charleston, and now it's time to come home. Do somethin' meaningful. Do your duty to this town that has done so much for us."

Only his father would insult him and ask something of him in the same entitled breath. Cooper looked around the table. His sisters were eating quietly, Dylan's glare had remained, his mother looked at him worriedly, and Maya had stopped eating the moment his father had begun talking, a hand slipping onto his knee beneath the table.

At least his father's words hadn't put her off.

How was he supposed to convince her, Colton, the world, anyone that he could change and be worthy of her if he couldn't even convince his own family that his life had purpose?

"You didn't feel this way when you used my accomplishments to schmooze voters. You had me go to every event in high school, purposely scheduled events around when I came home in college just so you could talk up my football. Now it's no longer convenient for you, and you just expect me to give it up?"

Something dark fell over his father's face. He stopped eating, angry eyes flicking back and forth between Cooper and Maya, as if she were the reason he was finally arguing his side.

And maybe she was. Maybe he was a little tired of being pushed around and she'd given him the courage to stand up.

"I *expect* you to do your duty to this family and this town. I *expect* you to take on more responsibility in this family."

Dylan scoffed across the table. "Cooper wouldn't know responsibility if it hit him in the face. He never has."

"Dylan," his mother scolded.

"Don't listen to him," Iris, the middle of his younger sisters said as she leaned toward Maya conspiratorially, rolling her eyes. "He's just bitter he got saddled with the *responsibilities* of the ranch."

"That's enough, Iris. Since Cooper left, Dylan has had to tend to the ranch more than anybody else. That's not how we raised you, Cooper. We raised you to give back to the community that has loved and supported you."

There it was. The guilting his father wielded like a weapon to make him feel bad for leaving. This was only the start, because inevitably, there would be a lecture about how hard his father had worked to get to this point and how ungrateful he was being.

Maya blinked at Cooper worriedly. Nothing about this was going the way he'd planned, but of course, what did? Cooper had known this conversation was coming, he just didn't know how to make his parents see reason. The word "no" meant nothing to them when it came to this sort of thing.

Still, he tried. "I'm sorry, but I won't be retiring this year. Maybe not next year either. I worked hard to get to where I am, and while it may not be the life you wanted for me or the labor you need from me, I'm happy. Even when I *do* retire, I don't think it'll be here. I have a life and friends in Charleston, and I have no intention of leaving them."

His father's utensils clattered against his plate as he stood, stomping out of the dining room into the mid-May evening.

"Oh dear." His mother was wringing her hands, glancing between Cooper and the door. As if to deescalate the tension in the room, most of which had left with Cooper's father, she asked, "So, when do you see yourselves not doing long distance, honey? Maya, will you be moving to Charleston soon?"

Maya looked at him with wide eyes, and Cooper brought her chair slightly closer to him before he slipped his hand into hers. He wanted her in his arms, but this would have to do.

"We haven't talked about that yet, Ma. Maybe we could hold off on this discussion for now?" Cooper pleaded.

Dylan hummed like his words made sense. They'd all probably taken that to mean serial player Cooper wasn't that serious about the woman beside him.

He hadn't thought the wave of frustration and itch to leave would come so quickly this trip, especially not with Maya.

Cooper sighed, leaning back in his chair, his appetite gone. When he noticed Maya sitting back from the table too, he excused them both.

⚾

Maya stepped around his childhood bed, fingers ghosting over his old jersey he'd hung up on the wall after his last season in high school. Green, just like the Sabertooths jerseys he wore now. If he believed in fate, it probably would've meant something.

"I'm sorry we didn't get a chance to see the town. I can take you tomorrow."

She turned around, a soft smile on her face. "I'd like that." Her finger ran over the trophies he'd received, mainly MVP, for all the glory he'd brought Oakridge Springs High, then over the couple of pictures of him with his high school teammates.

People he'd fallen out of touch with years ago, most of whom had only been friends with him because of his father anyway. Or because they had thought he'd make something of himself.

A couple of them had even had the gall to come out of the woodwork years later, once he was in the league, asking for favors.

He should toss those photos.

"Do you want to talk about it? I'm really good at talking about shitty fathers." She laughed.

His stomach roiled at that, remembering how much he hated her father for everything he'd put her and her brothers through.

"I think this is a *bit* different, since I think my dad generally means well. Or rather, he's not purposely tryin' to hurt me."

"Just because it's not purposeful doesn't mean it hurts any less," she pointed out astutely.

Cooper hummed in agreement, trying to parse his thoughts.

"Do they come to your games? Charleston isn't far, right?"

"Can't get a direct flight there, so it usually ends up bein' a three-hour trip. Or six hours by car."

He came up behind her, wrapping his arms around her as she looked at the framed photo of the ranch at sunset. Iris had taken it years ago, so much artistic talent in her from the time she'd been little. "The girls come sometimes. I always offer to pay for the plane tickets and even offered to buy a small house for them there so they could stay whenever they wanted, but my parents always reject the idea. Like my money insults them because it wasn't made off working on the ranch or something. I don't know."

"Why do you come back? If it's like this? Outside of the 'lying about medical emergencies' part."

Cooper rested his chin on her head. "It hasn't always been like this. Dad grew up real poor. He knew he wanted more for his kids, so he worked his ass off at the local construction company until he owned it. Built half this town. Maybe more. He kept the company for a while, even after he bought the ranch.

"Running for mayor was a piece of cake. He was widely loved, and the town was indebted to him. But he always believed he was just as indebted to the town, and so running it became his duty, his way of givin' back to the community that gave us so much."

She leaned back into him. "How long has your dad been hounding you like that?"

"There have always been comments here and there about it. That I left them. That I don't help Dad and Dylan with the ranch. Lord knows Dylan won't be goin' into politics after Dad. He's not exactly politician material. So I always knew it was something Dad wanted for me eventually. But this intensity is relatively new. January maybe? A lot of it has been him tellin' my mom to talk to me."

"And it doesn't seem like saying 'no' does much."

"Not at all. They don't seem to care what I do, how great it is, if it means I'm not in Oakridge. Mayor or nothin'."

"You *are* very charismatic," she offered.

"I always told Ma I'd end up a used car salesman."

Maya laughed, turning around and sliding her arms around him.

Cooper could tell something was on her mind, but she didn't voice it, so he continued. "But I'm sure she always saw me as a used car salesman *here*. Maybe coaching football at Oakridge Springs High. They didn't even know I was being recruited by Alabama until I made the decision to accept."

"Ouch."

"Yeah, not my proudest moment. I had to get out of here though. Like they say about small towns, everyone really knows everyone, and the moment they found a label to fit me, that's how every person here saw me."

She scoffed. "Like people are incapable of change. As if you're the same person you were ten, twelve years ago."

He shrugged, then squeezed her. "I like bein' here with you though."

"Liar. You don't like being here any better just because I'm here."

Cooper pulled Maya toward his extra-long twin bed, thankful he'd opted for dark-blue sheets in high school instead of something embarrassing.

"Get out of my head, sunflower." He sat, pulling her into his lap. "You make it more bearable though."

It was true. In Oakridge Springs, visits had always been sink or swim, and more often, he sank so fast, he had to leave within a day of getting in. But she'd thrown him a lifesaver and brought him to shore. Or maybe *she* was his lifesaver.

He never wanted to let her go. Cooper wanted to sit with her like this forever, just them and no responsibilities.

"You're quickly becomin' my favorite person, you know that?" he whispered. "Think you have been for a while."

"Better be. I didn't lock you down just to lose the best friend award to my *brother*."

"If it makes you feel better, I definitely lost to Lucia."

"Oh, absolutely. He was a goner long before they got together for real."

As they got ready for bed, Cooper knew he needed to try one more time to make things right, even if every bone in his body was telling him to leave. Just one more conversation before they left in a couple of days.

Because while this would never be *his* home again, this was his family, and while it may not seem so to his parents, he *did* value his family.

He just dreaded having to battle his father once more.

Chapter Twenty-Seven

Cooper

The spacious breakfast nook in Cooper's parents' house had always been one of his favorite places. When they'd been younger, he and his sisters would sit and eat before school together, looking out over the rolling green hills of the ranch. He'd listen to Lily Ann tell stories about her friends or give her advice about boys. He'd tell Iris how pretty her paintings or photographs were. He'd talk to Daisy about the flowers that bloomed in the garden she tended with their mother. Sometimes Dylan would join them, though usually silently.

It was the most at peace he'd felt in Oakridge Springs, other than on the football field. In a house that often turned into a warzone, with five children in close proximity who argued almost constantly, the breakfast nook had never seemed to allow that kind of negativity.

Cooper had even been sure to add one to his house in Charleston, imagining that one day, no matter the chaos of his life, he would still find the same peace there.

The next morning he sat there, watching Dylan and his father drive the truck until they were out of sight, likely dealing with downed fence posts from the last storm that'd blown through.

Maya was headed into town with his sisters, and he'd promised to meet them after he talked to his parents. Though it seemed he would have to wait until after his father came back.

Cooper's mother slid into the other side of the nook. "Did you sleep well?"

He nodded, then cleared his throat, looking out the window. "I'm sorry I haven't been the best about answering your calls and texts."

"Oh, that's okay, sweetie. I know you're busy."

Grass swayed outside, and Cooper could just make out the corner of his sister's garden, pretty pink flowers waving in the breeze.

"Do you remember when you taught me to ride a horse?"

His mother chuckled. "Of course. You hated every second of it. The complete opposite of your brother. And Tex knew too, because as gentle as he was with me, he had no interest in letting you saddle him."

Cooper smiled at the memory. He'd never been a big fan of the stables, and it'd taken him months longer than Dylan to learn how to ride. Dylan had always been a natural. "I think, even though I didn't realize it then, that was one of the first moments that showed me I didn't belong on the ranch. Not like Dyl," he murmured, turning to her.

"Oh, pumpkin. Don't say that. You were always so helpful. Any time your father asked you to help, you jumped at the chance."

That had more to do with wanting to be like his father than enjoying the work. For a long time, all he'd cared about was his father's approval. And then, when one of his middle school teachers had told him his height could be an advantage for their football team, he'd signed up.

Cooper had been like a god on the field, and over the years had earned the adoration of everyone in the town. And that seemed to be enough to get his father's attention and love too. So out went ranching, and in came football.

His mother clasped his hands. "I'm sorry he stormed out of dinner like that. There's a young kid running for mayor this time around, and he's just worried. You know how he is. He loves this town like family, and he'd feel a whole lot better knowin' the person taking over cared as much as he did."

"Ma, I'm tired of you bein' Dad's spokesperson just because he knows I struggle to say no to you."

She squeezed his hands, eyes sad. "Just want you to see things the way we do."

Cooper removed his hands from hers, crossing his arms over his chest.

"Do you know how impressive it is that I'm on a team that's won two championships? That I've scored touchdowns *during* those championships? Do you know how frustrating it is to stand before my family and know that they don't see who I am at all? That they can't even listen to me when I say I'm doin' something I *care* about, something I *love*?"

"Cooper, honey. We *are* proud of you. We just feel that there are things you could be doin' at home, closer to the family."

"Like running for mayor."

"Well, if you'd rather help with the ranch and try somethin' else, I'm sure your father would—"

"You want to know why I don't come home? Why I don't text as often anymore? It's because you're refusing to see *my* side of things. I'm an adult with a career that makes me happy. I have friends who I care about. And a woman I care about who sees me and cares for me exactly as I am. The more I have to have these conversations—the more I have to battle you and Dad—the less I even want to participate."

"I'm not sure what to say, sweetie. Your father's been pushing the issue a lot recently."

Cooper scoffed. "Yeah, I can tell. Look, Ma, if you don't want to stand up to him, that's fine—I get it. But at the very least, tell me you understand what I'm saying. This is gettin' to be ridiculous."

Quietly, she said, "Yes, I understand. I'm sorry if I've ever made you feel like I don't love you as you are. That was never my intention."

He rolled his shoulders. "I know. I *want* to want to come home, but with everything that's been going on the last few months, I've been less and less interested. I miss the girls and you. And even Dad and Dyl sometimes. I want to feel like I have a place here when I visit without feeling like it comes with strings. I know me leaving was what changed everything so much, but I'd like to fix that without havin' to give up all the things that I love."

His mother nodded. "I understand. Unfortunately, I'm not sure that—"

She was cut off by the back door slamming open. His father came in, grabbing a hat off a hook and searching the room. "Suze, I forgot..." He trailed off when he saw Cooper and his mother at the table.

"Surprised you're still here."

Cooper clenched his jaw. "'Til tomorrow. I'd like to talk to you. Just for a minute or two."

Cooper's mother was already sliding out of the nook, excusing herself and heading toward the kitchen. He wished she would go to bat for him against his father, but Cooper knew this was his fight.

At least she'd said that she understood.

"Make it quick. Dyl's waitin' in the truck," his father said gruffly, not moving any closer.

"I'd love to help you find a candidate you trust for mayor. But that person isn't me. This town hasn't been mine for a long time."

His father's frown lines, already strong from his daily work in the sun, deepened at Cooper's words. "One day I hope you understand how much I sacrificed to give you the life y'all got. I spent more time workin' construction jobs than you could ever know, just to make sure we had a beautiful place to raise our beautiful family. But with that comes obligations. As much work as I've put into this community, it's put just as much back into our lives. We'd be nowhere without the people of this town. It's why I've worked so hard to keep this place workin' the way it does."

"Dad, I appreciate everything you did for us. I really do. And I see all that you've done for this town. But I've built a life elsewhere. I'm not a puppet on a string you can yank back to do your bidding. I'm sorry I'm such a disappointment to you, but just like Dylan and the girls are all doin' what they love, I'm doin' what I love."

His father shook his head, pushing his straw hat farther down on his head.

"I want to be able to come home and see y'all. I don't want to have to be rushed out here because of a lie. But until you understand that I need football, Charleston, this charity, Maya, all of it in my life, I don't see myself wantin' to visit."

"Then go." His father turned, his boots loud on the floor of the house. The door slammed, and Cooper watched the truck disappear once more. His mother moved around in the kitchen, seemingly trying to give him space to think.

Cooper sat there for what felt like hours but was probably only a half an hour. The grass kept swaying in the breeze. Trees rustled together, dancing in the distance, and the sun moved higher overhead. He knew if he looked farther, the current of the Tennessee River, the far boundary of the ranch, would be as strong as ever.

Life went on.

And Cooper hoped that even if he never got his father's approval, life would go on.

Chapter Twenty-Eight

Maya

Getting along with Cooper's sisters was easy, even though they were all younger than Maya and liked to talk over each other. Daisy, who was more mature than her seventeen years, had shown her the small flower shop she'd just begun working at. Iris had a small studio down the street for her photography and painting, and she'd even started learning how to make pottery.

Into "town" was a stretch, because Oakridge Springs' downtown area was a square with a park and then a block of one-story shops along each edge of the square. Narrow streets hardly allowed for cars, and the parking lot behind Iris' studio was only large enough to hold six cars.

It was quaint, and though Maya had never been a fan of small towns, she could admit how beautiful it was.

Seeing where Cooper had come from made Maya think about where he was going, where his future would be. His mother's question from dinner the night before had been eating at her.

They hadn't talked about the future, and the more time Maya spent in Los Angeles, the less she saw herself being able to move away. Which didn't leave them with many options, certainly none she liked.

She would never ask him to move for her.

Lily Ann had been quiet as they walked through the little area, and Maya noticed she didn't seem to have a piece of downtown like her sisters. Maya wondered if Lily Ann was like herself—adrift and in need of a purpose.

It could explain why she was still living at her parents' house at twenty. Not that Maya could talk.

Daisy gasped, clapping her hands. "Oh! We can stop at the little coffee shop at the end of First Street! Maya, do you like coffee? They do some *wild* things to caffeine."

Maya wasn't a fan of coffee, but she nodded. "I'm intrigued by what you mean by *wild things*, so please lead the way." She laughed as Iris and Daisy linked arms and began skipping ahead, entering a pretty brick building a few shops down.

Maya turned to Lily Ann. "Are you having a good morning?"

Lily Ann nodded politely. "Of course."

"What's it like being one of five?"

A shrug. "Overwhelming sometimes. There's always somethin' to argue about."

"I can imagine."

Lily Ann looked at Maya out of the corner of her eye just as they walked into the coffee shop. "Did you go to college?"

Maya held back a grimace. "I did. Though I left early to pursue tennis."

"Do you regret that?"

Lily Ann with the hard-hitting questions. "Not really. I enjoyed every second I was on the pro tour. I did struggle to find my footing when I got injured, and I worried I wouldn't be able to find a job. But then Cooper helped me see that I'm capable of doing something else I love that's also impactful."

The younger sisters had already made it to the register, a few people in line between them and Maya. They waved bags of pastries in the air, and Maya smiled.

Lily Ann's lips twisted to the side. "He's lucky. That he got out. Ma's been so worried about losing any more of her children, she's been keepin' an extra tight leash on the rest of us. Not that any of the others wanna leave." Maya couldn't tell whether she was reading resentment toward Cooper, but she'd understand if she were. Seeing one of your siblings get the freedom you wish you had could do that to a person.

"But you do?"

Lily Ann looked away. "Thinkin' about it."

"It might help if you talk to him. I know he misses you all, and I think he'd be happy to help you any way he can." Because that's just who he was.

Lily Ann didn't answer, and Maya ordered a matcha, which came out pink, making her even less interested in drinking it.

The girls had gotten two croissants and a muffin, and they sat and talked about boys as they all tried the treats.

When they exited the shop, Cooper stood looking for them, hands in his pockets, shoulders just forward enough for Maya to know his talk with his parents hadn't gone well. Her heart took off at how handsome he was, beating wildly, and the moment his eyes fell on her, his face softened. Maya's stomach twisted.

If she weren't with his sisters, she'd have jumped into his arms.

Like seeing her had changed his day, his shoulders went back up and he smiled, walking the few steps over to them.

"I see you were swayed to get somethin' from Wack." He inclined his head to her pink matcha.

Maya turned to look at the shop, eyebrows furrowed, and found that *was* indeed the name of the coffee shop. She laughed at how on the nose it was.

"I was."

"Ladies, do you mind if I steal her away for a few minutes to show her my favorite places?"

"Actually, I was helping Daisy and Iris with some issues they've been having." It was his turn to frown. Maya looked at him, then to Lily Ann, hoping he understood what she was saying. "Maybe tonight?"

As his face lit up with understanding, Maya linked arms with his two youngest sisters and began walking with them, giving Iris advice on the boy she'd been crushing on since third grade and taking a couple more turns around the park to give Cooper and Lily Ann plenty of time to talk.

Night painted the sky black, though the stars shone brightly against the dark, and Maya marveled at what she could see without light pollution. She bumped along in the passenger seat of Cooper's old pickup truck, her fingers threaded through his as he took her to his favorite place in Oakridge Springs.

They'd spent most of the day in town, and she'd enjoyed seeing the dynamic between Cooper and his sisters. Lily Ann had opened up more after Cooper had talked to her, and Maya loved seeing their lively debates about which horse would win the jumping and racing competition the town held each year.

By the time they'd left, his sisters had been eager to get Maya's number and visit her sometime soon.

She liked feeling like a big sister for once.

They pulled onto the grass off the narrow main road, and Maya's eyes widened as they drove through some shrubs, then down a hill until they pulled next to a small watering hole.

"Did you bring me here to murder me?"

"Mm, not quite."

He helped her out of the truck, then pulled blankets and pillows out of the back, setting up a little area to lie in the bed.

Then he helped her into the bed, pulling her so she sat between his legs, her back against his chest.

Maya looked up, resting her head on his shoulder, taking in how brilliant the stars looked and breathing air that felt like *real* air, not the stale stuff she was used to in Los Angeles. "It's beautiful."

"It is. I've been wanting to bring you here since I realized we were comin' to Tennessee."

She turned her head, taking in his profile. "How's Lily Ann?"

"Good. She was always the smartest of all of us, so I'm glad she wants to go to college. She's gonna do great things."

They sat together silently for a few minutes, staring up at the sky. Finally, Cooper murmured, "Something's been on your mind since last night."

Maya blew out a breath, not wanting to ruin their evening. But they needed to talk about it. "What your mom said. About how we're going to handle doing distance and when we'll be in the same place."

Cooper intertwined their fingers, resting his head on hers. "I don't really have an answer right now, short of askin' you to move to Charleston. Do you?"

"Coop..."

"I'm not askin', sweetheart. Not yet at least."

"It's just...I *just* got the charity up and running, you know? I've made friends with people in the tennis world in LA, and now I've got my grandparents and my cousins. I have a community there now." In the span of a few months, she'd gained so many close relationships in Los Angeles. And she'd put *so* much into the charity, she couldn't abandon it now.

"I understand."

Though his words were kind, she felt like she needed to explain further. "Plus, you've done so much for me, you know? I don't think I'll be comfortable moving in with you until that's paid back. I feel like I'm already taking so much from you. And what would I do in Charleston?" She shook her head slightly. "I have to find a place where I can be reliant on myself. With this charity, I've done that."

Cooper smoothed a hand over her hair, pulling her tighter to his chest. "You don't have to explain. I understand. We'll figure it out."

Maya still felt something like anxiety and stress pulling at her chest. Not quite a panic attack, but nearly. To get out of her head, she asked, "How did it go with your parents this morning?"

Meeting his father had been...interesting. His storming out was childish, and she thought her father would get along with him well. They could spend hours talking about all the ways they could guilt their children into doing things that benefitted them.

Cooper sighed. "Ma seems to understand, but my dad doesn't." He told her about the conversation, and just listening to his voice calmed her heartbeat and breathing enough.

"I'm really proud of you for getting that off your chest. Now it's his turn—you've done all you can."

"Yeah." A beat, then two. "But I want to feel comfortable coming home. I want to hang out with the girls again. Maybe that's just somethin' we'll do in Charleston instead."

"Give your dad some time. He might come around when tensions aren't so high."

"Maybe."

Maya turned, putting a knee on either side of him so that she straddled him. She took his face in her hands and kissed him slowly, softly. Pulling back, she placed his hat beside them, running her fingers through his hair. "I've realized over the last couple of months why you and Colton are such kindred spirits. I watched my dad place his dream on Colton's shoulders as early as I can remember. And I see that same responsibility being placed on you. The expectation that you'll take care of *his* dream. I know it's hard to see it now, but life will be so much more fulfilling when you choose *your* dream. He might not be happy, but that's his issue, not yours."

Cooper's eyes flicked between hers. To lighten the mood, Maya moved against his hips, running her thumb over his bottom lip.

He groaned, grabbing her hips and stilling her. "Sweetheart, I'm still not deserv—"

"*Stop.* If you don't want to have sex, I can respect that completely. But I can't listen to you tell me one more time that you have to hold back because of what everybody else thinks.

The only person whose opinion should matter is mine. Not Colton's. Not reporters. Not the rest of the world. Mine. And you don't have to prove anything to me, Coop. I've never once believed that you aren't worthy of me. And I never will."

Something guttural left him, and then one of his hands was buried in her hair while he kissed her passionately, the other guiding her hips over his. She'd seen his bulge before, felt it even, but something about this was different. The dress she'd worn for the day was bunched at her hips, so all that was between them was his jeans and her panties.

Cooper groaned again. "Yes, yes." He moved against her. "*Fuck* yes," he panted into her mouth. Maya smiled, warmth pooling in her belly at the noises he was making and the feel of him against her.

She kissed down his neck, pushing up his T-shirt to kiss down his chest to his stomach, which flexed at her touch. Before she touched the button of his jeans, she flicked her eyes up to his face. "Can I?"

He was quiet for a moment. His hand came up to caress her cheek. "You're gonna ruin me, aren't you, sweetheart?"

"Only if you want me to," she whispered.

"It's all I want," he whispered back.

Maya unbuckled his belt slowly, torturing him for making her wait so long. She ran a hand over the top of his jeans, and his whole body shifted. She unbuttoned, then unzipped his jeans, pulling them down with his boxers, and his dick bobbed as it came out.

Maya smiled, even though she knew she wouldn't be able to take all of him. His balls were already tight, and she ran her fingers over them.

"Maya, please. I can't...*Please*," he pleaded.

She licked the tip, tasting the salty bead of precum there. He gasped, hand fisting in her hair. "Only because you begged."

She wrapped her lips around him and took him as best as she could, moving up and down and swirling her tongue. When he hit the back of her throat, he made a throaty noise she'd never heard from him, spurring her on. Up and down she sucked and moaned, adding a hand to his shaft as she moved. He mumbled praises, how pretty she looked taking his cock, how he loved hearing her moan, how good she made him feel.

It only took a few minutes before his mumbled praises turned incoherent, and the hand in her hair fisted tighter. "I'm gonna come. Oh, Mai, *fuck*." When she didn't pull away, he gasped, "You...don't have to...keep goin'."

But she did, and though Maya had never been a fan of swallowing, the look of adoration in his eyes made her wonder if that would change.

He came, salty and warm in her mouth, and as his shaking subsided, he grabbed her chin. "I wanna see me on your tongue. Open up, sweetheart." She listened. He used his thumb to swipe some along her lips, and he smiled at her. "Fuckin' perfect. Now swallow."

Maya licked her lips and listened again. Cooper pulled her up his body so she lay on top of him, kissing her passionately before flipping her onto her back. All words were lost when she saw the look on his face, the sky a beautiful canvas behind him.

"Did you have fun, sweetheart? If I reach down and touch you, let my tongue part you, will I find you dripping wet for me? Your pretty little cunt begging for me?" His hand ghosted over the top of her dress, down to the inside of her leg.

Not only were words a lost cause, but so was breathing, apparently. He placed a warm kiss to her jaw, then below her ear, then on her neck. His fingers moved softly over the flesh of her thigh, but he stopped when she didn't respond. Gruffly, he said, "I'm gonna need you to answer so I know if I can bury my fingers inside of you like I've been wantin' to for longer than you could possibly know."

"I-I—" She gasped in a breath finally, her body already tingling at the thought of him inside of her. "Yes, Coop. Please."

He moved away and pointed one finger at her panties as he sucked the pointer and middle fingers of his other hand into his mouth. Then he said, "Off. Now."

Maya ripped them down her legs, embarrassed that she was nearly panting for him. It'd been far too long, and even if it hadn't, she just knew it was going to be so much better with Cooper.

He kissed her in short, warm bursts, only a little bit of tongue until she was ready to beg him to kiss her like he meant it. Right as she opened her mouth to try to form the words, his middle finger was rubbing her center, and her entire body was shuddering.

"*Oh*," she moaned loudly. He circled her with slow, deliberate strokes as he pulled the neckline of her dress lower and sucked at the spot right above her breast, sure to leave a mark.

She quite liked the idea of that. Of being branded as his.

His finger moved slowly until he was sinking into her easily.

Cooper chuckled, pupils dilating further as he pulled back to look at what he'd done to her chest. "Guess I was right," he said, nodding down to her wet pussy.

Were those the hottest words ever uttered in her presence? Probably. Her legs shook, and she sank lower into the pillows and blankets. He kept burying his finger in her, circling her clit with his thumb.

Maya was dizzy, drunk with pleasure, waves and waves rushing over her like the Los Angeles tide.

Just when she thought it couldn't get any better, his sexy, stubbled face descended toward where he was touching her. He made eye contact with her and spit on her clit, his tongue slashing down over her in a way that had her body turning to jelly.

Cooper's eyes crinkled at the corners just a little, a wicked light in them. "You okay?"

The best she could do was nod, especially as he sucked her into his mouth, eyes still locked on hers. He used one finger, then two, and she stretched around them deliciously. Her body twitched at the pleasure that rolled through her as he nipped and sucked at her most sensitive spot, his fingers curling until she was crying his name, her hands buried in his hair as she practically rode his face.

Thrilling was the only word that came to her through it all. Then, "Fuck, Coop, *fuck.*"

"Mm," he moaned as he picked up the pace, like she was the tastiest meal he'd ever had. And suddenly she was hurtling toward that edge, his tongue traveling with her as she bucked against him a few times, blood rushing in her ears and the tingling of every cell in her body magnified.

Like the snap of a rubber band, she came all over his mouth, gasping and screaming until her body fell into a content hum. Cooper pulled away, licking his lips before shoving his two fingers into his mouth and sucking on them like he hadn't gotten enough of her.

They stared at each other as she came down from the high, and when she could finally move again, she pulled him on top of her, wanting nothing more than to fall asleep with him under the stars.

He kissed her lips lovingly, reverently, before setting his head on her chest, making sure his body didn't crush her beneath him, and joked, "Maybe there *is* some good in this town."

Chapter Twenty-Nine

Maya

A little over a week after her visit to Tennessee, Maya was in Charleston to celebrate Colton receiving the Buck Isaac Leadership Award. Only, her flight had gotten in late, she'd completely missed the ceremony, and she was now getting ready in the back of a car on the way to the club.

Still, she was excited for the evening, her low-cut maroon bodycon dress hugging her muscular figure. She smiled wide at herself in the mirror of her compact when she finished the look with a clear lip gloss, knowing it was the best she'd probably ever looked in Cooper's presence.

And they were right back where they'd started this flirtation: Frankie's. She could almost feel his lips on hers against that far, dimly lit wall.

When she arrived, Colton was waiting outside to let her in, and she threw her arms around his shoulders.

"Congratulations!"

Colton chuckled and then led her inside. "Well, I don't know about all that. It's just an award."

Maya could tell he was proud of the achievement despite his words. "Yeah, for being an excellent leader and stepping up when your team needed you. That's huge."

Colton shrugged. "Just glad you're here. Luc and I missed you."

"I'm excited to be here! And thank *you* for receiving the award on a Friday so I can stay a few extra days."

They neared the bar, where Cooper was talking to the bartender.

"Did you have lessons this week? You're not missing anything, right?" Colton asked.

Cooper finally looked up, and the look he gave her was entirely inappropriate for them pretending to be friends. The intensity of it as he took her in from head to toe reminded her of what they'd done in the truck bed, and heat slammed through her body, filling her veins.

She had to look away, but not before she noticed him in his signature jeans, tight-as-fuck black T-shirt that showed off his ridiculously ripped shoulders and arms, and his straw cowboy hat placed perfectly on the thick hair she wanted so badly to run her fingers through.

Colton looked at her expectantly, and she adjusted her dress as she remembered his question. "Oh! Lessons. Yes, I had private lessons and I coached for On the Line this week. I have Fridays off and won't have another private lesson until Monday afternoon, so I'm free for the weekend."

"Great." He hooked a thumb behind him. "Luc is on the dance floor if you want to join us."

Maya looked over to where half the team and their partners stood, talking and dancing to the music. Then she looked back at Cooper. "I'll catch up with you in a few minutes! Just going to get a drink."

Colton nodded his understanding, and they parted ways.

Maya sidled up to Cooper. "Hi! How are you?" she asked, like she hadn't been on the phone with him twenty-four hours ago, knowing plenty of Sabers players were in earshot of them.

"Doing well." The smile he gave her flipped her insides like a pancake, the promise of what he wanted to do to her clear. Oh, he *liked* this dress. "Colton asked me why you were in Tennessee with me," he whispered.

Maya closed her eyes, eyebrows furrowing in concern. She'd been thinking a lot about telling Colton, and she'd planned to talk to Cooper about it this evening, but she hated the thought that he'd found out like this. "I should have known it would have gotten out. What did you tell him?"

"Said you were on the phone with me when I got the call from my parents, and it was super last-minute. That I didn't want to bother him."

Maya opened her eyes, sighing. "Okay. Do you think he bought it?"

"Honestly, yes. He seems really oblivious to us. But I don't like lying to him, Mai. And you've shown me I don't need to hide this anymore. I want to tell him."

"I know. I wanted to talk to you about that tonight. I think we should tell him while I'm here this weekend."

"Really?" His hand began moving toward her, and then he dropped it, looking to the dance floor. Maya nodded. "Oh, thank God. I was worried you wouldn't be ready. Let's tell him tomorrow. I don't want to ruin his night, and I imagine news like that will—"

"You guys okay?" Colton had come back to grab his beer off the bar, and Maya jumped away from Cooper.

"Great!" Maya said, a bit overenthusiastically.

Colton nodded, sipping his drink. "I'm thinking we leave in an hour and hang out just the four of us at our house."

"I think that's a great idea," Cooper said, and Maya smiled wide.

"Great!" she declared again. *Subtle.*

Colton headed back to Lucia. After a few minutes of watching, making sure he wasn't coming back, Maya dared to slide the glass holding her pink drink across the bar closer to Cooper's hand, which held a glass of whiskey that he'd barely touched.

"Cheers," she said, licking her lips when her fingers brushed his, "to a job well done with the charity."

They clinked glasses and took a sip, eyes on each other the whole time. When their glasses came back down, he moved to wipe a small drop of the whiskey off his full bottom lip.

Before he could, her thumb swept it, catching and sucking it into her mouth. She hated the taste the moment it hit her tongue but didn't care because the look he gave her spoke volumes.

"Mm, forgot I'm not a whiskey girl."

"That's too bad. I would've offered you some of mine," he responded huskily, his heavy-lidded, lust-filled eyes dropping to her lips. As he lowered toward her, she shook her head once to remind him where they were.

"Careful," she whispered.

She didn't know when it'd happened, but they were toe-to-toe, and despite her being over six feet in heels, she had to look up at him.

"You want to dance?" he asked, inclining his head toward the dance floor full of sweaty bodies.

"Depends," she answered, a smirk curving her lips.

"On what?" The gruffness of his voice set her body on alert, just wanting a brush of his hand along her body, knowing she was already wet with want for him.

"Can I save a horse and ride my cowboy tonight?"

His throat bobbed at the whispered question. "I'm not taking you for the first time in a bathroom at Frankie's, as hot as we both know that would be."

"You know Colton's going to have you stay the night. Just sneak into my room."

Cooper looked around, then focused on her again. "That's even worse than lying to him about us."

"But *so* much fun. Think of how quiet we'll have to be. How great it'll be knowing how *wrong* it is."

Cooper looked up at the ceiling, like he was searching for strength. "You have no idea the willpower I've had to this point. How much I'm holding myself back from touching you right now." He looked down at her face, then her chest, down to the tips of her red-painted toes. "I want to rip this and anything underneath it right off you."

She leaned forward to whisper in his ear. "What if I told you there's nothing underneath?"

The groan he let out was animalistic, and his hands ghosted over her hips for just a second. Chills took over her body at the light touch.

"You are chipping away at my resolve quickly, sweetheart. The bathroom's not sounding so bad now."

"How about this: you sneak into my room and find me in just my dress in my bedroom, and next time we're out like this, you can do whatever you want to me in the bathroom."

There was that near-growl again. "Sunflower, if you don't take a step away from me, I'm going to let every single person in this club know who this pretty pussy belongs to," he muttered quietly, his hand ghosting over her inner thigh, inches from where she knew she ran slick with need for him.

She swallowed over the desire in her throat and took a step away. That didn't stop him from keeping his eyes on her for the rest of the night, their little game continuing into the car and all the way to Colton's house, until Lucia and Colton were drunk and ready for bed.

The soft, insistent knock on the door came only a few minutes after they had retired to their separate rooms in Colton's house. Maya let Cooper in and locked the door.

When she turned around, he was a few feet away, and she smirked at the devilish look in his eyes. "What are you thinking about?"

Cooper took a step forward. "You," he answered huskily. "Pretty much all the time."

"Oh," she breathed, her mind scrambling to find purchase on a single other word with him so close and those intense blue eyes on her.

"When I'm waking up and getting ready for the day? Thinking about you. When I'm at the facility or on the field? Thinking about you. When I'm out with the guys? Thinking about you, which is so bad because Colton is always sitting right there, and I'm terrified he can read my mind."

Maya giggled.

"When I'm in the shower, I'm thinking about you. When I'm stroking my cock, I'm thinking about you."

A muscle feathered in his jaw, and she saw the moment his control snapped. Cooper stepped forward, sliding a hand to cup her cheek, his fingers pulling at her hair, drawing a gasp from her mouth. His lips found hers quickly, and this kiss was punishing. *Is he punishing me for teasing him, or did he just miss me?* she wondered.

Cooper pushed her against the door, his warm mouth traveling to her jaw and then her neck, his hand moving to hold her waist. He strained against his dress pants, and she bit her lower lip to stop a breathy moan.

Maya was hot, feverishly so, and her entire body trembled with the knowledge that she was about to have what she'd been wanting for—well, who really knew how long? Since far before she'd admitted her feelings for him to herself.

Pushing the straps of her dress off her shoulders, he began kissing from her neck to her breasts, to her stomach over her dress, and then he was on his knees in front of her, looking up at her like she could control his every move if she wanted to.

Maya ran a hand through his hair as he slowly pushed her dress up her legs and over her ass, his breath warming the inside of her thighs until she felt like liquid, almost unable to stand on her own two feet.

Cooper's eyes still on hers, he hiked her right leg over his shoulder, like he knew she needed the support, and placed a chaste kiss to her clit. Maya inhaled sharply.

His eyes flicked down to her and then back up to her face. "Can I?"

Maya nodded, still speechless at seeing him on his knees for her. He swiped a finger over her and groaned. "You're always so *fucking* wet, sunflower. *Fuck.*"

Like he couldn't stop himself any longer, he licked up her slit, a strong arm wrapping around the leg thrown over his shoulder. The fingers of his other hand circled her clit, and the immediate thrill through her body pushed her head back against the door, breath coming faster and faster. As if he couldn't contain his joy at pleasuring her, he ripped his pants and boxers down and began palming himself.

"You think you're ready to take this cock, sweetheart?" When she didn't respond, he pulled away, and she frowned down at him.

"I asked you a question, Mai." Cooper spit on his cock, pumping up and down as he once again looked into her eyes.

Maya bit her lip, trying to slow her breathing before responding. "Y-yes."

Cooper raised an eyebrow, his cocky smirk making her heartbeat rocket through her body.

He was so beautiful.

"You don't seem so sure. Let's see."

Cooper slid a finger inside her, and she gasped quietly at how easily he slid in. When he inserted another, she gripped his hair in one hand, the nails of her other hand digging into his shoulder, and he moaned like he liked the pressure.

His tongue played with her clit as his calloused fingers continued pumping in and out of her until she couldn't take it anymore, blood pounding in her ears and legs shaking with her orgasm.

Cooper pulled away, setting her leg down and grabbing her waist as he stood, a self-satisfied smile on his face.

"You are a fucking wonder, you know that? I'm going to have somebody paint you in a hundred ways and plaster it all over my house."

Maya smiled at his words, knowing he meant every one. Not wanting him to feel like she didn't reciprocate, she grabbed at his cock, but he backed away, shaking his head.

"Maya, if you touch me, there is a very real chance I won't be able to bend you over like we both want." He stepped forward to grab her ass and squeezed once. "Get on the bed. On all fours, ass up."

The authority in his voice sent a shiver down her spine, and she complied eagerly. Maya rested on her forearms, shaking when his hands bunched the fabric of her dress and used it to pull her to him. His warm breath against her pulled the first moan out of her, and Maya had to push her face into the bed to keep herself quiet.

Cooper massaged her inner thigh for a moment and then stuck his tongue right inside of her, lapping up her first orgasm.

He pulled back. "Can I spank you?" he begged.

She let out something that sounded like *mm-hmm*, nodding her head, and the quick bite of his hand on her ass sent pleasure zipping through her.

"That's for teasing me at the bar when you knew I couldn't do anything about it," he said gruffly. Then he was kissing her inner thighs, his scruff rubbing against her. He found her center once again.

"Oh, *god*. Fuck, Coop, yes. *Yes*." His tongue continued lapping her up as he rubbed her, and she very nearly finished again, collapsing onto the bed.

Cooper chuckled. "You're lucky their bedroom is across the house from us right now or we'd be so busted."

She heard him spit onto his dick, stroking himself. "You ready for me, sweetheart? Want me to fuck you like you've been begging for all night?"

"Cooper, *please*," she whined.

He spanked her again, and she gasped at how good it felt. "Let me see that pretty pussy before I pound it, sweetheart."

Maya did as she was told. When she heard a wrapper being ripped open, she turned toward the noise. "I've got an IUD and I'm clean. I was tested a few weeks ago in case you were so inclined to fuck me. You don't have to use a condom."

"God damn it, Maya, you are so *fucking* sexy." She felt his teeth bite into the flesh of her ass, and she let out another delighted gasp at the sensation. Cooper licked the area. "Clean when I tested a month ago and haven't so much as looked in another woman's direction in months."

"We probably should've had this conversation before I came all over your face at the watering hole, but good news." She laughed.

He chuckled with her. A second later, the head of his penis was against her. "You ready, sweetheart?" This time, his words were sweet.

Maya responded by pushing herself into him.

"Guess so," Cooper whispered, words strained as he grabbed her hips and moved into her slowly. Her body stretched to meet him, and his grip on her tightened, like he was struggling to keep a hold on himself. He began to pick up the pace, his cock drilling into her until the only thing she could keep in the air was her ass, and even that was supported by him.

"This is the only fucking pussy I want for the rest of my life," he grunted as he thrusted. "Understood?"

Maya moaned in response, so dizzy, she could hardly enjoy the words she'd craved. Cooper filled her until she was screaming into the comforter again. The moment her middle finger began circling her clit in time with his thrusts, she came undone around him, and he groaned like he felt it.

"Jesus, fuck. Holy fuck."

She panted again, stars lining her vision. "Isn't that...a little...blasphemous?" she managed to get out.

He increased his rhythm as he said, "I would gladly go to hell for you, sweetheart."

And she nearly orgasmed again just at those words.

Just when Maya thought he was about to finish, his fingers digging into her sides harder and his thrusts getting faster, he said, "Fuck this."

Maya was flipped onto her back, light illuminating him in all his glory. "I need to see your beautiful face while I come."

Cooper pushed inside of her again, and this time, she got to watch his face as she took all of him. He captured her lips and kissed her hard while he continued thrusting, groaning low in the back of his throat as he filled her with his cum. She hadn't realized her nails were digging into his back until he'd stopped moving, his arms on either side of her body to keep him from falling on top of her, his face buried in her neck.

"That was…That was…Wow," Cooper panted, lying beside her, an arm draped over her.

Too in a daze to respond, Maya only hummed in agreement.

A few minutes later, he stood, walking into the bathroom and returning with a towel to clean her up. When he tossed it to the other side of the bed, she asked, "So, round two?"

Later, after they'd wrung each other dry, Maya lay on her back, Cooper on his side beside her, tracing his fingers along her thighs as he smiled down at what he'd done to her stomach.

"I like seeing you like this. Covered in me. I want everyone to know you're mine."

She threaded her fingers with his. "Let's see how Colton reacts tomorrow, and then we can talk about telling the world. I'm still worried about the charity."

He nodded thoughtfully. After a few moments of silence, he confessed, "I thought I could keep you off my mind when I only saw you a few times a year. But now that I get to spend time with you, I don't want it any other way. You've been dancing around my head for far too long. I want to show you how special and wanted you are, sunflower. I want you in every single way, from the morning kisses to the evening dates to this." He gestured at them and the liquid pooled on her belly from after their third round. "I want you."

The words brought a smile to Maya's face, and she grabbed the towel to wipe herself up a little bit. Cooper took over, gently removing all his spend from her body.

"I want that with you too, Coop. I want it all with you. I want to sit in your section at Sabers games and cheer you on. I want to kiss you when I first wake up and make breakfast with you before we start our days. I want to spend every free second I can with you."

Cooper tossed the towel to the floor, pulling her so she lay on top of him, tracing lazy circles along her waist. "I know I need to go back to my room for the night, but I want to lie here for another few minutes."

Maya beamed, her world suddenly so vast, and all she wanted to do for the rest of her life was explore it all with Cooper by her side.

A terrifying concept when she remembered the distance that divided them.

Chapter Thirty

Cooper

*B*ang. *Bang. Bang.*

Someone was pounding on the door, and Cooper was not happy about it in the slightest. He used the arm slung around Maya's waist to pull her closer to him, nuzzling his face in her hair and praying that one day this could be his every day.

Minus the door banging.

Maya began to stir, and Cooper squeezed her once, whispering, "Shh. They'll go away."

She sat up quickly, displacing him. Cooper's eyes blinked open, taking in the dimly lit room. What time was it? It couldn't have been later than six.

Then he remembered he'd agreed to lift with Colton this morning. And that Colton had probably found his door open and him gone.

Maya was already standing, shaking him from the other side and pulling him off the bed. "Coop!" she whispered urgently.

"Get in the bathroom and close the door. Hurry. And take your clothes."

Cooper quietly groaned, grabbing the clothes she thrusted at him and pulling them on. Maya was still naked from her waist up, and he groaned again at the knowledge that he'd been robbed of his chance to kiss every inch of her body this morning. By his damn best friend.

"Maya, what's taking so long?"

"Sorry!" she called, worried eyes pleading with Cooper. "Just putting on a shirt." She must've realized she actually needed to put on a shirt, because she searched frantically, running past him into the bathroom and picking one up off the ground.

Cooper held in a laugh at the state she was in but put up his hands in surrender and began walking to the bathroom when she fixed a glare on him. He stepped behind the bathroom door and listened to them speak.

"Hey, Colt! What's up?" Her voice was far too high-pitched, and if she was going for subtle, she was failing miserably.

Cooper hadn't realized his heart was pounding until both the Beaumont siblings were silent for a second.

Hiding in his best friend's guest bathroom after sleeping with his sister was quite possibly the *worst* way for Colton to find out about them.

"Can you come out here for a sec?"

"Oh! Sure. What's up?" she asked again, only slightly less suspiciously. Cooper watched her close the door, but it was slapped back open, like Colton had placed his hand on it.

"And tell Cooper he can come out too. But he better be fully clothed and not say a goddamn word."

Maya let out what sounded like a squeak, and Cooper closed his eyes, grimacing. "What! Is he not in his room? Maybe he left early."

All this because he'd fallen asleep and forgotten to go back to his room.

"I will come in there," Colton threatened.

Cooper cleared his throat, trying his best to keep his expression neutral as he walked toward his best friend. Colton led them into the living room, where Lucia was clearly trying to hide a smile behind her mug of tea.

"Good morning!" she exclaimed, chipper, like her boyfriend wasn't about to massacre Cooper in her beautifully furnished house.

Maya wouldn't even look at him, her wide eyes fixed on the couple in front of them. Colton placed a hand on Lucia's waist like she would steady him, then turned to face them, anger and hurt clear on his face.

Maya let out a forced laugh. "This? See, this I can explain. Cooper knew that I...um...He knew that I needed help getting out of my—" She cut herself off with a sigh. "How did you know?"

"Cooper and I were supposed to lift this morning. When I found his room empty, I figured he'd left, but the cameras around the house showed nothing, which made me wonder."

Even when he was being short with his sister, he was still kind, his eyes softening when he looked at her. He knew Colton's anger lay mostly on Cooper's shoulders, and Cooper hated that they'd allowed this to happen.

They'd been hours away from telling Colton anyway. How stupid did he have to be to forget to close his door, or to get up a little early to get back to his room?

Though he couldn't say he regretted waking up with Maya in his arms.

Lucia set her mug down on the dining table, a smile still clear in her eyes, even if her face barely showed it.

"Somebody better start explaining, and if it's Cooper, my fist has a mind of its own."

Maya stepped in front of Cooper, her hands up like she'd protect him. "Woah, okay, woah. There's no need for threats, Colt."

Colton looked at her expectantly.

"Okay. So, we're...seeing each other. It's new, but with the time we've been spending together for the charity, we've gotten a lot closer. And I can only speak for myself, but I like him a lot and...it's been really good." She turned and smiled at him, and Cooper smiled back, shoving his hands into his pockets to prevent himself from reaching out to pull her into a hug.

He knew Colton didn't want him to speak, but he also wanted to affirm what Maya was saying. "I like you a lot too, sunflower." He looked right at Colton, hoping to convey sincerity. "And it *has* been great."

Lucia let out a short squeal, clapping her hands twice like she was overjoyed at the news.

"Luc," Colton groaned exasperatedly, the anger disappearing when his eyes landed on her. "United front, remember?"

"Oh, right, right." She cleared her throat. "Bad, very bad. We do not condone this at all." And then she winked at them.

Cooper chuckled, but Colton's eyes were fixed on him.

"Why didn't you tell me when I asked what was going on with the charity on my birthday? I asked if you were okay working on the charity, and you didn't think to tell me you were sleeping with my sister?"

Cooper shook his head. "No, nothing had happened then. We—It wasn't like that then."

"So, when? How long have you been hiding this from me?" Colton looked between Cooper and Maya.

"About a month. Since the gala, but we'd been moving toward it for weeks before that," Maya responded quietly.

Colton scoffed. "I asked you why there was so much speculation about you two right after the gala. Why didn't you tell me? You had so many opportunities to just talk to me about it. I don't..."

Maya began to say, "Colt—"

"Wait, is this why you've been skipping team dinners and not coming with us to Frankie's? Why you haven't been coming to lift with me as often? Why I've barely seen you the last few weeks, even when you're in town?" Colton took a step back, right into the dining table. "When I asked you if you were looking to date someone specific, you *lied* and said *no*. Why wouldn't you have just *told* me?"

Cooper could see the hurt clear as day on his friend's face, and it only made him feel worse. Lucia's hand rubbed circles on his back, her eyebrows furrowed like her analyst brain was working overtime.

God, he was the worst friend.

"We were planning to tell you today, actually." Cooper looked down at the floor as he spoke, ashamed.

"It's my fault. I wasn't ready for anybody to know about it," Maya chimed in.

It was a lie, and one that Cooper was about to correct, but Colton forged on like he hadn't even heard them. "You guys lied to me. So many times. Maya, I can almost understand. She doesn't tell me about what's going on in her life much, and I can see how she'd be uncomfortable bringing it up, but you? You're supposed to be..."

Guilt slammed through Cooper so hard, he almost staggered back. He knew what Colton wasn't saying. They'd been friends for *years*, and Colton had taken Cooper under his wing when Cooper had first joined the Sabers.

This was the worst way to repay him.

When Cooper looked back up, Colton's jaw was clenched, and he looked angry, hands balled by his sides.

"And to find out about this *in my home*? For you to come here and keep it a secret in my own house..." Colton shook his head, seeming to only grow angrier by the second. "Look, I'm glad you're trying to change things for yourself, I really am. But I've known you for years, and I don't see this ending in any way but Maya getting hurt."

Cooper's heart lurched into his throat, and tears pricked his eyes, both angry at being spoken to like he was using Maya and hurt that even his own best friend felt this way about him. For Colton to talk to him like this proved Cooper's own best friend didn't even see him.

And maybe it was his fault for only expressing his feelings once, and only recently, but he'd be damned if he was going to let his past change how things were going with Maya. She was far too special, and maybe his prior mistakes meant he didn't deserve her, but he was willing to do *anything* it took to get to the point where he did.

Cooper had deleted every single woman out of his phone who wasn't his family or Sabertooths affiliated months ago, the moment he'd realized he wanted to be with her. He'd put countless hours into funding and helping with a charity, fielded *endless* press questions, to *show* he was capable of more.

And he would continue to do anything she needed for as long as she needed because he needed *her*.

Maya's hands were on her hips, and Cooper knew she was about to defend him, but he needed to clarify how far Colton would take this. Cooper set his hand on her shoulder, stepping beside her.

"So what does that mean, exactly? You want to dictate who I can and can't see? Who Maya can and can't see?"

"Well, I'm sure as shit not okay with this. Maya is my little sister, man. You know how much she means to me. You can have anybody you want. I just...She's already had one guy who wouldn't commit and...she's not temporary, you know?" Colton's voice broke on the word 'temporary,' like the betrayal was starting to sink in and overwhelm the anger.

"I *know* tha—"

"*Enough.*" Everyone snapped their heads to look at Maya. "Stop talking about me like I'm not in the room. And stop talking about Cooper like that. You of all people should know not to talk about him that way, especially when he's expressed that he wants to change. Cooper deserves far more credit than you're giving him. Just because he has a past doesn't mean it has to be his future."

Hope bloomed warm in Cooper's chest at her words. How she made him feel seen, like a real person and not some prized horse or dirty animal. Maya was speaking up for him in a way he had never expected anyone would, and something like love wiggled inside of him, opening its eyes and taking a breath.

"Mai, I just..." Colton sighed.

"I know you mean well, but stop treating me like a child. I'm a grown adult who can date who I like. If I want to spend my time with him, I will."

Colton hung his head. "I know you're right. I—I think I just need some time to think."

Cooper was already moving toward the front door at the words, his hand brushing Maya's as he went. "I'll go."

Giving his friend space to process this was the least he could do.

Before Cooper closed the door behind him, Maya appeared. She placed her hand on his cheek, her thumb rubbing soothing circles.

"I'm sorry," she whispered. "I'm so sorry. This is all my fault. I'll fix it. I'll apologize. It's my fault."

Cooper shook his head, taking both of her hands in his and kissing all ten of her knuckles. "Don't apologize, sweetheart. It's not your fault. I was the one who wanted to hide it at first. He's right to be upset with me. He needs to process, and then I'll apologize to him." He kissed her forehead. "I'll talk to you later, okay?"

Maya nodded, and Cooper called a car, at a loss for how the best twelve hours of his life had gone south so fast.

Chapter Thirty-One

Cooper

As if the day couldn't get any worse, George had called and left a message telling Cooper he was still working on his contracts. At least he'd mentioned he was pretty sure he'd be getting offers from all three teams, but it was no great joy to know Cooper's future was still so uncertain.

Driving around the city hadn't burned the feelings from the morning away like he'd wanted, so he'd gone to the Sabertooths facility, grabbed a pair of boxing gloves, and was now taking his feelings out on one of the punching bags in the gym.

Cooper couldn't remember the last time he'd voluntarily used the punching bags without being told to by a fitness coach, but he needed to expend the pent-up anger and anxiety that had been building in his chest since he'd heard Colton banging on Maya's bedroom door.

It had been months of worrying that he wasn't good enough for Maya Beaumont, and today, despite all he'd been trying to do to prove himself worthy of her, it was clear once again that he was not.

He wasn't even mad at Colton. He had no right to be. Cooper had been *notorious* for sleeping around for more than six years, since he'd joined the Sabers, and even long before then in Alabama. A couple of months of trying not to be linked with multiple women and working on a charity were not going to wipe that away.

The fact that he'd believed his reputation could be erased so easily had been imbecilic.

Sweat dripped down his face, and he swiped it away with his forearm angrily.

All because the old Cooper would have rather taken any form of love, no matter how fleeting, than none at all. How pathetic had he been?

Maybe it'd take six years to prove himself. Maybe he never would.

Cooper was glad he'd left his phone in the locker room because a voice in his head, the self-sabotaging one, told him to see if there was anything new about him on the news. He'd gotten better about it. He'd noticed he rarely checked when he was with Maya, or even when he was thinking about her.

But the reminder from Colton that he wasn't good enough had him sliding back down the hill.

Right as he began another set, he heard someone clear their throat behind him. When he turned, Colton was standing in a

Sabertooths sweatsuit, hands in his pockets and an unreadable expression on his face.

Cooper nodded in greeting, pulling the Velcro gloves off and tossing them to the side, wiping at his face with the T-shirt he'd discarded on the floor when he'd first started working out.

"Couldn't find you at any of your usual spots."

Cooper huffed a laugh. "My house and the beach?"

Colton nodded, taking a couple of steps closer. "That conversation didn't go the way I'd hoped. I was so blindsided, I just marched over to her room without even working through what was going on in my head."

"For what it's worth, I'm sorry. I didn't feel I was worthy of her and wanted to prove myself to you before we told you. Prove myself to the world, really."

Colton rubbed his eyes. "Well...I appreciate that. One of the things that hurt most was figuring out that this is why you kept dodging me this past month. It felt like you never wanted to be in the same room with me for longer than a few minutes."

Cooper ran a hand through his hair. "I hated keeping secrets from you. I wanted to tell you, but I wanted to show I deserved her first. And knowing I couldn't tell you made me uncomfortable. I thought as long as we didn't talk, I couldn't really be lying to you. I know that's dumb."

Colton looked away, almost haunted. "I just don't want you guys to feel like you can't talk to me, you know? I care about you both so much, and I'd hope you'd feel like you can. This is just a wake-up call, I guess."

"I really don't want you to take it that way. This was on us for not coming to you with it sooner. And you have every right to feel hurt and get angry with me. I really am sorry. I hadn't seen her in over a week, and I missed her. I just needed to see her in an environment where we could be us and not two friends who run a charity together." Like he'd *tried* to be last night. "But, that also isn't an excuse for keeping it a secret. We should've been honest."

"What did she mean by 'me of all people'?"

Cooper cleared his throat, looking anywhere but at his friend. "You and I kind of talked about how I was trying to make a change. I'd wanted to for a while, especially after seeing how happy you and Lucia are. But when I started getting closer with Maya, that want got stronger. I worried that you, her, the world wouldn't see it how I did, given my reputation. That there would be assumptions about who I was with outside of her. And I never wanted that for her.

"I never wanted to be like *this*." He gestured at himself. "I never wanted to be the guy people would be insulted to imagine dating their sisters. I've been trying to outrun that image since I left home. But that didn't work out so well for me, and when I came here, I just kind of fell into it again. It was clear nobody believed I was made for relationships." Cooper shrugged. "I don't know, it just seemed to stick. Why go against what everyone seemed to be able to see in me? If everyone thinks that way, it's got to be right, right?"

"I'm sorry, Coop. I'm a shitty friend for insinuating you're still like that. Especially after what you told me earlier this month. If I'd known it went this deep..." Colton shook his head. "I'm just sorry. I was hurt that two people I trust and care for so much were sneaking around behind my back, in my *house*"—Cooper grimaced at the reminder of how far his betrayal ran—"and I didn't think before I spoke. I know you won't hurt her. I've seen how you take care of her."

Something cleared in Cooper's head, and breathing got a little easier. "Thank you for saying that."

Colton held his hand out for a handshake, and Cooper pulled him in for a hug, laughing when Colton pinched his nose at the smell.

Colton asked, "So, Maya, huh? You really like her? I mean, what's not to like? But..."

And wasn't that the truth.

"I really do. She's changed everything for me. Makes me feel like I'm a human being and not what everyone sees me as. She makes me feel like I'm worthy of her, even when I don't see it that way. I want to be that person for her, who she leans on when she's struggling."

Cooper wanted to be that and more. He wanted to be there on her good and bad days, her happy and sad days. He wanted to hold her when she cried, tell her how strong she was and how proud of her he was. He wanted to show her how capable she was in every way, even when she didn't want to see it, even when she didn't feel worthy. He'd meant it when he'd said he wanted it all.

If he ended up staying in Charleston, there was always the opportunity to expand On the Line to another city. If he ended up in Los Angeles, he could see his Sabers friends during the offseason. And if he didn't end up with any offers, maybe he'd retire early and move to her. No one really played much into their thirties anyway.

Colton smiled at him. "I'm glad she's been the person I should've been this whole time. She always has been the best of us Beaumonts."

Cooper wrapped an arm around his friend's shoulder, his other hand patting his chest. "Well, you're not so bad yourself. Second best, but by a small margin."

Chapter Thirty-Two

Cooper

Maya had been absolutely correct when she'd told Cooper that if she ever wore jeans and cowboy boots for him, he'd be unable to take his eyes off her. The jeans she'd chosen for the night were a *very* snug fit, and the boots she'd purchased only a few hours ago on King Street looked like they needed to be seriously broken in.

She'd even worn a small cow-print top that made her stand out as an outsider, but she didn't seem to mind that no one else was dressed like a caricature of a cowgirl.

Cooper snapped his eyes away. He and Colton had worked through their issues this afternoon, but Cooper didn't want to test his luck by publicly lusting after his best friend's sister.

A crowd of people had lined up ahead of them, ready to go.

"Alright, any of you know how to line dance?" Cooper asked.

Maya, Colton, and Lucia all shook their heads. Colton looked ridiculous with a cowboy hat pulled low, trying to keep a low profile in a bar full of people who would probably recognize them in a heartbeat. Cooper did the same, but he knew he looked far more natural with it.

Cooper inclined his head toward where the line of people began kicking their feet to Copperhead Road. "Watch them."

They did as he said, and he added commentary. "See, it's kick, kick, kick, kick, then kick the foot up, kick the other foot up, then kick, kick, kick, kick," he said along with the music. Everyone in the line stomped, moving to face the left wall. "Stomp twice and start it again. Pretty simple."

"Elucidating, thank you." Maya rolled her eyes, a smile on her lips.

Cooper grabbed Maya by the hand and pulled her to the far end of the floor. She threw her head back and laughed as she stuck her feet out off beat, running into Cooper when she tried to stomp with the group. His hand landed on her waist to right her before he showed her again.

"I'm not the best dancer, as you can see." She laughed again as she tripped over her feet trying to hop and kick.

Cooper grabbed both her hands in his, and he instructed her quietly until she was finally on beat, even if she'd almost kicked him thrice. The smile she gave him was heart-stopping.

"You're perfect, sweetheart."

Her cheeks were red, either from the compliment or her body heating up.

A new song started, and a couple of lines in, the group of people yelled, "Honky Tonk!" with Brooks & Dunn, the name of the bar they were in. It took until the end of the song, but Maya finally had the basics down.

"You want to join the line?"

"You think I'm ready? Not gonna embarrass or insult you and your Southern roots?"

Cooper scoffed, pulling her into his side, glaring at a couple of men who'd been watching her a bit too closely. "You could never."

They hopped into line with the rest of the people, clapping their hands and stomping and kicking their feet, laughing together as they bumped into each other. Cooper stole a kiss between songs, and right before Watermelon Crawl started, Lucia joined them.

"Alright, I've been studying everyone the whole time, and I think I got this now."

"Hell yeah, let's go. Where's Colt?"

She pointed to where he stood, beer in hand and a frown on his face like he felt left out, even though it was his choice not to join them. Cooper chuckled as the line began moving.

Maya had started to get the hang of it, even if the rest of the line had changed up what they were doing. Her hair flew as she whipped her head each time they switched to a new direction, and as always, she was simply radiant, with a bright smile and an eager look in her eyes.

That feeling that'd begun to unfurl in his chest continued as he watched her while she danced, knowing how close he was to falling, teetering on the edge of the cliff.

He didn't care. *Bring it on.*

After a few more, the girls had to go to the bathroom, so Cooper grabbed a beer at the bar and joined Colton. When Maya and Lucia walked out, they were joined by a gaggle of other women, most of them circling Maya, who'd clearly made friends with them in the bathroom. She still had that brilliant smile on her face, and she turned it to him, stopping his heart again. Then she jumped into learning how to square dance.

Cooper watched her for a couple more minutes, trying to hold back a laugh at how she kept tripping over her feet and knocking into the girls who were too nice to say anything.

His girl was clumsy, that was for sure. At least on the dance floor. He'd spent hours the last couple of months watching her old matches, all of which proved that was nowhere near true on a tennis court.

Turning to Colton, he noted how his friend kept his eyes on Lucia, and even though he was still frowning, Cooper knew how happy Colton was.

"So, how long until you make her your wife? You waiting for someone else to sweep in and steal her?"

Colton turned that frown on him. "I need to find the right time. It hasn't really presented itself yet," he grumbled.

"Oh, shit. I was almost kidding. Y'all ready for that?"

"Hell yeah we are. But she doesn't want a long engagement." An almost smirk appeared on Colton's face. "Something about a guy she knew."

Cooper laughed. "Right. Can't imagine what that's about. Well, I'm excited for y'all. That'll be…"

"Different?" Colton offered.

"Not really. I don't think much will change. Y'all are already practically there."

"Yeah, I already got the ring actually, but…" He trailed off. His eyes were back on the dance floor, and he'd gone rigid, anger clear on his face. Cooper turned to look at what had upset him, and he saw a man standing over Maya, talking to her far too closely. Worse, the man had a hand on her arm, like he was trying to pull her into the line when she very clearly did not want the contact.

Lucia looked back at them with her eyebrows drawn, too far outside the group of people to do anything, though Maya's new friends were giving the guy an earful.

"Ah, hell," Cooper muttered, handing his beer to Colton, who seemed thankful to Cooper for what he was about to do.

He'd made it through the group of women who Maya had befriended in record time and placed his hat on top of Maya's long, black hair. It felt a lot like he was claiming her in front of everyone in that bar.

She looked up at him, relief clear in her face, and he hated that she was even in a position where she needed him to save her.

Cooper wrapped his hand around the man's arm the way he was to her. "That's enough of that."

The man glared at him. "Back off, man. We're just dancing."

Cooper turned to Maya. "You wanna dance with him, sunflower?"

She shook her head, still trying to yank herself from the guy's grasp.

"I think that there's answer enough, don't you? You'd better let go now." Cooper clenched his jaw when the guy didn't listen, moving his fingers to physically pry him off her. He shoved the guy for good measure, trying to create some space between them.

Cooper watched the guy ball his fist, readying for a fight. Cooper pushed Maya behind him, and right as the man came at him, the man dropped his fist, face slack.

"Holy sh—" The guy laughed. "You're Cooper Hayes. Holy *shit*." He turned to yell over the music. "Y'all, Cooper Hayes is here!"

The people around them turned to look at him in awe, and Cooper almost wished he could take his hat back, pull it low over his head, and walk out. But he nodded, smiling and waving as people began taking out their phones, disrupting the line. More and more people realized who he was, asking for pictures.

Colton was lucky. Cooper saw him against the wall, hat pulled low, Lucia at his side.

On his own then.

After a few minutes of waving at people for their pictures, he turned to Maya, who was smiling softly at him.

"Thank you," she whispered.

"You okay?"

Maya nodded. "I'm good."

"Good." He didn't reach out to grab her, not knowing how she felt about going public now. Just because they'd gotten through the conversation with Colton didn't mean she was ready to be in the limelight like this.

People continued chattering about the Sabertooths tight end loudly behind him, though the line was beginning to form again.

Maya looked up at him, her soft smile turning to a grin. She hooked her pointer finger through his belt loop and pulled him into her before setting one hand on the hat on her head.

And then she got up on her tiptoes and kissed him right there, for everyone to see.

It was so small. A kiss they'd shared plenty of times since they'd started dating. But the meaning was clear: she was his and he was hers, and she was claiming him as he'd claimed her.

Maybe he hadn't proved to himself that he was worthy of her yet, but at least *she* seemed to think he was.

Any lingering fears he had about this spiraling out of control or being anything like his relationship with Gabi disappeared, and he cupped her jaw and kissed her hard.

When they'd pulled away, Colton and Lucia were at their side.

"Local paps are gonna be here soon. We better go if we don't want to deal with that," Colton said quietly.

Cooper didn't take his eyes off Maya as he asked, "You ready to go home, sunflower?"

She nodded, taking his hat back and adjusting it on her head. "Hell yeah. Take me home, cowboy."

Colton made a noise like he was very uncomfortable, and Lucia laughed at him. Cooper looped an arm around Maya's waist, and they tried their best to shuffle out without attracting any more attention. It was moot, people following them out, but all Cooper could focus on were Maya's last words.

Home, she'd said, knowing they were going back to his house.

Damn it if that little critter in his chest didn't let out a cry and stretch its legs a little more. Maybe it was too late to talk about teetering on the edge.

Maybe he'd already fallen.

Chapter Thirty-Three

Maya

Striding toward a group of reporters posted right outside of her house, Maya decided never to go for a walk again. As if her face hadn't been plastered over the internet enough since she'd kissed Cooper publicly. She'd left the house half an hour ago, when it'd seemed the group had dissipated and found something more interesting to talk about.

Clearly, that hadn't been true.

Maya remembered the first article she'd seen, arguably her least favorite of the bunch, which talked about Cooper's long-term womanizing ways, speculating on whether his best friend's sister was "another notch on his bedpost or the woman to finally tie him down." She felt like she had the words tattooed on her forehead at this point.

She couldn't deny she'd been worried the first time she'd seen some variation of that, but the twinge of fear dissipated quickly when Maya remembered all Cooper had done that he'd never done for anyone before her.

Still, having to deal with this when he was thousands of miles away left their conversations heavier and heavier. If they could even catch each other. Since she'd seen him a week ago, they'd missed each other's calls almost daily until right before bed, when they were both exhausted from the day and could hardly talk.

At least she'd found joy giving lessons with the charity and to her other clients. And Maya had had a couple of game nights with Devi and her grandparents, which not only helped her feel more of a sense of community in LA, but also helped her get her mind off everything.

"Maya, can you tell us more about your relationship with Sabertooths tight end Cooper Hayes?" she was asked, as if anyone needed that introduction to know who Cooper was.

She kept her face neutral as she attempted to sidestep the group, noting a few who looked familiar. Probably because they'd been posted outside of her house for days, ever since she'd arrived back from Charleston.

One of them, a thin man with shoulder-length hair, sneered at her as he asked, "So you *were* given your role at On the Line because of your relationship, correct?"

Maya felt tears, maybe from anger, behind her eyes, and she finally walked up the concrete stairs to the house. This was exactly why she'd wanted to wait a while before they went public.

She didn't regret giving Cooper the assurance he needed though. She ached when she thought of the look on his face after everyone had realized who he was, when he'd had to find a place for his hands that wasn't on her. Maya couldn't bring herself to be sorry she'd kissed him.

A tear fell as she locked the door, and like her brother had grown a sixth sense for when she was about to spiral or needed comfort, Landon texted her.

He'd been checking in frequently since the news spread of her relationship, knowing the exposure was new for her and offering for her to stay with him to ease the stress for a few days.

Landon

> Doing okay? Still welcome to come stay here whenever you need a break.

Maya stared at the tips of a few strands of hair before wrapping them around her finger. She didn't want to put Landon out, plus she had so much going on in LA.

Maya

> Too many tennis responsibilities here, but thank you. I'm doing okay.

Landon

> Got it. Camp starts soon so I won't be able to come down much, but I'll see you for your birthday at the end of the month.

She didn't know what might happen with Cooper, especially now that June camp was getting started for him too, and she was glad for all the relationships she had with her family and friends near her.

Maya didn't bother to move from the door before she tried Cooper. He'd called her this morning before she'd woken up. She'd called when she'd woken up, before her walk, but he'd been busy, his phone sending her to voicemail.

She didn't know why she thought that would've changed within the hour. When his automated voicemail played, Maya sighed, dropping her head and tossing her phone a few feet away.

Maya missed him more than she could've ever imagined, and though she'd been keeping herself busy, she felt like Cooper was the one person she needed most right now with all that was going on.

Her phone buzzed on the floor, and she scooped it up, noting it was a call from Devi. "Hi!"

"Hi. I'm like a minute from your house, and I'm whisking you away to a birthday party to distract you from the evil media. Bringing you a lehenga to wear since I think we're about the same size. How long do you think you'll need to get ready?"

Maya laughed, wiping the few rogue tears from her face. Devi had been her superhero the last few days. "I just need a shower and then I'll be ready. Feel free to use the spare key. I'll hop in the shower now."

She ran upstairs, thankful she'd washed her hair yesterday after a short hitting session with Viola. Maya had gone to the center to work on additional transportation for On the Line, and since her wrist had been feeling better and Grayson had cleared her for light hitting, they'd decided to try it out.

Maya's shower only lasted a few minutes, and when she came out, Devi was sitting on her bed, an outfit waiting for her.

"Hi! I'll step out so you can put this on." They hugged briefly, and then Maya pulled the top and skirt on. Luckily, her cousin was almost as tall as her, so it wasn't too tight a fit. It was a vibrant blue with gold sequins dotting the short-sleeve blouse and striping down the long skirt. She didn't know how to pin the near-sheer swatch of light-blue fabric, so she walked out of her bedroom. Devi's face lit up.

"You look stunning! Do you need help with the dupatta?" She pointed to the fabric Maya was clutching.

"Please. I don't know what I'm doing."

Her cousin smiled widely, already pulling a box of safety pins out of her small purse. "That's okay. That's why you have me."

Devi pleated the fabric, tucked it into Maya's skirt, pinned it, and then wrapped it around and pinned the other portion to her shoulder. As she did so, she said, "So our twin cousins Nani and Nana told you about, Aishwarya and Jaya, went home for the summer, which is why you haven't seen them yet. They're staying with a friend on campus for the next couple of days, so they'll be at this party."

"Are you sure it's okay for me to come? I don't want to crash someone's party."

Devi stepped back when she finished pinning the fabric. "It's a really wealthy woman who invites almost every Indian in the city. Nobody will even know. I've only met her twice anyway."

Maya nodded, and when she looked at herself in the long mirror in her room, she hardly recognized herself. The lehenga suited her better than she could've imagined.

"Ready?" Devi asked.

"Ready," Maya answered, grabbing her keys and a small clutch, finger rubbing against the old, faded tennis racket keychain her mother had given her. She'd found it after looking through some of her old bins from high school. It felt right that a piece of her would be with Maya tonight while she learned about their culture with their family.

Her brothers weren't quite ready to embrace a culture that'd been so separate from them all their lives. She'd talked to Colton about why he hadn't answered when their grandparents had reached out, and he'd told her that he'd felt responsible for how their father had treated Nani and Nana. Even after talking through it with him, Maya couldn't say she understood why he felt guilty, but he'd agreed that he'd think about working them back into his life over the next few months, and that was progress.

And now that she was on better terms with Landon, she wanted to help him and Colton mend their relationship. She wanted the three of them to enjoy their culture and family together. They needed more family, especially as their father continued to be pushed out of their lives.

It only took a few minutes to get to the hotel where the birthday party was being held. Maya watched groups of people around her age walk in, women dressed in lehengas and men dressed in something Devi called kediyu. Maya hadn't even stepped foot in the ballroom and she was already learning so much.

Her finger ran over the keychain one more time before she put her keys into her clutch and walked arm in arm with her cousin into the noisy ballroom. At the front was a stage, DJ equipment mounted and a couple of beautiful women whispering to each other, a microphone in one of their hands. Vibrant tapestries of sequined curtains fell from a vaulted ceiling, the beat of the music reverberating around the large room.

They were a little late—which Devi claimed meant they were perfectly on time—so large clusters of colorfully adorned people already covered most of the floor. If Maya thought she had a lot of friends, this was on a whole other level.

Devi was already waving at a bunch of different people who had turned to look at them. Two women, only a year or two younger than Maya and Devi—who looked nearly identical save for their hairstyles and the outfits they'd chosen—approached them with big smiles.

"Maya, these are our cousins Jaya"—she indicated the one with shoulder-length hair—"and Aishwarya. They're your mom's brother's children. This is Kavya Aunty's daughter," she continued the introduction. Maya couldn't say she really remembered these cousins, but they both leaned in to hug her, and she felt welcomed even further into the family.

"Hi," she said tentatively.

"How have you been?" the one with long hair, Aishwarya, asked.

Before Maya could respond, Jaya interjected, "Wait, Maya? You're the one who plays tennis, right? Mom always talks about you. She loves watching you play."

Where Maya's smile might have once faltered, it stayed. "Yes, that's me. I've been doing well, thank you for asking. This is my first time at an event like this, so I'm excited to be here."

Aishwarya waved her hand dismissively. "Oh, we'll introduce you to everyone! A lot of our friends from Crestview are here tonight, and anybody we don't know, I guarantee you Devi does."

Devi laughed. "It's true, I probably do."

Maya smiled through so many introductions, and though she considered herself deeply extroverted, even she was wiped after trying to remember every one of their names. When Devi saw her face, she threw her head back and laughed.

"Don't worry. Nobody expects you to remember all these people's names. It's taken me *months*, and even still, I have to stand in the circle and listen in case they say a name I've forgotten."

Maya laughed with her as they walked to the tables on the side of the room laden with one-bite Indian delicacies, none of which looked familiar to Maya. She followed Devi's lead, enjoying every single one as her cousin named them. Dhokla, paneer tikka skewers, pani puri, gulab jamun. Each one made Maya want to throw as many of them in her clutch as she could and take them home with her.

They spent the next few hours mingling with Devi, Jaya, and Aishwarya's friends and dancing in a big circle, her cousins identifying all the songs the DJ played and giving Maya the titles of the Bollywood movies they came from. As the night ended, the four of them said their goodbyes and walked out together.

After getting their numbers, Maya hugged the twins, who were heading back to campus for the evening, and promised to see them at the next event. As she got into Devi's car, Maya marveled at how easily her cousins had embraced and welcomed her.

And how easily she'd forgotten about the shitshow that was awaiting her at home.

As if her cousin could read her mind, she asked, "Want to come over? I have at least ten Bollywood movies I think you'd like."

Maya thought about Cooper, who'd texted her an apology for missing her call and promised he would call when he got home. She knew he'd understand if she were busy, and she didn't want to miss out on experiences with others waiting for him.

"I have frozen margarita fixings too, if that entices you any further."

"I'm in."

"I knew that would clinch it." Her cousin hummed a song that'd played at least three times at the party and pulled out of the parking lot.

Despite the tightness in Maya's chest that'd developed over the last week of media terror and missing Cooper, she was excited.

Chapter Thirty-Four

Maya

The next day, Maya had physical therapy, two lessons, and a couple of hours of coaching with On the Line, so by the time she got back to the house, she was beat. Cooper had fallen asleep eating dinner the night before—something that made her both laugh and worry for him—so he hadn't called, but he'd promised to make it up to her in their video call this evening.

Maya showered quickly before eating some leftovers. She worked through emails as she ate, one from a tax attorney Devi had put her in touch with, a few from local coaches interested in helping with the charity, and an even larger number from families eager to get their children enrolled.

It was while Maya was finishing up the last of the tax paperwork that Cooper finally video called, right as the rays of sunshine in the backyard cast long shadows on the grass. She answered on the second ring, needing to hear his voice and see his face.

"Hi, sweetheart." Half the tension in her body melted away at his words.

"Hi, cowboy." Maya set the phone up against her water bottle so he could see her.

Cooper chuckled, and she saw his ceiling as he moved about. He looked tired, probably just getting home from a long day of camp, his body aching like it had been the past week. He'd told her June was the hardest month because his body got used to not practicing as much during offseason.

He lay down on his bed, an arm behind his head as he looked up at her. "I missed you all day. So much. Practice was a nightmare because I couldn't stop thinking about how badly I want to make pancakes with you in the mornings and drive you to get your disgusting ice cream with gummy bears every evening."

Maya huffed a laugh, saving her work and closing her laptop so she could focus all her attention on him. "Rude. And I could never eat ice cream every evening."

"Fine, just on the nights you want a sweet treat, then."

Cooper was too sweet for his own good, and Maya wished she could have him often enough that they could do all he said and more.

But that wasn't in the cards for them right now.

Maya smiled sadly.

"What's the matter?" he asked.

"Just miss you. And I worry I'm going to be doing a lot of that here for the foreseeable future."

"Yeah…" he answered, like he'd also been wrestling with the thought of that.

"Yeah."

"I don't know what to say, sunflower. I haven't come up with a solution that you'll accept yet, so right now, I *have* to be okay with the little I can see you. Because having you at all, even if it's mostly through video calls and texts, is better than not. I'd take a million days of only video calls if it meant I got to keep being with you."

Maya's eyes watered at the confession. "Coop," she groaned. "I feel the same way, but that's not sustainable."

"We'll figure it out. I know it's hard now, but…"

"It's only going to get worse. Once preseason really hits, we'll only get to see each other when I have time to travel to games."

"I can come every once in a while too."

Maya felt the well of her emotions open, and she fell right in, spiraling down.

Broadly speaking, their two options for staying together were for him to allow her into his space or for him to move his entire life for her, neither of which she felt comfortable with.

Maya wanted this to work out so badly, but she couldn't shake the feeling that it might not.

And if not, she'd have to be okay leaning on the community she'd built up in Los Angeles. Maybe she wouldn't be completely fine, but she'd get there.

The thought brought fresh tears to her eyes, and at her first sniffle, Cooper ran a hand through his hair, eyebrows pinched in concern.

"Sunflower, please don't cry. Please. I don't want this to be a sad call. I can see you're in your head. Let me help. Talk to me."

Maya swiped at her face for the second time today, sighing. "Why do you call me that?" She pushed her thumbs over her closed eyes to stop the tears.

"Sunflower?"

Maya nodded.

"Because you brighten up everything around you. You're brilliant and beautiful, and you have this air about you that just...lights up the world. And when I found you again here all those months ago, even with the grief of your injury, you immediately brightened up my sad, bleak, and boring life. You've made every single day since so much better."

"Oh, I—" Maya tried to respond but only managed a squeak as another tear fell down her face. "Sorry," she breathed. "I don't know why I'm so emotional. I think I'm just uncertain about the future."

His words gave her hope. Maya knew she'd probably spend the rest of her life wondering if he was getting tired of her, getting ready to leave, but at least she knew where he stood now. As long as she did all she could to prevent his wanting to leave, like being sure she paid him back for all he'd done for the charity, maybe they stood a better chance.

Maybe things with Cooper really *could* be different. Even if they had to be different across the country.

"How can I make the future feel more certain to you? What if we get matching tattoos? I'll get a giant *M* across my face and you can get a *C* on your left butt cheek since that one's my favorite."

Maya let out a watery chuckle, and Cooper laughed alongside her. She wiped away the remainder of the tears, sucking in a breath. Damn if he didn't always know how to make her feel better. "I want you. Ideally beside me, but in whatever form I can get."

Cooper's smile was wide and bright, and she wished she could kiss it.

After a few seconds of staring at each other with big grins, he asked, "Are the reporters still outside?"

"Let me check." Maya walked to look out the curtained windows to the front yard and sidewalk, where there were indeed a couple of reporters.

"Yeah," she called, walking back to the dining room. "One of them asked me if I have the job with On the Line because we're together."

His expression changed lightning fast, eyes angry, jaw tight. "Describe them."

Maya cocked her head but answered, "Shoulder-length dark hair, kind of pale, and—"

"Kind of thin and spindly?"

Maya nodded.

"Yeah, I know the one." His words were harsher than she was used to, though she knew they weren't directed at her.

"I'll be okay. They don't bother me when I'm in the house. I only went for a walk because I thought they'd left, but now I know better."

Cooper's face relaxed, marginally. "You know all those things they're saying aren't true, right?" He said it so quietly, she almost missed it. "You are so special to me, if I haven't made that abundantly clear, sunflower. You could never *ever* be a notch on my bedpost."

Maya had known that. She'd known it the minute she'd seen the article on her screen, only a split second of fear before she'd known how wrong it was.

Still, his reassurance was soothing,

"I know. You've never made me feel otherwise. I know it's different with us." She paused, realizing how he must be taking the news as well. Cooper had been trying so hard to change the narrative around him.

How did *he* feel?

"You know all those things they're saying about *you* aren't true, right?" she asked him the same question he'd asked her. "Who cares what any of those people think? The only people who matter are the people who care about you, and all of us know you're not like that. Don't let their boredom-induced speculation tear you down, cowboy."

Cooper's lips twitched, and she knew she'd done well. "Let's talk about something that isn't depressing before we sleep. Or are you planning to stay up longer?" he asked.

"God, no. I'm exhausted. I was just passing the time until you called so I could hear your voice."

They did their nightly routine together, him asking her to double check that all the doors and windows were locked before they brushed their teeth and slipped into their beds.

Maya set her phone down on her charger, her eyelids growing heavy.

"Have I ever told you when I knew you were going to change things for me?" The quiet confidence in his voice had Maya turning around to look at him on her nightstand.

"Don't think so."

"It was the first time we met, at Frankie's, when you were here for a few days before a tournament, I think. I knew Colton had a sister, but you'd been so busy with college tennis and then starting the tour that I didn't meet you until I'd been on the team a couple of years."

"Mm-hmm," she mumbled sleepily.

"You came to hang out with Colton, and I was lucky enough to be invited. He didn't want to be there, unsurprisingly, so he was at the bar, but you were out on the dance floor making friends with everyone around you. And I don't know what it was, something about the way you looked at me when I talked, like you really saw me, really cared to hear what I had to say, but I knew then that you were going to be different for me."

"Of course I cared what you had to say. Everyone should."

Cooper chuckled. "I was so scared that every birthday or holiday I saw you at, I tried my best to stay away. It was hard, and I usually failed. I always wanted to know more about what the tour was like, and every time I asked a question, you treated me like I was the only person in the room, even though I tried so hard to make sure we were never alone."

Maya yawned, trying to keep her eyes open, a smile slipping onto her face. "I always thought that was odd. How you used to leave the room with Colton if he was going to get something. Tried not to think much of it but..." Another yawn. "What changed on my birthday?"

"Your friends had gone to the bathroom, and when you begged Colton to come dance, he told you to take me instead. So, you did, and I watched you dance with the rhythm of a one-winged penguin."

"Hey!"

Cooper laughed. "It's true. It was adorable, and all I could do was hope your friends would come back because I really wanted to kiss you and I knew that was a bad idea."

"You should've kissed me."

"I'm glad I didn't. I wasn't ready then."

"Mm. And are you ready now?"

The words tumbled out of her right as she felt the edges of consciousness fraying, and as she fell asleep, Maya thought she heard him say, "More than you could ever know."

Chapter Thirty-Five

Cooper

It had been two weeks without seeing Maya, and missing her today had pulled his focus all practice. Not even the news that he'd gotten both an extension on his Sabertooths contract and an offer from both the Los Angeles teams had made him feel better. After an ice bath and a lengthy shower to scrub off the grass stains that somehow painted his body, Cooper tossed on his change of clothes to grab dinner with the guys and joined them outside the locker room.

It wasn't a team dinner tonight, just a few teammates who didn't have plans and wanted to have a chill evening before preseason really began to pick up. Plus, it was a good way to show the rookies some of the best places in town.

They'd chosen one of Cooper's favorite seaside restaurants and were led to the waterfront patio, the umbrellas already closed for the night as the sun began to set, a light breeze cooling them from the hot Southern summer air.

Ordering only took a few minutes, and then the table grew loud with chatter.

"Did you see the Palmettos last night?" Chris asked.

"Man, I was so pissed there at the end. Kelly told me to be quiet when I started yelling at the screen, but they were so damn close." Sam, an offensive lineman, slapped the table.

"At least they have another chance tomorrow."

"Yeah, but it's way more pressure this time."

TJ, their running back, groaned. "Baseball has to be the most boring sport known to man. You old geezers need to get into MMA."

TJ was a third year, only twenty-four, but most of the guys listening were in their late twenties or early thirties, and many of them rolled their eyes at him.

"What would you like to talk about, little guy?" Sam asked jokingly.

Devin planted his hands on the table, a wide grin on his face. "I know what we can talk about. My party next week."

"Devin, that's hardly news—you always have a party. Especially during offseason. If I drive by your house, I can almost guarantee something is going on," Chris, their center, retorted.

"Alright, then we can talk about Cooper. Who was the hot girl you were kissing a few weeks ago at the Honky Tonk?" a rookie called from down the table.

There were a few hoots from other rookies who hadn't yet met Maya, but most of the rest of the team, who knew exactly who she was, went quiet, looking to Colton like he would explode.

Colton's jaw was clenched. Cooper was on the same side of the table as him, so he could see his balled fist. Unfortunately, this talk wasn't unusual, and Cooper hated to admit he'd once been a part of it.

Never about Maya though.

Colton gave him the subtlest of nods, and Cooper knew that was Colton passing the baton, telling him it was okay to let the cat out of the bag to the few who didn't know.

"Colton's sister."

The rookies who'd hooted got loud, banging on the table and cheering before they saw Colton's glare and shut the hell up.

"Yeah, actually, I was gonna ask about that. No offense, but what the hell are you doing?" Devin asked. "I thought you were my fellow *can't be tied down* man."

Cooper ran a hand through his hair a couple of times. He couldn't tell a table full of his teammates that he'd run from the possibility of Maya since he'd met her, trying to keep his distance. But like they were destined, they kept getting pushed together until Cooper had been forced to admit what he'd known that whole time: he'd been running from the one woman he knew had the ability to change everything for him.

When Cooper didn't answer, TJ asked, "Or are you still like that and this is a casual thing? Are we all allowed to hook up with Colton's sister?"

Across the table, Chris shook his head like he knew Colton was about to snap. Instead, Cooper was the one who said, "*Don't*. Don't talk about her like that. It is *not* casual."

TJ held up his hands, almost hanging his head like he knew he'd fucked up. "Sorry, man. I was just messing around. Didn't mean anything by it."

Dinner conversation remained harmless from there, though the interest in women didn't fade. Devin spoke at length about all the things his waitress from a few nights ago knew how to do with her tongue. TJ joined with talk about the woman he'd hooked up with at a bar a few nights ago.

Cooper tuned them out for the most part, and when it was finally time to go home, he couldn't get out of there fast enough. Since his minor outburst at the table, his thoughts had remained glued to Maya. He was going to change into some sweatpants, turn on the TV to get some white noise going in his very quiet house, and video call the woman who'd taken up residence inside of his head and his veins.

Now that he had more clarity about his options, he was finally going to ask the question he'd been wanting to ask for weeks. They'd skirted around the topic a few times, and he was afraid he knew her answer, but he was finally going to come out and ask her to move in with him, even if only for the season. It was the only logical way for them to see each other often while he was playing. And if she didn't see herself being able to do that, he now had the choice to move to an LA team.

It only rang a couple of times before her beautiful face popped onto the screen.

"Hiii," she said, drawing out the i, a huge smile on her face. "Devi's here. We made margaritas, and I'm a teeny tiny bit drunk." She chuckled, and he heard a snort from somewhere behind her.

His spirits simultaneously fell and soared, sad not to be able to voice his question but overjoyed she was making friends with her cousin. He knew how much she'd wished her mom's family had been more present in her life growing up and after her passing, so the fact that they'd become such fast friends was heartwarming.

"I'm so glad, sunflower."

"I miss you," she whispered.

"I can hear you! Do you want me to go upstairs so you guys can have phone sex?" her cousin called from behind her.

More giggles, but Maya shushed her. "Don't listen to her. She's just jealous."

Cooper grinned at the state she was in, flushed cheeks, eyes half-glazed from the alcohol. "You're adorable. And I miss you too, sweetheart. You think you can swing a visit this week?"

Maya blew a raspberry, her features flattening a bit like the question saddened her. "I can't this week. We have new kids coming in for the charity and I have an event I'm going to with Devi. And I have to plan my birthday party."

"You're not planning anything. I'm already working with Lucia on it. You just have to tell me what your favorite bar is and we'll handle the rest," Devi yelled.

Cooper smiled even as his heart sank. Logically, he knew this was just how things were going to be. If they were going to do distance, he had to be okay with weeks like these, where the need to hold her squeezed his chest so painfully, he thought he'd stop breathing. It wasn't a feeling he wanted to get used to, but if it meant getting her, touching her, holding her, tasting her, laughing with her on the good days, he'd deal with it as long as she wanted him.

Just because she was building up her social life again didn't mean she was leaving him in the dust—something he'd had to remind himself every once in a while. She was nothing like Gabi, and he knew how much she cared for him. Cooper had seen it first-hand every time she'd stood up for him. In every smile and laugh and kiss.

"I understand. Are you still being bothered by reporters?"

Maya shrugged. "Less, but they're still outside the house or the tennis center sometimes."

Cooper remembered the conversation he'd had a couple of days ago with the paper where the man who'd been bothering Maya worked. He'd called the guy's superior the first time to report his behavior, but this time, Cooper had threatened a libel suit for what he'd been saying to Maya in an effort to run a lie of a story. If the guy hadn't been in serious trouble the first time, Cooper hoped he would be now. At this point, the only news he was checking anymore was about her, making sure no one was saying anything untoward.

If he weren't so upset about it, he might've been proud of himself.

"Have you seen that specific guy we talked about? With the long hair?"

Maya thought for a moment, looking above him before shaking her head. "No, I don't think so. Not the last couple of days."

"Good." Wanting to take the conversation away from something they were both unhappy about, he winked at her and said, "I can't wait for you to see your birthday presents."

He'd come up with a few ideas, all of which he'd purchased for her already. There were two wrapped, exquisite, and expensive gifts waiting to be packed for when he flew to LA next week. His mother and sisters had helped him with those and provided him with feedback on the third—and his personal favorite—gift.

Cooper had worked with her grandparents to get it for Maya, and he had tracked it every step of the way until it was on his doorstep. Now it stared back at him, unwrapped.

"Presents plural?" She narrowed her eyes playfully, barely able to contain the smile that quirked her lips. "You got a crush on me or something, Hayes?"

"Or something."

A big grin spread across her face like she couldn't contain it any longer, and Cooper knew in that moment that no matter how he and Maya ended, there was never going to be anyone else for him. Not from the moment he'd met her and had watched her tuck her hair behind both ears so he knew she was listening to him, hanging onto his every word in a way no one else had, like they were meaningful. Like his thoughts mattered. She saw the real him, the one so many others refused to see.

There would be nobody who could so perfectly make him laugh until his sides hurt, who listened to him even when he was being an idiot, and who made him feel simultaneously so human and yet so invincible. Nobody in this world could smile at him and make his chest tighten like this, his whole body tensing with the knowledge that her attention was wholly on him. Nobody in this world could brighten his entire evening, even the worst ones, just by giggling like he was the funniest person she'd ever met.

There would be no "after Maya."

Chapter Thirty-Six

Cooper

Maya's birthday evening ended with her, Cooper, Colton, Lucia, Landon, and Devi at her father's house. Her tennis friends hadn't been able to come, since they were all training for Wimbledon, but she'd seemed to be in good spirits throughout the night nonetheless.

The rest of their party was pretty intoxicated, so they each went to their respective rooms with Devi in the guest bedroom. Cooper's insides knotted at the knowledge that she was about to open his presents.

Maya closed the bedroom door behind them, then turned her sweet smile on him, and the knots intensified.

"Hi," she breathed.

"Hi, sweetheart. Did you have a good night?"

She nodded her head aggressively, that smile widening as her eyes flitted closed. "The best. Having everyone there was perfect and I think they all had a good time."

His hands were behind his back, holding the three gift bags, but he set them down on her desk and pulled her into his arms. She always cared what others were feeling, making sure everyone at *her* birthday party was having fun even when it was her night. That piece of her that'd always been the invisible child in her family showed itself in her actions every day. In every push for independence and quiet determination to work through her own issues.

He loved and hated it at once.

At least she'd been getting better about letting him take care of her.

"You want to open your presents now or wait until tomorrow?"

She hummed, thinking it through. Cooper knew she was tired, and after practice earlier that day and the time difference, he'd have been happy to sleep, but she pulled away just enough to look past him toward the desk.

"All three of those are from you?"

Cooper ran a hand through his hair before scratching the back of his neck sheepishly. "I might have gone a little crazy, but I wanted to make sure you had the best birthday."

Maya had taken her heels off, so she pushed up to her tiptoes and pecked his lips. "You being here made this the best birthday. You didn't have to get me anything."

He chuckled, seeing the way her eyes kept finding the bags, clearly intrigued.

"Why don't you open my favorite one tonight, and then if you decide you want to open the rest, you can."

Maya nodded, and he grabbed the handles of the bigger bag. Luckily, Lucia had made them look presentable, because on his first attempt, he'd done a pretty poor job.

They sat on the bed, the bag in her lap, and she weighed it a couple of times before she slowly pulled the light blue paper from inside. The knots traveled up to Cooper's throat until it was hard for him to swallow. He held his breath as she pulled the first part, a flash drive, from the bag.

Maya looked at him expectantly, so Cooper grabbed her laptop and began setting it up. When the video was up, he turned the laptop so she could watch.

In it, a young woman who looked a lot like Maya smiled at the camera, a very young and chubby Maya in her arms. They stood in someone's living room, the woman leaning against a couch.

At Maya's sharp inhale, he pulled her closer to him comfortingly.

"Ma," Maya's mother said, rolling her eyes at Maya's grandmother behind the camera. There was a smile pulling at her lips.

"Kavya, show, show," Maya's nani urged.

Her mother set Maya down on the ground, her feet landing on the tile floor, her chubby hands still in her mother's. Maya began trying to move her foot, like she was just learning to walk, and when she planted the first foot and started on her second, clapping could be heard in the background, others at the party cheering her on and laughing.

At the sound of her laughter, baby Maya looked up at her mother lovingly, a grin on her face like she was happy she'd made her mother smile.

"Great job, honey. Look at Nani, Maya." Maya didn't listen, still looking up at her mother reverently, and her mother laughed again.

Maya's mother picked her up and placed her back on her hip. "How old are you today? Did you turn one today? Can you hold up one finger?" She used the hand not supporting Maya to pull one of Maya's chubby fingers up, holding it up to the camera.

"Great job! Look at you." Maya's mother kissed her head, beaming down at the little girl in her arms. "Is it your birthday today? Happy birthday!" Another kiss.

Cooper paused the video. There were plenty more on the flash drive, but that was the part he'd wanted to show her. When he turned to the woman who'd upended his entire life so quickly, he saw the tears trailing down her cheeks.

Cooper set the laptop down and dropped to his knees in front of her, taking her head in his hands and wiping at the tears. "It's okay, sunflower. It's okay."

Maya pulled him against her, her body shaking. He rubbed her back.

"Whenever you're ready, there's something else in the bag. I want you to have the sound of her voice near you whenever you need it. You mentioned that you stopped hearing her in your head around the time of your injury, so this is just something I hope will help."

Maya choked on a sob, pulling more paper out of the bag. She pulled out a soft brown teddy bear, with a paw that read *squeeze me!*

She looked at Cooper with watery eyes, and he nodded. Maya squeezed the paw, and the sounds of her mother's laughter and the words she'd spoken in the video could be heard.

"Great job, honey." Then she squeezed again, and it was "Is it your birthday today? Happy birthday!" followed by more of her laughter.

A strangled sound left Maya, and she pulled the stuffed animal to her body, then Cooper, until she was clutching both of them like they were her lifelines, tears still streaming down her face. Cooper rubbed her back as she let it out, and he hoped these were good tears and not ones that meant he'd completely ruined her birthday.

After a few minutes, Maya stilled. Cooper stood and sat beside her on the bed, pulling her into his lap and dragging his knuckle under her eyes to wipe away the last stray tears. She stared lovingly at the teddy bear, and he asked softly, "Do you like it?"

Her beautiful eyes turned to him, and his heart skipped a beat or two. Even with reddened eyes and a mix of grief and happiness flickering across her face, she was the most heart-stopping sight. Cooper had never seen anyone so beautiful in his entire life.

"I love it," she whispered, hugging it once more and setting her head on his shoulder. "It's the best present I've ever gotten. This is...How? How did you do this? This is the most thoughtful present anybody has ever given me."

He kissed her temple before pushing a few strands of her hair behind her ear. "I had Colton put me in touch with your grandparents. Hopped on a call with them to get it all figured out, and they sent me the flash drive. Then I got it specially made. Oh, and..." He turned the bear in her hands so she could see the Velcro seam in the back of it. "You can put the flash drive in here so you have all the videos in one place. If you want. You can put it wherever you want, though, if you don't like that."

Maya traced the seam. "It's perfect, Coop. It's the most perfect—"

She cut herself off with a shuddering sigh, setting the teddy bear on the bed beside them, and then she swung her leg so she was wrapped around him in the tightest of hugs. "You are perfect. Nobody has ever done something like this for me before, and I can't even begin to thank you."

Cooper tightened his hold on her, pressing his head into her chest. "I'm so glad you like it, sunflower. So glad."

Maya let out a watery chuckle. "I *love* it. I can't believe you were worried about that. And that you got me more presents. I've never..." She pulled back and looked into his eyes, placing her hands on either side of his face and tracing his jawline with her thumbs.

"This is the most loved I've felt since before my mom passed away. I can't ever repay you for the feeling you've given me this evening."

"Oh, sweetheart." His eyes were watering at the words, both because he was glad he could do that for her but also because it hurt him to know that she'd felt so unloved for so long. He wanted to make her feel this way every day for as long as she'd let him. Like she put the stars in the sky. Like she was the gravity to his planet.

If she let him, he'd find a way to help her see how special she was every damn day for the rest of their lives.

Maya kissed him gently, her hands in his hair. It started sweet and slow, but then she began to move her hips against him, and he groaned into her mouth.

She pulled away and stared at him.

"Sweetheart." He panted at the friction, resolve fraying thread by thread as she set the bear on her nightstand and began unbuttoning his shirt, pushing the material over his shoulders. "Sweetheart, you don't have to do this. We can—"

"I want to," she said firmly, taking the shirt and dropping it to the floor. Then she was unlacing the red leather top that'd pushed her breasts up so perfectly all night. Her fingers pulled at the strings deftly until her toned upper body was exposed and the top had followed his onto the floor.

She continued like that, slowly removing every item of their clothing, and Cooper let her take the lead, not sure what she was ready for after the turn the evening had taken. When Maya had laid him down, completely naked, poised above him, her wet, warm pussy teasing the head of his cock, he said, "I just want to make sure one more time that *you're* sure." His words came out gruffer than he'd intended, and she cocked her head, her movements so feline.

Maya slowly slid down over him, and he had to bite down on a knuckle to quiet the throaty moan that left him. "Does this answer your question?"

And then she rode him, slowly at first before he felt her clenching at the pressure, and then she picked up the pace, her tits bouncing as their bodies slammed together. When her legs tired, he flipped her onto her back, thrusting in and out of her as he whispered every thought that flitted into his head. "You are wondrous" and "I have never known anybody like you" and "I'm so glad it's you in the end."

When she finally came, screaming his name into his mouth as he kissed her senseless, he emptied himself inside of her.

Cooper had known after the first time with Maya that things were different with her. It was the first time he'd allowed emotion, real emotion, into the bedroom with him. Not young, idiotic love, but real, unfiltered, uninhibited love that filled his every vein and artery, pumping through every single part of his body.

As she lay panting, he kissed from the tips of her fingers, up her arms, her neck, and down her other arm to the tips of the other hand's fingers. Cooper knew words wouldn't do justice to what he was feeling, so he hoped the reverence with which he held and kissed her told her what he couldn't.

When they'd cleaned up, he lay on his back, her on his chest. His fingers traced over the curves of her body, memorizing the feel of every inch of her.

"Move in with me." He had wanted to wait to ask her until another day, but now, as he lay holding her, knowing he had to leave tomorrow with no certainty about when he'd be able to see her again, the words tumbled out of him. Cooper hardly regretted them.

Her body tensed. "Coop..."

His heart sank. "If not in with me, come with me to Charleston. Just for the season. Just so I can have you nearby. I don't know when I'll be able to get away to see you, and I hate doing distance." His hand stilled as he pleaded, "Please, sunflower. *Please.*"

Maya's finger began absentmindedly tracing lines through the smattering of hair on his chest. "Cooper, I want that too. I don't like being away from you, and knowing that we may not be able to see each other as often terrifies me." His heart soared again, even as he knew there was something else coming.

"But I can't. You've already done so much for me with the charity and everything else. I've been saving as much as I can to repay all the starting costs, but I'm not there yet. And I certainly can't swing rent while I'm trying to save."

Confusion slammed into him. What did the charity have to do with anything? What he'd done for the charity had to do with his own personal issues, and now that he'd spent so much time working on it, he put in the time and effort because he believed in it.

"You don't need to pay me back."

Maya pulled away from him and sat up, leaning against the wall and crossing her arms. "Yes, I do. I'm not just going to accept all that money from you and not pay it back."

"Mai, what...What are you talking about?" he asked exasperatedly.

"I'm not a child who can't afford to pay their own way. You spent a lot of money getting the charity started and you paid for the opening gala on your own. I have to pay you back at least half of that."

"I'm not treating you like a child. I didn't agree to this charity because I think you're somebody who needs to be taken care of. I did it to help myself, and then when I saw how much you started to glow and how much change we could really make, I realized I *believed* in it, and that's why I'm doing all of this. And none of that has anything to do with why I want you to come with me." Cooper looked away toward the far wall. "I just want my sunflower by my side."

"I'm scared you're going to leave," Maya whispered, putting a bit more distance between them.

"I don't know what else I can do to make it clear that I'm here for as long as you'll have me."

Maya placed her head in her hands, her shoulders drooping, and he felt like an asshole for doing this on her birthday. "You *have* shown me that, Coop. But that's now. I don't know what that will look like in months or even years."

Cooper sighed, pressing his back to the wall beside her, wrapping his arm around her shoulder and pulling her body into his. "Nobody knows what the future looks like, Mai. I don't need you to pay me back, I just want you to…"

Maya moved her face from her hands and turned to look at him. "Want me to what?"

He'd been ready to ask her to love him, but it seemed too soon, even if he felt it vibrating inside him, between them. "I just want you, Mai."

Her head fell back to his shoulder. "I'm sorry. I don't want to fight with you. But I've built my life here. I've got the charity and Viola and the tennis community in LA, and my grandparents and cousins. Landon's nearby, and I'm just…I care about you so much. More than words can express. But I can't."

Cooper ran his hand through his hair, eyes fixed on the glow-in-the-dark stars hanging from the ceiling, trying to find his breath after the rejection. He completely understood her reasoning, but he couldn't help but feel that it meant they might never be able to come together and end the distance.

"Of course, sunflower. Whatever you want. I, uh...I actually have an offer from LA, so I could move here instead. If you want. Something we can talk about in the next few weeks before I have to decide." He didn't have to give his final answers until mid-July, three weeks from now.

"*No.*"

Something had constricted tight in his chest as the conversation had moved along, but it tightened to the point of pain at that word.

"I can't ask you to move your life for me. I would never forgive myself if you left Charleston, the team, your friends, everything, for me. You can't. I won't be the reason you uproot yourself."

He wanted to push, but it wasn't the time. It was her birthday, and this conversation was clearly draining them both.

"Okay, we'll figure it out," he said over the tendrils of hurt that flooded his body.

They lay back down and fell asleep like that, uncertainty hanging over their heads. Long distance wasn't the problem. Having no end in sight for the distance was.

The next morning at the airport, Maya said goodbye to everyone who'd flown out for her. She stopped at Cooper last, her eyes brimming with tears as he pulled her into his chest. They held each other tightly, refusing to be the first to let go until Lucia told them they needed to leave if they were going to make their flight.

Maya pulled away, nodding, wiping at the tears on her face.

"You're my favorite person," she whispered.

"And you're mine," he whispered back, her hair falling from his grasp as she took a step away.

Neither of them said the words he thought they were both ready to. He didn't want the first time saying them to her to be as he said goodbye. Instead, he kissed her forehead and joined Colton and Lucia, walking like a zombie toward airport security. The claws gripping at his beating heart squeezed tight, and he gritted his teeth.

This couldn't be the end of the line.

Chapter Thirty-Seven

Maya

The moment the tennis ball came off Maya's strings, she knew something was wrong. She'd just been cleared to hit at a slightly higher level without a brace, and she'd been so excited that she'd come to the tennis center during Viola's first free hour so they could practice.

But now, her wrist hurt more than it had before she'd started going to physical therapy in February, four months of work down the drain. Maya's racket fell from her hand to the court, and Viola rushed to her in an instant.

"What's wrong?"

Maya just stared at her wrist in disbelief. "I...I don't know."

It felt like it was on fire for another few seconds before the pain began to dull, though it didn't recede completely. Maya twisted it, wondering if it needed to pop, but it only ached more. She walked over to the bench, thankful she'd brought the brace just in case, and slipped it over the injured hand.

Maya was too upset to do anything but sit on the bench. The hot June sun beat down on her, sweat slipping down the back of her tank top.

It had been over a week since she'd seen Cooper, and his absence felt like a physical weight. They'd been so busy that they'd barely been able to talk on the phone or even text.

Maya had more lessons than usual this week, and she was using them to distract herself from thinking about their last conversation. She'd hoped training would clear her head like it used to, but now that seemed out of the question.

It all felt so *unfair*. And Maya was becoming more and more frustrated with it all as the days went on.

Cooper's offer had weighed heavily on her from the moment it'd left his mouth, and while she'd wanted so badly to say yes, there were so many reasons she couldn't.

The charity was thriving, she was *just* getting to know her grandparents and cousins again, she was near Landon. But even more than that, she was terrified that if she didn't do all she could to pay Cooper back for all he'd done, one day down the line, he might resent her.

And Cooper *had* done so much. He'd talked her through her injury and helped her see why physical therapy was so important early on. He'd helped her find the thing she was passionate about, and then when she'd needed help getting it up and running, he'd offered to put his hard-earned money into helping her. Cooper had given so much to support her, and knowing she'd never be able to repay him made her nauseous.

Plus, she loved the charity too much to abandon it just as it was getting its footing. She and Viola were looking to expand into other areas of Los Angeles now that more and more people were interested.

She couldn't move in with him, and he certainly couldn't leave everything behind to live with her here. Maya wouldn't allow him to do that.

So where did that leave them?

"You're awfully quiet today. Is it your wrist?"

Maya gave Viola a small, apologetic smile. "Just thinking."

"About your man?"

"Kind of."

Viola leaned back on the bench, intertwining her hands. "What happened?"

"I think we're struggling to figure out how to make this work long term. He wants me to move there, at least for the season, and if not that, he wants to move here. But I can't let him leave everything behind to move across the country just for me. I can't."

"So why not go for the season? You know I can handle running On the Line while you're not here. You can stay with him during the season, fly out occasionally, and come back during the offseason."

Maya shook her head. "He's done so much for me. It's hard to explain, but...I've been mostly on my own my whole life, you know? After Mom died, I became wholly invisible. I had to do everything myself, and any time I asked for anything, it felt like I was asking too much. Burdening everyone too much. So I pushed myself hard, worked myself to the bone to get to a point where I could go to Crestview on a scholarship. And then when I wanted to go pro, I spent every free moment on the court, morning and evening, so I could make it to the tour."

"You've had to do so much on your own."

"Exactly. It made sense to put my head down and stay out of people's way. Do my own thing. And then I got injured, and then suddenly I was a twenty-four-year-old living at my dad's house, the one thing I'm good at out of grasp forever.

"Cooper waltzes in and encourages me to take care of myself. My brothers come out to see me, worried about me, and I feel horrible for worrying them, because that's never been me. I'm supposed to be the easy one, the one nobody has to stress about. Cooper helps me find what I love and then funds it. Suddenly, when I've been so independent my entire life, done everything for myself, I've become this annoying little sister who everyone feels the need to take care of. I don't want to be in that position again. I don't deserve that kind of attention or care. I don't want him to ask me to move in with him for the convenience, and I certainly don't want him uprooting himself for me."

Viola sent her an incredulous look, but her voice was soft and sweet when she spoke. "What if he's asking you to be with him because he cares about you and wants to be with you, not just because it's convenient?" When Maya looked at her, her sympathetic smile nearly brought Maya to tears.

Maya shook her head. "I can't. I've just made something of myself here. And my grandparents and my cousins are here. I can't give up what I've built."

"Nobody's asking you to give that up, hon." Viola's hand landed on Maya's knee. "But maybe for once, you should let somebody in. Go for the season. Be with him and your brother and enjoy living with the man you love, and then when it's over, you can always spend the rest of the year here. You can have both."

Maya's head snapped to Viola at the word she'd said so easily, like it was so obvious. And Maya realized it *was* obvious.

Of course she loved him.

Cooper was the most selfless and caring person she'd ever met. He knew how to make her laugh and just what to say when she was sad. He'd made her feel more loved in the last five months than anyone ever had, besides her mom. Most of all, when she was wrapped in his arms, her heart rate could slow and she finally felt wholly safe.

He was her very best friend.

It made her dizzy just thinking about it.

But it was that selflessness that worried her. How far would he go, how much would he give her, until he realized that she didn't deserve it? That she wasn't worth it? What happened if she did move in with him and he realized these feelings, all this effort, had come about as some sort of sympathy for the situation she was in?

Before she could agree to do any kind of moving, she needed to pay him back. That was the clear next step.

Unable to play anymore, Maya moved to Viola's empty office, staring off into space, a bag of ice wrapped around her injured wrist and a rock heavy in her stomach.

It didn't seem to want to disappear no matter how much she pushed and prodded at it.

Chapter Thirty-Eight

Cooper

Practice ran later than Cooper would've liked, so he ran home to grab a sweatshirt and met Colton and Lucia at the beach as the sun set. When he found their secluded little area, a tray of cheese and crackers between them, Cooper set out his blanket and sat, taking in the lights of the city coming off the water.

"Hi, Coop." Lucia smiled sleepily.

"Hey, Luc. Am I that late? I assumed y'all ran home after practice too."

"Nah, Lucia's just been extra sleepy recently," Colton assured him, looking her over with a worried expression.

Small waves crashed against the rocks that kept this section of the beach off most people's radar, the sound calming after a very hectic day. They'd had a lift, watched film, then done field work and more film. Cooper was still getting back into shape after the few months of offseason, and his body ached everywhere.

Or maybe he was just getting old. Being a professional athlete was one of the few careers where being twenty-eight meant you were ancient.

"How's Maya?" Lucia wondered. "She hasn't called yet this week. She must be busy."

Cooper nodded. "She's working on a potential expansion of the charity into more areas in Los Angeles."

"Is she thinking about expanding anywhere else? Say, across the country into Charleston?" she asked, not so subtly.

"Nosy." Colton nudged her.

"What! I'm just wondering how things are going with you guys."

Cooper's lips twisted as that piece of him that had been going through the motions of his life surfaced for air.

He missed her. There was no other way to say it. Cooper hadn't seen her since her birthday two weeks ago, and it sucked. They still texted every day as their schedules allowed, even if just to check in, and they tried to call before bed, but he couldn't help but feel there was just a sliver of separation that hadn't been there before.

"Wait, are you guys okay?" Lucia sat up, eyes wide. "That was an awfully long silence."

"Nosy," Colton hissed again. Still, he leaned in a hair, like he too wanted to know what was going on.

"I miss her. Doing distance is fucking awful. And…"

"And what?" Colton asked quickly.

"Now who's nosy?" Lucia grumbled.

"I asked her to move in with me for the season—or at least to move to Charleston—so we could be closer once things pick up since I can't really get away much."

When he looked over at his friends, he could see he had their undivided attention.

"She said she couldn't. And I get that, because she has On the Line to run and your grandparents and cousins she's just found again and Viola and all the kids. I just don't really know how we're going to bridge this distance ever. Colt, you and I talked about my offer from LA, and I volunteered to move there, but she shut that down because she doesn't want me to give up being so close to you guys and the team and my family. But if neither of us can be uprooted, where does that leave us?"

Cooper heard the anguish in his own voice, and when he caught the couple looking between each other, he knew they'd heard it too.

"You love her," Lucia stated quietly.

"Of course I do," Cooper said without hesitation. The words slammed into Cooper's chest like a hammer, and he let out a sharp exhale. He hadn't voiced it before, but now that he had, it was like he'd been struggling for air without even knowing it, and now he could breathe again.

"Have you told her?"

Cooper shook his head. "We don't get to see each other much. So often when I want to say it, I'm about to leave and not see her again for at least a week. I don't want to leave it on that note, and I don't want to say it to her over the phone. Plus, I'm..." He sighed. "I'm scared. Because if we don't work, I don't see myself with anybody else. I wouldn't even *want* to be with anyone else. I want this to work so badly, but more and more, I'm not sure how I see that happening if she can't leave Los Angeles and I can't leave here."

"Well, I don't know that you necessarily have to listen to her whole 'you can't leave here' thing. If that's what you want, then you guys should have that conversation."

Colton shook his head. "Maya is very serious about that, I'm sure. If there's one thing I know about my sister, it's that she has constantly been made to feel like she has to do things on her own. After Mom died, she needed someone, and Landon and I didn't do a good job of being there for her. I tried my best, but she needed a parental figure, and my dad made it clear from the beginning that he didn't give two shits about her. She'd never forgive herself if you left everyone you know here to be with her there."

Cooper had had a hard time piecing it all together when they'd talked about it on her birthday. She'd seemed resistant to move because she hadn't paid back the starting costs, which hadn't made sense to Cooper in the moment. But now, after Colton's words, it all became a little clearer. Was she worried about being a burden if she moved in with him? And if so, how could he change that?

"So that still leaves the question—how do we get to the point where we can live together, or at the very least in the same place, sometime in the near future? I don't know anybody who's done long distance for their entire relationship."

Lucia leaned into Colton almost subconsciously, and Cooper had to turn toward the water to stop the grip around his heart from squeezing too tightly.

She spoke softly. "Maybe you can find a way to split your time between the two places. She could expand On the Line to here, and since it would be local, I'm sure we could all find a way for the Sabertooths to help fund the new location. You could do seasons here and then during the offseason, you guys could be in Los Angeles with her family and friends. And she can always visit LA whenever she wants during the season."

Cooper's shoulders slumped. He knew Lucia was trying to help, but she'd basically come up with exactly what he had, and Maya had already nixed the idea, which put him right back at square one.

The waves continued to break against the rocky shore as the three sat in companionable silence, broken only by quiet small talk and Lucia's request that they keep eating the cheese and crackers so she *stopped* eating them. Cooper kept thinking through his options, though they seemed bleaker and bleaker the more he considered them.

Almost an hour later, Lucia was stretching and pushing to a stand.

"Okay, I know this peaceful beach enjoyment situation was my idea, but I'm tired as hell so I'm ready to head out. We should do it more often though—it's nice at night."

Colton began picking up their things, sending an apologetic look to Cooper. "I'll see you tomorrow. And I'm sorry we couldn't be more helpful. She might be my sister, but women in general are enigmas to me."

Lucia scoffed, setting a reassuring hand on Cooper's shoulder. "Colton, that is entirely by choice. But I am also sorry, and I really do hope you guys get it figured out soon. I've been rooting for you two since the Thanksgiving before Colton and I were even together, and I know Jenna and some of the other girls agree."

"Thank you." Cooper stood and followed them toward where they'd all parked. With one last wave, he got into his car and dropped his head onto the wheel.

He wondered if he should call his mother. Or maybe his sisters. He'd never really gone to them for advice, especially not with women, but he was desperate for help. Plus, since the last time he was in Tennessee, his relationship with his mother had improved greatly. She'd stopped texting him about his *duty* or sending him the news articles about himself that he'd been sidestepping like the plague. His father too, though he seemed to just be ignoring him.

Cooper debated it as he pulled out onto the highway.

Maya had trouble taking up space in other people's lives. So what did he have to do to convince her he *wanted* her to take up space in his life?

He needed to show up. Keep proving to her in his words and his actions that he was here for the long run and that he wanted her, needed her, in his life.

Cooper would tell her every day how much he cared for her, with his words and his actions. The next time he saw her, no matter how long they had to talk, he was going to tell her how he fully felt.

Colt and Lucia were right. He loved her, and if she didn't even know that, how could she know he didn't see all of this as some kind of obligation? He had years worth of trauma—created by others who made her feel that way—to undo, and the least he could do was tell her his feelings.

Maya had made him feel seen in a way no one else ever had. Rather than ignore his past or see him as a trophy or someone to use for financial gain, she saw it all, knew every piece of him and showed him how much she cared about him. All of him.

To the point that he'd stopped getting the urge to check the news about himself when he was with her, because she made him see how much what others saw didn't matter.

Cooper continued down the highway, almost on autopilot. When Maya's name flashed across the screen of his car's dashboard, his heartbeat picked up.

It was earlier than she usually called, just past dinnertime for her.

He answered the call immediately, hearing blood rushing in his ears.

"Sweetheart, are you alright?"

In the shakiest voice he'd ever heard from her, she whispered, "Somebody's in the house."

All at once, his heart stopped.

Chapter Thirty-Nine

Maya

Someone was definitely in the house. And Maya was pretty sure she knew who it was.

She dialed 911, breathing in and out deeply. Did she try to get into a suitcase? Hide behind the door and hope the person didn't notice? The moment she'd heard the thump downstairs, she'd turned off the lights, grabbed her pepper spray, locked her bedroom door, and run into the closet.

"911, what's your emergency?"

"I think there's somebody in my house," Maya whispered.

"Okay, sweetie. Can you give me an address?"

Maya relayed it, even softer than the first time she'd spoken.

"Just a second, okay? Stay on with me while I get the word out."

Maya nodded like the woman would be able to see her. Adrenaline coursed through her as she considered how she could make herself more inconspicuous.

"Are you still there?"

"Yes," she whispered. "Please hurry."

"We have a unit en route, okay, sweetie? They should be there in just under five minutes. Stay hidden if you can, okay?"

"Okay," she breathed.

Maya felt so stupid. She should have trusted her gut. When she and Devi had been out to eat earlier that night, they'd been approached by the creepy reporter who'd been bothering her the last few months, claiming Maya had gotten him fired. After they'd left, Devi had offered to stay the night, but Maya had said no despite feeling uncomfortable. Now she stood in her closet, unable to find a place to tuck herself into in case whoever was downstairs found their way to her room before the police got to the house.

She picked up two of her biggest suitcases and propped them up, trying to make them look haphazardly pushed in rather than meticulously placed. Maya pushed her hanging clothes out of the way, stepped over the suitcases, and then pulled the clothes back so that when she sat down, she had a wall at her back and side, a suitcase in front and beside her, and clothes above her.

It was the best she could do.

And even though she hadn't wanted to worry him, she knew this could very well be her last chance to talk to Cooper, so she dialed his number.

"Sweetheart, are you alright?"

His deep, velvety voice filled her ear, and that alone helped calm her.

She swallowed over the stone in her throat. "Somebody's in the house."

Cooper was silent for a second, and she heard honking. She turned down her volume.

"Coop, I'm scared."

"Okay...okay. Okay," he repeated. "I know you probably did this already, sweetheart, but tell me you called the police?"

"Mm-hmm," she hummed quietly. "They should be here soon."

"Okay. I'm here. Okay, sunflower? I'm here. You stay on with me, even if you have to stay quiet."

"Okay." Maya hadn't realized she was crying until a tear landed on the hand holding up the phone. She tried to sniffle quietly, and Cooper made a strangled noise.

"Did you find a place to hide?"

"Mm-hmm," she hummed again.

"Okay, good. Good."

"Cooper, I just wanted to tell you in case anything happens and I'm not able to that I lo—"

"*No*." He sounded pissed. "Don't you dare, Mai. Don't you dare say it. You wait to tell me how you feel until you're in my arms the moment I can get a flight to you, you understand me? *Stay. Safe.* You...you have to. Stay quiet and stay hidden." His accent was coming out more, like it had when they were in Tennessee.

A couple of minutes later, a loud crash sounded, closer to her than she'd expected, and she slapped a hand over her mouth to stop the cry that tried to push through. She bit down on her fist to prevent herself from panicking, willing the tears away. If she needed to fight, she needed to be able to see.

"Maya? Are you alright?" When she didn't respond, he went through a series of curses, each more vile than the last. "Where the fuck are the police?"

Footsteps pounded, and from the closet, Maya couldn't tell if they were coming in her direction or moving the other way.

Ignoring Cooper's earlier plea, she closed her eyes and whispered, "I love you."

And then someone crashed through her locked bedroom door.

Chapter Forty

Maya

Maya heard a grunt and then her name. "Mayaaaaa," the man called, and she was almost positive it was the reporter who'd been thrown out of the restaurant.

At some point in her shock, her phone had fallen to the ground, and at the muffled sounds of Cooper speaking, she ended the call. Then she set her phone on *Do Not Disturb* so it wouldn't ring if he called again.

Maya hoped he would understand.

She heard things being knocked around in her room. "I know you're in here," the man called in an almost sing-song voice that made her heart still.

This was really it for Maya. She could feel it.

Her closet door creaked open, and she could just make out a stream of light through her clothes. Was she breathing? She didn't think so.

When she heard her hangers being moved, screeching along the metal bar, she knew she wasn't.

Get it together. Breathe.

She shifted the cover on the pepper spray, situating her pointer finger on top of it. Maya felt the tears streaming down her face but was too afraid to wipe them away in case any movement let him know where she was.

He took a step inside the closet. More hangers screeched until the light shone on her and she could just make out his face. He didn't see her at first, and in the second Maya had before he did, she realized she'd been right.

The reporter who'd been bothering her for months was inside her closet.

And now he was scowling down at her. "Filthy little whore," he spat. "You little shits got me fir—"

Maya didn't wait for him to finish. Through watery eyes, she pressed down on the pepper spray trigger. His words turned garbled, and even as she felt the burn of it in her own eyes, she pushed him, hard. As fast as her shaky, adrenaline-filled legs would take her, she dashed out of the room and down the stairs, hearing screaming and pounding footsteps behind her.

The stinging of tears and the spray made it impossible for her to see straight, but she knew this house well, and she bee-lined for the front door, hoping one of her neighbors might be able to help her.

Maya slammed into something, hard, and when she felt arms around her, she struggled against them, smashing her head into the person's chest and screaming. Maybe the guy had brought a friend. And if so, she was well and truly fucked.

"Shh, shh, I'm a police officer. You're okay. It's okay." The words didn't register, and she continued struggling. "Miss, please." There was a crackling, like that of a walkie talkie.

All the fight left her when another man stepped beside them and yelled past her, "Police! Don't move!"

There was a scuffle and a thump.

"Let me go! I didn't do anything!" the reporter screamed.

Maya wiped at her eyes, taking in the uniformed man holding her gently. Behind her, the reporter glared at her.

What had she done to make this man hate her so much? Clearly he'd known her name and her address, so he hadn't mistaken her. But she had no idea what he'd meant when he'd claimed she'd gotten him *fired*.

"Is there anybody else in the house?" the officer let go of her, but his words were quiet.

Maya shrugged and shook her head uncertainly. Did this man have an accomplice? He hadn't been with anyone at the restaurant. "I'm not sure. I was alone, but he might have brought someone else," she murmured. Her words didn't sound like her own, so raw.

The other officer walked out, dragging the reporter with him. "I'll read him his rights outside."

When they were gone and Maya began to hear the blood rushing in her ears, the man in front of her started speaking. "Do you need medical attention?" Maya shook her head. Her eyes were already feeling better. "Okay. We're having a photographer come out to take pictures of everything. We do need a statement from you and then we'll be out of your hair, okay?"

Maya nodded wordlessly.

"Do you have any family or friends nearby you'd like to call to come be with you before we take your statement?"

Maya thought of Devi and her grandparents and nodded again.

"Okay. I'll be outside to take your statement when you're ready."

She thought it would be useless to nod again, so she walked upstairs to get her phone. Maya texted Cooper that she was okay because she was sure he was worrying. Then she called Devi and shakily told her everything.

"Can you tell Nani and Nana? And my brothers?"

"Of course I will. And I'm coming over right now."

Maya felt like grass, pushed and pulled in different directions by the wind. The officer asked her questions, and she answered to the best of her ability.

No, she didn't really know him. She'd seen him outside her house once, and maybe at a press conference for her charity months ago. Then she explained what had happened at the restaurant.

Sometime during her statement, her grandparents and Devi had shown up. They'd held her until she needed to pull away to breathe.

It all felt like everything moved in slow motion and so quickly all at once. The officers told her they would call when they had more information, because it seemed this was a targeted attack. They took pictures, let her know the house was no longer a crime scene, and took the reporter into custody. She'd called Cooper and let him know she was unharmed and with family and that she would call again in a few hours when things had settled down.

Maya hadn't wanted to worry him after all, and he'd been frantic when she'd first spoken to him.

She'd tried to eat something, some leftovers from her fridge, but she couldn't remember what. Devi had put the TV on, and she'd stared at it wordlessly, her cousin on one side and her grandparents asleep in the armchairs beside them. Even when Devi finally fell asleep, Maya couldn't.

It was like she was existing outside of her body, watching everything unfold.

Right around midnight, Maya jumped at the sound of the door opening, and there Landon stood like he'd forced someone to fly him out as soon as he'd heard the news.

Maya stood and walked into his open arms. She stayed there until she remembered that he'd probably been awake as long as she had trying to get to her.

She grabbed him a water bottle, and they sat on the stairs, not wanting to disturb their sleeping family. Landon's eyes kept straying to their grandparents, like he couldn't believe he was seeing who he was seeing. Even though she had grown closer with them, Landon hadn't been able to visit them the couple of times he'd come to see Maya.

"I'm glad they were here," he whispered, leaning back against the stair and rubbing his chest, looking up at the vaulted ceiling of the foyer.

"Me too."

"Do they talk about Mom a lot?"

"Only when I ask them to."

"Do you think...Do you think they'd be open to me coming by more?"

Maya leaned her head against his shoulder. "I think they'd really like that. And so would I."

Landon nodded. "I'm glad you're safe. When Devi called and told me, I nearly dropped my phone. I called like twenty people I knew trying to find someone with a private plane, and then when I did, I pestered the crap out of them. I would've flown that shit on my own if I had to."

"Thank you." Maya knew how difficult it was for Landon to express his emotions. Not like either of her brothers had ever been big on talking about their feelings, but Landon especially had kept them bottled up for as long as she could remember.

"We need to get you a security system in this house. I'm surprised Dad doesn't already have one considering there's no one permanently living here to keep an eye on the place."

"Yeah..." Though she hadn't thought much about anything since the break in, Maya's brain had certainly flitted across Cooper's offer to live together multiple times. She hadn't made much of a decision, or really one at all, but she kept it in her mind, continuing to mull it over.

At the very least, she needed a security system and to spend more time at her grandparents' house or Devi's apartment. But the thought of asking them to allow that made her insides turn. That was far too much to put on them.

"You can stay with me too sometimes. If you want. There's a ton to do in the Bay Area, and you wouldn't be far. I could show you Santa Cruz and all the silly sightseeing things in San Francisco."

"That's so sweet of you. Thank you."

Maya wouldn't take him up on his offer though. She already knew that. As badly as she wanted to spend more time with him, she would never be okay taking up that much space or time.

This whole situation was a nightmare. Without the adrenaline, Maya's body felt like it was shutting down. And every single person in her life was offering for her to move closer to them so that she would be safe. She couldn't do it.

Maya felt like she was twelve again, held together by Colton as her panic attacks ebbed and flowed. Taking up too much space in his life. In everyone's life.

She had never forgiven herself for what she'd put her brothers through. They'd lost their mother too, and rather than having the space they needed to grieve, rather than being able to work through their own issues and get a good night of sleep after their father forced them to work harder than anyone else on the field, they'd had to take care of her.

Maya began to get choked up, and she sat up, putting her head in her hands.

Landon placed a hand on her shoulder, but before he could say anything, she said, "I'm sorry. That you and Colton always had to take care of me after Mom."

Landon's hand slid around to her other shoulder, pulling her into his side. "There's nothing to be sorry for. I wish I had been there more. Colton was always in your room, helping you, and I felt like shit for not trying to do something too. I didn't know what to do, and you never seemed to need me, and I didn't want to intrude on something that seemed to be between you and Colton. But you needed someone, especially after Colton went to school, and god knows Dad wasn't there for you. You needed me and I didn't step up. *I'm* sorry. That it maybe wasn't enough."

"You were there. That was enough." She leaned into him a bit more. "I'm glad you're my big brother."

Having him back in her life these last few months, more than since she'd been a kid, had meant the world to her.

They dozed off on the stairs after talking a bit more, startled awake by her phone vibrating, her father's contact flashing. Maya stared at it groggily, noting it was almost seven in the morning, before looking at Landon. He was also frowning but shrugged.

"Hello?" she answered. Her father never called her first.

"Colton told me something happened at the house. Is there a lot of damage?"

The first words spoken to her since January, and they weren't even to ask if she was okay. He only cared about the house.

"I...I don't really know. Somebody followed me home and broke in through a window."

"Did you lock everything?" he asked accusingly. Landon bristled beside her, clearly listening in. He reached for the phone, but Maya shook her head.

Landon's relationship with their father was bad too. Maya didn't want him making it any worse on her account.

"Of course I did. I double-checked the doors and the windows before I went upstairs."

He sighed like she'd told him the worst news, not like she'd just said she'd tried her best to make sure this didn't happen.

"Great. Well now I have to come out there and make sure I take stock of the damage."

A headache speared through her left temple, and she rubbed at it. "I can do whatever you need me to."

The front door flew open, and dressed in a wrinkled sweatshirt and jeans stood Cooper, his hair in complete disarray and his beard longer than he usually allowed it. His eyebrows were drawn together like he was in pain.

Maya's world stopped when she noticed him.

"Dad, I got to go," she said. It felt good to be the one pushing him off the phone for once, rather than the other way around.

She'd spent so much of her life waiting for him to care about her, to give a single damn about her, and over the last year, she'd slowly realized that wasn't going to happen.

But Cooper did care about her. So she hung up and ran into Cooper's embrace, throwing her arms around his neck and burying her face in his chest.

Chapter Forty-One

Cooper

The moment Cooper walked into the house and saw her, the flight time calculations, the extra fees for the short-notice flight and first-priority boarding, the nearly five-hour drive to Atlanta, and the five hour flight to LA had all been worth it. Having her in his arms, wrapped tightly like she might fly away otherwise, settled his body in a way nothing else had been able to since her brief call during his drive.

"I'm okay," she'd breathed into the phone, and he'd sobbed like a baby because the thought of something happening to her had made him feel like every organ in his body was shutting down.

"I'm here now," he whispered into her hair over and over until he felt her body shaking with sobs. "I'm here. I've got you. I've got you, sunflower." Cooper nodded at Landon, who had an odd expression on his face. He noticed her family, who had clearly been woken up by his entrance, and tried to smile at them as he carried her into the study so they could have some privacy.

Cooper set her down, leaning her against the empty desk and scanning her body from head to toe to make sure she was really okay.

"Coop," she hiccupped, wiping at her face. "I'm okay, I promise. I pepper sprayed him and ran downstairs where the officers were. I'm okay. I just finally feel safe now that you're here." Maya pulled him up and wrapped her arms around his middle. "Safe enough to finally let out the emotions I didn't know I was holding in until now."

She continued crying softly, her warm tears seeping into his sweatshirt.

"I'm sorry I wasn't here. I'm so sorry."

There were a million and one things he wanted to say to her, but they were stuck in his throat, pushing hard against whatever was lodged there. His eyes watered as he realized how different this situation could've been if she hadn't called the police early enough or hadn't thought to grab the pepper spray.

His smart girl.

Cooper tightened his arms around her, rubbing her hair to comfort himself as much as it was to comfort her.

"You don't need to apologize. There was nothing anybody could've done."

Cooper pulled away, feeling the anger in his chest shift. He'd been so furious when she'd called, all at himself. He'd been worried something like this would happen from the moment he'd learned she was living here alone all those months ago, and he should've done something.

"Maya, I understand if you don't want to move to Charleston. That's fine. But I'm paying for a security system or a rabid dog or something because I can't do this. I can't be across the country not knowing whether you're okay or not at any given moment." He cupped her face, wiping at the tears that remained under her eyes and on her cheeks.

"You are the most important person in my life, sunflower. I need you to know that. I need you to see that there is nothing in this world that matters more to me than you being safe. So something has to change here because I..."

Words failed him once again.

"I'm sorry," she whispered. "And I'm sorry I hung up on you."

He moved his right hand to grip her chin so she looked into his eyes, his left hand slipping to her waist. "Don't you apologize. You did everything right."

Maya opened her mouth, and he shook his head. "Listen to me, sweetheart. The only reason I'm upset is that I wasn't here. I am not even remotely upset with you, okay? You didn't do *anything* wrong. I love you so fucking much, and the thought of anything happening to you made me crazy. Fuck, babe, after you hung up, I found a direct out of Atlanta and drove so fast, I made it there over half an hour earlier than my phone said I would. I'm sorry I didn't tell you the moment I realized it, but

I do. I love you, and I don't give a fuck that we live across the country from each other, I want to be with you."

Maya's bottom lip was wobbling, and he ran his thumb over it to steady it.

"And I want to live with you, Coop. I really do. But even if I didn't have the charity and my family here, I don't think I'd be okay moving in with you until I can pay you back for everything. If I can just give you back the starting money you put into the charity, I won't feel like I owe you, you know? I won't feel like there's something hanging over us. I want to pull my weight."

Cooper stepped away, hands dropping from Maya, one of them bracing himself on the wall. He swallowed over the fire in his mouth before he asked, "I need to ask you some questions, and I need you to think real hard before answering. Did you agree to date me because of some strange, clouded view that you *owe* me something? Do you feel obligated to be with me because I helped with On the Line?"

She was already shaking her head. "No! That's not what I'm saying. Of course not. I just want to feel like I'm pulling my weight. I've done everything on my own for so long that not doing the charity by myself was hard for me, so I told myself I'd find a way to pay you back. But that was entirely separate from us. I love you, Cooper. I meant it when I said it on the phone. I called you and wanted to tell you, wanted that to maybe be the last thing I *ever* did, because I meant it. I love you so much, and our relationship is completely separate from all of that."

"Okay, good. I thought so. So now, ask yourself this—if it's separate, why does it impact you coming with me to Charleston?"

"I—I—"

"Have I ever made you feel unwanted?"

She shook her head.

"Have I ever made you feel like you're a burden to me? Not you overthinking but anything that I've actually *done*."

Maya paused for a second before shaking her head once more, more vigorously. "No," she whispered.

"And I never will. I'm sorry that's how people have made you feel, but I'm not them. You have never, ever been a burden to me. Everything I have done has been because I care about you. The reason I want you with me during the season is because I love you so much that the thought of us being apart that long makes me want to quit football just so I can be with you. I want to be able to hold you after a crazy win or a tough loss. I want to fall into bed, dead tired, bruised beyond belief, and know you're right there with me."

The words fell out of him easily. He'd been thinking it through the entire trip here. She'd shown him that she was the one person who didn't care about anything but him, even as others, like his own family, were still learning. Maya had never wavered in that.

And now he would do the same for her.

Cooper ran his hand through his hair once, twice, a third time. "I need you to stop seeing everything so *transactionally*."

Maya sat on the desk, crossing her arms over her chest. "I don't know how not to see it that way. I mean, look at what's happening here. Look at all these people who left their lives to be here for me. Even Colton and Lucia are on a flight here right now, and all I can think about is how I've disrupted everyone's life."

All of Cooper's frustrations fell away at that admission. Right now, all he saw in her was the twelve-year-old girl who had lost her mother and needed someone to step in, and when they didn't, she'd felt she had to do life on her own. That people around her were temporary, and that she needed to be invisible so her problems didn't become the problems of others.

Cooper gently removed her crossed arms to clasp her hands. "Sunflower, that's what people do when they care. They show up. I'm sorry your dad is a piece of shit and he didn't show up for you after your mom passed away, and I'm sorry he didn't let anybody else show up for you either. But you have us now, and you're gonna have to get used to people caring about you. Because that's what love is, and that's what every single person in this house feels for you."

He bent down so his face was right in front of hers, his forehead touching hers. "I'm not going anywhere, and I'm gonna keep showing up for you. Every step of the way for as long as you'll allow me, I'll be here. We're a team, sweetheart. We don't do things on our own anymore."

Maya leaned in and brushed her lips against his. "Okay. I'll work on it." And then she kissed him like she hadn't seen him in months.

A few minutes after their conversation, Maya got a call letting her know she needed to go into the police station to answer a few more questions. Cooper joined her for moral support, though he wasn't allowed to come into the room with her. He sat just outside, staring straight ahead as he thought through their options, trying his best to keep his exhaustion at bay.

He was absolutely purchasing the craziest gate and security system for her. Whether at her father's house or wherever she lived next.

A commotion to his left startled him, and when he looked over, he noticed a familiar face screaming at him, his hands in handcuffs.

"You piece of shit! You're the reason I'm here." The man kept spitting the same words out over and over.

Cooper blinked. Then blinked again. In all the craziness, he hadn't thought to ask *who* had broken into her house. Now, as he looked at him, anger, red and hot, pulsed through him, shoving that exhaustion away.

The man's mousy brown hair was a lot longer and greasier, and he looked different without his evil grin, but it was most definitely the reporter who'd needled Maya during their first press conference, who'd shown up to bother Cooper after the gala in Charleston, and who'd been sitting outside her house after she'd kissed Cooper at the Honky Tonk.

So threatening a libel suit against the paper he worked at had worked then.

Cooper stood, walking toward the door through which Maya had gone to talk with an officer. Another officer, whose desk was right next to the room, looked up at him.

"Hi, I think I might have additional details about the break-in at the house on Sunnyvale Avenue."

The guy stood and knocked on the door, and after speaking with the other officer, Cooper was allowed to go in. Maya looked at him, confused.

Cooper explained it all. How after the press conference, when Maya had been so brave and that reporter had kept questioning about their relationship status, he'd called and left a strongly worded message for his boss. How the man had traveled all the way to South Carolina to ask Cooper his dumb questions. How after the man had asked Maya if she'd gotten her job with On the Line because of her relationship with Cooper, Cooper had threatened a suit. And how the reporter must've lost his job because of it and seemingly took that out on Maya.

Maya decided she wanted to press charges, and she was given information on how that would proceed. After the officer told them they were free to go, Maya whirled on Cooper in the parking lot, arms crossed.

"What happened to us being a team, huh? You want to tell me about how I have to let you be on my team and let you take things off my plate or help me with the charity, but you didn't even tell me about this until after the fact! What, it only applies to *me* telling *you* things?"

Cooper raised his hands in surrender. "Mai, I'm very sorry. You're absolutely right. I should have told you. I thought I was handling it. I just wanted to make sure he left you alone after he treated you so poorly."

"*Us*. He treated you poorly too."

"Okay, yes. I just wanted his boss to know how he treated *us*." He'd definitely only cared because it'd made his sweet and bright Maya upset, but he'd give her this.

Now he was pissed at himself because it was his fault for putting her in this situation. If he'd kept his mouth shut or done a better job of protecting her, she would have never been in danger.

"You should have told me. No more secrets. No more doing things on our own. Those were your words."

Cooper nodded. "Agree completely. An oversight on my part that will not happen again."

Maya rolled her eyes. "Stop talking like that and get in the damn car, you big idiot."

She'd been down all day, stressed about the situation and clearly still shaken up, but with that sentence, Cooper finally let himself smile.

His sunflower was back in full bloom.

Chapter Forty-Two

Maya

By the time Maya and Cooper got back to the house, Lucia and Colton were there with the rest of Maya's family, and both of them embraced her for minutes until she wiggled free and assured them she was okay. They apologized profusely for not getting there sooner, but they'd used Colton's connections to get on the first flight out of Charleston. Maya began playing the role of hostess, grabbing stuff from the fridge for people, until Colton set his hands on her shoulders and asked her to follow him.

Maya took in the rooms her family had made every effort to clean up, almost like new, though she knew if she looked up toward her room, she'd still see a splintered door. She followed Colton into the study and sat in the wheeled chair. He looked like he had something serious on his mind, so she waited for him to speak.

"Maya, it took me a lot of thinking recently to realize that you've always been so scared of letting other people take care of you. Or maybe scared is the wrong word, but hesitant to allow it." He paused, his hands fisting into the pockets of his pants. "If that's because of what happened after Mom, then I want you to know that being there for you my senior year of high school were some of the best moments of my life."

Maya was startled by the admission. "You had just lost Mom too though. You needed someone there for you, and instead, you had to come home from hard-as-fuck practices—I'm sure wishing for sleep—and make sure I was okay. You talked me through panic attacks for months."

"Yes, and it occurred to me that you think I viewed taking care of you as a duty or responsibility, and I can't allow you to keep thinking like that. It was a *privilege* to help you work through your panic attacks. The time we spent counting your stars as you figured out box breathing and orienting yourself to the world was the only time I really had to grieve Mom. It was my one reprieve from football, football, football. It gave me a purpose I *wanted* to fulfill."

Maya's eyes burned with disbelieving tears. "I don't understand."

Colton looked at her meaningfully. "The nights I rocked you to sleep and helped you through your attacks were the nights I felt worthy of being your big brother. I never did a very good job before Mom, and I honestly didn't do a good job after, especially since I left for Crestview so quickly, but those few months where I could help you were the ones that made me feel worthy of calling myself your brother."

"But Dad told me I was taking your focus away from football and I needed to stop crying over something that had happened months before. He said you needed to sleep and you didn't have time to help me like that anymore."

Colton's jaw clenched and he sighed, closing his eyes. "I should've known it was his doing. That's why you stopped asking for help?"

"You didn't feel that way? That I was pulling your focus and you didn't have time to coddle me?" she asked, repeating her father's words from that night.

"Never. Not once. I always want to be there for you whenever you need it. I'm sorry you ever felt otherwise."

It was like the shattering of a glass wall around her. A dam broken.

The tears came and kept coming, and she let Colton hold her until there were no more left to cry.

And for the first time in twelve years, she let the people who mattered most to her take care of her and worry over her as she sat beside them and enjoyed having them all in one place. Devi found boxes of old board games, and they sat around the dining table, cycling through them for hours. Her grandparents held her, telling them all funny stories about her mother. Landon made sure she was well-fed. Colton and Lucia worked on getting the rest of the damage in the house fixed and a security system in place immediately. Devi quoted their favorite sitcom with her and made everyone their drinks of choice.

Cooper never left her side.

Seeing how they'd banded together, how Landon and Colton especially made an effort with their family, healed something in her she hadn't known was broken.

Maybe they were there to take care of her, and maybe this had disrupted their lives, but it seemed like a worthy disruption.

It wasn't easy to displace years of feeling like she wasn't allowed to take up space in other's lives, but she did her best.

Maya stole a fry from Cooper's plate, tossing it into her mouth and ignoring his faux annoyance. Everyone else had flown back or agreed to go back home after a couple of days of making sure she was okay, but Cooper had gotten a few days off from football to be with her.

He had finally convinced her to try a new restaurant to get her out of the house, which was incredibly thoughtful. She hadn't known how much she'd needed to leave until she was sitting across from him, listening to the waves and the chatter of other patrons. It was something to get used to, but she found she enjoyed being taken care of, especially when she'd spent such a long time forcing herself to be independent.

"I don't want to leave On the Line behind. I feel like I'm abandoning my baby," she said like it was a brand-new thought, when in reality, they'd been over this ten times at least. She and Cooper had talked about his offers and had decided the Sabers were the better option, which meant figuring out their next steps.

"Sweetheart, if I have to tell you one more time that I've already talked to the Sabertooths' philanthropy department and have gotten funding for a new branch all but approved, I'm going to come over there and give you the loudest, wettest kiss right here on this boardwalk for everyone to see and hear."

Maya laughed harder than she had in days. "But still, even if I can start a new one there, what about—"

"You know damn well Viola can handle the Los Angeles branch. She'll absolutely kill it, and she'll be ridiculously excited about it too."

She smiled at his newfound ability to read her mind. "Should I bake her cupcakes that have tennis balls on them and ice the top with letters that spell out *be my LA director*?"

"You can bake? You wear so many hats."

She grinned. "You should see my collection."

Cooper winked. "I plan on seeing it plenty, in my house."

"What about my lessons? I've been making a lot of money by coaching rich people around here." Her flare-up seemed to be over. She hadn't noticed the twinge of pain in her daily life, and Grayson had said it was a good idea to get back to it.

"Luckily, I'm rich and I want tennis lessons from you. Coach me."

Maya rolled her eyes. "Cooper."

"Fine, I'll find a few rich friends who want to learn, okay?"

Her grin widened. "And what about my family? How am I gonna be okay living so far from them?"

Cooper chuckled, shaking his head. She'd asked all these questions multiple times already. "Well, lucky for us, planes exist and you can visit them whenever you want."

"What about during offseason? Will we live in Los Angeles or Charleston?"

"You can live wherever you'd like, sunflower. Once I retire, I'll go wherever you go. We can have two houses. We can have a million houses wherever you want, I don't care." His face grew serious. "But they will all be decked out with a state-of-the-art security system."

Trying to lighten the suddenly serious mood, she asked, "And how will I repay you for all of your generosity with these million houses?"

He grinned from ear to ear, like he'd caught her.

"Move in with me. That's the only repayment I'll take."

"And what about in a few years?"

"What do you mean?"

"Will that change down the line? What if you want something more?"

"Maya, Maya, Maya. Now you've gone and done it." His grin grew more mischievous. "The only thing I'm gonna want down the line is you kissing me at an altar and maybe one day giving me some ridiculously athletic children." He took her hand in his gently, squeezing once. "But only if you want those things then."

Maya's heart skipped three beats hearing him talk about a wedding and children. She knew they weren't ready for it now, but the thought of it sometime in their future excited her.

She obviously had to keep pushing him though.

"You know, if you think about it, we've been dating for less than three months. What will you say to the people who will ponder that? About how it's a *little* fast to be moving in together?"

"I'll say fuck them. I'll say we've known it's us for longer than that. And then, if that's concerning to you, I'll buy you the house next door to mine so we can have space apart and time to ourselves whenever you want. Or a tiny bungalow all the way across town from me. Whatever you want."

"Coop, I don't deserve th—"

"You deserve that and more, Maya. I didn't understand the meaning of going to the ends of the earth for someone, but now I know that's not even a strong enough way to describe what I'd do for you. To keep you feeling safe and loved."

The part of Maya that hated taking anything from anyone writhed in pain at his words, but she knew with him, it was nothing but the truth. He wanted to give her all these things simply because he loved her.

"I'm going to be making tons of dough coaching tennis to your rich friends. I can buy those things for myself."

"I know you can. I'm just trying to sweeten the pot here. As long as I get you with me during the season when I can't travel to see you, I will do anything you want."

"What about—"

"Sunflower, if I didn't know better, I would think you're coming up with all of these flimsy and debunked excuses because you don't want to live near or with me this fall."

She smiled, tossing another fry into her mouth. "I guess it's a good thing you know better."

"So you'll come with me to Charleston?"

Maya sat and stared at him for a long minute. She'd already made her decision after she'd asked these questions the fourth time, but she wanted to see him squirm a little.

He didn't. He knew her answer already too.

"Fine. But you're doing all the heavy lifting with my boxes."

Cooper rolled his eyes and scoffed. "Like that was ever not the plan."

Quietly, she said, "Colton and Landon agreed I should take the pictures on the wall. I don't know if I see myself ever living in my dad's house again after everything, and we thought it would be good for someone to take them. They thought they'd be best in my possession, since nobody ever really comes to the house anymore."

Cooper nodded, leaning back and rubbing the back of his neck in a way that made his bicep bulge a bit. Maya tried—and failed—not to get distracted by it.

"Did you talk to them or your nani and nana about taking some of your mom's clothes?"

"Yeah. Colt and Landon don't care, and Nani and Nana said they're mine, they just want to look through them one last time."

She didn't know what'd happened when her mom had passed and why some of her things hadn't gone to her mom's parents. Maya had been too young to pay attention to any of that, and now she certainly wasn't going to ask her father, who couldn't care less about Maya or her mother.

If Nani and Nana said they were hers, she was taking them. And she would take her mother's journals too, because even if it'd been a year since she'd heard her mom's voice in her head, she still had the sentences she'd memorized written in her mother's handwriting and her lovely laugh and cheery voice in the form of Maya's favorite present.

If her mother was looking down at her or could somehow see her in whatever plane she was in, she hoped she was proud of her and her growth. Proud of her for all that she'd achieved on the tennis court in honor of her. Proud of her for clawing her way out of the well of grief after she'd passed, and again after her injury. Proud of her for learning how to let others take care of her, and how to allow herself to take up space when she'd gotten so used to being invisible.

And she hoped she was proud of her for the legacy she hoped to leave behind with On the Line.

None of it would've been possible without her.

Chapter Forty-Three

Cooper

Three weeks later, the day after the Sabertooths won their first preseason game, Cooper went through the motions of pool recovery, then watched some film and showered before meeting Maya at the entrance of the facility. She looked breathtaking, unsurprisingly, in a loose tennis dress, her long hair down and a folder full of papers in one of her hands.

Cooper hadn't seen her in two days, since he'd left for Minnesota for the game, though it'd felt like eons. Her smile was beautiful, and he took her by the hand and pulled her into an empty meeting room past the front desk, waving at the guy behind it.

Maya giggled as he closed the door of the dark room. "I should say hi to Colton before we go talk to the philanthropy department, right?"

"Screw Colton—we'll see him tonight for dinner." Cooper dropped his forehead to hers, taking her face in both his hands and kissing her deeply. After a few seconds, he pulled away and whispered, "I missed you."

Maya grabbed him by his T-shirt and pulled him back for another kiss. "I missed you more."

"You think we have time to have a little fun in here before our meeting?"

She shook her head, fixing her dress. "Definitely not. Krista's going to be expecting us any second now."

Maya had spent the last few weeks painstakingly putting together a proposal for the Sabertooths' philanthropy department in the hopes that they would be willing to create a board and provide funding to allow for a branch of On the Line in Charleston, with the potential to expand all over the country. Cooper had tried to be helpful, but it often ended in Maya telling him he was distracting her, or with them in bed.

Cooper knew she hated the idea of using his and Colton's team for better funding and exposure, but she was doing much better about accepting help, even when she wasn't completely okay with it. Often, she found ways to still be independent, because at the end of the day, she was his stubborn sunflower.

He was so proud of her.

Maya's hand slipped into his, and she led him out of the meeting room. She was almost bouncing, either with nervousness or excitement, as they waited for an elevator. If one hand wasn't gripping her proposal, the other in his, she'd probably be twirling her hair around a finger.

Cooper turned her by her shoulders to look at him. "You are going to be amazing, okay? You've spent hundreds of hours working on this, and you're already established in Los Angeles. They'd be crazy to say no, especially considering some of my teammates' charities they *do* help."

Maya sighed, nodding. "Okay. I'm just nervous because if I can convince them, this could mean big things for On the Line. Imagine an expansion into other states. That would be incredible."

"And she's going to see your passion and be excited to help in any way she can. What you're doing is amazing, sweetheart. Krista will see it."

"What *we're* doing."

Their eyes met, and they smiled at each other. When the elevator finally arrived, they walked in. Cooper pressed the level, and when he turned to her, Maya was pointing at the piece of paper sticking out of his sweatpants. Her eyebrows furrowed. "What's that?"

Cooper pulled it out of his pocket sheepishly. He held it up for her.

"Is that from minigolf?"

Cooper nodded. There, right below the eleventh hole, was a frowning face.

"You kept that?" She laughed. "Why?"

"It was the first conversation we had where…" He looked away from her. "Where I felt maybe we didn't just have to be Colton's best friend and sister anymore. I don't know. Something clicked for me then. Maybe hope." Cooper looked back. "I like to think it's good luck."

Maya's eyes searched his. "Hope," she murmured, then smiled. She pecked his lips. "You're the sweetest man in the world."

Cooper's chest constricted at the healing words. "Only for you."

When the elevator opened, Maya took a step back. "For professionalism," she whispered.

He pocketed the scorecard and they walked side by side into the philanthropy department, waving to Josh before heading down the hall to Krista's office.

Krista looked up from her computer and smiled. "Good afternoon! I'm glad you're here."

"Thank you so much for having us. I'm excited to talk to you about On the Line."

They sat in the chairs in front of Krista's desk. "Is that folder for me?" she asked, and Maya nodded, handing it to her.

"Wow, this is thorough," Krista murmured as she flipped through each page. It took her a couple of minutes, and Maya turned to look at Cooper nervously every few seconds. His smile never wavered.

Cooper was certain Maya's hard work would pay off. Like he'd said, some of his teammates had questionable charities that the department was helping with, so something of this magnitude that was already established and strong should be no problem.

"This is impressive. Everything I was going to ask for is here and more. You clearly know what you're doing, and based on how well everything is going in Los Angeles and the interest we've already received for a Charleston branch, I could absolutely see expanding into more cities in the country." Krista set the documents down. "I know we could've done this over email, but I wanted to meet you in person. Philanthropy can be life-changing, and I always want to know who we're working with before we do."

Maya was nodding enthusiastically, twirling her hair around her right pointer finger. Cooper bit back a smile.

"I'd love to hear what it's like on the court. What has running this charity meant for you?" Krista looked between the two of them, but they both knew Maya would answer.

"I spent most of my life playing tennis competitively, and it's been one of my greatest joys in life. It brought me and my mother together before she passed, and it helped me feel close to her after. It gave me a team to root for in college, great friends when I went pro, and it gave me a means to support myself in a nontraditional way. But honestly? None of that would've been possible if I hadn't been born into a privileged family."

Maya stopped twirling her hair, like talking about this elevated her confidence. "My best friend was born with almost nothing and learned early that she had to choose between a lot of things that I took for granted growing up. Food or clothes? Save money for her siblings or spend a little to pay for something she liked? She battled that constantly. Only because she made a friend whose parents were in the tennis world was she given an opportunity that so many others aren't.

"So, in many ways, this is about helping those talented kids break away from their life experiences and find something that they can use to support themselves and their families. For others, it's a great opportunity to give parents some reprieve for after-school care while teaching them a sport that they may grow to love. Making tennis accessible to lower income families is something that can help them, even in a small way. I love being able to be on the court and do what I love while also giving back to a community that needs it."

Maya finished, putting her hands in her lap, and Cooper's chest almost burst with pride for her. He couldn't believe he'd accepted the title of cofounder when she put so much love, energy and hard work into it. He wanted to give her a standing ovation for that, even though he'd known everything beforehand.

Because she spoke from the heart and she truly meant it.

Krista seemed to be thinking the same way, a smile curving her lips as she put her hands on the desk.

"Well, if I wasn't convinced before, you can bet I am now. Your passion is infectious, Maya. I don't have final say in these decisions, but I think this is the exact thing we're looking to help with right now. I'm going to give you some paperwork to fill out in the lobby and leave with us, and then my hope is that we can get back to you in the next couple of weeks. Is that okay with y'all?"

Cooper nodded. "Thank you for being so helpful throughout this process."

Maya nodded enthusiastically. "Oh, yes! I never got to thank you for all the invaluable information you gave me via Cooper when I was first starting out. I appreciate it so much."

Krista stood. "I'm just glad it went to such good use."

She handed them the paperwork she had clipped together and walked them to her door. They thanked her again, and this time, Cooper was sure Maya's bouncing was from excitement.

"You okay, sunflower?" he asked as they walked to the lobby.

"More than okay," she whispered back.

It took them a little over half an hour to finish the paperwork, even with both of them working on it, and when they finished, they handed it to Josh, who still sat at the front desk. When they were finally in the elevator, Maya breathed deeply, and Cooper pulled her into his side.

"You are wondrous. Brilliant. Passionate. Beautiful." He kissed her hair between each word.

"I think she liked it. I think...it seems like we have a good shot. I don't want to get my hopes up, but I really think there's a chance."

"Of course there is. Did you hear what she said? She was absolutely enchanted by you."

Maya leaned into him. "If this works out...I think I'd be so happy I could die."

Cooper squeezed her to him. "I would not appreciate that. I would like to keep you happy and *alive* until well after I'm gone."

"You are *so* old," she mused. "Won't be long now."

"The oldest. Soon I'll be playing geriatric football."

Maya snorted as the doors of the elevator opened onto the main floor, where Maya had parked. "That'll be the day. Imagine an old you and Colt running routes."

Cooper dropped his voice as they stepped out. "I think I like when you talk football to me."

"Too bad our meeting room is in use." She pointed to the small window of the room they'd been in less than an hour ago, where a light was now turned on.

"We have hundreds of empty rooms, sweetheart. You just give me the word, and I'll have you screaming in one in no time." Cooper kept his voice quiet as they smiled and waved to the guy behind the front desk of the facility.

Maya shoved him. "Inappropriate, Mr. Hayes."

Cooper grinned. "You like that last name?"

Her cheeks pinked, but she rolled her eyes, pushing the door to the facility open, the cool, air-conditioned air giving way to the oppressive August heat.

Once upon a time not so long ago, he'd been dodging away from women as they exited buildings because he was so concerned with what would be said about him or who he would be linked with. Now, he kept his arm wrapped around Maya's shoulders as they moved to the outdoor parking lot in search of her car.

Let everyone see how absolutely gone for her he was.

They could print what they liked. If Maya didn't care, no matter how often they tried to pin some ridiculous cheating allegations on him, he didn't either. Cooper hadn't even checked in weeks.

"Maybe tonight after dinner. I'll wear that dress you like." Maya looked back at him, shy, despite knowing what she did to him.

"I have never been tortured more than now that I'm with you."

"Would you want it any other way?" she asked, clicking her car unlocked.

"God, no. Never."

Maya turned, her back against her car. "Aren't you forgetting something?"

Cooper leaned down to kiss her, assuming that's what she meant, but her chuckle and hand on his chest stopped him. "No, cowboy. You drove here this morning for practice. Are you going to come to my apartment and leave your car here?"

He shrugged. "I haven't seen you in two days. I don't give a fuck about my car. I have plenty more at home, and I can easily get it later."

Maya kissed his lips quickly, just a peck, before opening her door and hopping in. "Well, then you have to be okay with me getting on the phone with the girls for a couple of hours while we figure out what we're doing when I visit them in Florida in December."

Cooper knew how excited she was to visit them. It was one of the many reasons she'd agreed to live in Charleston, especially during the season, since the women's tour was usually finished by mid-November.

"That's fine. It's time I get to know them better anyway." He walked around the car and jumped in her passenger side while she turned the car on, air conditioner blasting.

Once she got on the highway, she got a notification in her sibling group chat from Landon.

"Are you still flying to San Jose for his first home game of the season?"

When Cooper had talked to her before he'd left for Minnesota, she'd planned to meet up with her grandparents and Devi in Northern California to see Landon's game and visit some of the tourist sites her nani and nana wanted to see while they were there.

"Yes! I know Colton's going to be sad I'm missing your season opener, but Landon deserves some family support too." Her eyes flicked to his for a second before they were back on the road. "Will my geriatric football player be okay if I'm not in his box for one game?"

Cooper pretended to think about it, trying to hide his grin. "If we lose, I'll blame you publicly for not being in my box to support me."

Maya rolled her eyes. "I'll be sure to check the play-by-play every five seconds to see if you've scored."

"Well, in that case, I'll score two just for you." He reached for the hand that wasn't on the wheel, threading their fingers together. "Actually, I asked my family if they wanted to come. My sisters and my ma are coming to watch. Called them right after I called you after the Minnesota win, and Ma told me how proud she was of me."

It'd taken a few tries, but his mother had finally figured out the right things to say to him when they did their new weekly calls. His dad rarely talked during them, and Cooper wasn't sure he'd ever fully forgive him for not coming home or be proud of him for his accomplishments, but at least he wasn't being berated for being selfish anymore.

A win was a win, however small.

Maya squeezed his hand, turning her blinker on. "Coop, that's so exciting. I'm sad I'll miss them though."

"Oh, my mother was emphatic that she see you, so they'll either come early when you're still here or leave after you get back. She's very excited about it. Though, I must warn you, she's definitely going to bring up us getting married and having children."

She had practically been chomping at the bit when she'd learned Cooper had bought an engagement ring for Maya, though she'd been less than thrilled to learn he wouldn't be asking the question for a while.

Maya was still getting her footing in Charleston, and he wanted her to feel comfortable, live in their house together, before he proposed. He knew she wouldn't be ready until then anyway. Still, that hadn't changed the fact that he'd known from the moment he'd seen her after that asshole had broken into her home that he was going to marry her someday, if she let him.

"Don't worry. Nani and Nana have been asking the same thing. I keep telling them I'm waiting on you."

Cooper whipped around before he saw her playful smile. "Sunflower, you know damn well that the minute you're ready, I'm going to ask the question. Probably before you're ready, a hundred times, until I wear you down."

"You'd better."

Maya

TWO AND A HALF YEARS LATER

Maya pulled out of the tennis center parking lot, waving at one of the children she'd just finished coaching. She was already late to Cooper and Colton's retirement party, and if she didn't step on it, she was sure to get that specific look from Lucia that told her they would be having words. Kind, but very firm words.

Speeding down the road and then the highway, she made it to Colton and Lucia's house in record time, dialing the number so that she could be let into the ridiculous security gate that encircled their property.

Colton didn't mess around. Especially now that Maya's two-year-old niece was in the picture.

Half of the Sabertooths team spilled out of Colton and Lucia's house as Maya pulled into the driveway, even though there was absolutely space for all of them inside. While the team was generally saddened that they weren't in the conference finals, the watch party festivities were in full swing, and a bounce house was erected for the Sabertooths children on the large front lawn.

Maya jumped out of her car and rushed toward Colton and Cooper, who stood watching the inflatable house. When she was only a few steps away, Cooper noticed her, opening his arms for her to run into.

She'd seen him just this morning before she'd gone to the tennis center to coach for the day, but she'd missed him in the hours they'd been apart. He hadn't changed much in the few years they'd been together, his cowboy hat still worn proudly, jeans and tight Sabertooths T-shirt showing off the work he'd put into his last season.

Walking into his arms and being held by him felt like home.

"Hi," Maya whispered into his chest.

"Hi, sunflower."

"Happy retirement. Also, I missed you."

"Thank you. I missed you more."

She hummed in disagreement. "Well, I *love* you more."

Cooper squeezed her tight. "Say it again," he murmured against her hair.

Maya giggled. "I love you more."

Colton grumbled something that sounded an awful lot like "get a room" and playfully stomped toward where Lucia was putting little bows in her daughter Lyla's hair.

"Now you know how I feel!" Maya called after him. "And happy retirement!"

"Thank you!" He laughed over his shoulder.

"Good one, sweetheart."

Maya snorted at Cooper's sarcastic tone, turning in his arms to take in the late January day and all the people who were important to her and her family. Kids ran around screaming and chasing each other, chaotic in the best way.

She looked around for her father, already sure he wouldn't be here. Despite the fact that neither her nor her siblings had expressly cut him out of their lives, he had quickly become like a vestigial organ—existing as a semblance of a family member, though rarely appearing at family events and being excluded or asked to leave quickly when he inevitably erupted.

Plus, he was probably distraught that Colton was leaving the league in his prime.

"Are your mom and sisters here?"

Cooper set his chin on her shoulder. "Ma and the girls are inside with your Nana and Nani, fawning over the food and insisting on taking pictures of anybody and everyone who walks into the house." He waved his hand toward the opposite side of the yard, past the inflatable bounce house, where Devi and a teammate's wife stood talking.

Cooper's sisters had visited often, and Maya had grown close to them. His mother too. His father still wasn't the most present, and Maya imagined he was upset that Cooper's retirement had come and yet Cooper still had no plans to move back to Tennessee, but Cooper didn't seem bothered by it anymore.

"I'll go say hi. Has the game started yet?"

Landon, after spending so long in Colton's shadow, was finally playing in a conference final on the way to the championship, and Maya and her family couldn't be happier for him. Her brothers had done a lot of growing in the last year, together and separately, and now more than ever, Landon was becoming a shining star. He'd risen to be one of the top tight ends in the league, trading off with Cooper, much to Cooper's dismay, and he'd finally met a woman who could put him in his place.

"Not yet. Few more minutes and then we can go inside and watch with everyone."

"Okay. Meet you inside?" Maya turned back around in his arms and placed a chaste kiss to his lips.

He smiled into the kiss. "I'll get us good seats. I'll be the one waving wildly with a bell around my neck. You won't be able to miss it."

"If you can't get good seats, plead man of honor."

She began to walk away, but Cooper grabbed her hand and pulled her back to him gently. He put his hat onto her head and whispered gruffly, just for her ears, "You decided whether or not you're gonna marry me yet?"

Maya felt her cheeks warm. She'd given it lots of thought, and she already knew her answer would be a yes. "I don't know, cowboy. You calling in your favor?"

"If I have to use funding our charity as a means of convincing you to marry me, I've done something so very wrong in this relationship."

Maya tapped her chin. "I guess we'll have to keep thinking about how I can pay you back then."

Cooper cupped her chin, and she quickly put a hand on the hat that threatened to fall off her head as he pulled her gaze to him. "You know damn well you paid that off long ago, and I wouldn't have cared even if you hadn't. Now don't make me beg at my own retirement party in front of all of my teammates."

"You know how I love when you beg," she said, knowing the smirk on her face was only fueling a fire that would spread through her later that night, especially by the way his pupils dilated and his gaze shifted to her lips.

"Big. Sloppy. Kisses."

Maya pulled out of his arms as he descended toward her, running away from him, a hand still holding his hat to her head. "Get us good seats to watch the best tight end in the league, please!" she called over her shoulder as she made her way to Lyla and Lucia.

When Maya reached them, she swooped down to grab her niece in her arms, spinning her around once before placing her onto the ground. "How's my little athletic genius?"

"Stop throwing my child around like she's a stuffed animal, please," Colton grumbled, though Lucia sent Maya a wide smile.

"He's grumpy because he has to watch Landon in the con-ference final this year." Lucia laughed when Colton's eyebrows furrowed. Maya knew it was all in good fun, as they'd already agreed they'd be at this year's championship game if Landon made it through the conference final. Plus, both Colton and Cooper were content with their three championship wins.

"You know I'd rather be here than anywhere else."

Down the lawn, a few of the rookies on the team yelled for another to chug his drink, and Maya's nose wrinkled. "It's almost like you're raising a frat baby."

At Colton's disgusted frown, Maya snickered.

"How dare you." Then he moved toward the group of guys, yelling, "Hey! There are kids at this party," and Maya almost felt as though she'd tattled.

Her niece waddled to her mother, who scooped her up. "I'm gonna take her inside. I thought about putting her down for a nap, but the frat house is only going to get louder once the game gets going. We'll see how she does."

"Auntie Maya would be happy to take her off your hands anytime. I'm going to make her into a tennis superstar," Maya cooed at her, waggling her fingers as Lyla laughed and clapped her hands.

"Noted, and I will put you in rotation," Lucia joked, heading up to the house.

Maya walked the few yards to where Devi stood, smiling at her like she'd been waiting for years to be reunited with her, and not like they'd just seen each other last week.

Maya had officially moved into Cooper's house before his last season, but she traveled to Los Angeles a lot, checking in with Viola and the LA branch of the charity as well as visiting her cousin and grandparents. While she coached a lot in Charleston, both for the charity and on her own, her schedule was flexible and allowed her to be gone for a few days at a time, which meant she didn't have to do virtual margaritas with Devi anymore and could instead be with her, slurping them down by the gallon in person. Even Landon, when he had a few hours, would fly down to hang out with them, or they'd meet him in San Jose.

The Sabertooths had loved On the Line, and over the months after she'd moved to Charleston, had created a board and taken over some of the bigger logistical aspects of the charity that were over Maya's head, like expansion and tax work. She and Cooper were still cofounders, and Maya continued coaching and handling day-to-day oversight in Los Angeles and Charleston. She also made sure to work with the board often on everything she could, especially expansion efforts, but she had learned to let other people help her when she needed it.

They now had branches in Austin, Denver, and Kansas City, and were on the lookout for more locations now that the season was over.

Her friends stopped by when they could to help with On the Line, which was fun for her *and* for the kids, who were excited to meet professional players. She knew their support was a way for them to show their love, rather than out of obligation to her, and she was eternally grateful to them.

Maya was forever in awe that her small dream from three years ago had yielded something so spectacular and that On the Line had helped so many children and families.

"Hi!" Maya pulled her cousin into a hug. Devi didn't often come to visit them but she'd grown closer to Lucia and Colton and had wanted to be here for his retirement party. Plus, she had a soft spot for Lyla.

"I see you're embracing Cooper's Tennessee roots." Devi nodded her head toward Maya's hat.

"You like it? I'm going for a hybrid, tennis slash horse riding thing here." Maya grinned as she waved her hand at her tennis dress, which she knew did *not* pair well with the hat.

"It's great. Wouldn't be surprised if you started a trend with it." They laughed, turning to face the lawn as more and more of the team began filtering into the house, readying for the big game.

Despite all his claims of getting them good seats, Cooper still stood talking to Colton and a couple of other teammates near the front door. They were going to end up sitting on the floor, if they were lucky.

Devi caught her look and gave her a knowing smirk.

"He ask you to marry him yet today?"

"You know it. Once a day for months." Maya couldn't contain the smile that split her face as he threw his head back and laughed at something Rudy said. "Yesterday, he said the moment I say I'm ready, he's going to throw me over his shoulder and marry me right then and there."

"And are you ready?"

Cooper's eyes met hers across the lawn, and the smile on his face matched hers. She gave him a small wave of her fingers, and he winked at her.

Maya's heartbeat increased as though she hadn't been in love and loved by this man for years.

Her life made her happier than she ever thought possible, even more than when she had been on tour.

And though Maya couldn't hear her mother's voice, she liked to believe it was because her mother had been guiding her to this better purpose, and when she'd found it, she hadn't needed guidance anymore.

It was a bittersweet sentiment, but she loved it nonetheless.

Everything felt like it had fallen into place, and she finally felt ready.

"I'm getting there," she lied.

Because Maya Beaumont was already there, and the moment they were alone together, she was going to say yes to him in nothing but his cowboy hat.

Acknowledgements

I cannot describe how difficult this book was to write, especially after *Gridlocked on the Gridiron* seemed to come out of my head so easily. I will never be able to thank those that helped with this book enough but let me try.

To my alphas: Georgia, Marja, Miah, Elaine, Lisa, and Heather. Thank you for helping me see all the ways this book wasn't working so that I could get it to the point that it was. To my betas: Rachel, Casey, Hannah, Alex, and Kie (+Marja and Miah again!), thank you for helping me fine tune Cooper and Maya's story to get it to a point where I didn't want to light it on fire and throw it away.

To Rachel for being the greatest editor. Thank you for hyping me up but also giving me feedback that made this book the best that it could be. Sorry for sending you a million messages all the time, and for saying one thing and then immediately changing my mind five seconds later. You are so much more than my editor, and I'm thankful for every single thing you do.

To Chelsey, thank you for helping with the alpha draft, and for finding the little things during proof. Your excitement made me feel like this book was worthy of being seen. To Laura, thank you for always being willing to put your degree to use for me. I miss you endlessly and love being able to talk books with you.

To Victoria, Courtney, Vaidhs, and Aly, thank you for all your support on Instagram. Being an indie author can be so difficult at times and you make it worth it.

To my family, for being far more supportive than I ever expected with my debut and future projects. Thank you for believing in me and championing me. Especially Mom, for getting me hooked on tennis as a kid.

To Marja, who has become one of my biggest champions in the year that we've been friends. I'm so glad I've had you along for my entire indie journey, and that that will be true for however long our careers are and beyond. Thank you for always being willing to alpha *and* beta for me, for formatting my book babies, and for being one half of Frog and Toad with me. I know we hate emotions, but I love you so much. To say I wouldn't be where I am without you would be the world's greatest understatement.

To Miah, who has superseded every other person in my phone for time spent texting or calling, I cannot thank you enough. From mental breakdowns over this book or other projects or life events to all my wins, personal or professional, you have become someone so important to me in such a short period of time. Thank you for reading this book so many times and for loving my brain children as much as I do (especially

Colton lol). Honestly, I could probably write a novel's length list of reasons why we're so perfect for each other, but I'll leave this at I love you.

To Ethan: thank you for your no-questions-asked support in everything I do and for being my biggest fan always. Every book I write will be a love letter to you, and this one is no different.

And finally, to anybody who picked this book up: thank you for supporting me. I hope you enjoyed reading about Cooper and Maya as much as I loved writing about them.

Also by Vai Denton

The Beaumont Legacy series
Gridlocked on the Gridiron – Colton's book
Tumbling Over the Tight End – Landon's book

The Off Court series
Drop Shot
Cross Court
Kick Serve

About the Author

Vai Denton is an American author, romance enthusiast—especially if sports are involved—and book lover. She has spent much of her life struggling to find her identity between her two cultures, using books as a sanctuary. Her hope is that her stories provide readers with the escape she once sought. In each of her books, you can expect swoony, healthy relationships that will have you kicking your feet.

If she's not reading or writing about love, you'll find her playing tennis, watching football, Pride and Prejudice (2005), or any number of her favorite romcoms with her two cats and fiancé.

If you'd like to contact Vai, find her on instagram @vaidentonauthor or via email at vaidentonauthor@gmail.com